electrified

electrified

rachel blaufeld

dedication

This book is dedicated to my mom. For most of my life, it has been
just the two of us, and I know you think you made
mistakes and have regrets.
You didn't. Not one, *except that time…*
Really, you're perfect, and I'm doing exactly what I was meant to be
doing in life, thanks to you.
I love you.

one

Friday night

Sienna Flower had only been at the Electric Tunnel for an hour when one of the younger exotic dancers, Sydney Luv, knocked on her dressing room door.

"Too many bachelor parties to count, every private room is filled, and the front of the club is lined with couples having drinks and watching the dancers," Sydney reported to Sienna. "And I'm totally nervous to go onstage right before *you* tonight!" She wiped her brow, pretended to be faint, and then jumped up and down as if she'd just won the lottery.

Sienna smiled, patted her shoulder, and took in Sydney's big hazel eyes brimming with excitement, her wavy auburn locks bouncing all around, and her sweet freckled nose. She nodded toward the quintessential all-American beauty, the complete opposite of herself. "You'll be fabulous, Luv Bug. Plus, Petal is going to be there with you. She wouldn't have asked you to join her if she didn't believe in you, honey."

"I know," Sydney admitted before her eyes went wide. "But still... before *you*, Sienna Flower. That's the most sought-after slot! Dancing right before your act made Petal a star!" She continued to prance around the dressing room.

Sydney was twitchy with nerves, excitement stealing her breath, forcing her to push her words out rapid-fire. Her enthusiasm was contagious, making Sienna feel warm and bubbly to know she was part of that.

"Aw, sweetie, just have fun! Only everything good is coming your way." She leaned over to give the girl a quick hug, just as Petal popped into the dressing room to grab Sydney.

Before making her way out to the club, she surveyed her look for the evening. Tonight she had decided to wear a hot-pink lace thong and matching bra covered by a sheer light-pink baby-doll shirt, her blonde hair pulled up in a messy side ponytail, silver sparkle eyeliner to bring her baby blues to life, and five-inch-high strappy silver platforms to top it all off.

As usual she was ready early, so Sienna went to hang out by the side of the stage where she could watch her friends perform their first act together. She was a big fan of the idea of the two of them doing a duo, hoping that Petal's new popularity would give Sydney a boost. Although Petal's initial impetus had come from going on just before Sienna, her star was now shining brightly on its own.

She settled near the club's back door stage entrance with Petey, an oversized young man who had recently moved up from bouncer to being in charge of security. She was chatting with him, automatically flashing her smile at a few patrons who spotted her in that out-of-the-way corner...when she saw *him*.

Tonight her new fan was sitting close to the front at a table for two, alone as usual, his big frame consuming the large leather chair he occupied.

Just past the stage, deep red and purple leather club chairs were tucked around mahogany cocktail tables in the area they referred to "the pit" in the club. Most men looked small in the oversized chairs, but this man was broad-shouldered and muscular, and barely fit in the chair.

Somehow he took masculinity to a higher level, even in the über-masculine decor. He was so dark with black hair, deep brown eyes, and olive skin. His persona screamed *danger*, but Sienna didn't believe it. The man was as sleek a predator as a tiger at the zoo, yet she wanted to reach out and pet him with no regard for his bite or claws.

Standing there near the back door, Sienna had a fantasy of him sitting in one of the deep purple leather booths in the VIP area, resting his arms against the plush, midnight-blue velvet along the back wall, his legs stretched out in front of him, assessing her with those dark, brooding eyes while she did a lap dance for him.

Lap dance? Where the hell did that thought come from? She never thought about giving lap dances.

Sienna quickly yanked herself back to reality and curiously watched Mr. Tall-Dark-and-Handsome as he took a sip of his drink.

Is he going to look up at me?

Not fully knowing what possessed her, she turned and whispered to Petey, "Radio up to Ash that I'm going down front so I can see the girls' act from there. Tell him not to worry." She ignored Petey's raised eyebrows and pushed off the wall. As she turned to walk away, Petey frowned while speaking quietly into his earpiece.

Ash is going to have the fit of all fits. Asher tended to be a bit overprotective of her, more a big brother at times than a business partner.

Giving Petey's huge shoulder an affectionate pat, Sienna slipped out a little farther into the club with only thirty minutes left until she had to be onstage herself, even though she never did this on a Friday. She took a deep breath, taking in all the smells surrounding her. Sweat, alcohol, lingering secondhand smoke, and a mixture of cologne—scents that meant nothing alone, but when mixed together formed a unique scent that she'd come to identify as home.

Moving like a caged animal set free, she wound her way around to the front of the club, flashing a few more dazzling smiles mixed with her signature innocent-yet-electric gaze to those who noticed her on the move. Like a heat-seeking missile, she landed right next to the dark-haired gentleman of her fantasies.

Coincidentally, the only empty seat up front near the stage was the second one at his table. Coming to a stop next to that chair, she gripped the edge of the wine-colored leather, praying she didn't faint from nerves.

There was no way she could sit. She was already going rogue with being out in the club on a Friday. She felt Petey's gaze on her back and saw the other bouncer, Big Mike, clenching his hands and watching her from the front entrance, and knew as sure as she was breathing that Asher was counting backward from a hundred before he barreled his way over there to rescue her.

The problem was, Sienna wasn't acting on her own volition. Something altogether new was driving her.

Animal instinct.

Sienna made her own rules for a reason, and her most important one was staying safe and off the floor on weekends, when the club was filled to the max with adoring fans. Yet here she was, standing out in front, pretending to watch Petal and Sydney while a man stared at her profile. A man she wanted.

She wasn't even sure what "wanted" meant, but there was some strange desire burning inside her. A fire whipped through her entire body, setting a blaze to her heart and sending tingles to the area down below, barely covered by the tiny scrap of pink lace.

Unsure of herself, she gripped the chair for balance, and had nearly convinced herself to walk away when she heard a deep *hello* directed her way.

A response bubbled up in her throat, but when she glanced at him and his intense dark gaze snared hers, she wasn't able to get it out.

The music that pounded loudly around them seemed to fade away, the people surrounding them becoming suddenly insignificant, and the cavernous room shrank until it was only him, only her, just the two of them left in the universe.

Sienna gave a small nod and smiled back.

"Well," he said slowly, "I guess I'm pretty damn lucky, Sienna Flower..." He ran a hand through his hair, obviously not knowing how to finish his sentence.

She ripped her gaze from his and gave herself permission to quickly check him out a little closer. Sienna guessed him to be almost forty due to the touch of gray at his temples, although his body said mid-thirties. His hair was cut short on top, just long enough for natural waves to form, and left a little longer on the sides, enough to curl around his ears. She couldn't help but wonder what it would feel like to run her hands through the thick black ripples.

He was really something special. Sienna saw men all day, every day, not to mention each night, and not one compared to the man staring at her from across the cocktail table. She might not have feared his type from high above on the stage, but with him right in front of her eyes, inches away, she was petrified.

Not of the man, but of the way he made her feel.

"That's me," she finally stuttered in response. In an effort to save face, she said, "I just snuck out to see my friends in their new act," then nodded her head unnecessarily to indicate the stage.

"They are very good," he agreed, then narrowed his eyes slightly

4

and cocked his head. "But not as talented as you, or as beautiful." A tiny dimple formed when the corners of his lips tilted up slightly, and there it was...his smile. Not a full one, but the hint of what it could be like if expressed fully. It would be glorious, beyond glorious.

Seeing the large, strong man flash a small smile at her made Sienna shudder. It was what she'd been waiting for since the night before, or maybe even weeks.

Suddenly she wished she could be the one to put an even bigger smile on his face. It would be decadent, and she knew if she experienced that, she would be like an addict, wanting more.

The thought was too much for Sienna to take, and she started to move away. She'd never felt an intense attraction like she was experiencing now, and she might have wanted to explore it more, but she couldn't afford to allow herself that luxury.

"I'm up next," she said with a tinge of regret. "I have to go."

His eyes darkened, the brown turning nearly black. "That's what I'm waiting for. You, Sienna Flower."

Against her will, she leaned forward slightly, forgetting for a moment that she was out on the floor on a Friday. This beautiful man drew her in, making her want to break every rule she'd made for herself.

But reality came slamming back along with the loud music, the crowd that surrounded them, and the knowledge that this was a really, really bad idea.

Her heart pounding, she said simply, "Enjoy the show," then she waved and turned to slip away.

"Wait," he called out, and against her better judgment, she stopped and turned back. "I know you really never do this, but would you join me for a drink later?"

She shook her head. "I'm sorry. I can't."

"Okay, it didn't hurt to ask," he said, looking slightly disappointed.

She hated seeing his frown. Sienna wanted that little smile and dimple back from him.

"I can't because I perform a second time tonight, and I usually stay backstage between acts," she explained, not wanting him to feel bad.

Forget performing twice, I don't have drinks one-on-one with customers. Do I?

"Perhaps another time, then?"

Sienna couldn't even think straight. Normally she was all about protecting herself, staying safe, and not getting close to anyone, but she found herself saying, "Maybe. I don't really know, not on a weekend."

Shocked at what she'd just said, she muttered, "I have to go," then turned and fled backstage before anything else ridiculous could come out of her mouth. She hadn't made it two steps past the backstage curtain before she ran into Asher, his expression a murderous thundercloud.

Uh-oh.

He grabbed her arm and pulled her to the side. "What the fuck? You *are* the one who says no weekends on the floor," he hissed in an undertone, before adding, "You scared the hell out of me, Li...Sienna."

Sienna realized in that moment just how nervous her unexpected detour to the floor had made Asher. It was only when he slipped into his crazy protective mode that he sometimes accidentally called her Lila, the name she'd been born with.

She sighed. "I'm sorry, Ash. I know. I wanted to see Sydney dance with Petal, and then I saw him sitting there. I don't know, but there's something about that guy. He's the one I asked you about, remember? He's here a lot lately, and he only watches me, never smiles, and..." She waved her hands about in frustration as she tried to articulate her feelings. "I was just curious. That's it, I was intrigued, but now I'm not. I guess some type of sick curiosity came over me, and now I've satisfied it."

Asher's expression relaxed. "It's okay, doll. Just keep me in the loop when you decide to break protocol. It's my job to keep you safe. You okay, for real?" He gave her a reassuring smile and pulled her into a hug.

Sienna nodded and wrapped her arms around Asher to give him a big squeeze.

With that, he playfully slapped her ass and pointed her to the stage. "Time to do what you do better than anyone else. And, Sie, you don't have to apologize for being curious. You deserve whatever your heart desires and more."

I can't have more, but you can.

Sienna wasn't really okay, but she knew if she didn't let him think she was, he would pull her from dancing, and that was the last thing she wanted.

Most people would think it would be hard to get up and perform after the unsettling encounter she'd just had, but Sienna loved losing herself while dancing. Dancing was her safety net, her security blanket, and gave her sanity. Without dancing, Lila would still be lost, or even worse…back with her husband.

With performing in mind and the calming of her nerves that came with it, Sienna headed to stage left and prepared to make her entrance as the lights dimmed.

She climbed the pole while it was still dark so that when the sparkly spotlights went up, she was already hanging upside down, the hem of her baby doll shirt flipping forward to reveal luscious, creamy, shimmering skin and, of course, the hot-pink lace lingerie underneath.

For this routine, she'd chosen straight rock for her music. When the hard-core, steady rhythm of the electric guitar quickened, Sienna picked up the pace of her routine to match the drum solo in the song. Her hips swaying to the pulsing beat, her hair swinging with the music, she trained her eyes on the audience.

On everyone in the audience except for *him*.

She didn't even know his name, but was considering having a drink with him, which was crazy. What in the world was wrong with her? Maybe she needed a few days off.

Sienna broke free from her thoughts, becoming fully engaged in her act as she left the pole and stalked toward the front of the stage. That was the effect dancing had on her. It was cleansing, detoxifying, allowing her to drop all her negative thoughts and be transported somewhere else.

Dancing delivered her courage.

She wrapped her arms around her body as though she were enveloping herself in a tight embrace, then lifted the nightie off in one seductive swoop before flinging it to stage right.

Down to her bra and panties, Sienna strutted to the front of the platform. She tugged her hair loose from the elastic band that held it, then bent over to shake her long locks loose. When she flipped back up, hand to hip, dancing suggestively, swaying her middle while letting her hair fall down her back, she saw him.

He was staring. Not gawking or watching awkwardly like most fans, but gazing possessively at her. A mysterious warmth flooded her body, seeping out from her veins to her muscles, skin, and most private parts, making her want to touch, feel, and gaze openly.

That was all she could handle. Sienna turned and went back up the pole to finish the song, avoiding looking at the audience. She couldn't stand another second of the heat between their gazes.

Twisting and wrapping her lean body around the pole, never

breaking a seductive smile, Sienna had the crowd twisted in lust. She could feel it in the air. It was heavy, blanketing the audience in a fever. Unable to cool down, the crowd's only choice was to take in more sensuality.

At the end of the song, Sienna didn't wait to see if the man she'd already spent too much time thinking about had left. She did a quick spin around, giving the crowd one more long look at her toned bare butt, blew kisses to her fans, and sashayed off the stage.

To look at her, one would never know her insides were churning with anxiety, that her thong was soaked…not from sweat, and her heart was beating hard…not from exertion.

The crowd probably expected her to head to the back to get laid. There was nothing else to do after a performance like the one she just gave other than melt into another person. She didn't have a significant other, though, so she went to her dressing room to be alone.

As always.

two

Twenty-four hours earlier, Thursday night

THE OVERHEAD lights were dim, the stage dark with a single spotlight focused dead center. It was showtime. Sienna waited backstage, inspecting herself in a full-length mirror one last time to be sure her minimal costume covered what it should. She checked her makeup, then ran a hand over her skin to ensure the lotion she'd just applied had been absorbed completely; it would make her skin shimmer and sparkle when the light hit it. Her audience had come to expect her lush, creamy skin to radiate onstage, and she wouldn't disappoint them tonight.

The music in the main room began to pulse, sending vibrations throughout the entire building, and marked the time for her entrance. Counting backward from ten, Sienna entered stage left as if she owned the huge platform rising above the crowd. Her demeanor actually said more than that; her moves suggested she owned the whole club.

Actually, she did own the entire club…now.

Well, half of it, to be precise.

It had only been three months since that fateful change of fortune; only time would allow the idea to settle with her.

She now owned half of all this. This being the Electric Tunnel, the one and only route to Vegas's heady, lust-filled underground, and a fiery inferno of deep, hot, anything-goes fantasies of the sensual nature.

Asher Peterson, the club's owner and the top purveyor of everything and anything sensuous in Sin City, had brought Sienna in three months ago as a partner in "the Tunnel."

"You deserve it," he had told her one night as they left the club. She had just stared at her closest friend—her only true friend—watching him run a hand through his thick, wavy blond hair and thinking he needed a haircut, and a goatee trim while he was at it.

"Without you," he'd said, "this would still be just a small strip joint on the outskirts of the Strip. Now it's the most sought-after place to go to in Vegas. I won't take no for an answer. From now on, Sie, we're fifty/fifty partners." Asher had kept his eyes trained on her, waiting for a reaction, his serious expression letting her know he would accept nothing short of "yes."

She had continued to stare. No longer distracted by her boss and closest friend's facial hair, she had pondered the idea.

Me, Lila, the sweet little religious girl who's only ever slept with one man, owning a strip club? Imagine that.

It had been enough to make a little laugh bubble up in her throat at the absurdity of it, but Asher had insisted he wanted her to have it.

Warming up to the subject, his silver-gray eyes had been intense with sincerity as he'd said, "*You* bring in the big money, the men with hundred-dollar bills to burn, the couples with serious cash to spend on a decadent time in Vegas, the bachelor parties with guys who drink like fish and buy lap dances like they're candy, and the lonely businessmen who would pay anything to get off and go to sleep. They all come to see you. You're their fantasy come true. They wait in line, fill the crowd, buy booze, and book private rooms months in advance to simply dream of you. It's Vegas, baby, and you make the whole experience for them. You need to own that, love."

With those words, her heart pounded even more furiously. She was indeed all of what Asher had said—a stripper, the best one out there—but she had a past. One she couldn't risk becoming public knowledge, which was why she did what she did. Sienna took her clothes off for money. She bared her skin so she didn't have to show her soul.

As Sienna, her secret was safe in a city full of secrets, because what happened in Vegas, stayed in Vegas.

Sure, it was a cliché. But it was exactly why she had run there seven years ago in the first place. She'd felt she was safe in Vegas, so she was staying put. Why not take Asher up on his offer?

Her onstage career would be limited by her age, and she hadn't had a ton of options when it came to earning money. At some point she would need to retire, and everyone needed a nest egg. Even a woman who had left a life serving God for bright lights and a stripper pole deserved to not be destitute.

And that was how Sienna came to be an owner of the Electric Tunnel, the naughtiest, classiest, and most exclusive strip club in the United States.

She still had to dance at this very moment, not only because the music had started, but the club relied on her. Without Sienna Flower, the Electric Tunnel was just another gentleman's club. With her erotic beauty, sleek curves, lush breasts, and virginal eyes, she was the main course who lured everyone inside to be tempted by other appetizers and side dishes. Everything else at the club was à la carte: drinks, having a nubile young woman rub up against you, as well as venturing to the private areas.

Sienna Flower captivated the audience and demanded their focus, night in and night out. Not only did she own the Tunnel's stage, but every other adult dancer in their attempt to be her, even if for just one single performance.

By necessity, she was an owner in heart and mind, but not on paper. It would never be official. Her past prevented that, so that a paper trail would never lead anyone from her past to her present. Sienna Flower was a mirage, a figment of the imagination, hiding who she really was from the real world.

The applause and cheering were deafening as she took the stage to perform. This wasn't something new. Every night for the last four and a half years, the clapping and catcalls only got louder, the audience demanding to be pleasured with Sienna's tantalizing curves and smooth moves. She loved and adored the noise the crowd made; it never got old. It wasn't as much about adoration as it was longevity for her. The louder it was, the greater job security she had. For Sienna Flower, security was everything.

Men and women alike lined up outside the club six nights a week to gain entrance to the Tunnel, paying no mind to it being an all-female strip club. The people who pressed against the velvet rope outside didn't discriminate by gender; each of them wanted to catch a glimpse or more of Sienna Flower. The season of the year made no difference. In the brutal heat of summer, or the chilly evenings of winter like now, they came in droves to get "electrified."

They knew that if your name wasn't on the list for Friday or Saturday nights, you could forget about even trying to get in the door at the Tunnel. "Try coming back on a Tuesday," one of the bouncers would say, turning you away with no regrets before moving on down the line.

The first six months she danced were quite a different story. No one knew who she was, and her less-than-sultry moves met with vague stares and drew only small crowds, but then she started coming into her own. Back then she was still Lila, playing dress-up as a stripper. It didn't take long for Lila to hold tightly to perfecting the role of Sienna Flower.

Like an empty, hollow Hollywood set, Sienna Flower was a stripper with no real sexual history to speak of, no experience with intimacy, and certainly no fantasies other than surviving.

She could never be Lila again, couldn't go back to her old ways, so she was betting the house on Sienna Flower.

If not Sienna Flower, who would I be?

Asher was the only one who knew the real Lila. She was certain this was why he wanted her to have half the club. He knew what she fought against. Everyone else just assumed the personal and business relationship between the two was based on Sienna being the main attraction at the Tunnel.

Turning her focus to the crowd, her skin was glowing, her hair shining, and her smile radiant as she took center stage. Sienna was ready to thrill and entice like she did every time she performed.

Fully settled in her routine, Sienna's thoughts drifted again.

"My name is Lila," she'd told Asher when he first interviewed her all those years ago, "but I'm thinking about going by something different." She had felt safe immediately with Asher. Something about him had made her feel protected, allowed her to talk freely.

He just shook his head, because he got it. It was Vegas. Everyone was hiding from someone or something, so she didn't need to explain anything more to Asher. Most of the locals were hiding from one thing or another, and she blended in.

Asher hadn't seemed one bit nonplussed with her two-bit story, which made her breathe a sigh of relief.

He'd looked her up and down, finally settling on her eyes. He'd given a final nod when he looked straight into her eyes. At the time, Lila had no idea what the big deal was.

Now, almost seven years later, she knew they were her calling card, despite the fact she always wore sky-blue-colored contacts. One prominent entertainment magazine had recently noted:

> Sienna Flower pulls you in with her eyes, a tunnel straight
> to the desires of any man's soul, an electromagnetic
> doorway to baser desires from what feels like a virginal
> source.

Seven years ago, with long, straight blonde hair thanks to a bad home-dye job and a motel hair dryer, and wearing what she considered to be a skimpy black halter top, too many bangle bracelets, bad boots, and skinny jeans hung low on her hips, Lila had answered Asher's help-wanted ad in the paper for a cocktail waitress. She didn't have any experience, unless one counted entertaining company—silently and begrudgingly—in her old life, although slinging drinks while showing a fair amount of skin certainly hadn't been part of entertaining in her former life.

Lila had dressed how she thought she should as a potential cocktail waitress. She needed to at least look the part. Actually, what she needed was to hide, fade away from her former life, and immerse herself in a world so different from the only one she'd ever known.

She knew she had to play the person she wanted to become in order to get the job, which was a woman so intrinsically different and more sophisticated than the one she had been raised to be. It was a massive task considering the sheltered world Lila had been raised in, yet the seedy, sin-filled land of Las Vegas was her only choice in destinations when she fled years ago.

Once there, she decided to insert herself even deeper into a place where she'd never be found. While letting the bruises heal, Lila looked for a job with cash tips. One that was far removed from any of her old values.

Seeing an ad for a cocktail waitress in an out-of-the-way strip club, off the Strip, was the answer to her prayers, and she had a lot of those. Prayers. Much different from the ones she used to pray, but prayers nonetheless.

These days, when Sienna looked in the mirror, Lila wasn't there at all. Her former nondescript brown hair was perfectly dyed and highlighted golden blonde. Her eyebrows matched her locks, showing off her big, beautiful, innocent eyes. She never went out without her blue contacts, so no one even considered her to have any other eye color.

Sienna was a blue-eyed, blonde-haired, supple goddess.

Lila had light green eyes the color of the sea and a slight bump in her nose. Sienna didn't have even the tiniest bump in her button nose, thanks to another gift from Asher. After her first successful run at the Tunnel, Asher had a close personal friend, a regular at the club who happened to be a plastic surgeon, fix Lila's nose.

It wasn't just about making the club money, though. She'd become Asher's family as much as he'd become hers. Their financial success was only the icing on the cake for them. The two had both been left without any family, so their bond ran deep. Deeper than blood. That was what happened when two people who had been abandoned found and learned to rely on each other.

When Lila began dancing, she was scared and timid despite the fact she'd already been waitressing in the club for close to a year. The slightest clap of hands made her shudder during her first performances.

With a little experience, some added confidence thanks to Asher, and a few dances under her belt, Sienna Flower bloomed in the bright lights, loud music, and throbbing pulse of the club.

This was the only place Lila felt safe anymore—shimmering in her solo spotlight. The club gave Sienna Flower life when Lila was dying.

I'm onstage right now, Sienna Flower, not Lila. Sienna Flower to everyone but Asher, and that was the way it would remain.

She snapped out of her memories as the beat of the music deepened, causing the floor to shake from the vibrations. It was a mash-up of a rock song mixed with rap, made just for her by a local DJ. This wasn't uncommon. Sienna Flower only danced to original music.

With her head tilted, Sienna's hair flowed all the way down her back. It was loose tonight with a light wave accentuating her perfectly and professionally colored tresses. Wearing only a metallic gold bustier and matching thong, she slid her leg up a pole.

The thong crept farther into no-man's land as she stretched her leg higher up the pole, giving her audience a hint of the goodness underneath. Just a hint. Everything else was left to the imagination. She knew how to show just the right amount of skin.

It was the beginning of her act but Sienna's skin was already glowing, compliments of her signature sparkling body lotion. Every inch of her skin from the neck down was waxed smooth; the veteran dancers had taught her about this in the beginning.

The lotion was all Sienna from the beginning, though. Most of the other girls used baby oil to make themselves look sweaty, but she didn't like that look. Sienna Flower was sparkly, iridescent, soft, luscious... yet very untouchable.

Sienna lowered her leg and swung around the pole twice with her eyes closed and a sensual pout on her lips. She knew what she was doing. This had been her life for the last several years, six nights a week. Playing Sienna Flower, enticing her audience with something in between innocent mystique and overt sexuality. Being a good girl with the moves of a seductress was her calling card.

She might not have believed this would be her life a decade ago, but it was, right down to the tiny tattoo of a flower permanently imprinted underneath her right collarbone.

Her moves had become more flawless as the years went on, but she finally learned it was her innocent eyes coupled with her illicit moves that captured her audience.

Sienna's persona was her very own suit of armor. They would never find Lila here. Lila would have never dared to be in a place like the Tunnel.

The music sped up, snapping Sienna to full attention. She moved away from the pole, strutting up and down the front edge of the stage, and running her gaze along the faces of a few men watching. All the while she stared straight into the crowd, creating the feeling she was looking into the soul of each individual, reading their wants, and focusing on them and them alone.

With a flick of her hip and a toss of her hair, Sienna was back in the middle of the pole, hanging upside down, her bustier firmly in place with just enough of her breasts spilling out of the top while she was inverted. A quick flip had her climbing up to the top of the pole before sliding down in one quick motion.

Once firmly back on the ground, she took her right hand and seductively pushed the hair out of her face while holding on to the pole with her left. Slowly, she snaked toward the ground with her legs bent on either side of the phallic symbol, pushing and rubbing herself up against it. She knew the audience assumed it felt good and that she was getting off. She wasn't.

When Lila became Sienna, she gave up the quest to ever really feel good. This was about survival for Sienna, though she did take pleasure in making others feel good. Sienna knew it was sick, but the smiles of appreciation did something to her. She had never really been appreciated; now she could make others glow and be valued in a twisted way, but important nonetheless. Men, women, and couples all came to see her, and she made their fantasies come to life. It was true beauty.

Disturbing, but it still made Sienna happy.

The music was coming to an end. It was Thursday, so Sienna only danced one act. The only nights she did two were Friday and Saturday. She used to do a double every night, but once her popularity exploded, Asher decided she should save her doubles for the weekend.

Weekdays and Sundays, Sienna went on around eleven, but Fridays and Saturdays, she was front and center at midnight and once again in the early hours of the morning. By two a.m. Mondays, she was truly off.

During the week, when it was only slightly less crowded, Sienna worked the room once or twice a night, saying hello personally to some parties and flashing a seductive smile at whoever looked her way. It was impossible to do this during the craziness of the weekend, and Asher, with her input, had decided long ago, there was too much pawing at Sienna during weekend nights.

She was hands-off, no lap dances, and no touching. Sienna was for looking and fantasizing only. The most expensive eye candy out there, the stuff sexual dreams were made of was who Sienna Flower was in and out of the club.

Years ago, she didn't realize leaving her old life would mean never really being able to live fully. Since then, she played a role and never broke character in order to remain breathing. She never bared who she truly was because she actually had no idea.

Sienna went up the pole one more time at the end of her act. Her legs were once again wrapped tight around the pole, her gold stilettos pointed toward the ceiling, ass pointed to the audience. She didn't need to twerk or hump the floor. She just looked seductive while entangled with the pole or performing her signature dance moves, and she had

16

the whole crowd riveted.

Another write-up about the club and Sienna had said:

> *Sienna could simply stand onstage batting her long eyelashes over her deep, mysterious eyes filled with innocence and promise, and the audience would be titillated, turned on, and amped up. How the hottest stripper in Vegas creates that look, no one understands or knows, but everyone wants to sneak a peek.*

Sienna finished her act by blowing the crowd a kiss after turning herself right side up on the pole. She always took the time to look out at the crowd when she did this. She liked to see them smile, and feel the electric charge. She liked to know it was an act well done at the Electric Tunnel.

That was when she saw him. She didn't know him, but had seen him in the Tunnel a few times over the last few weeks. Dark black hair cut short with a little wave running through it where it curled around his ear, a scratchy shadow on his face, a day or two old, and jeans with a white dress shirt rolled up at the sleeves, a masculine tattoo peeking out. He was always there on a Thursday or Friday, sat up front for her act, and quickly left when Sienna finished.

This wasn't completely unusual, since many fans came to see just Sienna Flower regularly, but this guy seemed almost uncomfortable at the club, as if he wasn't sure why he was there. Fidgeting in his seat, always running his hands through his hair and never smiling, yet being completely focused on her. He was her mystery guy, something she never had or thought about having before.

Most of her regular fans stopped her to say hello on the nights she walked the main floor of the club. They weren't allowed to touch or take pictures, but most of them just wanted to tweet they met Sienna or be able to brag about meeting her at a party at a later date. Not this guy, though.

He just watched her on the nights she never made an appearance in the outer club, and when her set was over, he headed out. He didn't even try to flash a grin her way, let alone meet her.

She wasn't afraid of him; he didn't give off that vibe. But Sienna was curious—she wanted to know why he didn't smile. Was he nervous about being at the club?

He's so big and masculine...there's no way he could be afraid of overt sexuality.

Did he want to ask her something? Maybe he was a journalist? A writer? But he looked so strong and tough; he couldn't be a writer.

His eyes, even from far away, were as captivating to her as many claimed her very own were to them. Deep brown like a chocolate bar begging to be savored, his eyes called to her. They were forceful, uncompromising eyes that had seen a lot. She envisioned they would hold pools of warmth, and a touch of sensitivity if you looked far enough into their depths.

Stop looking.

But Sienna couldn't help herself. She looked back over her shoulder, batting her eyelashes for cover as she exited the stage, and as usual, the guy with the jet-black hair, the man who never smiled, was leaving the club. Giving her a perfect view of his ass.

Strangely, she was a bit saddened by his lack of response, his strict composure versus outright pleasure, and his avoidance in trying to meet her. Sienna made a mental note to mention it to Asher. Asher could get a read on the guy when he worked the room. If the guy came back.

But do I want him to?

three

CARSON GRAHAM shifted into fourth gear as he hightailed it away from the club toward his hotel. Why did he keep coming back to Vegas? Who the hell knew. If there was one thing he didn't have any trouble finding or getting, it was willing women.

He knew women weren't really "things." They were interesting, often complicated creatures, and he both appreciated and respected them. He just happened to like women in his bed who came with no strings. It was the twenty-first century, after all, and there were plenty of women who liked that kind of deal.

He had never settled down, and he sure as hell wasn't about to start now. At closer to forty years old than thirty-five, he felt the bachelor life suited him just fine. Or maybe it was that he only deserved the single life. His particular circumstances hadn't exactly set him up for success in the relationship department.

Picking up a little speed, he changed course and steered toward the mountains, needing more time to clear his head.

It would be great to be on his motorcycle right now, to be able to lean into the steep and winding curves, but it was back in his garage on the East Coast, grounded—just like his life at the moment. The sports car he'd rented here in Vegas would have to do.

As he shifted the engine into fifth gear the car jetted forward, allowing the tension to bleed from him with the increased RPMs. He was trying to drive away from the pull as fast as he could; the pull coming from an insanely gorgeous stripper he was lusting after in a big way.

There was something magnetic about Sienna Flower, dragging him in deeper and deeper. More than her sleek, toned body and her sensual moves when she wrapped herself around the pole, there was a draw deeper than the physical. Carson wasn't a hard-up kind of guy. He never got like this over a woman. Ever.

Growing up without a mom, he was fairly certain there was nothing lasting about "love." If a mother could actually up and leave her child without any notice, like his did, there was no such thing as forever. His dad had done the best he could to be everything to Carson, but the fact remained: When a six-year-old's mother left and never came back, that fucked with a kid.

It fucked with a grown man, too. As a result, Carson never considered love an option.

Lust, a few cocktails, dinner out, and then a good roll in Egyptian cotton sheets—that was Carson's modus operandi. He definitely didn't have any delusions of long-term love.

In reality, his thoughts on the subject of love didn't really matter. His lifestyle and career didn't allow for love; at least, that was what he told himself. After joining the FBI, he traveled all the time, leaving at a moment's notice on any number of classified assignments. He was wise enough to know the FBI lifestyle didn't lend itself to successful relationships, so he never pursued them. If he were honest with himself, he might admit maybe that was why he originally chose to take the FBI job, but who wanted to look that closely at their own motives?

He certainly couldn't be hunting down a suspect in a different time zone while pretending to be at a sales conference in Orlando when he called home in the wee hours of the night…or morning, depending on where he was.

Eventually all the lies, fibs, or whatever you wanted to call them caught up in a field agent's relationship. As a man who avoided conflict in his personal life for fear of being deserted, he knew the lying would eat away at him.

After cracking a high-profile missing person's case at the FBI a few years ago, Carson had struck out on his own. Going solo, he built his own firm, still traveling and having a grand fucking time doing what he did best, which was remaining uninterested in a long-term relationship. Now he was an independent private investigator, making his own rules, and it suited him just fine. His reputation followed him and he took the cases he wanted—except for this current bitch of a case—which allowed him to have a good time living life.

To most people, he introduced himself as a bounty hunter or some shit like that. No need to have every Tom, Dick, and Harry asking him to take this or that heartbreaking case. Carson worked, traveled, and enjoyed the finer things life offered. He liked getting paid too much to take on pro-bono cases.

Although his recent case was starting to feel like one…that and a big, annoying crock of shit.

A vibration in his pocket partially dragged him out of his funk. Holding the wheel steady with his knee, Carson pulled the phone out of his pocket and hit ignore. Speak of the devil who got him involved in this crap. His best friend, Alex. He should have answered; the guy's family had practically raised him. He owed him that but he wasn't in the mood, since it was Alex's fault that he'd taken this damned case.

Guilt overtook him as he traveled the long, dark desert road, and Carson dialed his friend back.

"Hey man, what's up?" He focused on the open road ahead of him, the mountains bleeding into the skyline, the moon lighting his way.

"Not much. Just checking in. Making sure my oldest friend is still alive and causing trouble wherever he may be at the moment."

"Yeah, yeah. All good here. Kicking around out west, trying to solve that shit case you sent me. Taking a much-needed break in Vegas as we speak." He pushed his speed a little more, feeling the car purr.

"Way to make me jealous. I'm stuck at home watching the baby while my wife is out on a girls' night out, and you're probably on your way to getting laid. What's wrong with this picture?"

"Nah, Alex. You go be with your baby and let your wife have a good time. You're not missing anything. Except for a few strippers." He laughed out loud.

A small chuckle came from the other end. "I'm gonna get you for that one. Have some fun for me, will ya? Keep me updated on the case. I know I can't be much help, but if you need anything, let me know."

Carson chuckled. "I wish you could help with the case. It's turning into one hell of an adventure. I'm trying my best to help out your relative's friends, but for the first time I just don't know. Hell, listen to me rambling like I'm a spoiled bitch. Forget it, man. Go love your baby."

"Okay, but stay in touch, Carson. Don't go MIA so often."

"I hear ya."

As he disconnected, he thought about Alex's comment. Going MIA, doing his own thing, was part of who he was.

His current personal life lined up with his new career perfectly. He had a few women around the country who knew the 411 when it came to him. Lavish times with no commitment; that was how he rolled. Period.

Now here he was, rushing back to Vegas every weekend. Why? What the hell was the draw? Carson sighed because he knew damn well.

Sienna Flower, adult entertainer with moves that would ignite a dead man, and eyes like a virgin, making him feel like a young kid all over again.

Christ, he had a problem.

The case he was currently working was burning him up and playing with his mind, besides displacing him to the West Coast. Although the job was lining his bank account—even at his lowest rate—it was taking much longer than he expected. He needed it to be over.

Am I losing my touch already?

He sighed and turned the car back toward the Strip while something nagged at his gut over this assignment. There was something odd, some piece of the puzzle missing, which was why the case was taking longer than expected.

What was wrong with him that he couldn't find it? What was he missing?

It was a first for him, and he didn't like it. Not. One. Fucking. Bit. Which was why he found himself running off to Sin City every weekend.

He needed to let off steam, and where better to do so than Las Vegas? It was an occupational hazard of his...letting loose. Going back to his FBI days, Carson always needed a little fun, a tiny walk on the wild side to let go of the stress of the job. Otherwise, he lived and breathed his cases, working late into the night to solve them.

He needed a good time to release the pressure, which he currently was finding at the Electric Tunnel, but the pressure only mounted more after visiting the club. What originally started out as a method to clear his head and make way for him to solve the case, was clouding his judgment even more.

Sienna Flower had happened...that was what.

His latest client—or *clients*, since it was a married couple—was able to pay him. Yeah, they were making good on his rates, but their friends raised the funds, not them. They were willing to keep transferring money to him, yet he didn't like the eerie feeling that had begun to dog him. They were lying to him. Withholding information, at the very least.

For the first time ever, Carson was considering giving up the case. The only thing that stopped him was the worry that nagged him over the missing person he was hunting down.

Shit, I'm going soft.

He was turning into an emotional cream puff, which was a bigger occupational hazard than having a grand time in Vegas.

Originally, he'd needed a respite from the bone-deep worry that something was terribly wrong with the case, so he started heading to Sin City for the weekends. Now, his gut was messed up from the case *and* his head was fucked up from a stripper.

The family who had hired him was pretty certain their missing relative had fled out west or thereabouts. Why were they so convinced of that theory? Carson had been stuck scouring small towns for the last month and a half. He didn't like small towns with strange people all up in each other's business. Almost as little as he liked the case.

He was starting to need his weekly adventure to Vegas by Tuesday of each week. It was a place where he could disappear and enjoy himself for forty-eight hours. After all, he was still a man with baser needs.

The problem all began when he went to check out the infamous Sienna Flower the first night he got to Vegas. He hadn't been able to tear himself away from her image, nor enjoy himself at all since that night. He couldn't figure it out. He'd had many women over the years— gorgeous, seductive, exotic women when he was traveling—and now he was stuck on some Vegas showgirl. No, not a showgirl. Exotic dancer.

Carson downshifted the car as the lights of the Vegas Strip came into view, rolling around what little he knew about her in his head. Nothing about her made sense. She'd arrived on the scene a few years back, and before long became the biggest thing Vegas had seen in years.

She didn't do private rooms or parties. Ever. Asher Peterson, king of the adult dance club world, pulled her from lap dancing after only a year of dancing at the Tunnel. Now all she did was grace billboards, shake her ass onstage, and bring millions of dollars into the club.

He knew all this from Google. Fuck, after the first night seeing her, he couldn't get her tits, firm ass cheeks, and electrifying eyes out of his mind. He'd googled her like a horny teenager, and decided she must have been a local Asher had taken a liking to.

Were they romantically involved? Was Asher tapping that?

And why was he even thinking about Sienna's potential bed partners? He was fairly certain that wasn't a role even he could fill.

Do I want to?

Unfortunately, Carson had developed a nasty habit of heading to the Tunnel every Thursday through Saturday nights for the last month. Tonight was no different. He went to see Sienna dance. Then he left to go back to his hotel to either pick up someone in the hotel bar or jack off. Lately, his preference was to stroke himself to recent memories, those of a striking, gorgeous, naturally curvy woman with a heady combination of innocence and salacious moves.

He might as well have been in high school all over again, lusting after the prom queen, not knowing what to do about it other than rub one out.

This evening was different, though, because he had felt Sienna lock gazes with him. She looked right out at him as her act ended. She was smiling, but he could see right into her eyes. She was examining him back as though she wanted to know more about him.

It was disturbing on so many levels. He was a private eye. He should be able to read people. Yet she seemed to be reading *him*, looking deep within him.

He couldn't begin to figure out Sienna Flower, and now she was trying to figure him out? The thought made him harder than he normally was when he exited the club. Tonight he was practically limping as he walked out.

He needed to get laid, stop coming back to Vegas, and leave his thoughts of Sienna Flower at the door.

Of course, he knew he'd be back at the same place tomorrow night with his eyes homed in on one stripper, his dick standing at attention. Weeks ago, he'd paid the concierge at his hotel extremely well to keep him on the weekend list for the Tunnel. Open ended. No need to waste that.

Leaving his rental sports car at the front of his hotel with the valet, Carson bypassed the gaming tables and slot machines and went straight to his favorite bar for a drink. He grabbed a seat at the far end of the bar and nodded at the bartender, Victor, who now viewed him as a regular and brought him a drink without his even needing to order. Top-shelf scotch on the rocks.

Fuck, he was officially a Vegas groupie. The valets knew him, the bartender knew his drink and had it ready as soon as he stepped foot in the lounge, the front desk gave him the same room each weekend, and he was lusting after a woman who starred in Lord only knew how many other men's fantasies.

If his FBI buddies caught wind of this, they'd never let him live it down. Most of them were settling down, either resolving themselves to living double lives, or trading in their FBI badges for white-collar jobs. Not Carson, he was living the dream. Fast cars, motorcycles, big money, booze, high-end escorts—or dancers, depending on how you looked at it—and his current bullshit case.

He needed to relax and get a handle on all this shit. Carson caught Victor's eye and then lifted his chin, smiling when Victor made his way over to him.

"Hey, Vic, how's it shaking? You got any cigars back behind the bar, or do I have to move my ass to a special bar to smoke one?"

Victor chuckled as he wiped his hands on a bar rag. "You're in luck, buddy, this is Vegas, where anything goes. I just happen to have a few select ones in a humidor under the bar. Let me grab it and you can pick your poison."

Moments later Carson inhaled deeply, scotch in one hand, a fresh cigar in the other, his view on the casino floor. Actually, he was relaxing for the first time all week, coming down from his dark mood, and found himself not wanting another woman. He wasn't even sure if he wanted to take care of himself either, which was new.

Surprised at that revelation, Carson decided he was content to only finish his drink and cigar before heading upstairs to go straight to sleep.

There was always the promise of tomorrow night, and Sienna locking eyes with him again.

four

Sienna's mood dampened when she couldn't put even the slightest grin on the face of the dark and mysterious guy who'd been watching her that night. He was clearly watching her and only her; this she knew. After years in the business, she could read patrons from afar. Some visited the Tunnel to see the myriad of titillating scenes, whether it be whoever was on the main stage or the vast landscape of lap dances; they were at the club to soak it all in. Others visited to see Sienna. Just Sienna.

This didn't bother Sienna. She thought it should, but it didn't. She was bringing in customers, who were often derailed from their mission to see only her and became smitten with another dancer, or two or three. Sienna Flower was a business ploy. She was the draw, a force of nature who brought them into the Tunnel. Once they were inside the club, they couldn't help but to be sucked into the hedonistic den of pleasure and passion where they could enjoy any number of sexual fantasies.

Not her person of interest, though. The man she had suddenly found both curious and somewhat lust-worthy was gone. He was a ghost after Sienna left the stage, and never engaged in anything more with the other dancers in the few weeks he'd been regularly coming to the Tunnel.

He always quietly exited as she finished her dancing for the evening. Tonight was no different and for some odd reason, Sienna felt isolated and lonesome. This was uncharted territory for her. Being the center of attraction at Vegas's most popular adult entertainment venue wasn't only a business move, but also one for protection. Her role as Sienna existed to keep her secure, and embodying Sienna meant she didn't get attached to anyone.

Her safety rested in no one knowing the true her. Developing a relationship with a customer wasn't only an occupational hazard for any stripper, but a major risk for Lila.

Forming a bond with a man, other than Asher or the bouncers, meant he might get to know the real person underneath the stripper persona.

Which was a horrible idea. Disastrous. Period.

In her newfound state of confusion, Sienna headed out to visit the club floor and check on her "girls." She caught a glimpse of Asher leading a disgruntled customer up to his office with Big Mike bringing up the rear. Standing by the somewhat hidden stairs to the office, Sienna overheard Asher going ballistic as the threesome climbed the steps.

"Mike, can you believe this gentleman asked Sadie to go home with him? As if my girls are low-class hookers. Bullshit."

She paused by the bottom step so she could hear a bit more. Asher really hadn't been himself lately.

"Nah, man. Guy is whacked if he thinks we would allow our sweet little Sadie to do that, or anyone else," Mike answered with his typical dry humor, while keeping a firm grip on the customer's shoulder.

"Well, yeah, it gets better, Mikey boy. He then asked Natalie when Sadie said no."

Sienna shook her head. *Natalie, of course. That's why Ash is laying it on so thick.*

Mike's head went from side to side. "Fuck, dude, that's so wrong. You have no fucking clue." Mike ran his hand over his short buzz cut before giving the guy a little shove up the last step.

Asher leaned in and whispered something else to Mike that she couldn't catch before the three of them entered the office and closed the door. Fearful for what might or might not be happening, Sienna decided not to make her second round walking the club.

It was no biggie. She did that sometimes.

Being unpredictable was another facet of her dirty-diva persona as Sienna Flower. Yet she never let go of the facade; she was Sienna all the time. She never broke character. Her sanity and safety relied on upholding her good-girls-can-be-naughty reputation, and a large part of her success with that was based on acting like the prima donna everyone assumed she was. Lila was nothing but a memory, and in order to keep Sienna alive and well, she had an image to live up to… all the time. And she played it so well, only she knew it was nothing but a role.

Skipping her walkthrough of the club floor reminded her fans she was unpredictable and wicked. Sienna Flower was a big mystery and untouchable, but her rounds circling the Tunnel were widely anticipated. She didn't like letting the crowd down, but one time was no big deal. It would definitely ensure the current customers would return in hopes of an up-close peek at Sienna.

If she hadn't been out on the floor once already, she wouldn't consider bailing, but she'd done a few laps earlier in the night. She had her usual cocktail, sparkling water with a splash of cranberry and lime in a lowball glass, knowing better than to drink the hard stuff when so much was riding on her success. Tonight she decided to enjoy it with her protégée, Petal, and a gentleman she was entertaining. The gentleman was being nothing but polite and keeping her friend well occupied and flush with cash.

She liked to keep her eye on what the dancers were up to when she was out on the floor, so she made it a point to join small groups here and there for a little while. This served a dual purpose of making customers feel special, and helped out the dancers with the extra tips they got from the delighted customers. Every night she did this for as many dancers as possible, but Petal was her favorite.

Ravyn Petal, or Petal, as everyone affectionately came to call her, was often mistaken for Sienna's little sister despite the contrast between Sienna's golden hair and Petal's silky black. Petal had started at the club about a year and a half ago, her popularity helped by her soft, smooth skin and round, firm, natural breasts much like Sienna's.

Both her parents had died in a car accident when she was little, after which she became a victim of the foster care system. Without a stable adult in her life and no real ties to anyone or anything, she had hopped on a bus to Vegas the day she turned eighteen, with stars in her eyes.

Sienna met Staci, now "Petal," when the girl was answering the phones at the Cat's Meow, Sienna's preferred waxing studio and one of the few places she ventured out to on the Strip.

When she did go out to the glitzy side of town, she dressed very low-key, shoving her long blonde hair under a baseball cap and donning super-large shades. Typically, Sienna wasn't very social when she went outside the club; in fact, she tried to avoid talking to anyone, especially on the Strip. There were too many fans, pawing, touching, and asking her for photos, so she usually grabbed one of the bouncers from the club, often Mike, before heading that direction.

The problem was that Sienna Flower was known all over Vegas. Her picture graced a large billboard right before the famous Welcome to Las Vegas sign. There were Internet chat rooms devoted solely to her performances, the lingerie she wore onstage, and her bad-girl secrets; whatever they might be was anyone's best guess. Thankfully, no cameras were allowed in the Tunnel.

There was a brief period where all this publicity made Sienna nervous, but the fact she looked nothing like Lila anymore put her at ease. Not to mention, her looks only mattered if she even remotely thought anyone from her old world would be delving into adult entertainment. They would never, ever think, let alone dream she was a stripper who danced onstage and took nearly all her clothes off, baring everything she had to offer.

Still, even if they did, Sienna didn't look one bit like Lila. She was reinvention, both physical and mental, at its finest.

With this in mind, Sienna seldom went out unless it was a occasional publicity event Asher asked her to do, or her salon trips. For waxing, she went to the Cat's Meow, and for her hair, she went to the posh private salon for high rollers at one of the luxury hotels on the Strip. Those were her only destinations; everyone else came to her these days. Her manicurist came over on Tuesdays, a personal shopper came as needed, and she ordered her dance clothes shipped straight to the club.

On the day when Sienna had first met Petal, Big Mike had driven her down to the Strip, but he needed to run a quick errand, so she had some time to kill after her waxing was done. Mike was going to swing back and get Sienna at the Cat's Meow, since she felt more than comfortable waiting there, typically hanging out in the back.

Except on this day, she didn't stay in the back of the studio; she went to check out the candles in the front of the store. A new girl—Staci, according to her pink pussycat nametag—was answering the phone and booking appointments at the reception desk, but stopped what she was doing to step out and help Sienna with the candles. She was so fresh and innocent, a rarity in Vegas, that Sienna was captivated with what she recognized as a younger version of herself.

Deep in thought over what could have been, and where she might have ended up had she not met Asher, Sienna had heard Staci drawl, "Can I help ya?"

Sienna thought back to her early days in Vegas, to her awful outfits, bad hair, and zero clue as to what it took to succeed in Vegas, and she felt something toward the girl. But it wasn't pity. Sienna had contemplated the girl in front of her, her mind spinning. *If she's going to make it here, Staci needs to be way more cosmopolitan, polished.*

And a rescue fantasy was born.

Vegas was a town of mystique and make-believe. It was an adult fantasy come to life, and there was no room in that fantasy for "hick talk." Visitors to Sin City wanted to believe they were indulging in a lavish playground for adults. They didn't want reminders of the farm town they grew up in, or the very image, accent, or background they were trying to lose.

Sienna had answered the question quietly, wanting to strike up more than a conversation with Staci, but needed some time to think about the best way to approach her.

"Yes, will you help me find a few soft scents for my bathroom at home?"

"Whatcha like? Somethin' flowery? Vanilla?" The girl cocked her hip to one side while her hand rested on it, making her look formidable.

Trying not to show how much the accent was grating on her nerves, Sienna maintained a neutral look on her face and answered, "I like more natural scents. Lily of the Valley…water."

"Well, I got the water scent right here for ya. Thunderstorm. It smells like rain. Ya want me to add it to your bill for the wax?" More hip cocking, side to side.

Sienna cringed, even though she was trying hard not to show it. "I have an account here. Just have Penelope add it to my charge."

"What do ya mean, an account? I don't know nothing about accounts here." Petal frowned and waved her hands in the air helplessly.

30

Taking pity, Sienna decided to step outside her comfort zone and explained softly, "Staci, my name is Sienna. Sienna Flower. I'm one of a few women with personal accounts here. Penelope does it as a courtesy to a few of her more frequent customers."

"Oh! Oh my God! I didn't recognize you with the hat and the glasses and all the clothes. Sienna Flower from the billboard!" Staci shrieked while jumping up and down.

"Shh, right. That's me, but let's keep it quiet. Staci, why don't you send your calls to voice mail and let's go have a cup of tea in the back."

Staci stopped jumping, her eyes widening to the point she looked downright frightened.

"You're not in trouble," Sienna assured her. "I just want you to succeed here. I can tell you want to, but we have to chat about a few things so you can do that. I'm doing it as a favor to Penelope."

Staci had frowned and took her bottom lip between her teeth, then said, "Is that going to be okay with Penelope?"

"Don't worry about that, Staci. Penelope and I are close friends. I'll handle this."

Once they'd been seated at the table in back with some hot tea and sliced fruit, Sienna got to know Staci and shared a little about her own background.

Silence fell between them for a moment, as the girl digested what she'd told her, then Sienna leaned forward and said, "Staci, you could make a really nice life for yourself. I had a bad life and now I have a good one."

Good, but lonely. So lonely, I'm taking you under my wing.

Sienna had omitted anything specific about Lila and why she ended up in Vegas. She simply left it at the two women sharing difficult upbringings.

With a compassionate expression on her face, she said, "I had a tough beginning like you, and I want to help you make something of yourself, so you can stay here and be happy, Staci. I was able to transform myself, and now I can help you."

The young girl had just stared at Sienna. Most likely, no one ever had showed an interest in her, let alone someone she saw as a celebrity.

"You don't have to dance if you don't want to," Sienna went on, "and I definitely don't want to take you away from Penelope, but we have to work on your manners and speech. There's a lot of money to be made here in Vegas, and opportunities are at your feet. Let's help you take advantage of all of this. The first step is assuming the role of what people expect in Vegas. Anything but reality." She tilted her head and looked at the younger, more naive version of herself.

Sienna decided helping Staci make it on her own in Vegas was a start at paying it forward in the same way Asher had taken her under his wing. The Electric Tunnel and its people—Asher, Mike, and Petey, who all gave her refuge when she needed it, helped her achieve success, and made her feel warm and welcome—were her current inspiration.

Staci probably saw her as a stripper with a heart of gold. The truth was that she was alone and craved a friend like a drowning person craves fresh air.

Sienna was an extremely giving person deep down inside, and Lila had never been able to fully express that side with all the beatings and lies she'd had to endure. Lila was someone who craved to love and be loved, something she never truly had. And since she couldn't afford to fall in love now, Sienna chose Staci to be her family.

The two women had bonded quickly. Lila never had a sister, but always wished she did. Maybe if she had, she would have had someone to go to when she was secretly being abused.

As Sienna, her only family was Asher. These days she took care of Asher as much as he took care of her, but she had more love to give. Knowing she'd never get married again and have a family of her own, she saw Staci as a chance for her to take care of someone else, so Sienna took her under her wing.

Initially, Staci would spend time with Sienna at her house, or the two would meet for a quiet lunch somewhere way off the Strip. Quickly, the two women became as close as Sienna could be with anyone; like sisters, but Staci could never know about Lila. Sienna felt bad, as if she were lying by omission, but not only was it dangerous for Sienna to reveal her true identity, she didn't want to involve Staci.

The less connection to my past, the better for everyone.

Soon enough, Staci became Petal. Ravyn Petal, the Electric Tunnel's newest dancer. Petal still worked at the Cat's Meow while she was learning to dance, until she earned herself the spot right before Sienna went onstage. Petal also happily did lap dances and trips to the private room with customers. Going onstage right before Sienna elevated Petal to most-wanted status, and she left the Cat's Meow after eight months, since she was making big bucks at the Tunnel.

Sienna was proud of Petal's success in making a new life, and taught her how to save and manage money. To Sienna, there was nothing to be ashamed of in developing a career as an exotic dancer. For many, it was more money and security than they could have imagined, and under her wing, the girl would learn to prepare for the future.

Sienna didn't judge Petal for working the floor and doing whatever she did in the VIP rooms. She watched her lead the gentleman from earlier to the back area, his hand on her lower back, and she was smiling. With her soft raven-black hair flowing down her back and brushing against the small booty shorts she wore that revealed hints of the round bum underneath, Petal was now a confident young woman, very different from the insecure girl she had been when they first met.

The pair stopped to be vetted by the head bouncer that evening for the VIP rooms. After learning from Asher, Petey was as tough as nails when patrons entered the secluded area. Wearing his usual bad-boy getup, that was enhanced by his very muscular tattooed arms, he only had to focus his midnight-blue eyes on someone to instill fear, demand respect, and maintain decorum. Sienna watched him frisk the very willing man before arranging terms and explaining the code of conduct, taking his credit card for safekeeping, and opening a tab for time with her girl.

This was part of the life, and thankfully at the Tunnel there was absolutely no funny business when it came to the dancers performing one-on-one for the customers. With high-tech security cameras and the toughest bouncers in the business all over the club, customers couldn't get away with anything raunchy or disrespectful.

Sienna had done a lot of lap dances—with no touching—in her short career on the floor before Asher had said it was enough. When Asher saw how customers gravitated to simply watching her perform, he determined there was no reason to ever place Sienna on the floor. When her stage persona clearly became the main draw to the club, Asher started paying her even better than he had been to simply dance.

She knew it was both a personal and a business decision. Asher was well aware how difficult it was for her to work the floor, but he also realized the benefits of Sienna dancing exclusively. Her shows brought customers back over and over again, while being good for the other girls on the floor. Following her stage numbers, the floor dancers were flooded with requests for lap dances. There was no denying Sienna was the draw, and limiting her to the big stage only amplified her pull.

Sienna never worked the private rooms, though. She refused to enter a space where she was alone with a customer, ever, even before she was famous. Asher understood this and never pushed it, even without knowing the entire reason. He seemed to sense that being in one of the rooms would push Sienna over the edge.

Years ago when Asher had first approached Sienna about getting on the stage, he'd rubbed his hands soothingly up and down her arms. "Sie, doll, you know I'm never going to make you go back there to those rooms, don't you? I just think you should dance, and make more money. That's it." It was his gentle, assuring way with her that helped her find the path to a brand new identity, one that saved her life.

These days, there was absolutely no reason for Sienna to do anything she didn't want to, now that she was an owner. *An owner.* It might not be what she dreamed of when she was a little girl, but she was a part owner of the Tunnel.

If my destiny was to be a stripper or strip club owner, so be it. Safety first.

Sienna was living life on her own terms, which was why she had no reason not to allow herself to head out early upon occasion. She was confused by her fixation on the dark-haired man, who only watched her and seemed immune to the sexual hum of the club, and she needed some time to herself, to appreciate what she did have and not what she was missing.

Like a gorgeous, dark, brooding hunk.

five

As SIENNA exited the club Thursday night on Big Mike's arm, unconditional love and affection emanating from the big bruiser in his running pants and matching warm-up jacket, she thought about her new family—Asher, Petal, Sydney, Penelope at the Meow, and her sweetie, Mike. It was more than she could ask for to have five people so intimately involved in her life.

Sienna had dreamed of having a big family with a bunch of kids when she was younger. When she ran away from the only family she'd ever known, she'd expected to be alone for the rest of her life, but she wasn't. And for this, Sienna was grateful. The gang might not be much, but they were all she had.

Mike was the one who had surprised Sienna the most. He sort of crept into her life, and now was permanently fixed as her biggest fan and buddy. Not only did he take Sienna out when she needed to venture outside her house or the club, but he walked her to the club's town car each evening.

Asher didn't like Sienna driving herself to and from the club. When the billboard went up two years ago, he put an end to Sienna coming and going on her own. Tuesday through Sunday, Asher sent a town car to pick up Sienna, and then the same driver would return her home safely. Typically, Sienna found herself hanging on to the elbow of Petey or Mike, who escorted her out the well-lit back entrance to the Tunnel and deposited her safely into the soft, luxurious leather backseat of a town car. Like tonight.

The time each night when she was escorted out was special. It was something she looked forward to, relished even. It was a quiet moment when she truly connected one-on-one with another person.

As the town car whisked her effortlessly home, Sienna found her thoughts centering on Asher. She wasn't stupid; she knew Asher provided this service more for his own peace of mind—and his sex life—than her general safety. He was a man, after all, and had his own physical needs. It wasn't like that between Sienna and Asher, although many speculated it was, and sometimes, Sienna wished it were. She wouldn't be forced to be alone for the rest of her life if she could be romantically involved with Asher, but their relationship was nothing more than a deep friendship, or brotherly love.

Asher would probably go for her sexually out of some weird sense of responsibility, but that wasn't what Sienna wanted, nor would she ever force Asher into a life like that. She cared for him too much to allow him to tie himself to her out of obligation.

No one who *really* knew the two of them, which was maybe ten people in total, believed they were a couple. Only the media and the crazy paparazzi speculated, which was fine with Sienna. The upside of the rumors of her having a steamy affair with Asher was that they didn't link her with anyone else.

Secretly, she liked this aspect of her relationship with Asher, even though it was false. Not having to publicly be linked with someone else was a relief. But if Asher actually met someone special, Sienna knew she'd easily give up the act.

He deserved that.

Like her, Asher had come from a shitty life. Although he didn't publicize it widely, he wasn't nearly as secretive about his past with everyone at the club as Sienna was. His mom, a showgirl who had never married, dropped a seven-year-old Asher off at a neighbor's house one afternoon and never came back. With no clue who his dad was, the neighbors took Asher in and raised him as their own. At least his mom had taken a calculated risk in leaving him with people she must have known wouldn't turn Asher over to the system, even though he gave them plenty of reason to do so once he hit his teens.

The couple, who both were lifers in the Vegas nightlife industry, ran a small bar and casino off the strip. They were decent people who never had kids of their own, but gave Asher as good a life as they were able. In turn, Asher could never repay them enough for keeping him out of the foster care system. He bought and paid for a luxury condo for the couple he thought of as parents a few years back, and they never wanted for anything.

Asher had told Sienna he was certain he wouldn't even be alive today if he had been passed through the foster care system to people who couldn't have given a rat's ass about him.

A major rebel through his teen years, Asher was left with few options when he graduated from high school. Because of his grades, college wasn't realistic, and he despised the idea of the military. So Asher gravitated toward the only life he knew...the Vegas nightlife.

Working his way from bouncer to club manager to young owner of the very run-down strip club, Tunnel-O, he slowly found success. Over time, Asher transformed Tunnel-O into the Electric Tunnel, and his business was on the upswing when he met Sienna.

With a desperate need to make sure he had security in life, Asher built the Tunnel into what it was today. Well, with Sienna's help, Asher had always insisted. Her dancing was a big part of the club's success, but Sienna knew Asher was well on his way to making it even before she came into the picture.

Sienna knew Asher's personal needs were often met after a long evening of work at the club, when she was already safely at home. Although he typically said he had to "stay and work late" after the club closed, his version of working late was entertaining in his office, which he couldn't enjoy if he was worried about Sienna getting home safely. So when he suggested she start taking the town car back and forth to the club, since he couldn't "get any work done" if he was worried about her, she didn't put up a fuss. She didn't like to upset Asher, and it wasn't any of her business anyway, so she didn't argue about the town car.

Asher didn't make a habit of dating any of the girls from the club, yet he made an exception with Natalie. There was something going on with Natalie and Asher, but Sienna didn't pry, since it was clear at the moment they were on some type of break. What kind of break was anyone's guess, since no one quite got what was going on in the first place between the two.

Sienna knew Asher was only distracting himself with the other young women who visited him at the club, but he genuinely liked Natalie. Again, none of her business, but still she sort of liked the thought of Asher ending up with Natalie, and hoped they could work out whatever it was they were going through and move forward.

She bit her tongue from saying this directly to Asher, though. Sienna stayed out of Asher's dating life.

Stay out of his; he'll stay out of mine. Which was probably wishful thinking.

Sienna's silence didn't stop Asher from meddling in her dating life, or lack thereof. He asked her more than once a week, "Sienna, you ever going to date, baby doll? Find a nice guy for yourself and settle down?"

"Ash, you know I'm not," she always answered. "I have all the men I can take staring at me at the club."

Sienna knew Asher saw right through her response, but she also hoped he was smart enough to let it be. He knew more than anyone about her marriage. He just didn't understand that she could never really see herself having another one.

Asher, always trying to make sure I get everything I want out of life and more.

She knew Asher's heart was in the right place, but her inner Lila really didn't want anything other than to be safe. Exposing herself to a level of intimacy again wasn't in her future.

But could it be? Her thoughts floated for a minute to the guy who had sat front and center the last few weeks and never smiled.

What would he be like in person?

No, she couldn't open herself to a man again. Besides, she wasn't divorced. There was no chance of moving forward, even if she wanted to, with the man who had suddenly taken over her mind.

Just because she was destined to be alone didn't mean Asher shouldn't date, have fun, and make a good life, though. Why he didn't make a life with someone, Sienna had no clue. He was successful, beyond wealthy all on his own, and had a huge heart. Maybe she should break her own rule about getting involved with Asher's love life, and help him figure it out. Pay it forward some more, like she did with Petal.

She knew he liked Natalie a lot.

Earlier, as Mike had leaned in to kiss her on the cheek before settling her in the car, she had whispered to him, "Watch out for Asher. He's like a live wire after what happened a few weeks ago. You know what I mean? In the VIP room?"

Mike had nodded his head. "Yeah, kid, I know. Petey feels responsible, and we've all been treading lightly with the boss. We know there's something more there with Nat and him, but I got you. I'm keeping an eye out."

Snuggling in for a tiny bit more affection, she had said, "He deserves to be happy. If it's with Natalie, he has to resolve his issues with her at the club, and trust you guys. You and I both know Petey was there in a heartbeat."

He had pulled her in for a brotherly hug. "Don't you worry yourself over it. I'll watch him, and Petey knows, love." He rumpled the hair on top of her head and gave her a push toward the car.

"It's not that easy, Mike! I'm going to talk to him, too." She laughed and put a playful frown on her face as she settled herself in the backseat.

"Good night, Sie." He had gently closed the car door and turned on the heel of his high-top basketball shoes to head back inside the club.

Just a few weeks before, things got a bit wild in one of the private rooms. It happened occasionally at the Tunnel, despite all the bouncers and security equipment. Some customers tried to get away with crazy shit. That was what went down with Natalie and one of the other dancers named Sadie, who were entertaining of all patrons, a married couple.

The husband and wife showed up on the VIP list from one of the upscale hotels, flashing a ton of cash and wanting to have a good time, which was a common occurrence at the club, especially on the weekends. Natalie, who was always looking to earn a little extra money so she could do more for her son, had no problem with dancing for the couple in the back room. The husband and wife also wanted a second dancer, so they could simultaneously get lap dances. Not an outlandish request for the Tunnel, where people played out all kinds of fantasies.

Natalie pulled Sadie in with her, and both of them were perfectly fine with tantalizing the man and the woman with their solo moves along the sensuous deep purple banquettes in the farthest back room in the VIP area. It was the dancer's call in the back rooms to loosen the no-touching rule as they felt comfortable. Usually, girl-on-girl touching was no big deal. There was never any type of penetration allowed, but a good feel was pretty much standard back there.

Sadie was performing for the wife, and from what Sienna heard, the two of them were having an extremely good time. The woman was amped up on hormones and loving every second of Sadie grinding up against her, blowing in her ear while whispering sexual suggestions for her to share later with her husband. This was all pretty standard for a backroom all-female experience. The woman was softly caressing Sadie's side cleavage, teetering on the verge of orgasm just from the provocative lap dance while her husband enjoyed Natalie.

Time was ticking by, and the couple was running up a huge tab at a thousand dollars an hour to enjoy Nat and Sadie in the VIP room. Well into the second hour, the husband stuck his finger inside Natalie's mouth, despite the fact that no penetration was allowed of any kind— oral, vaginal, anal, it didn't matter.

Even though Natalie was allowing the man's hands to roam a bit, she wasn't down for his finger entering her body. To make matters worse, the guy had palmed an ecstasy pill, which he tried to slip under Natalie's tongue.

Drugs were a hard no-no at the Tunnel. They were reason for immediate expulsion and your name blacklisted forever. With two bouncers at opposite ends of the VIP room and video cameras all along the overhead lighting, it didn't take long, maybe twenty seconds at most, to catch Natalie wincing and struggling.

Within a minute, the couple was swiftly removed from the premises, and Natalie and Sadie were ushered directly to Asher's office suite in the club. Sadie was fine, no worse for the wear, only concerned for Natalie.

Sienna had popped up to check on Natalie and caught Asher in a rage, completely beside himself. He was bitching Natalie out, going on and on about how she didn't care about herself, her son, and him. Not wanting to be a part of it, she excused herself.

Witnessing the strong emotions Asher had for Natalie confirmed what Sienna already knew. He cared for Natalie more than he let on to her, and to himself. She just didn't understand why Asher didn't allow himself to follow through on whatever it was he felt for Natalie.

I hope he's not holding back because of me.

That was one big reason why guilt plagued Sienna. Did Asher not want to hurt her by dating other people, and possibly starting a relationship? Did he think she would feel deserted?

She wouldn't. She loved Asher, but not like that. So now that Petal was settled, Asher would be her next project.

Sienna let Asher have his no-strings fun and took his town car home to be by herself each night, hoping he'd do more than have a casual fling in his office. She needed to be by herself, but Asher didn't, and now she was going to help move him toward something she could never have herself.

Sienna was still thinking about Asher and how he shouldn't be lonely as she was when she got home and dipped into her bath. No matter what time she arrived back home, at night or early morning, Sienna took a hot bath. It helped her soak off the sweat and energy of the club.

Sinking into her tub full of bubbles, lathering herself with a clean, fresh scent, and washing away the sultry air of the Tunnel transported Sienna to a good place. Closing her eyes, she imagined not being the lonely woman she was, but rather a lover, partner, wife, caretaker. In any one of these roles there would be someone else to whisper to, joke with, or sleep next to after a long day.

A long day of what? Stripping?

There was no denying she'd pretty much seen and heard it all at the Tunnel. She didn't wish to experience every single act she had knowledge of over the years, but somewhere deep, she longed for something sensual of her own. She'd never experienced making love, let alone dirty, kinky sex with anyone, and a small piece of her wanted that.

Making love. She knew she'd never have it, but still she wished on some level she could.

Her bathroom was her refuge, the only place she truly let down her hair. The room was her favorite part of her carriage house, and where Sienna allowed her thoughts to drift and wander to what she might desire.

For the most part, her entire home was the one thing that made her smile, leaving her not feeling totally bereft from what had become of her life. Actually, her home was the carriage house at the rear of Asher's property; he had renovated it and was looking for a tenant when he met Sienna. When he'd learned she was staying in a dingy extended-stay motel, he moved her in to the carriage house, saying she would pay him "back rent" when she could.

At some point, it became clear he was never going to charge her back rent, so Sienna abruptly handed him a lump sum for the value of the place. Although not one bit necessary, she knew Asher would transfer the deed to her, which he did.

She turned on the water, adding a little more warmth to her bath, taking pride in the fact that she was now a homeowner. Sienna Flower owned her own home. Something else Lila had only dreamed about.

It felt liberating, even though without Asher in her corner, none of this could have happened. After all, she couldn't exactly apply for a mortgage using her old social security number.

Originally Asher had run her paychecks through his own account and then cashed her out. It was an arrangement they struck when she was moving from cocktail server to dancer. As a server, she earned cash tips and a tiny off-the-books base. Moving on to dancer, she started with a small salary and lots of cash benefits, which only grew. The cash was all good because she couldn't declare her own salary, forcing Asher to come up with a more unique solution.

After some time, Asher set up a small LLC and paid the corporation Sienna's money. Then he withdrew a salary in cash for her. Asher made it work, no matter what.

He told his accountant it was a little talent-search business he set up on the side to find new dancers. Despite the fact that she hated lying or deceiving the IRS, there was simply no way around it. Thankfully, Vegas wasn't a place where many looked into one another's personal business. There was too much shit to hide on everyone's part, so Sienna Flower wasn't a target.

Everyone took it for what it was worth: She was Sienna Flower, queen of the strippers in Vegas, and made a shit load of money. Period.

She had an extremely well-done fake driver's license to prove she was in fact Sienna Flower; yet another benefit of living in Vegas. She only had to hope and pray no one ever really ran her social security or driver's license numbers.

After thinking too long and hard in the tub, Sienna's skin was wrinkled like a prune and the water had cooled off. She climbed out and wrapped herself in a huge terry robe before slipping into bed.

Her bed was another of her favorite purchases. It was a huge king-sized sleigh bed with silky sheets and way too many throw pillows. An indulgence so contradictory to her austere upbringing, she couldn't help but smile every time she crawled into it, despite the fact she was crawling into it alone.

Often Sienna drifted off to sleep as she watched the early-morning news, typical of the life of someone in the adult entertainment industry. As the sun came up, the strip clubs closed for the night. Days and nights were forever mixed up, but she was used to it now. In fact, she liked not having to be home alone in bed in the dark, when her thoughts jumbled in her head.

Sienna turned off the TV and snuggled deep in her soft sheets and covers. This was the time she felt lonely, with no one to warm her feet or bring her a cup of hot tea. Not that she'd had that in her marriage, but somewhere deep down she dreamed of it.

Maybe I should get a dog?

six

AFTER FINISHING his nightcap and cigar, Carson exchanged a few good-natured jokes with Victor and closed out his tab. Slot machines clanged loudly all around him, and a chorus of excited shouts went up at a nearby roulette table. He shook his head and bit back a smile, darkly amused that someone's luck was obviously better than his.

Fueled by the oxygen being pumped into the casino, his long legs ate up the luxurious carpet covering the casino floor as he approached the elevator, intent on a good night's sleep. By himself. But all his good intentions were derailed when he heard someone call his name from across the elevator lobby.

"Carson! Carson Graham!" a woman called out as she walked toward him. "Wow, look at you, still as striking as ever. I'm not one bit surprised to find you walking around one of the nicest hotels in Sin City."

Has she always been this loud?

He allowed himself a mental sigh, then arranged his features into a welcoming expression. "Lucinda Field. Wow, right back at you," he said carefully as he was flooded with a mixture of emotions. "I haven't seen you in over a decade, and here we are, running into each other in

Vegas."

A decade? Actually, it had been slightly longer than that since he'd last seen Lucinda. Since college, in fact. They'd had the same major, which meant they attended many of the same classes together. And as luck would have it, were frequently paired together as study partners or part of the same project group.

Carson knew she'd always liked him more than a friend, but he never went beyond friendship with her. Mostly because he was sure she would want more, and he wasn't that type of guy, especially way back then. With his abandonment issues at their absolute worst, Carson hopped from bed to bed throughout college. Like now, he never made promises. Although, he might have been a tad worse back then.

He was always up front about his preference for a lack of strings in his relationships. He knew his good looks, charm, and penchant for the good life helped in this department. Without any family keeping him tied down and no real visions of a white picket fence in his future, he lived life fully during college. Nice dinners, expensive beer, and fast motorcycles were his calling card.

Lucinda always pushed him to let her take a taste of the wild life with him, but he never bit. She was a good girl from a nice family. Although they both graduated with double majors in history and political science, Lucinda was smart and went to law school, while he was recruited by the FBI.

Unlike him, Carson was certain Lucinda dreamed of two kids, a dog, and the same white picket fence that gave him nightmares. He never wanted to lead her on, so he didn't. Perhaps he was a bit of a man-whore back then, but one with a heart.

Am I still a man-whore?

Running into Lucinda in Las Vegas all these years later, seeing her reminded Carson he hadn't changed much. When he thought about it, he was still driving fast bikes and cars, indulging in good food, liquor, and women, with no intention of settling down. And he suddenly wondered whether that was a good thing.

Carson reluctantly agreed to Lucinda's invitation to grab a drink together, and took her gently by the elbow to lead her back to the bar he'd just left. They had no sooner received their drinks than she was invading his personal space, much bolder than she had been in college.

"I'm in town for a conference, and since I have nothing holding me down at home, I thought I'd have just a touch of fun." She winked and licked her lips.

She leaned into Carson, letting him know without a doubt that he was currently the brand of trouble she was looking for. He glanced up to see Victor smirking at them from behind the bar, confirming what he already knew, mainly that he was horny and lonely. Which was a very bad combination.

He answered, "Is that so?" Despite knowing it was the wrong choice, he winked back. It was halfhearted at best, but she didn't seem to notice.

"Definitely," Lucinda purred. "I deserve it. I work hard, do it all on my own with no one having my back, and I'm a woman with many interests. Why not let loose?"

Lucinda was giving all the buying signs, but he wasn't in the market. She droned on, not stopping to notice that Carson wasn't even listening.

It was his own damn fault he was so desperate for a female's attention or touch. He was the one tied in knots over a stripper—a beautiful woman with supple curves, all the right moves, and bluer-than-blue eyes so deep they revealed she was actually much more than who she appeared to be onstage.

A woman who was completely inaccessible to him and untouchable to everyone. Yet he was so hung up on her, he was about to head up to his hotel room by his lonesome without any intention of trying to find another woman or even take care of himself.

Carson shook his head, annoyed at himself and confused by his current disinterest in pursuing anything female. He knew it bore some type of significance. A meaning, perhaps, that he shouldn't ignore.

If he had taken a longer drive before heading back to the hotel, maybe he wouldn't have run into Lucinda. Unfortunately, he didn't let the speed of his car take him away longer, and with tension still rippling through his body, he couldn't help but react a little when Lucinda ran her hand over his chest. She was no longer a bright-eyed, bushy-tailed, innocent coed. She was a grown woman now, and if she still had an itch when it came to him, perhaps he should scratch it.

At least, that was what he was thinking when he looked down and saw her red nails smoothing down the front of his white dress shirt. He imagined he could take her upstairs and have his way with her any way he pleased. While she was chatting his head off in the bar, he was envisioning a long night of tasting her, pushing inside her heat, and no telling what else.

His dick was saying yes, and his head was nodding in agreement.

Carson had nearly convinced himself to take her straight up to his room when Sienna Flower popped back in his mind. Her legs wrapped around the pole. Those long limbs, firm and toned, yet feminine. He couldn't think about anything other than running his tongue up and down the length of her smooth skin.

Her body was soft in all the right places, especially her eyes. There was an understanding and a softness about them, as though she deeply cared about the crowd watching her dance. Sienna made each and every person in the audience feel special and unique. It was such a contradiction to what she did for a living, but it made Sienna Flower who she was. A stripper with the most trusting eyes he'd ever seen, making him wonder what she would be like in person, one-on-one.

With his head filled with floating images of Sienna dancing and batting her long lashes over her seductive blue eyes, Carson could no longer even stomach the thought of taking Lucinda upstairs.

Not because she wasn't good-looking. Lucinda had matured into a beautiful woman, but she was so hard and direct, practically begging him to fuck her, that he couldn't get away from her fast enough.

When he finally reached his breaking point, he said, "Lucinda, it was so great seeing you, catching up and all, but I'm afraid I'm not very good company. I'm flat-out exhausted from all the travel I've been doing, and I have to catch some shut-eye."

She pouted like a schoolgirl.

From the corner of his eye, Carson could see Victor containing his laugh by covering his mouth with his hand, then pretending to cough.

"Well, let's at least exchange numbers," she suggested coyly. "Maybe we'll cross paths again?"

The woman just won't take no for an answer. Unbelievable.

"You know what?" He shook his head, then stared straight into her eyes. "It's not going to work. I'm married to my job these days." He picked up his drink and downed it, signaled to Victor for the bill, and gave Lucinda an apologetic half smile.

Lucinda stood up, her shoulders straight and rigid, but the quaver in her voice betrayed her. "I see. Well, it was nice to catch up with you, Carson. Safe travels." She then swept past him regally, holding her head high as she walked quickly away.

Watching her leave, he mumbled under his breath, "Hope you find your happiness."

Exhausted from their exchange, Carson ended up going to his room all by himself as he'd originally planned, then proceeded to toss and turn in his hotel room's king-sized bed.

He couldn't get settled over the fact he had turned down a woman who was ready, willing, and able, all because she seemed too direct, available, and loose. He hadn't been one bit attracted to the woman throwing herself at him.

Which was somewhat ironic considering the fact that he was fixated on a stripper. Didn't women who shed their clothes for a crowd say *Please fuck me* in not so many words?

Not Sienna. No, she was a different story altogether, and he was going to uncover it and take a big bite. Maybe even two or three bites, but that was it.

He wouldn't bite off more than he could chew. Just enough to satiate his appetite.

On that note, it wasn't until morning Carson felt himself begin to relax. Just before he thought he was about to drop off to sleep, he decided he would get in a long workout tomorrow—although technically it was already today—before he headed back to the Tunnel that night.

It was a good plan in theory. Unfortunately, Sienna insinuated herself in his thoughts once again, and sleep still eluded him.

seven

Friday night, after Sienna's first performance

B ACK IN her dressing room after her performance, Sienna sat down at her vanity while sipping from a bottled water, thinking of *him*. She picked up a towel, and was running it over her damp body when she heard a commotion outside her dressing room. When she peeked outside her door, she found Big Mike arguing with their newest bouncer, Billy, a young guy who was working on his criminology degree at University of Nevada, Las Vegas.

"I'm sorry, man," Billy was saying. "That guy only asked me to bring this message back to Sienna. I looked at it, and it wasn't anything rude, so I agreed. I know, it was stupid." The guy stood at the ready, obviously worried that Big Mike was going to pound him. And from the look on Mike's face, he wasn't far off in that estimation.

Mike's huge fists were hooked on his hips, his eyes narrowed at Billy as he said sternly, "Dude, I get it, but nothing gets delivered to Sienna, just like no one gets back here either. This is private space, and Sienna is not in the habit of taking names and numbers." He leaned into Billy's face and dropped his voice lower in warning. "Do *not* let this happen again."

Worried that the two of them were about to go to blows, Sienna stepped outside her dressing room door and interjected, "Uh, guys, I'm standing right here. What's going on, Mike?"

Billy lowered his head in shame. "Sorry, Ms. Flower, but some guy gave me this slip of paper for you with his number on it. He only asked if you wanted to go for coffee and to give you his number. I thought it might be okay to bring it back, but I made a mistake. I won't do it again."

"Okay, Billy," Sienna said carefully, not wanting for Billy to get into trouble on her account. "Yes, Mike is right. I don't normally take messages or numbers, but no one got hurt or bothered, so no worries. Since you're already back here, let me take that." She brought her hand up to take the slip of paper, then crumbled it in a ball, but held it tight in her palm. "By the way, what did the man look like?"

Mike swung his surprised gaze on her as she accepted the piece of paper, which was about as unusual as her walking the floor on a Friday night. For the second time that evening, Sienna was breaking her own personal code, and he knew it.

Great. Not only were Asher's hackles up, but now Mike's were, too.

Billy didn't answer, he just looked to Mike to see what he should do after the dressing-down he'd just received for bringing the note backstage.

Mike ignored him, and with curious eyes glaring down at her, answered for Billy. "I saw him. It was the man at the table you stopped by earlier."

"Oh." Sienna paused to collect her thoughts, not wanting to raise any more speculation. "Thanks, guys. I've seen him here before. I don't think there's anything to worry about, he's just a harmless fan. He asked me to have a drink with him tonight and I turned him down. He was probably just looking for another chance." She gave them both a smile that she hoped looked genuine, and went back into her dressing room.

As she settled onto her chaise longue, her one indulgence in her private dressing room, she realized she still had the slip of paper in her hand. Sienna knew Mike wasn't going to let this go. He had been with the club since she came to work at the Tunnel. Big Mike might cover up the silver-spoon upbringing he was always trying to shed with a scary face and demeanor, but he was also a softie like Asher when it came to her. He would never let anything make her scared or sad, and had been telling her this since she first came to work for Asher, promising he would always protect her. The bouncer was younger than she was, but he had taken her under his wing with a tenderness that at first had surprised her.

"Sienna, sweetie, we're gonna take care of you, Asher and me. Nothing is gonna scare you. Nothing," Mike used to say as he drove her home to that gross motel when she first started to dance. It wasn't as if he had designs on her. Big Mike was a one-woman man even back in the day, and his girlfriend lived with him. He just cared for Sienna and considered her family, unlike the wealthy parents he had turned his back on years before.

And just like family, she knew he wasn't going to drop this.

Sienna unfolded the slip of paper.

> *Name is Carson. Coffee on Saturday or Sunday?*
> *Nothing too crazy. I promise.*

That was all it said, along with his cell phone number.

Sienna put the note away. She couldn't think about this now. She had to go back out and dance again soon, and she was pretty sure Asher would be showing up any minute to check on her. Mike had a big mouth, and Asher was already concerned. *Shit.*

Locking the door, Sienna started to change her outfit for her next act. Unable to stop her thoughts from whether Carson was still out there, she began to choose a one-piece lace negligee with him in mind, and then caught herself.

Wow. I'm losing it.

Maybe she needed a little vacation? Perhaps a few days of R&R at one of the spa resorts near Red Rock Desert?

She was obviously not herself with all this thinking about a man, dressing for said man, and that tiny part of her that was considering having coffee with that man.

A little vacation was the answer.

A moment later, Asher knocked on her door as she'd predicted. After a quick check to be sure she was "decent," Sienna opened the door.

Asher brushed past her and turned to confront her, his protective mode in full swing. "Sienna, are you okay, honey?" Before she could answer, he raked his blond hair off his forehead and frowned. "I'm always telling you to make some time for yourself and date, but let's not get carried away with some guy from the audience. I know I told you it was natural to feel curious, but did you throw his number away?"

Sienna tried not to sigh. Asher meant well; she knew that. But sometimes he went a little overboard with his big-brother act.

So she smiled and, ignoring his question, said, "I'm good. Really, I am. I had a moment or something, I can't explain it, but there was a thing with him. Something I never had before. A pull."

The look that flashed over Asher's face looked suspiciously like pity. "Oh, doll, you're so lonely. That's it."

Sienna ignored the brief annoyance she felt at the thought of Asher pitying her, and did her best to mollify him. "I know, Ash. I'm all good now. It's passed, whatever it was. I think I need a few days off. A little vacation will do me good."

His face brightened and he instantly perked up. "Sounds great, I can go with you. How about Tuesday? Wednesday? Mike can run the place."

She laughed. "Perfect. Thanks, Ash, love you. Just a little break, a night off will do me wonders."

"I know, doll. Now it's time to dance and bring the house down, before we ride off into the sunset."

With a kiss to her temple, Asher headed back to his office, and she was left alone with the note again. No, she hadn't thrown it out, and she wasn't sure why. After all, there was nothing she could do with it.

As much as she loved dancing and it was her ultimate relief, she needed to break away from this place for a day or so. Thank God for Asher and the upcoming getaway. She would go away with Asher, take a breather, and return home restored and renewed to live life. By herself.

As for him, Carson, he was nobody to her. There was no "thing." No pull. Only a big blip of loneliness filled with need and want, one that could never be filled.

Taking a deep breath and allowing her mind to go blank, Sienna hit stage right before heading out to entice the crowd with nothing less than what they expected. They wanted to feel seduction and sex in the air, so that was what she would make them feel. The more charged the performance, the more anxiety relief Sienna felt—and the more sexually entranced she became.

As she hit center stage, Sienna's line of vision locked with Carson's, and her moment of relief was lost.

She'd only learned his name less than an hour ago, but she felt like it had been on her tongue for years. Carson. He watched her intently, as always. He didn't smile like earlier, but his eyes bore down on her with a look she had never experienced. Want? Intimate need?

How would her name sound coming off this tongue? Sienna...Lila. She wasn't even sure of her own name. His stare was turning her inside out, something else Sienna had never experienced.

Finding it harder and harder to lose herself in her number, she tried to avoid Carson and his molten chocolate eyes for fear she might melt into a tiny pool herself. Her heart was pumping and it wasn't from dancing, heat was gathering once again in her tiny panties, and she had to look far away into the back of the crowd to keep from leaping off the stage.

Sienna wanted to jump right into Carson's lap, an animalistic urge that bubbled up in her entire body. It was a force of nature she never had to control before, but one she had to tamp down, because she needed to survive on her own.

The truth was, she had no clue what came next if she did jump on his lap. Because even though Sienna might have the right moves onstage, up close and personal in real life, she had no idea what to do.

eight

Sienna was both emotionally and physically drained by the time Mike walked her out to her car after her shift Friday night, happy to know that Simon was waiting to drive her home.

She loved Simon; the grandfather of two little boys always brought a smile to her face. He'd been a driver in Vegas for thirty-six years, and he always made her laugh with his tales of Las Vegas, then and now. After the night she'd had, Simon was just what she needed.

Mike opened the car door for her, but touched her arm before she climbed in. When she looked up in question, he frowned slightly. "Sienna, I know Ash is worried and you think that something weird is happening. Nothing weird is going on, you just need a life outside of here," he said as he motioned behind him to the club.

"The guy with the note seems like a good guy," he went on as she gaped at him. He slung his big arm around her slight waist. "You need to take a leap with someone, even if it's not him, but why not him? What I'm trying to say is, you need to get back out there. You need to live."

And before she could say a word, he handed her into the backseat of the big black town car.

Sienna was shocked; no longer looking forward to Simon's sweet stories.

Am I going to take advice from a twenty-five-year-old bouncer?

Advice was what she needed, and Mike was one of the few trusted people she had in her little world. Petal and Sydney were still at the club working a few private parties, but she could wait and ask them. She could, yet she was their role model.

What would they think about her indecision? Both Petal and Sydney would think she was crazy not to follow her heart, but like Mike, they didn't know her real history. They didn't know why it was imperative that she stay alone.

Sienna knew Carson had stayed through her second dance. He didn't get up right away as usual. Did he think she was going to come out and talk with him again?

She knew he was gone when she finally left for the night, because she had peeked at the club from the one-way mirror in Asher's office before leaving.

Was she in high school, checking up on a guy?

As the town car carried her home, Sienna found she couldn't stop thinking about him. He was probably still up. Could she have coffee with him tomorrow?

No one would have to know. She didn't have to tell Mike she took his advice.

Without thinking, she pulled out her phone and texted the number on the slip she'd tucked into her bag.

> *Sienna*: It's Sienna. Got your note. I don't typically do this, but coffee tomorrow may work.

Before she could put her phone away, it pinged with an incoming text.

> *Carson*: Hi, Sienna. Didn't expect to hear from you, but glad. Coffee sounds good. Where? When? You name it.

Her heart in her throat, Sienna enjoyed a quick back and forth with him as she broke another of her own rules.

> *Sienna*: Canyon Coffee in Henderson? 1 p.m.?

Carson: Meet you there?
Sienna: Yes.
Carson: Looking forward.

Once the plan was set, buyer's remorse immediately set in.
Oh God, I've done it.

As the bright lights of the Strip faded away and suburban Las Vegas passed by her window, Sienna tried to calm her nerves. Perhaps the sexual hype of the club clouded her judgment? Surely, the serenity of her neighborhood with its perfectly manicured rock gardens and well-lit porches would give her a better perspective. She looked out the darkened window, unsure of exactly what time it was, but caught sight of the moon hanging in the black velvet sky over the distant desert. She leaned back into the soft seat and stared at it as her thoughts whirled.

The problem was, she wasn't strong enough to resist the desire and urge to connect intimately with someone else. Her heart and her body had another plan, and somehow she had to get a handle on it all.

She would have coffee with Carson, and give the curiosity a chance to bleed out of her system. Afterward she would go away with Asher for a day or two, and then she'd be ready to move forward on her own, just as she had been doing for years.

The fact she was an adult star scared her less than getting attached to a man. The adult entertainment world was a place the only other community she'd ever known shied away from, ignored, and pretended as if they weren't even part of the same secular space. The two universes would never collide. She was safe in the little web she'd spun for herself.

But she wasn't safe opening up her heart.

Sadly, Sienna arrived home before she knew it, having ignored Simon for the entire ride. As he opened her door, held her hand as she exited into the chilly evening air, and walked her all the way up the narrow path lined with tiny pebbles, she felt bad. She shut the door behind her, the lock clicking into place, and made a mental note to make it up to him later in the week with some cookies. Getting her priorities straight was more important.

A short while later as she slipped into her nightly bath, letting the water warm her skin, Sienna felt solid in her resolve. One cup of coffee and she'd be done with Carson. An hour of mindless adult chatter would ease her ache for the intimacy missing in her life, and then she could continue to move forward with the plan she had set for herself a long time ago.

Even as her brain worked overtime, trying to convince her heart that this tactic was the right one, the rest of her body tingled, remembering how it had pulsed earlier.

The feeling radiating through her was something she couldn't identify. Lust? Desire? It had been years since she'd been intimate with a man, and the only one she had been with did nothing to satisfy her. Which explained why, at the moment, she was having trouble pinpointing why her body was so heated with physical need.

Since arriving in Vegas, Sienna learned all there was to know about sex, acting sensual, playing up the more naughty ideas, and how to please herself. She even had a vibrator. Growing up, Lila didn't even know something as miraculous as a vibrator existed. When Penelope gave Sienna one as a gift, she was mystified, but after a few times experimenting with it, she was sold.

Taking care of herself with the tiny little "pocket rocket" was the only sexual pleasure she had ever had. Sad that it was at the effort of her own hands and a little battery-operated friend.

She was pretty sure it would be different with a real, live man, but since that wasn't a reality, Sienna had figured out to take care of her own body's needs. Now it suddenly didn't seem enough.

As her hand slipped into the tub and ran along her soft heat, she couldn't help but think of Carson.

She'd never touched herself or gotten off while thinking of a specific man before; no one had attracted her like that. But since she worked in the sex industry, she needed a release after breathing the sexually charged air at the club, so she took care of herself.

Allowing herself to feel some sort of pleasure was a big step for Lila. She'd been raised to service a man in his release and making babies. Never once had she thought about her own body and its needs when growing up.

Even now as she took care of feeling good, it wasn't the kind of multicolored fireworks Sienna had heard other women talk about around the Tunnel.

It just took the edge off.

But at the moment, her own finger was deep inside herself, the palm of her hand hitting her most sensitive spot, her mind on Carson, it wasn't even beginning to take the edge off.

No man had ever captured her attention enough to warrant what she was doing with him solely in mind.

Thinking of his broad shoulders, his dimple, and the glimpse she'd had of his tattoo, shivers burst through Sienna as her orgasm hit, and she wanted to do it all over again.

She wanted to push her fingers deeper, increase the pressure where she needed it most, and feel herself explode to thoughts of it being Carson's hand strumming her.

This thought shocked her to her core, and she froze. She was in trouble, deep trouble, because her plan to stay safe was based on not getting attached to a man. She further reminded herself of this as she stepped out of the tub and dried off, then put on her silky camisole and pajama bottoms.

Her reminders were fleeting because all it took was the soft feel of the silk on her raised nipples to cause her thoughts to move immediately back to Carson.

His hands on my nipples, pulling them, then putting his tongue on them. That's what I want.

Despite being worn out from the emotional roller coaster of her day, Sienna thought sleep would elude her as she crawled into bed with her rapid thoughts and ideas. With her body still humming from her orgasm, she drifted off quickly, though, to thoughts of more. More Carson.

Unfortunately, her body wasn't in agreement with her thinking. The Carson of her dreams was on top of her, his head buried between her legs, then sliding back up her body and plunging his hardness deep inside her.

CARSON COULDN'T sleep when he got back to his room. She was all sizzling sex and natural beauty with something else he couldn't put his finger on, and she had stood right next to him. Somehow over the last few weeks, Sienna Flower had become something more than an obsession for him.

An addiction? He couldn't stop going to the Tunnel, and he wasn't sure he wanted to stop.

The "dirty" dancer with sparkling eyes stole all his fantasies since he first saw her. Christ, he had turned down a night of hot, no-strings-attached sex with Lucinda the night before because he couldn't get Sienna out of his head.

Tonight when she came over to him, he didn't even know what to say. He lost his words over a woman, which was about as unusual as Sienna walking the club floor on a weekend night.

Actually, fucking rare, as in it never happened to him. Ever. And from what everyone said, Sienna Flower never walked the floor on Fridays, and she definitely didn't approach patrons alone.

Yet she had walked right out into the crowd and stopped at his table, waiting for him to say something, make the first move. And he simply said, "Hi."

Smooth. Real smooth moves, idiot.

Carson had really wanted to ask her to dinner. Somewhere nice. Go to a quiet place and stare at her. Have her all to himself, not in a room full of men who were all fantasizing about her. He wanted her to have only eyes for him while sharing cocktails, and then ravage her afterward.

Fucking ravage her. Every inch of her.

What did all this mean? Did he want to date her? Have a relationship with her?

She's a stripper. She takes off her clothes for money. And I don't date.

Christ, he was hard just thinking about her standing next to his table, leaning up against the chair. He had never wished to be a damn chair before in his life. Her little nightie-thing with the pink thong peeking through it had controlled his thoughts from the second she walked up next to the empty seat at his table. He'd never wanted to touch a woman so badly, and he couldn't stop thinking about who else had touched her.

He needed to forget about who else had touched her, because the thought made Carson want to kill them.

What the hell was he thinking? How could he become addicted to a stripper? Let alone, ask her out to coffee on a little slip of paper like he was in high school? Fucking fool.

He was a good-looking dude; he knew that. He didn't need to pay someone to fuck him, but she didn't have sex with men for money. She made an honest living stripping.

This was what was rolling through his head when the text came through. He could tell she was obviously on edge with her curt text message, but he was still happy as all fuck to get it. He'd bet that when she sent the text, she probably hoped he wouldn't reply. Oh, but he did.

Carson was ex-FBI and he knew how to read a person. He knew that if he didn't respond quickly to her text, there would be no second chance with Sienna. He knew enough from watching Sienna dance (and googling her) that she was a loner, stayed to herself, and let no one in close. But she was texting *him*.

I am going to get her in bed and fuck her right out of my system.

Then he was going to wrap up his current case, spend some time in the Bahamas, and come back and only take well-vetted jobs. He'd agreed to coffee with Sienna, but in reality wanted much more. And he was unsure about whether he could get it.

Do I really want her?

And if I have her, will I be able to let her go?

The plan was set to meet the next day, and now Carson was even further away from sleep as he lay on his king-sized hotel bed. His hand roamed down his own abdomen and he gripped himself hard. For a man who prided himself on his lasting power, it didn't take long to get himself off with his own hand.

Like an adolescent male opening up a nudie magazine for the first time, Carson grasped his dick and pumped his hand up and down his shaft, thinking of the one and only woman he'd been able to conjure up in the last few weeks.

He wasn't ashamed of taking himself to pleasure. He was a hot-blooded male with a pretty large sexual appetite, and he'd been watching Sienna Flower week in and week out with very little release.

Taking himself over the edge had recently become his greatest pastime with a mental Rolodex of images of Sienna onstage, but it was doing less and less when it came to his sexual hunger. The more he jerked himself off, the greater the need he felt to sink deep inside the woman he only recently began to think of as more than sexual eye candy.

His palm was working fast and rough on his dick, and before he could control himself, he came all over his hand to the mental images of a mouth-watering and dick-hardening adult dancer.

When he stepped into the shower to clean up, his dick was rock hard again. The only choice he had was to lean up against the wall and rub another one out, or turn the water temperature freezing cold.

Leaning up against the tile in the shower with the hot water beating down his back, Carson wrapped his hand around himself for the second time that evening. This was getting to be ridiculous. He wasn't really that big a fan of beating off, but something about Sienna and her eyes pulled him in…all the way in.

He didn't want to go down to the bar and seek the company of someone else. He wanted her. Only her. This was definitely a first.

After relieving himself twice, Carson tossed and turned for a few hours before getting up and working on his current case a little.

He called back east, where he knew some of his contacts would be hard at work already. He pressed the speed dial on his phone for Rich, a fellow PI, and didn't bother to say hello when he answered.

"You ever work with cults? People you just don't get? Maybe don't even want to get? That's what I got going on here in hell. Talk to me."

Rich chuckled. "Hello to you, Carson, too. Yeah, I worked with some people out toward the Amish community. Fuck, they're weird, but those psychos were rolling in the dough. Made it worth my while."

Carson scratched his head, messing his hair while thinking of what he wanted to say next. "Starting to think my recent case with my very own sect of weirdness is not worth my while. Not only is it a huge time suck with no end in sight, but the shit is fucking with my head, making me do things I'd never ordinarily do. Like date."

"Uh, buddy, what do you want to do? Talk like we're high school chicks going to the prom? No way." Rich snorted. "As for your case, run it by the big dogs at the Bureau."

He pinched the bridge of his nose. "Nah. Too early to admit defeat and ask for their help. Thanks, Rich. You've been a dreamboat. Remind me to call Ray next time."

Rich laughed good-naturedly, then disconnected the call.

Carson's zigzag thinking moved to how he'd acted like a teenage boy the night before, and he decided to do something to get himself in check. How many times could he masturbate? He was going to get calluses on his hand and his cock.

So he hit the hotel workout room with a vengeance. He went for double his usual workout, grabbed a protein drink, and was shocked when he wasn't one bit exhausted. He was practically buzzing with energy.

In an effort to kill time and his raging hard-on, Carson decided to do some more work until it was time to meet Sienna. He was starting to despise his current case, and looking it over was like dumping a bucket of cold water on his erection. He reviewed the notes he'd made when he initially met with his client.

Call the big dogs? No way in hell.

Originally, he'd thought this was going to be a cake case. Find missing person, deliver to family, collect money, and move on. Instead, he wasn't one bit closer to finding the victim.

But was the person really a victim? Or were they just seeking a different life than the fucking cult family who'd hired him?

He needed to make a visit back east to collect more details. What they gave him was shit, and he was starting to think he'd been set up. He had the strangest feeling that someone, a third party, was planting information in their minds, leading them on, and screwing with his investigation.

They were wasting their money and his time. Time he could be spending watching Sienna.

Noon approached quickly as Carson was deep in thought over his next course of action in his current assignment. Sunday night, he planned to start researching what he wanted to do next. Monday, he would go back east and make arrangements to see the client. He couldn't call them now; that would be a waste of time. They wouldn't answer on their weekend.

For now, Carson decided to put the missing person to rest, get ready to meet the woman of his fantasies, and desperately try to convince himself he was making a stupid mistake.

He hoped that gorging on her would get her off his mind.

Yeah, right. As if she's going to just fuck me at the coffee shop.

nine

Saturday

SIENNA WOKE up sweaty and restless, itching for the dreams to be reality.

Typically, she lounged around on Saturday mornings. Her little carriage house was the best place to do this with a gourmet kitchen that opened into a comfy sitting room, perfect for baking and watching TV at the same time.

There was also a beautiful stone patio off the sliding glass doors in the back of the kitchen. Often on Saturday or Sunday, she would venture out there with something from her to-be-read pile of books.

On this Saturday, Sienna couldn't settle down with a book or baking. After a few hours of extremely restless sleep, she dragged herself out of bed and into the bathroom. Even her luxurious stall shower with beveled glass, multiple shower heads, and steam wasn't enticing her. Frantic with nervous energy, she decided to walk across the yard to Asher's house.

During the week, it wasn't unusual for Sienna to go over to Asher's and have coffee while reading the paper, but on weekends, she usually stayed put at her place. She had a routine, and generally stuck to it.

Today was an exception. Sienna needed to talk her current situation out with someone.

While Asher wasn't the person the other girls went to with their emotional problems, he was all she had, so she turned to him often. Sienna trekked through the path lined with cacti up to the side door of Asher's main house on the front end of the property.

It was Asher, after all, so Sienna didn't even think to change out of her pajama pants and tank that she briskly put back on after her shower. With her hair in an insanely messy bun on the top of her head, no makeup, and a cardigan sweater wrapped around her, Sienna unlocked the side door with the keypad and walked right in...to see a very naked Natalie sitting on the kitchen counter, barely wrapped in a blanket, swinging her legs while sipping coffee.

"Oh boy! I'm sorry, Nat. I didn't realize Asher had company." She pushed the air in and out of her lungs, and jumped as she heard Asher coming down the hall. *Shit.*

"Nat, I'm here, baby. I had to chat with Mike on the phone for a sec, but now I'm all yours." He rubbed his face, scratching his goatee, clearly having no clue that Sienna was there yet.

Seeing Sienna, Asher changed gears midsentence, turning all his attention on her when he noticed he had a visitor other than Natalie. "Sie, honey, you all right?"

"Yep," Sienna said, thinking fast on her feet. "No worries, Ash. Just wanting to chat about our trip. I was so excited thinking about it this morning. But it can wait." She waved her hand with nonchalance and turned to head back to the side door, desperately trying to escape.

Asher strode over to her quickly, grabbed her shoulder, and turned her to face him. "Me, too, doll. Can't wait. Nat came back for a drink last night, and well, she's still here as you can see. We're going to make breakfast. Want to stay?"

There was no way she was going to talk about her coffee date with Natalie there. Not because she didn't like Natalie; she just didn't share too much of her feelings with anyone.

"No, sweetheart. You two have breakfast. We will have our whole trip together. I'm going to go home and change, so I can run some errands." Attempting not to be fazed by the completely bare woman with her butt cheeks pressed to the granite countertop, she stood on her tippy-toes, gave him a quick peck on the cheek, and immediately went out the door she entered, pulling it shut tight behind her.

Sienna also didn't want to make Asher feel awkward. She'd wanted him to make up with Natalie for some time, so this was good. She just hoped that was what he was doing with her, and that he didn't mess it up.

Natalie had a son, an adorable little nine-year-old boy named Quinn, who Sienna knew she took a lot of pride in raising. Natalie's mom pitched in with childcare since the child's dad was long gone from the scene, and it wasn't easy being a young single mom.

This wasn't a situation for Asher to dick around with, and she planned to tell him that on their trip now that she could see they already made amends. She'd held her tongue long enough, especially after the episode a few weeks back.

But first, she had to survive her own personal crisis. Coffee with Carson.

Her phone beeped as she walked back into her carriage house.

Wow. I'm popular all of a sudden.

She looked at the screen and found a text from Big Mike.

Mike: Call me.

That was all it said, so she did. First it was late-night advice, now phone calls?

Mike answered on the first ring. "Hi, Sie."

"Hi, Mike," she said warily. "What's up? Everything good?"

"Yeah, it's all good. I wanted to see how you got along last night after the note. That's never happened before, and you know I care for you, girl."

Big Mike is my fairy godmother all of a sudden?

She so desperately needed to talk with someone about Carson, she took him up on his offer to chat. "I'm all right. After getting in the car last night, I texted that guy. Carson, that's his name. It was a weak moment, but I guess I was curious."

"I got you, Sie."

"Well, anyway, we're going for coffee today. I'm hoping to just get the curiosity out of my system. I know you and Ash want me to settle down with someone, but that's not going to happen, so I figure an afternoon out with some adult conversation will do the trick. He seemed nice enough."

Mike sighed heavily over the line. "Sienna, that's a bad attitude. I told you, girl, you deserve a good life and more."

Geez, Mike is quite the romantic.

"Maybe you'll like this guy," he went on. "I'm no matchmaker, so that's all I can say. Uh, the real reason behind my call is you. I thought you might take a leap and see this dude. When you do, I'm gonna tail you."

"What?" She plopped onto her sofa, shocked at what she was hearing.

"That's right, girl. I always go with you, so you're not sneaking off to coffee with a strange guy."

"Mike, we're meeting over here in Henderson at Canyon Coffee. I was planning on wearing big glasses and a baseball cap," Sienna said with a giggle.

Who else wears a baseball hat to meet a guy for coffee? A stripper needing anonymity.

"Nope," Mike said. "I'm going with you. As much as I want you to meet someone, I need to get a feel for the scene." Sienna didn't even have a chance to reply before he asked, "What time? You can drive there yourself, if you want, but I'm gonna follow."

"One o'clock. And I'm only telling you because I can tell there's no arguing."

"See you at twelve thirty, Sienna. Still wear the cap and glasses."

"Okay. 'Bye."

He disconnected, so Sienna decided to get dressed and clean up her desk. She had to do something to calm her nerves. She hadn't checked her e-mails yet, so decided to get that task out of the way.

Except when she booted up her computer, Sienna found herself feeling sentimental.

She wished she could keep in touch with a few of her friends from her old life. She wondered if any of them ever thought of her. Lila had turned her back on all of them when she ran, but they didn't know what she was going through. She knew better than to be honest with them; it would be difficult for them to believe who her husband really was and what he did.

Besides, very few women took a stand against any man where she grew up. Being transparent with her friends would only stand to hurt them, and in the end, would make life worse. She'd never before had someone who had her back, like Mike or Asher did now.

Back then, she was forced to take dramatic measures to survive.

Still, she couldn't help missing and worrying for the women she had known for most of her life.

H ER CARRIAGE house was clean and Tunnel e-mails returned. Sienna had killed as much time as she could, so she headed to her bedroom to get dressed to go out for coffee. Coffee with a man. A man she couldn't risk letting in, but she was pretty sure had already barged in where he didn't belong, settled where he absolutely shouldn't and couldn't be, and would have to be pushed out. Fast.

This was all on her; it was all her own fault.

Sienna walked into her large walk-in closet off her bedroom and decided to go for understated. Chocolate-brown leggings, a big chunky oatmeal-colored sweater, suede boots, light makeup, and a Los Angeles baseball cap that one of the other girls had brought back for everyone after a trip. With her hair in a low ponytail underneath the cap, Sienna looked like a suburban housewife, except for her body.

She knew a stripper's body when she saw one. The pole dancing and certain dance moves they had to do just did something to women in their line of work. Sienna had come to recognize the unique curves of dancers, like her, who took their clothes off for a living.

She was barely recognizable even to herself, and the feeling wasn't exclusive to what she saw in the mirror. It had been so long since Sienna had any friends other than Asher, Petal, and Mike, she barely knew what her personality was other than Sienna Flower, adult dancer. She internalized the idea of her body, her stage persona being the entirety of her.

There were times when Sienna yearned to have more friends, to have someone special to wake up next to, but she couldn't allow it. She'd sacrificed all that when she left her old life to recreate herself.

In her old life, she might have woken up every morning next to someone, but to him she was a nothing. Her husband thought *he* was someone, especially when he was throwing her into the bookshelves or raping her against her will. She still wore the faint scar on her hip from when her husband had brought a candelabra down on her repeatedly when she'd resisted him, with no regard to the pain radiating through her hip bone.

Everything he did went against all she'd ever been taught. Growing up, she'd been led to believe that as a wife she would be considered precious, that she would be doted on by her lover and partner, and together they would create a family. But that was far from her reality.

Within a few weeks after the marriage ceremony, her dreams became a living nightmare. Beatings, rape, and emotional abuse were all doled out on a regular basis, yet kept secret from their tight-knit religious community in New York City, where they lived.

She had absolutely no one to turn to when the torture started. She knew that the clergy would turn a blind eye, her family wouldn't risk being shamed in front of their friends, and her in-laws would never believe anything but the best about their son.

Intent on staying alive, she had slowly conceived an escape plan, and executed every detail with precision and caution. When she crawled out of the window on that dark and cold night, her body had burned with fear. But the fear of what would happen to her if she stayed was worse.

Lila crawled out the window wearing ratty jeans and a tight black turtleneck with her hair uncovered and flowing freely down her back. The clothes she had found in a thrift shop outside their neighborhood when she went to the dentist. Her hair hadn't seen the light of day since she was married, so it was longer and darker. Minutes before leaving, she had hidden in the bathroom and cut long bangs with shaky hands to partially conceal her eyes.

This quick disguise got her to the subway and into one of the other boroughs, where she boarded a bus to Chicago, then Kansas. Her plan was to make a few stops, which she hoped would throw anyone off her master plan to land in Vegas.

She'd come a long way from the scared young woman on the run who didn't know what to do next.

Thankfully, now she was firmly planted in Vegas with a very different appearance than she'd had back in her early twenties. She was gorgeous but unattached, lonely, and remained an enigma to most.

She didn't have anything even remotely close to a social life, and now she was walking out the door to have coffee with a man. A man she only knew because he had watched her dance at the Tunnel, and now she was dreaming of having more with him.

God, I'm stupid.

Canyon Coffee was a ten-minute drive from her house. Nestled in an upscale shopping center near an organic grocery store, yoga studio, and a small Italian bistro, it was a quiet location. Sienna rarely took her car out except for quick local errands, but today she put the top down on her little foreign convertible and enjoyed the ride. It was nice being chauffeured in the back of a town car, but there was something liberating about driving on her own. It gave her yet another small sense of freedom, one she'd never had in her old life, and could rarely enjoy in her new one.

As she pulled into a parking spot, she saw Mike in his big SUV. Parked in a front spot with a direct line of sight to the coffee shop, he was in position to watch her every move. Warmed by the thought of his careful diligence, Sienna made a mental note to grab Mike a coffee when she was on her way out later.

Sienna got out of her car and started making her way to the coffeehouse. She didn't glance Mike's way, careful not to make any overt gestures toward him. She didn't want to give him away, since it would be somewhat awkward for Carson to know she had someone watching over her.

Taking a deep breath, she walked toward the coffee shop like she met a random man for coffee every day of the week.

Sienna startled slightly when the chimes above the door jingled, signaling she'd entered the coffee shop. She kept her head slightly down, although a quick survey of the store revealed no one showing interest in the latest customer to enter. There were two tables occupied with suburban housewives in yoga clothes, who were probably gossiping over their lattes. In the corner, Carson was sitting in one of the large brown leather armchairs with his black down vest laid over the one catty-corner to his. She glanced at the counter, noting there was no line for a drink, and nothing left to distract her.

Carson stood up and walked toward her. He looked good in daylight. Instead of his usual white button-down shirt, he was wearing a light gray henley tee, worn-in jeans, and brown motorcycle boots. He still hadn't shaved, and Sienna had the strangest urge to rub herself like a kitten against the stubble on his face.

He looked rugged, but refined. A gentleman who could take anything that came his way. Tough on the outside, but soft on the inside, as evidenced by the warmth in his eyes when he caught sight of her, and in the way his brow furrowed in anticipation as he approached her.

"Good morning." One corner of his mouth lifted slightly, acknowledging the irony of his salutation although it was early afternoon. He obviously knew she kept late hours.

She was a stripper. He was a patron. Sienna needed to keep

reminding herself of that little fact. This wasn't a fairy tale. Fairy tales didn't exist.

"Same to you," Sienna whispered back.

Carson suggested they sit down, and lightly placed his hand on the small of her back to escort her back to where he'd been sitting.

Although she was a stripper, she'd never been touched so intimately. The faint brush of his fingertips along the bottom of her spine sent chills all the way down to her toes and back up again. Sienna automatically pulled away from the slight touch despite wanting to sink into it, confused by the unfamiliar sensations that seemed to ripple right through her.

"Is this okay?" Carson frowned and immediately removed his hand, but it still lingered, hovering near her back. The cute little lines where he furrowed his brow appeared again, making him hard to resist.

"Sorry," she said. "Actually, it startled me a bit. I'm so used to the no-touch policy at the club." She shrugged, unsure of what to do, where to turn, or if she should make a beeline for the exit.

Actually, I want you to rub me up and down with your big, strong hands, touching me like no one ever has before.

"No worries. Let's go sit, start over, and I can grab us some coffee," Carson said, and gestured toward the comfy chairs he had been saving.

Before they sat, he reached out a hand and said, "Carson Graham. Nice to meet you...formally."

She hesitated for a second, then extended her hand and said, "Sienna Flower, but you already know that."

He took her hand in his and shook it lightly, making their introduction official, sealing Sienna's fate that she was doing this. Her hand felt like it was crackling on fire as she shook his, touching a man for the first time because she wanted to, not because she was handed over to him or being paid to dance in his lap.

An electric current ran through her whole body, traveling through her veins and straight to the one part of her she never revealed to anyone. The only area that stayed tightly hidden away, even at the Tunnel.

With formal introductions out of the way, he politely asked for her coffee order and then walked back to the counter as she settled into the chair opposite his.

His ass looked so good in his jeans. Noting his back pockets were slightly frayed, Sienna wanted to slide her hands in them and feel what

70

was inside. She'd never done that before, but the idea popped into her head as though it were the most natural thing to do. Was it?

I'm screwing this whole damn thing up, Sienna thought to herself as Carson ordered a cappuccino for her and something for himself. So stupid. *No-touch policy at the club? That's the best I can come up with?*

Sienna decided to move conversation away from the club when Carson came back to the chairs. *Talk about him, act polite, and then end this coffee date on a nice note.* In no time, she would be home for a warm bath and go to work.

Why did that tug at her heart?

Unlike normal teenagers, Sienna had never been on a date; it wasn't part of her culture growing up. Boys and girls were separated from one another once they hit ten years old, and on that birthday, gone were the days of playing together at recess or the local playground. Their classes at school became single sex, their roles at home steered by whether they were male or female, and every second of free time was closely monitored.

Of course, as puberty arrived and their bodies changed, the boys and girls noticed one another behind lowered gazes or when no one else was watching. It was impossible not to be curious, but if one were overly curious, they were scolded and labeled as deviant.

As the baby girl of her family with three older brothers, even if she had wanted to rebel, it would have proven difficult. Lila did as she was told. She went to school, was taught by her mom to cook and run a household, prayed each day, and when the time came, she accepted an arranged marriage her parents set up for her.

So she'd never dated unless you counted the two or three times she'd shared a cup of coffee with the man she was betrothed to, under the close supervision of an adult chaperone.

Her brothers were all married off to young women her parents had hand-selected for their sons. Plain, family-oriented, religious, with no real goals other than to take care of their husbands and eventual children, all three wives were cookie-cutter models. The same model Elon thought he was getting in her, but he also wanted a punching bag who could spit out a baby each year.

Although Asher had been begging her for the last few years to get out and date and make a life, she never allowed herself that dream. Not so much because she was still legally married. She definitely wasn't looking to get married again so that wouldn't come into play, but she was scared to death about sex.

Forget sex, being intimate in the smallest way frightened her. Coming from an arranged marriage with all kinds of crazy rules about relations, she had little to no experience being intimate with a man.

She glanced toward the counter, assuring herself she had a few more moments to gather herself. Carson waited by the barista for her beverage, standing there as if this was their regular Saturday morning routine, making small talk with the young girl behind the massive espresso machine.

Sienna looked around for a stray newspaper. It would finish off the "young couple out for midday java" look.

Early on in her dancing days, Sienna read a lot of romance books. Sienna Flower was a creation of who and what women in the books were portrayed as being, both in fantasies and happily-ever-after romances. Perhaps the romance novels were the reason women loved Sienna just as much as the men did. She embodied what women thought they should be like for a man.

Surely, a man wanted a real woman rather than a fictional character?

Sure as she was sitting in a room filled with the aroma of fresh coffee being brewed and steam filling the air around the latte counter, Sienna had no hard-core knowledge of "being" with the male species. No more than servicing a man while lying on her back motionless, taking his penis inside her as if she really wanted it, and accepting his punches when she wasn't lying down.

A chill ran down Sienna's spine as she remembered her husband coming to the room they shared for two weeks of every month. He never touched or kissed her. He didn't even take her clothes off, rather left them as a barrier between his skin and hers. He would push her underwear to the side and enter quickly and without warning, then he would finish as quickly as he entered. With a few rough jabs of himself inside her, he would ejaculate and be done.

Sienna wasn't sure whether there was a problem with her or him, but there must have been one because she never got pregnant. Thankfully. He wouldn't allow her to use birth control, and they only had sex during her fertile periods.

Sienna dragged herself out of her fog. She was so nervous over one cup of coffee, her thoughts had taken a negative path. She needed to redirect herself to somewhere positive, especially since she overheard Carson thanking the barista for the beverages, and would soon be back.

Although she'd never really been out with a man, she placed a smile of confidence on her face as Carson made his way back to their seats, juggling the steaming drinks and a small plate.

"One cappuccino for the lady, and I took the chance of buying a scone for us to share. In case we get hungry," Carson added with a wink.

"Thank you. I'm actually hungry." When Carson raised an eyebrow at her comment, she asked, "What? Isn't that why you bought the scone? To eat?" She busied her hands, rubbed her thumbs over each other, and tried to still her nerves.

"Yes, of course. It's just that in all my years of dating, I've never heard a woman admit she was hungry on a first date. I kind of like it."

He laughed, and the sound shot right to her heart, warming the muscle she'd frozen over years ago, relaxing her everywhere.

Sienna gave him a tentative smile. "Well, believe it or not, I don't have much experience with doing this," she said with a wave of her hand indicating their surroundings. "I'm just being myself, and I'm hungry. Truthfully, I wanted to avoid talking about what I do, but the fact is what I do, I can eat whatever I want. Pretty much."

Carson just smiled at her. She had no idea where all her boldness was coming from; she was a regular Chatty Cathy at the moment. Admitting she had little dating experience and telling secrets of her job? What personal information would she reveal next, that she was on a perfect twenty-eight-day menstrual cycle?

Desperately trying to curtail her rambling, Sienna reached over and took a piece of scone to shove in her big mouth.

"I'm a runner, so I eat whatever I want, too," Carson said, defusing the tension even further.

Of course he ran. Just look at his gorgeous, lean body.

"I run about twice a week," she said. "I just go around my neighborhood, and one of the guys from the club typically comes with me. I don't know why. Without makeup and my hair in a cap, I'm not recognizable." She motioned her hand like a game show hostess across her face to prove the point.

Carson leaned back in his chair. "You're still gorgeous, if you don't mind me saying. I like this natural look. I didn't know what to expect when you agreed to meet. I've only seen you at the club, so I had no idea what you'd wear outside in the real world, but I like it. I don't know about the baseball team itself, but the cap is good. And you're even more stunning without all the makeup." He gave her a once-over, allowing his eyes to roam before he stopped at her eyes and gave her another wink.

Before she could blush, he pressed his forehead into the heel of his hand. "God, I'm such a dumb fuck. I told myself I wouldn't make this meeting all about your looks, but rather get to know you. Yet here I'm going on about how you look."

She smiled. "It's fine. I've never done this before. I really don't have much of a life outside the club. Just work, the other girls, and the rest of the time, I enjoy the quiet of my place. I don't know what I'm doing here either."

Sienna took a deep breath and somehow found the courage to add, "You're handsome, too. I liked the way you looked when I saw you at the club, but you never smiled when you watched. It made me curious about you."

Carson leaned back in the leather chair and stretched out his long legs beneath the tiny table between them. He laced his fingers together over his midsection as he said, "Well, it's good to know that we're both fascinated with each other. And that we're out of our element."

"Do you think this was a bad idea?" she asked while she sank back, trying to lose herself in the large leather chair she occupied.

His eyes widened. "Is that what you think? I don't think it's bad at all. I was captured by you and your mesmerizing eyes weeks ago, and I'm pretty damn happy to be here. I'm not one to go to a gentleman's club every weekend, but your eyes drew me in deeper each time I saw you. You seemed like such a contradiction up there with your innocent stare under your big lashes, when your moves were so sensually loaded." He reached a hand reached across the two armrests and stroked a finger up her arm, motioning for her not to drown in her seat.

"But you didn't smile." She stared deep into his eyes, determined to understand him better. "You really didn't seem to like it."

"I don't think I smiled because I was trying to figure you out. I'm a private investigator, ex-FBI. I solve mysteries for a living, but I couldn't put my finger on you. You were enticing and inviting, yet private at the same time. To say I was intrigued and riveted is putting it pretty mildly," Carson explained.

Suddenly Sienna was overwhelmed, swimming in a sea of scents—cinnamon, fresh-roasted coffee beans, and spicy aftershave. She felt a tiny frisson of nerves wash over her when he mentioned solving mysteries. Schooled in appearing to be something she wasn't, she hid her reaction and held on to her casual expression, even though she didn't know if she wanted to climb the mountain of a man or bolt.

Of all the guys to meet and go to coffee with, I pick one who's an expert in uncovering mysteries.

Taking a sip of her cappuccino, Sienna changed the subject. Aiming for something more mundane, she asked, "So, do you live in Henderson?" then winced. Asking where he lived wasn't casual at all.

Carson raised an eyebrow at the abrupt change in conversation. "Actually, I don't live here."

She was in way over her head. The upside was that he didn't live in Vegas, so he wouldn't be around for long. And likely only looking for a good time.

"You don't? But you come in to the club a lot. Where do you live? What brings you to Vegas so often?"

"I'm based in Philadelphia. I grew up outside Philly in the suburbs with my dad, and moved into the city when I got older. Now I travel a lot, so I just keep a small condo there. At the moment, I'm on a case out west. It's silly to keep flying back and forth, so I come here on the weekends to unwind."

He grabbed the last bit of scone and an exaggerated look of guilty pleasure washed over his face. She didn't know if it was about the scone or being a regular at the Tunnel.

Is he sneaking around on a wife?

She sat forward and pulled her long ponytail out from the back of her chair, splaying it to the side of her neck, and tilted her head. "Don't you miss home? You must have family or someone special back there." Then realizing she was being pushy, Sienna said, "Oh, I'm sorry. I didn't mean to pry."

Carson shook his head. "You're not prying. We're out for coffee, which I wouldn't be doing right now if there was someone special. I travel way too much to be a tied-down kind of guy. My dad died before I went to college, so I don't really have any family. I guess my situation makes me pretty well suited for what I do."

"Oh." Sienna looked down at her coffee cup, unsure how to respond. Something had stirred inside her when he said he didn't have someone "special." She should be glad he didn't live in Vegas, but Carson interrupted her thoughts.

"Don't get me wrong, that type of thing works for some people, and I get it. It must be nice to have that type of deal, I don't really know for sure. My mom left when I was little and never came back, so I don't really remember that between my parents. I imagine it feels secure, nice, but my life is too crazy." He shook his head, as if to shake away the memories, and caught her eye. "But enough about me."

Oh no.

"Did you grow up here in Vegas?" Carson asked, lightening the mood with a grin.

Between his smile and the toffee-colored glint in his warm brown eyes, Sienna had no idea where to look first. She was completely captivated with the man in front of her, and feared she was falling hard and fast for something that wasn't even a possibility. Even if Carson wanted it.

She had to think quickly. If she allowed herself to hesitate, Sienna was certain Carson would coax all her secrets from her. "I didn't grow up in Vegas," she said carefully. "Military family, so I moved a lot growing up, mostly Eastern Seaboard." She wrapped her hands around her still-warm coffee mug, seeking its heat and comfort since she was rattled by both the conversation and her train of thought.

"Tell me more. What are you into? What do you do when you're not working?" He leaned in toward her.

Her heart pounded. She smelled his unique scent, mostly manly, a bit woodsy, although now it was mixed with the leftover essence of chocolate-cinnamon scone and strong coffee. It was captivating.

"Actually, I don't do much other than work and dance. I read when I have a chance. Oh, and I garden around my place and Asher's." She busied her idle hands with her hair again.

"Asher, he owns the club, right?"

"Yes. Asher Peterson owns the Tunnel. He's also my neighbor and closest friend. My house is behind his." Sienna added the last tidbit as a little deterrent.

Deterrent to what? She wasn't sure if she wanted to keep Carson from getting close, or remind herself to stay far away.

"Do you have hobbies when you're home?" She finally steadied her hands and reached for her cappuccino.

"Other than running, which I try to do everywhere, I boat during the summer, and I have a motorcycle." He flashed a huge grin when he revealed this little fact. "Otherwise, I work and enjoy a couple good cocktails on the weekend. That's it. Pretty simple."

Carson shifted his big frame in his seat before leaning in once again toward Sienna. She had no idea what he was doing, and was fearful for the first time since seeing him in the club. Was he going to reach out and touch her? Kiss her?

She wasn't ready for that…was she? She might never be ready.

I want to kiss him, but what if I'm not good at it?

Biting her lower lip, she stole a quick glance out at the parking lot. Seeing Mike still in his spot with his eyes on the coffee shop relaxed her a little.

Still, what would she do if he got any closer? Jump up and run out to Mike? Start waving her hands in the air to get Mike's attention? Either way, she'd look ridiculous. She had no choice other than to focus on Carson and try to finish the coffee date.

Still chewing on her lip, Sienna tried to focus on what was happening in front of her. She quietly inhaled his scent, smelled the pungent combination on his breath, and almost wanted to lean in herself and taste the cinnamon and coffee right from his mouth.

"Sienna, look. I know this is pretty unconventional. I've never hung out at a place like the Tunnel a few weeks in a row, let alone asked a dancer out before. From the little I know and what you've told me, I also know you don't typically go out with customers. So this is odd for both of us, but there's something that keeps drawing me to you." He paused for a second, his gaze roaming from her eyes to her lips, then back again. "I really don't know what it is or means, especially since I told you I'm basically a no-strings attached kind of guy, but I'd like to find out."

His breath tickled along her cheek as he talked, continuing to assail her senses. She found herself speechless, both from what he said, as well as how he made her feel.

She opened her mouth to respond, but hesitated, pressing her lips tightly before she was finally able to put a few words together. "Yes, this is a bit out of both of our comfort zones. For me, everything is awkward because I don't date. Ever. And you're more like a love-'em-and-leave-'em bachelor."

Carson shook his head. "But that doesn't make it bad. Yes, a little awkward, but not bad at all. Now that I see you outside the club, I want to know you better. You have a quiet beauty to you when you aren't onstage. Sure, we both have our reservations, but I want to get to know you. I don't know how long this West Coast case is going to take, but

I'm not wrapping it up anytime soon. Can we get to know each other? That's all I'm asking."

"I don't know," she said with a sigh. "I've never done this, and like I said, I'm kind of inexperienced when it comes to dating."

She was such a liar. Sienna wanted to get to know Carson in the worst way. She wanted to know all of him, even his little quirks, what he looked like in the morning, and whether he would like her running her hands through his thick black hair.

"And to be honest, I'm pretty sure I wouldn't live up to any of your expectations," she said so softly she almost couldn't hear herself. Why was she sabotaging herself?

He pitched his broad chest just an inch or two forward. "Seriously," Carson said sincerely, "no expectations. Just dinner, a movie, a run, maybe see your gardening? No big deal. Can't we just explore this?"

"I guess since I already put my foot in my mouth and was honest about being hungry earlier, I can go for a second time and eat. But I hope you're not expecting me to be fast on a first date or anything. I'm not like that." She lowered her gaze and bowed her head with the admission.

Or experienced, she added silently. At all.

At that, Carson burst out laughing, showing off a full, genuine smile and beautiful teeth. He reached one finger under her chin and tilted her face back up so they were eye to eye. "We're drinking coffee in the middle of the day with you sitting there in a baseball cap, and I couldn't want for anything more. Crazy as it seems, this is good for right now."

Sienna was pretty certain her heart melted a little bit, fully warming for the first time since Asher took her under his wing. She sat there in silence with no clue what to say or how to respond.

What was Carson really looking for? He seemed nice and wasn't looking for a happily-ever-after, and appeared to respect her limits. All winning him points.

Then there were his looks. He was a striking man. He didn't look anything like her husband, a small-minded man who made up for his insecurities by physically hurting women. No, Sienna could see a passionate soul in the depths of Carson's dreamy eyes and expression. He might act like a tough guy, but she was thinking he might not be so tough underneath it all.

Just because she wasn't experienced in dating didn't mean she couldn't understand people. She had stared into the eyes of an evil man long enough to know a good one when she saw him.

Carson was good and she was lonely, which was why she said, "All right. I'm open to trying to get to know each other. I have no expectations and I live a pretty quiet life when I'm not at the Tunnel. So I'm not sure if I'll be the good time you're looking for right now, but I'll try."

He reached his hand over, bridging the gap between the two of them, and covered hers.

Sienna had never felt anything as intimate or sweet as that simple gesture in her whole life. With their hands entwined, she sat quietly, the lump in her throat not allowing her to say anything more. To cover up her silence, she smiled, even though she felt like crying. Crying over the promise of what could be one day in her life, or what she left behind; she didn't know. Maybe both.

Carson broke the silence. "I'm sure you need to go relax before work tonight. I have to head out of town on Monday, first thing. Do you think we could have an early dinner on Sunday?"

"I work on Sunday nights. I dance once around eleven thirty, and then I go home to rest for twenty-four hours. Mondays are my day off. Since I don't eat a big dinner before work, how about a late lunch around two tomorrow?" She stumbled over her own words, sat on her hands, and longed for another bite of scone to shove in her big mouth.

Sienna couldn't believe she had just asked him to a late lunch. It was as if she had no control of herself.

He nodded and squeezed her hand. "Sounds good. Why don't we go to the little Italian place right here in this shopping center? I assume you want to avoid the craziness of the Strip."

"Definitely. That sounds good. I can meet you here then." She retrieved her hand and shifted in her seat, preparing to stand up.

"Or I could pick you up? If you're not ready, I get it."

She shook her head and braced her hand on the arm rest to push off. "I'll meet you." Then, before she lost the courage, Sienna asked, "Are you coming tonight?" She sat on the edge of her seat, literally and figuratively.

"I want to, but I was afraid to show up without your okay. I know it's your job and I don't want to disturb you."

Sienna nodded slowly. "I think you're right. I was just thinking that I may prefer to wait and see you for lunch tomorrow."

"Okay. Until then," Carson said as he took her hand back, lifted it to his lips, and placed a gentle kiss on the inside of her wrist.

She had never been kissed on the wrist before. It felt so erotic, and yet affectionate. The warmth that shot through her surprised her, since no one had ever made her feel that way.

Suddenly, she knew she had to get away before she stuck her foot in her mouth any further, before she deluded herself into thinking they could have a life together, and begin wanting the fairy tale. Yet a few minutes ago, she had wanted the whole coffee date to end, and was glad that he didn't want a commitment.

With her thoughts all jumbled, Sienna stood up and gave him a smile she hoped looked genuine. "Good-bye."

Carson lifted an eyebrow and looked up at her. "Are you going to take something back to the big guy watching us from the SUV, third row, front spot?"

She inhaled sharply; his question had shocked her, but she wasn't going to lie. "What? How did you know he was there, watching me?"

He chuckled, stood up, and gathered her slightly into his side. He whispered, "I'm a detective, Sienna. And after working at the FBI, I know when I have a tail. Besides, I'm pretty sure he wanted me to know he was there watching you, he didn't exactly try to hide it. I made him as soon as you parked, and knew right away he wasn't a jealous boyfriend. He's obviously a friend looking out for you. You must be important to a lot of people."

Sienna blushed, not sure how to respond to that or the semi-embrace she found herself in. *He's not the most obvious choice for me to get mixed up with—ex-FBI and all—but I want to.*

His expression turned serious, and he said, "To be honest, I'm happy to see you have someone watching you. You're a bit of a celebrity. I just hope you trust me enough one day to allow me to do the protecting."

At a loss for words, Sienna pointed to the coffee bar and finally found enough breath to say, "Actually, I'm going to get Mike a coffee before I head out. Thanks for the cappuccino and the scone, Carson." She freed her body from his warm grasp and felt a cold chill almost immediately.

Carson gave her a big grin that warmed her to her toes. "See you tomorrow, Sienna."

ten

CARSON THREW his room key onto the desk, cracked open the mini-bar, and sank into the couch in the corner of his room. Not accustomed to dealing with emotions all that well, or regularly for that matter, he decided a large shot of scotch was in order.

As he tossed back the liquid, wincing with satisfaction at the burn sliding down the back of his throat, Carson tried to organize his thoughts. He needed to be with a woman. Not just imagine being with the woman of his fantasies while he used his own hand, but really *be* with a woman.

Obviously, it had been way too long and his body had grown desperate. He was so starved for sex—for some type of release or *something*, he didn't even know what—he was actively seeking a relationship with someone he didn't really know.

A *relationship*, for God's sake!

One moment he was telling Sienna he was a no-strings-attached type of guy, and in the next, he was making gentle declarations of wanting to see where they were going.

What. The. Fuck?

As they'd talked, Sienna had kept chewing on her lip, which to him looked like part nerves and part sexual tension. No matter what brought it on, the action drew him to her like a card counter to a casino.

Carson knew he had a heart deep down inside, but yearning for a relationship was completely out of character for him. It wasn't that he was a cold and soulless man, but he never really allowed much of that side to show. It was a vulnerability that he couldn't afford.

Why now? And what was it about Sienna that coaxed his more caring and sensitive side to come out?

He kept calling her "Sienna," and yet he wasn't even sure if that was her name. Didn't all strippers go by stage names? Was that why a little flash of panic crossed her face when he told her he was a PI?

So she was probably using an assumed name. Was it really such a big deal? After all, she was in the entertainment business, and that was par for the course.

Could her expression have been his imagination? Or was she hiding something else?

Questions and possibilities banged around the inside of Carson's head like the ping-pong balls in a bingo cage, turning and tumbling in a chaotic whirl. Needing a distraction, he grabbed the remote from the bedside table and turned on the flat-screen TV that sat atop the low dresser, then pressed the channel button distractedly, trying to find something else to think about.

But it didn't work.

Sienna wasn't hiding anything in the looks department. The irony was that she was even more appealing when she wasn't all done up in makeup and a sexy little outfit. She was a natural beauty, and seeing her in a baseball cap and oversized sweater made her seem more approachable, more a real person. The way her leggings clung to her legs, shifting with her ass as she moved, simultaneously hiding yet revealing long limbs, had made his cock hard. But her soft features had his heart pumping.

She was multidimensional. The woman who took the stage like a pro and provocatively twirled around a pole, baring most of her body, wasn't the same woman who showed up for coffee. The Sienna he shared coffee with was stunning, interesting, and thought-provoking.

Yeah, he got wood from that version of Sienna, too, but his mind was as equally stimulated as his body by the time he left the coffee shop.

Carson had been the best of the best in the FBI. He was the guy who could read a person better than anyone else, yet he must be losing his edge. An hour with Sienna, or whatever her name might really be, and he was questioning the only thing he knew for sure about himself—that he wasn't a commitment kind of guy.

His thoughts flew around his brain so quickly, he could barely keep up with himself. Jesus Christ. How did he get so freaking obsessed with an adult dancer?

"I just hope you trust me enough one day to allow me to do the protecting."

Really? He couldn't believe he'd actually said that. And meant it.

He needed to go out, and not to the Electric Tunnel. Thankfully that was already predetermined; she didn't want him there. He was wound too tightly with this crazy case of the missing cult member. He didn't like the people who hired him, and he was beginning to resent looking for the person. He didn't like the clients, didn't want their money anymore.

He just wanted to move the fuck on…with Sienna.

Nothing about her outside the club said stripper. Her eyes were all innocence. Clear, blue, wide, and open to life, her eyes weren't those of someone hardened by selling herself. She had looked so young and pure wearing that ball cap with her hair pulled back, her face practically bare, as if she had nothing to hide.

Come on, Carson, put two and two together. The innocent look can't be real. Is it just an act to reel in a guy?

His initial pull toward her at the club had been purely sexual. He was a warm-blooded male in need of an orgasm, and he liked her, wanted her in that way. The way that involved hot, steamy, sweaty sex without getting tangled up in each other's lives.

Meeting her outside the Tunnel was a bad idea, as it brought other latent needs to the surface for him. Desires he'd never had before. All of a sudden he wanted to get to know her, protect her, let her into his life. And she was a stripper.

Carson turned the volume down on the TV and tossed the remote aside, then poured himself another scotch and tossed it back, biting against the burn it brought.

He needed to solve this whole West Coast case and get back to Philly, to his actual life. His life with no one significant in it, but at least he had his bachelor pad, good takeout nearby, his motorcycle, and the occasional date. He didn't even have the agency to worry about anymore; he was a one-man show. He made his own decisions and rules, both in work and in life.

For some reason this stripper, Sienna, was making him abandon all his own rules, but until he got back to all that was great about the bachelor life in Philadelphia, there was nothing wrong with getting to know her. She was an enigma and the investigator—screw that, the man—in him wanted to know more. His dick wanted to know her from the moment he saw her, and now after talking with her, he was even needier.

He felt the insatiable urge to dive into her head-on, body and mind, and take whatever she would give him, all the while knowing he would be asking for more. But she'd made it very clear that sex with her wasn't on the menu just yet, which left him with two choices at the moment.

Another woman, or his hand. Again. Fucking hell.

Since he was only a few fingers of scotch in, he decided to step downstairs and see what was going on in the hotel bar, have one more drink, then consider the possibilities.

He was pretty sure that made him an asshole.

Yeah, definitely a jerk.

Ignoring his conscience, Carson dressed to go play some table games in the casino. He was burning up with a feeling he didn't quite recognize, nor was he sure he liked very much. Jealousy lodged like a bad case of heartburn in his chest as he thought of Sienna dancing tonight, and everyone but him watching her on the stage. He imagined hundreds of other men salivating over her.

Christ, she was a dancer. That happened every night because it was her job to take her clothes off and dance sexually, to make men's mouths water, and allow them to go home and jerk off to thoughts of her.

Men just like him, only he was dumb enough to pursue the fantasy and think he had a chance of scoring with her.

After a few rounds of blackjack, Carson stepped away to check his cell phone and found he had a voice mail from a number back east. His client, of course. Saturday night brought the end of their weekend, and they would want a progress report, as well as his plan for the following week.

Hell, it was still the goddamn weekend for him, and he was going to enjoy it. They could wait until *his* fucking weekend was over.

Carson went back to the table, ordered a scotch with some water this time, and placed his bet. He was up for the night, letting loose for the first time that day, and placing some high-stakes bets when a gorgeous redhead sat down next to him.

"Hey," she said.

Carson slid a sideways glance at the woman and gestured for another card. "Hey."

"You look like you're doing pretty well tonight," she said, eyeing his chips.

He shrugged. "Yeah."

She tilted her head and offered her name. "Madalyn."

"Carson," he responded.

She leaned in and he caught a whiff of her arousal. Rather than being disgusted at the scent of sex permeating from her body, he felt exhilarated. *About fucking time I'm turning someone on.* He had been so strung out at being constantly aroused the last few weeks, that he failed to realize he was hardly the one making this woman hot and bothered until it was too late.

"Want to quit while you're ahead? Get a drink?" Madalyn asked.

"Sounds like a plan," Carson said automatically, then immediately began to regret it. For the second time in a week, he didn't want to follow through with a heady, lush, and ready woman. This one was on the prowl, and could have suggested a drink to any of the other available men in the casino. It certainly had nothing to do with him.

Since he'd already agreed to the drink, Carson cashed out and walked over to the small lounge with Madalyn, not his normal haunt. The two of them found seats along the ornate marble bar lined with expensive liquor. He imagined Victor would be rolling his eyes at him having drinks with yet another overly-willing woman if they had chosen his bar instead of this more formal, Grecian goddess-themed one.

After ordering, Carson tried to engage in conversation with the woman, but she kept purring and cooing while rubbing her hand up and down his chest in the same way Lucinda had given him the go-ahead signal. He practically rolled his eyes at this point. He hadn't even heard one word she said.

What might have turned him on a few months ago seemed pathetic and desperate at the moment. He wasn't even getting any movement down below from a willing and able woman running her hands all over him. In fact, her behavior was making him sick to his stomach.

Carson leaned back slightly, then picked up Madalyn's hand that was sliding its way toward no-man's land and placed it back on the bar, thinking how different her pawing was from Sienna's sweet demeanor. This woman was like a lovesick puppy, trying to crawl her way into bed with her new owner.

Madalyn gave him a practiced little pout, then brushed her breast against his arm as she leaned over and asked, "Are you staying here? Let's go up to your room."

Shit, she's desperate…and it's fucking gross.

He couldn't do it. He was whipped by a woman he'd only shared a cup of coffee with. A woman who put her naked body on display for any man to see, yet seemed innocent, untouched, and genuine, which was diametrically opposed to her stage personality. A woman who had shyly declared, "I'm not fast."

His mind made up, Carson gestured to the bartender for his check. "You know what? I'm sorry, Madalyn, but I'm not feeling it. Really sorry, but I'm going to go back to the blackjack table."

Watching the aggressive ginger strut away from the bar looking for another wealthy stud really stirred up shit again for Carson. Normally, he would have contemplated whether she was a natural redhead or not, but tonight his thoughts were on a blonde. A blonde he couldn't care less whether she was natural or not. He wanted her no matter what secrets she was packing. They couldn't be worse than a bad ex-boyfriend in her past, and a good hairdresser on speed dial.

Carson rubbed a hand over his face, tossed back the remnants of his drink, grabbed his chips, and headed to the elevator. Time for bed. He had to put thoughts of Sienna to sleep for the night.

Good luck with that.

He was less than successful in saying good night to the Sienna in his mind. Her soft skin and delicious curves filled his thoughts. The way she'd said, "You're handsome," in that hushed tone that was so seductive, yet seemed so innocent. It was borderline shy. Much like the contradiction between her face and body, her personality reflected a much more intriguing person than her celebrity persona suggested.

At the club, she wore a sexual little pout while she danced. But when they were having coffee, her mouth was relaxed and natural, downright delectable, desirable. The small smile she had flashed him was bright, and her lips were full.

Carson wanted those lips on him. All over him.

electrified

SIENNA WAS half-dazed by the time the town car came to pick her up before work on Saturday night. She was in such a haze that even Simon asked her if she was feeling well.

She told herself to snap out of her funk as she entered the club through the back door, and was happy to see Petey at the rear entrance. He was looking rough and impassive as usual in his leather jeans, white T-shirt wrapped tightly around his biceps, and silver chains dangling from his belt loop to his pocket. Petey minded his own business, and Sienna was in no mood to deal with mother-hen Mike now. She had given him his coffee earlier in the parking lot of the coffee shop, and had sent him on his way before he could ask too many questions.

Putting on her unflappable and confident face, Sienna walked like a gazelle into the club. With long strides, her hair loose and swaying behind her, she decided to put Carson in the back of her mind. She was an exotic dancer, adult entertainer, and half owner of a gentleman's club. She wasn't the type of woman men wanted to form a lifelong commitment with.

Men wanted sex from her. Only sex. Sex with "Sienna Flower," without even really knowing who she was. Or all she could be if she weren't hiding.

Normally the thought of sex, especially sex without strings, turned Sienna off, which was why she was so inexperienced. If she wanted, she could have a different flavor of man every night of the week.

Settled at her vanity, carefully applying her makeup, she only glanced up from time to time when she heard footsteps outside her dressing room door. Except no one ever knocked or entered. Wishing one of the girls would come by and give her a report on the floor, Sienna realized she was only looking for an excuse to talk to someone, get her head out of the gutter, and put her one-track thoughts to rest.

She actually had to reapply her eyeliner four times because she jumped each time she heard feet approach, and she would smear black glitter clear across her cheek. The sexual banter in her head wasn't helping matters. The mere thought of a certain man's hands touching her were making her body quiver.

With Carson, she was starting to believe she could be persuaded to take a taste test, and this was precisely what was so troubling. She was sexually attracted to Carson in a way she'd never been to anyone else. Ever.

She had no idea why or what sparked the change. Perhaps because he was drop-dead gorgeous with a strong exterior, but clearly not indifferent to feelings on the inside?

Which is a hundred percent different from the man I'm still married to.

Carson was a real man, and all man at that, physically fit with broad, thick muscles. He was confident with a touch of arrogance, yet kind at the same time. His eyes were like a dark pool with moonlight shining down through them, and so compelling it was hard to pull your gaze away. She itched to touch his tanned skin and explore that mysterious tattoo she'd only seen glimpses of. And his hair, oh how she wanted to thread her fingers through those dark waves. Carson was an attractive package, and she liked it all a little too much.

He would be her flavor of choice if she could pick one, and she wanted a nice, long lick.

Sienna knew it was really her mind playing tricks on her. Forbidden fruit was only desirable because you couldn't have it. Carson was intriguing because he was so different from any of the boys she knew while growing up. Those boys were slight, bony, messy, unkempt, and boring. There were definitely no tattoos to be found anywhere on their bodies; it simply wasn't allowed.

She gave up on makeup for the moment and moved to her soft purple velour chaise. She didn't know why it had to match the rest of the club. No one ever came back to her room other than the girls or Asher, but it did. She reclined on the sumptuous fabric, smoothing her hands down its plush sides, letting her head fall back, and sighing deeply. She had no idea what was happening to her mind. She resigned herself to the fact she couldn't stop herself. Her heart was on its own path, just like her fingers trailing up and down the sofa, making their way back and forth, skimming the edges of her thighs, leaving soft touches here and there, perhaps even reminders of what she really wanted.

God, was she one of those women who chased after bad boys? No, she was just lonely. If she really thought about it, she'd been lonely her entire life. Growing up with an austere, devout father concerned with impressing the neighbors, a mother who made her father's happiness her main role, and three brothers who had paid no attention to her since she was a girl, she hadn't felt much affection.

Then there was the man she was arranged to marry. No love and affection lost there. Her husband was the type of man her parents wanted for her—a religious man from a wealthy family with good standing in the community who would provide her with the best. She was expected to make a life and babies with him. Her parents demanded nothing less.

On paper, Elon Finder had been the perfect match for Lila Dasher. He was well-learned and devout like her father, and came from a much wealthier family, one that would help elevate her parents' status. Unfortunately he was one of five sons, and desperately wanted to be the center of attention.

Marrying Lila was one way to get that attention, for procuring a wife enabled him to secure the reins of the family business. Lila was pretty back then, took care of herself, and was considered a good catch in their community. Yet Elon acted like he'd won a prize at a carnival when he brought Lila around his family.

He didn't seem to realize that she wasn't actually a stuffed animal, and it hurt when he threw her around. The pushing and shoving left marks. There was a reason she was dry and never ready, making sex hurt. Pain didn't turn her on, neither did verbal slights. In this respect, they definitely weren't a perfect match.

But that life was behind her now. Lila was Sienna, and she needed to stay true to character, which meant not getting involved. Being Sienna meant she was safe. Underneath it all she was lonely, but that was a small price to pay for living a long life.

She didn't have to be lonely, though. Why not explore the character of Sienna a little deeper with Carson? *Sexy Sienna gets some…*it made her giggle to herself just thinking about it.

Carson wouldn't be around forever. He had a job to do and a case to solve. There were probably dozens of other cases waiting for him, and he didn't live out west. He was a prime candidate for testing the waters. For all she knew, he could be married back home, despite what he'd said. A lot of men ditched their wedding bands when they came to Vegas; everyone knew that.

Being with Carson would soothe her growing isolation, and becoming more social would get Asher and Mike off her back. Plus, she might learn a thing or two. It was a smart move to test the waters with someone who wasn't local, a man she would never see again when it was over.

She stood up from the chaise and went to the full-length mirror framed in lights. She stared at her reflection for a very long time, marking the differences from years ago, noticing her pulse quicken in her neck with her most recent thoughts of Carson, and wondering what was going to become of her. Examining her full lips, natural breasts, and slim yet shapely hips, she tried to instill some type of resolve to stop what was happening because it was dangerous. Extremely.

Get real, girl...he's ex-FBI. The man works on big, important cases, and is only interested in my girl parts. Sienna told herself she was safe; there were no worries concerning him and her past.

With that thought in mind, Sienna found a fresh fortitude to make a move for herself, go after the man, and started to get ready to wow the crowd so she could get back to the main task at hand. As she was doing her makeup for the millionth time that evening, perfecting her cat eyes with sultry black glitter, adding a touch of sparkle to her high cheekbones, and dusting her chest and shoulders with even more shine, she silently wished one of the girls would pop back and tell her what the floor was like.

And that Carson was out there.

Flipping through her outfits, Sienna realized she sort of wished she was dressing for Carson. *Geez, stop it; you told him not to come tonight.* After choosing a silver bustier and matching thong with a few crystals on the front, Sienna was contemplating red or pink patent stacked platform Mary Janes when Sydney knocked softly and then just barged into the dressing room.

"Hey, Sie, we have a huge bachelor party tonight. Petal is bringing down the house, reeling in the big bucks on the floor, and she asked me to go on with her again later tonight before your second act." Sydney bounced around the dressing room as she delivered her report, and squealed, "Sweet!" as she picked up one of Sienna's costumes to admire it.

"Sounds great," Sienna told her as she finished applying her makeup. "You two were awesome last night. A big hit!"

"I know, right?" Sydney gave her a huge smile. "It was so much fun. There's always such an energy in the room before Sienna Flower takes the stage. Oh, by the way, seated right next to the bachelor party is a Sienna stalker. Keeps asking when you're going on."

This caught her full attention, and she paused brushing on eye shadow to look at Sydney directly. "What did you say, sweetie?"

I thought I asked Carson not to show up tonight.

"Some dude, kinda tall, not real wide, blond crew cut, jeans, and a cowboy hat. He keeps ordering another beer and asking for you."

90

"Oh, I don't know who he is." Relief mixed with disappointment as Sienna asked, "Did you tell Ash?"

"Of course I told Mike and Asher. They're on it. Keeping an eye. They sent Laurel over to give him a dance, keep him occupied. Anyway, I'm out of here. Just wanted to give you a heads-up. I got a big party to work!"

Sienna set down her eye shadow brush after Sydney left, wondering at the vulnerability she found herself feeling. She'd never felt disappointment over a fan not being there, but Carson wasn't just any admirer. At the rate she was going, before long she'd be wearing her feelings on her sleeve. She had almost jumped for joy when Sydney mentioned someone asking for her, thinking it was Carson, then felt the sting of tears when she realized it wasn't him. Even though she'd told him it would be better for him not to come, did she wish that he would show up anyway?

She sighed and grabbed a tube of her lotion, then began carefully applying it to her skin.

Who was this new guy asking for her? No one ever really did that; they knew she would be onstage soon enough. She should be more concerned over the stranger in the hat than mooning over Carson, and decided that after her dance, she would make it a point to get a better look at the dude in the cowboy hat.

The whole scenario made her shiver. It was just a bit too weird, strange, and out of the ordinary. Customers wearing cowboy hats weren't an everyday occurrence in the Tunnel, and the guy's going out of his way to ask for her made her wonder if her past was catching up with her.

For the first time in years, Sienna thought about the possibility of Elon sending someone to look for Lila. *Elon.* Just thinking his name in her head gave her goose bumps. She was never going back to him, even if she had to cross the border to Mexico.

No way. It wasn't possible, Sienna told herself. Elon would never think to look for her in a strip club. It was a world not even remotely on his radar. The new life in which Sienna existed was so distinctly different than the one they shared back in New York.

The stage was her security blanket, the only place where she checked her past memories at the door.

When she was ready, Sienna alerted the crew to black out the whole stage so she could climb the pole and be ready to surprise the crowd when the lights went on. As the R&B beat started to build through the speakers, she clung to the pole, waiting to be revealed to her fans. In the dark, she could barely make out the silhouette of the cowboy. Laurel was sitting with him, fawning over him seductively. Good. Maybe she was just the right distraction. Doubtful, but maybe.

Sienna didn't need any more men sniffing around her personal life. She needed to get back to being alone, but first she had to get Carson out of her system. She deserved one little bite of sweetness.

She had enough to worry about with Carson, the upcoming lunch date, and staying alive. Her cowboy was going to have to find a new interest.

Ten, nine, eight... Sienna quietly counted while entering her zone.

The lights came up, and what seemed like a thousand twinkly spotlights shined on Sienna hanging from a pole, thanks to a mirrored ceiling and twenty-five strategically placed light bulbs. Everything at the Tunnel was make-believe, but it felt unbelievably real. Not only the decor, but Sienna herself was a large part of the illusion.

The vibe was smooth and subtle tonight as her bustier clung to her cleavage, revealing the natural round curve of the top of Sienna's breasts, hinting at more. With one leg stretched up the pole, the other facing the other direction and twisted around it, Sienna looked out into the crowd with her pools of mysterious blue from her split on the pole. She teased their senses, luring them into her world where anything was possible.

The customers might catch a glimpse of her nipple and think they know her intimately, but they would never really know her. The true her. Her looks and her moves might captivate, entice, and scintillate, but she held everyone at bay, never fully letting them in deep. That was the tease, the hook that kept everyone—men and women alike—coming back for a better glimpse of nipple, vagina, or just about anything Sienna.

The slower rhythm and blues vibe blended into a hard-core rap, so Sienna picked up her pace, working the front of the stage, running her hands through her hair, squatting down low, her legs bent and spread to the side, giving the men yet another peek. She was feeling the pulse of the music, the collective heartbeat of the club, the expectant air that always settled on the room when she danced, but she was missing her dark and mysterious pair of eyes.

She was so caught up in missing Carson, she was oblivious to the man who stood up and swiftly moved toward the stage.

It was only when Sienna turned to head back to a rope dangling from the ceiling—she was going to climb it and twist herself in it for the finale—when a ruckus broke out behind her. She willed herself to ignore it and grabbed the rope, but when she spun around, there was Petey and Mike escorting the man in the cowboy hat out of the club.

In the middle of her act, Sienna knew she couldn't break her concentration. She finished her dance. Sweat beaded on her chest as she hooked her ankle in a loop on the rope and climbed up, the rope squeezing her cleavage and forcing her calf muscles to contract while she gripped it. She knew the audience was hypnotized by this athletic and raw, sexual side of her, and that the sight of her butt, round and completely revealed, heightened the whole experience. Her thong, which only covered the most sacred of private areas, kept the crowd's gaze focused on one person. They had no clue what was happening with the cowboy because there wasn't an eye in the house not focused on Sienna.

Finally, the song came to an end. Sienna dangled from the rope by one arm and one leg, throwing her standard kisses into the crowd, but she couldn't wait to get the hell off the stage.

As soon as Sienna walked backstage, Asher was waiting for her. He paced back and forth like a lion waiting to pounce on its prey. He watched her walk toward him with rage in his eyes, although she knew it was not directed toward her.

"Shit, Sie. Shit, babe. I'm so sorry. I know Sydney pegged that guy as being strange, but I didn't expect him to rush the stage. Scared the fucking crap out of me. Fuck!" He yelled the last few words and slammed his open palm into the wall.

"It's okay, Ash. Shh. You guys were right on it." Sienna placed a comforting hand on his arm, willing him to calm down even though her own nerves were equally shot. She knew if she let him know how rattled she was, he would clamp down on her with extra security. Despite all that just went down, Sienna couldn't stop thinking about her date with Carson the next day. If Asher started amping up security, he'd know about the date, and she wanted to keep that part of her life to herself for the moment.

"Sienna, if something happened to you, I'd never forgive myself. You're family. Nobody's going to hurt you on my watch."

"I know, sweetie, I know. I'm good. No worse for the wear." Sienna stood up straight, threw her shoulders back, and flung her hair behind her back.

"Do you want to skip your second dance? I get it if you do, doll." Asher moved away from the wall he'd just pounded, shifted close, and ran a soothing hand down her arm, stopping to grasp her hand tightly as if he never wanted to let it go.

"No, I need to dance. You know better than anyone, dancing is when I feel free, liberated." She squeezed his hand, leaned closer on her high heels, and kissed his forehead. She lingered a few extra moments, her steady breath hovering over his face, telling him what he wanted to hear with her actions.

He trained his entire focus on her face, scrutinizing her sincerity, and bought it. "All right. I'm going to sit up front for your next act. Go unwind and take a rest before you go back out."

Sienna gave Asher another peck, this time on the cheek, spun on her heel, and returned to her dressing room. She locked the door behind her and slid down the smooth wood to the floor. Convincing Asher she was okay had stripped her of whatever strength remained inside her body.

The club had been her refuge, her little nest of safety for the longest time, but the guy in the damn cowboy hat and his specific questioning had her on edge. Not to mention his storming the stage and Asher's resulting rage.

She made herself a cup of tea to calm her nerves and changed her outfit. She wouldn't let them see her rattled. Fear is going to get the best of me, she thought as she picked out a red cat suit and gold boots. It was a dominant choice. The red combined with the gutsy zipper down the skintight bodysuit made a statement. She wasn't to be messed with. Not now, not ever.

I'm not broken. I'm strong.

The rest of the night went without incident. Sienna danced. She lowered the zipper, gave the crowd a hint of everything good inside, and then let them go home to make their fantasies come alive. The man was gone, but she noticed Asher had stationed himself out front, with Mike and Petey flanking the stage, and other security personnel visible around the room.

With only a little sliver of fear running through her, Sienna settled back to being herself, or the self she thought she should be as a stripper.

Happy with making others' dreams come alive, Sienna went home

electrified

later to her carriage house. She went through her relaxation routine, lit a candle, took a bath, and thought about how she really didn't have any fantasies of her own, but wanted a few.

Not ones with her vibrator.

With Carson. And I'm going to make some.

eleven

Sunday morning

SIENNA SLEPT in until ten thirty on the next morning, which was something she hadn't done in a while. She had been exhausted once she got home the night before from her churning emotions. Her heart and mind were at odds with each other, and she'd tossed and turned trying to fall asleep, even after the relaxation of her bath.

She told herself she had to be rational and go back to her plan. A plan where she definitely didn't open herself fully to anyone of the opposite sex, other than Asher, of course.

Yet her heart pounded with an urgency to get to know Carson like it never had before. She could feel the muscle throbbing in her chest, blood flowing in and out, desire building within the walls and seeping out into her bones. The night before she easily gave in to the organ, which pumped life into her blood, allowing herself to dream of frivolous, steamy sex with Carson, but that wasn't on the docket for survival.

But her body wasn't listening to her more pragmatic side.

Sienna had never had true intimacy. Certainly not in her marriage. She had been taught that sex was mainly for procreation. In her one relationship, there was never any emphasis on feeling good, orgasms, or pleasuring each other, yet she knew her husband forcing himself on her wasn't the way it was supposed to be either. This was a large part of the reason why she loved her new world. The club was about feeling good, going deep with sexual desires, and fulfilling dreams without ever being shamed.

Many critics thought the adult entertainment world was rife with violence and altogether dirty and shameful in its pursuits. Sienna knew this to be largely untrue, other than the few lousy sons of bitches in the business.

She had lived in a world of violence and dirty gestures shrouded as holy. The life surrounding the club might not have been holy or wholesome, but it was liberating and satisfying, which was why there were so many couples who came to the club. There was a purpose in pleasure for them.

For the most part, the bachelor parties got wild and a little crazy, but never out of hand. They were really not the way the movies portrayed them. Mostly the "batching" guys were out to have a good time, bank away fantasies for later, drink too much, and have a great night out with their friends.

After being immersed in this world for more than half a decade, it was only natural that a piece of her yearned for some kind of intimacy. The pleasuring kind. The only thing was, she couldn't have it. Her brain, her logical side, told her that opening herself up to any kind of relationship in order to have intimacy was risky.

Her body was on a separate mission to feel something, to touch and be touched. It was a deadly mission, yet she couldn't stop herself.

To KEEP her mind busy and avoid cleaning her place for the second time in two days, Sienna texted Sydney and Petal and invited them over for coffee. A morning with the girls was a good way to steer her mind away from her lunch date with Carson.

Do I tell them about the date?

Throwing back on her cardigan from her adventure at Asher's the day before, Sienna shoved her feet in soft slippers and padded out to the kitchen. She knew the girls would come in similar outfits. They relished their time to be casual and comfy after working late hours with all the makeup and uncomfortable outfits.

While waiting, Sienna baked a small banana loaf for the three of them. As she was pulling the loaf from the oven, her phone pinged with a text. Her first thought was that maybe one of her friends changed her mind, which made her nervous at the prospect of having to occupy herself for a few hours. To be left alone with her warring thoughts seemed torturous.

Then panic ran through her…maybe Carson was canceling? While that would be the best thing for both of them, the thought plagued her every fiber and assaulted her soul.

She grabbed the phone and peeked. It was neither.

> *Mike*: What's the plan? You know what I mean.
> *Sienna*: Late lunch. 2 p.m. Bella's near Canyon Coffee. Didn't tell Ash.
> *Mike*: OK. I feel you but you'll have to tell him soon.
> *Sienna*: No. This is going to be it after this lunch.
> *Mike*: I'll be outside your place at 1:30.

He didn't respond to her mention of this being the last time. *Does he think this is going to be an ongoing thing?*

Sienna didn't bother to argue with the arrangement. Mike was going to tail her again, and Carson knew she had someone watching. Maybe it would be a big turnoff. With that thought, her doorbell rang and in walked her friends. *Thank you, God.*

Sydney, sporting doggie print pajamas and her auburn hair knotted in a bun on top of her head as though she just rolled out of bed, went straight for the coffeepot. Petal plopped down in the big blue and white damask floral armchair, her jet black hair fanning out around her, the color rich and seductive, a complete contrast to the softness of the chair Sienna chose for her living space. All three of them were chatting at once, the smell of banana and coffee permeating the room, a feeling of easiness in the air. It was times like this that made Sienna feel she'd survive in this life…forever.

A few friends were all she needed. She had a warm and cozy house with nice furniture, and at the moment it was filled with smiles and laughter. She never had that once in her old life.

As she grabbed a coffee with Sydney and brought the banana bread over to the coffee table, the girls were giggling about the bachelor party the night before. The group of young gentlemen had taken a private room for three hours, and couldn't stop throwing cash the girls' way.

Asher had plenty of security on the private rooms, so fortunately nothing went wrong like it did with Natalie a few weeks back.

There was nothing more than heavy touching, but the money was worth it to Sydney and Petal. Both of them grew up with the bare minimum, and now they supported themselves, plus were able to save for the future, thanks to Sienna. Nobody could take that away from them.

Sienna listened and laughed as they told stories of the guys with tented pants watching them dance and move as if it was their last breath before tying the knot. The tented pants were a little inside joke between the three of them. Privately discussing which ones were bigger than others was a bad weekly habit. Apparently, last night's bachelor partiers were fairly well-endowed, and Sydney was fascinated. She was newer than Sienna and Petal, so it figured. Petal threw her whole body backward into her chair in a fit of laughter as Sydney demonstrated with her hands how high one guy's pants were raised.

Sienna was only half listening when Petal abruptly asked, "Sienna, where'd you go, honey? You were off in space while I almost choked to death from my own laughter."

Busted, Sienna thought. She was really thinking about Carson and couldn't imagine he was small in the pants. Oh. My. God.

No way was she going to cop to that, so she said, "I have a lunch date today. I really don't even know what to make of it."

"What?" the girls cried out in unison.

Sienna looked at the two of them. Petal had her knees curled up in the huge armchair with a pillow squished over the side and her head resting on the top of it. Sydney was lying on the floor with her head propped up on her hands, her coffee cup in front of her. If this wasn't safe enough, Sienna didn't know what was, so she went out on a limb.

"Yeah, a date. There's been this guy coming to the club on the weekends, and he sent his number back to me. Since Billy was too new to know better, he brought it back to me. I guess I kinda liked him from afar and was curious these last few weeks, so I texted him. Oh my God, that's so embarrassing when I say it out loud. I texted him. I must look so needy." She buried her face deep in her hands, afraid to look up, but when she did she saw their softening expressions.

"No way," Sydney said. "It's adorable, you liked him enough to text him. This guy is one lucky dude with all the men who are dying to get a text from you!"

Petal chimed in, "Even better, he gets to know you, the real you. Not just the gorgeous Sienna Flower all men dream about, but you, the sweetest person on earth." She pulled up to her knees in the chair and looked straight at Sienna, driving the point home.

She shook her head and chuckled. "Chill out, ladies. We had one cup of coffee yesterday and planned for this late lunch today. He doesn't live here, just visits, which is good. I don't think this is the smartest idea, but I just sort of like him, so I want to have this date."

"You're crazy. If you like him, go after him." Sydney grinned at her, then popped another piece of banana bread into her mouth.

Petal got up to refill her coffee, and patted Sienna's shoulder as she passed her. "You deserve a life. I know you had it rough and don't like to talk about it, Sie, but you're kind and loving. You deserve everything good and sweet, baby."

"Ugh, you two are killing me. It's only lunch. That's it. No more. Just to get the guy out of my head." Noticing the dreamy look in both Sydney and Petal's eyes, she knew they were no longer listening to her. She was saying this more for her own benefit.

Before she could say anything more, the girls had Sienna in the shower with a cleansing mask on her face, and were rummaging through her closet to pick out an outfit for lunch.

"I was just going to wear jeans and a ball cap. You know I don't like going out all exposed," Sienna protested.

"No way, girlie."

"Agreed. No way," Sydney said with a nod to Petal.

T HE HOURS passed quickly with the mini-makeover. By one thirty, Sienna was buffed, polished, lightly made up with makeup, and had soft waves cascading through her hair. She was wearing skinny jeans, an untucked white blouse with the sleeves rolled up, and knee-high brown boots. Wearing no jewelry except hoop earrings, Sienna pulled her dark purple suede blazer over her blouse and walked out with Petal and Sydney still in their pajamas.

When Sierra walked outside, Mike was already waiting. He lifted a hand in greeting, then smirked as he looked over from his car. She was certain he was glad he missed the estrogen-filled coffee klatch. Sienna kissed both her friends, then hopped into her car and pulled out with Mike following close behind.

Her heart was racing on the drive over to Bella's. Coffee was one thing; lunch was another. Yesterday Sienna wore her uniform for going out in public—nondescript clothes, hat, and glasses. Today she was dressed up in what Sydney and Petal pulled together for her, with her hair down and her face made up like she was an ordinary woman.

She felt exposed.

Sienna didn't do "ordinary woman." She was either made up like the adult dancer she was, or she went incognito in the ball cap. This was a whole new look. She didn't dress like this in her old life either, and at the moment, she had absolutely no idea how to act in her current getup.

Not to mention that she was going on a lunch date, which aside from the coffee she had with Carson yesterday, was also a first. The newness of everything had every nerve in her body tingling.

Sienna parked and got out of her car, then gave a quick nod to Mike before walking over to the restaurant. She usually got takeout from Bella's for Asher and herself during the week. Dining in was definitely new to Sienna. No wonder she felt like her heart was going to jump right through her chest...how many firsts could a woman take in one day?

Carson was waiting for her in the little lobby. Sienna had to lower her gaze upon seeing him; he looked that good. Today he was wearing dark jeans, not tight or baggy, but just right for him, a cream-colored henley with the sleeves pushed up, and the same brown motorcycle boots peeked out from his jeans. His whole tattoo was exposed since his sleeves were rolled up so far. It was a series of ancient symbols along his forearm, such a contradiction to the serious PI she knew him to be.

In a move that took her breath away, he reached out and softly lifted her chin so they were eye to eye. "Hi." The look he gave her was so warm, yet sizzling with promise, she couldn't even answer back. When she didn't respond, he said, "I already told them we were going to need a table for two. I was just waiting for you to come in so we could be seated together. Do you want to sit near the window or toward the back of the restaurant?"

Finally pulling herself together, Sienna breathed out, "The window actually sounds nice."

"I see you have eyes on you again today. I just thought he'd prefer for you to be near the window. Wasn't sure what you would want."

"Well, yes," she said, both pleased by Carson's thoughtfulness, and at the same time taken aback by it. "I think it's better for me to be in his sight line, but I've never dined in here and the window space looks nice, so that works. By the way, that's Mike. He's the head bouncer at the club. He's also a friend and a bit overprotective of me."

"Okay, no worries. A window table it is."

With that, Carson led her into the restaurant with his hand lightly resting on her lower back. Unlike the day before, she didn't flinch at his touch. Instead she wanted to sink back into it and take more.

Sienna didn't understand how a man could be so strong, yet so gentle at the same time. She barely had any experience with men; the men she'd known before were either sheep or wolves, and Carson didn't seem to fit neatly into either category.

As they arrived at the table, Sienna felt lonely and naked when Carson had to take his hand away, then mentally chided herself for her weakness. *I survived twenty-eight years without a hand on my back; I can handle lunch in my seat like a big girl.*

She took in the candles burning softly on the tables, the tiny flickers casting shadows around the room, the various rows of wine bottles lining the walls, and caught the scent of aromatic herbs drifting through the air. It was the most perfect setting for a first date.

Once they were seated, Carson said, "You look stunning. I mean, at the Tunnel everyone knows you're gorgeous, but this right now... you're a natural beauty."

The breath whooshed out of her. "Thank you."

"How was work last night?" he asked, looking nowhere else but straight at her. He gave her his full attention just like when he was at the Tunnel, as though nothing were more important to him than she was.

She stole one more quick look up at his eyes before looking at her place setting and studying the napkin. He couldn't know how she wanted to forget last night happened. That damn guy with the cowboy hat. "It was pretty good, we had a lot of bachelor parties. None of them got out of hand, though." She felt her nose twitch a little with the white lie.

Carson noticed. "Really? I bet you it was more exciting, by the way you're looking."

"Really, it wasn't. There was this one guy who rushed the stage when I was dancing, but Mike threw him out. After he was gone, the night went smoothly." She lifted her eyes to meet his.

He frowned. "Does that happen often? I haven't seen anything like that when I've been there. Seems like Asher runs a tight ship."

She shook her head, and reached out to toy with the menu in front of her. "It rarely happens, and almost never to me. If there's a problem, it's usually in the VIP rooms, but Asher's, I mean *our* team is top-notch, so it doesn't go on too much."

"Hmm," Carson said with a teasing smile. "Now I wish I didn't listen to you and had been there to rescue you."

Sienna let out a laugh, her cheeks flushed, and she caught a tiny fluttering in her chest. "They had it covered, and here I am in one piece."

Although she really didn't want to discuss the situation at the club, it was better than small talk about their lives growing up. That was a topic she wanted to avoid, not wanting to lie about her past any more than she already had.

"Did you have a nice evening?" she asked. "Did you hang out on the Strip?"

"I did. Played some blackjack, indulged in some pretty good scotch, and smoked a cigar with my favorite bartender." He raised an eyebrow and shrugged his shoulders like a happy-go-lucky kid. "What's a guy to do?"

She chuckled before becoming more serious. "I couldn't say. I don't go to the Strip much. To be honest, I've never been there all made up. With the billboard, I just attract too much unwanted attention. But sometimes I think I want to check it out, just as someone else. So I guess I should thank you for meeting me out this way again."

"I imagine going anywhere in this town is a crush for you, so I'm feeling damn lucky to be with you here right now." Carson moved forward in his seat, his gaze directly on Sienna's face, and winked.

She blushed and looked away, knowing she needed to turn the whole atmosphere down a notch before she climbed across the table, especially since she had no idea what she would do once she got over there.

"I get takeout from this place a lot, but like I said, I've never eaten in before, so this is a treat. Asher will be jealous. He loves it here."

"You two are tight. Is he that tight with all of you at the club? Should I be nervous?" Carson's eyes were unsure as he asked this, as though he was actually worried about competition for her affection.

Sienna shook her head and laughed. "No, no. Ash is my family out here. Well, my family, neighbor, and business partner. Thank God we have a high tolerance for each other. We seem to always be together, but it's nothing intimate."

"Partner?" Carson's brows pinched together. "What do you mean? Do you guys have a business together?"

Sienna realized she'd put her mouth in her foot a tiny bit. She really needed dating lessons.

"Yes, we own the club. Actually, I own half the Tunnel with Asher now."

"Wow, I'm impressed. I didn't realize." He sat back and assessed her, a half smile on his face. "You're one smart lady. Do you ever want to give up dancing to run the business full-time?"

She frowned.

As soon as it was out, he said, "Shit. I didn't mean it that way. Of course, you're smart whether you own the club and dance or not. Your dancing is gorgeous. For selfish reasons, I don't want you to stop. I like watching, but I wouldn't be offended if I were the only man you were performing for." He ran his hand over his face, up over his forehead and back down his hair, stopping at his neck, resting his head in his own palm with his eyes boring down on her.

She knew he was only half joking, but she had to explain and set him straight.

"No, I couldn't stop. Not now, it's part of the club and me. Sienna Flower is so synonymous with the Electric Tunnel. I don't mean it in a bragging way, I just couldn't do that to Ash. We grew that club together with his management and my dancing. So, now he keeps up his side and I dance, which gives the other dancers a chance to learn. And to earn a slot near mine." She took a much-needed sip of the water the busboy had just placed in front of her.

Carson took the hint and picked up his menu, but kept his eyes trained on her. "You really have a good handle on it, I'm even more impressed. I could tell you were the real deal, though. Brains, beauty, and the most beautiful smile."

Sienna didn't know what to make of all this. She didn't know how to accept the compliment, so she changed the subject while picking up her menu. "You already know I eat, which you find so 'real,' so I'll say this...I love the food here." She looked down at her menu, but Carson didn't. He remained exclusively focused on her.

"The way you keep it real is so refreshing, Sienna. I can't imagine ever getting bored with you. So, what do you like here?"

Trying to keep from blushing, she said, "The salad with the creamy house dressing. It has all kinds of crunchies and goodies in it, the stuff that falls to the bottom. I usually get that and one of the pasta dishes."

He nodded. "Sounds good to me. I'm thinking of chicken marsala."

"Oh, that's good, too," Sienna said, and gave him a big, genuine smile. She was turning into a cheese ball, but she decided she liked that. She was starting to enjoy dating. A lot. Maybe a bit too much.

Carson ordered a glass of wine for himself and Sienna opted for club soda. She was working later that night, and needed to be on her game.

The conversation flowed, but stayed pretty neutral after their chat on her deal with Asher. She steered the conversation toward him, and relaxed as he told her more about himself.

Carson couldn't discuss much of what he used to do at the FBI, and now he was basically for hire, mostly on hard-to-crack missing persons cases. He liked to travel and blow off steam in between assignments due to the volatile nature of what he did, and apparently Vegas was his go-to place only when he was in the middle of a job. He saved the Caribbean for when he put a case to rest.

Lucky for her, Carson revealed he didn't have much family. Sienna followed suit and said her parents were gone, fibbing that she was an only child. This made Asher and the girls being her only family much more plausible.

Sienna found herself relaxing and enjoying herself. The fact that she was out in public, surrounded by people, and without a hat to hide her very recognizable face faded into the background with everything else. Carson seemed genuinely interested in her owning part of the club, while resolved to the idea that she was a dancer.

She wasn't going to change. Dancing was her salvation, although he didn't know it.

Carson set her at ease. For the first time in forever, she felt like she wasn't being watched. From being a small girl under constant scrutiny for modest behavior, to her chaperoned dates with Elon where an elder took in her every move, to feeling like she needed to have eyes behind her back, this was the "first" that hit home the most. A feeling of being completely at ease.

Not that it mattered too much. She was only having fun, making a memory, and that was it. After today, Sienna was going back to erecting the walls that were solidly placed around her heart, body, and soul, protecting her from anyone who might destroy her safety net. But God help her, Carson became more and more irresistible as the awkwardness of their date wore off.

A small touch brought Sienna out of her fog. Sadly, they were finished with their food and the bill sat looming on the table.

Her hand tingled when Carson placed his big one over it. "Do you have time to get a coffee next door before you go back?" he asked, while his touch continued to burn through her palm. His eyes twinkled, inviting her to dive in, but she couldn't right now. It was all too much.

She couldn't deny there was a sexual fuse between the two, but she was inexperienced with how to handle that other than the overt sexual flirting she used while performing. In a one-on-one situation, she was at a loss. *Carson must be so frustrated with me.*

He probably thought he was going out with a sex goddess, a woman on the frontier of sexual experimentation, and most likely a slut. Unfortunately for him, she was none of the above.

As much as she wanted the date to go on, she felt it was a good idea for her to go home now. Mostly because her hand twitched to grasp Carson's and never, ever let go.

Her traitorous heart was willing her to do just that, but her brain won.

"I think I'm just going to grab a tea to go," she told him. "I have a quick errand before I go back and prep for my night."

Carson looked disappointed, even though he had to know this was only lunch. She'd warned him she wasn't fast. Oh, but she wanted to be, which was why taking a tea to go was the smart move. After all, he had said earlier she was smart.

"Sure. I get it. It must be hard working opposite hours as everyone else," he said as they stood from the table.

"I guess for some, but not for me. I told you, I don't have much of a life outside the club, and my friends are all there. I guess it's easier that way."

"Well, I hope you make room for someone not from the club," Carson whispered in her ear as he helped her up from her seat. Once standing, she found herself face-to-face with him, and before she could move, he leaned in and left a trail of feather-light kisses from her ear down her neck.

He was marking her right in broad daylight in front of anyone to bear witness. His actions told her he wanted her, and he was going to make sure everyone knew it. Including her.

Stunned, Sienna couldn't move, and Carson took advantage of yet another opportunity to lean in and place a small kiss high on her cheekbone. It was sweet, chaste, but full of promise. A promise that Sienna knew she couldn't make good on. Ever.

Or could she?

She wanted to skip work and lose herself in the man who just took her on her first lunch date. Instead she asked, "Are you coming to the club tonight? I think I might like that."

If her brain was winning before the tiny electromagnetic kisses still burning their way down her neck and her cheek, her heart was victorious at the moment. Shock waves ran through her body making her bold, asking and saying things she shouldn't be saying. Now there was no way of retracting it.

"You know what," he said, "I think I will. I leave tomorrow, and there's nothing more that I would like than to see you dance."

Uh-oh.

He gently put his arm around her shoulders, almost as if he knew she needed to be treated with care, and led her to the exit. It was the most divine feeling.

"Okay, see you there then. This was great, Carson. Really, so much fun. And thanks for making it easy. I'm going to see if Mike wants something. Actually, I'm going to see if he wants to go in with me. His legs could use a stretch, I'm sure." She was rambling on and on, and she couldn't stop. It was time to say good-bye. She slipped out of his embrace and gave him one last sweet smile.

One, she had to leave so she could breathe.

Two, she needed to get away so she didn't ask him to move in with her or something ridiculous like that.

Three, she needed to escape before he kissed her anywhere again. Ear, cheek, neck, lips. Anywhere. Period.

Sienna knew Carson was watching her as she walked over to Mike's car. Something about it felt so right and amazingly wonderful with his heated gaze on her back. She knew she shouldn't wrap herself up in some false notion of security with him, but she couldn't help it. She was so far gone already, unable to pull herself back to reality.

Right now she was a girl. A girl in "like" with a man who was far from a young boy, and she needed to get her head right again.

She tapped on Mike's window and he rolled it down.

"You want a coffee or tea?"

"I thought you were coming over for relationship advice," he teased, a big grin on his face.

"Ha, real funny, Mike! No, I actually have to run to the Meow before going home, and I thought you could just follow me down. I was being nice, you big jerk! I was going to treat you to a drink before we left."

Sienna gave the sass right back to him while realizing Mike gave her the comedic break she needed. He must have noticed how deep in her head she was when she walked to his truck. Her new family knew her unlike the family she had been born into.

"Yeah, sure, babe. I'll take a large coffee with cream and sugar. You sure you want to drive yourself to the Strip? I could follow you home and we could dump your car?"

She knew he was looking for an excuse to chat, but she wanted some time to herself to daydream about Carson. "I think I want to take my car, let the top down, and enjoy the day. Rain check?"

"Yeah, yeah. I got you, babe."

He really does.

WITH A coffee delivered to Mike, the top down on her convertible, and iced green tea in the drink console, Sienna pulled out of the parking lot and headed toward the Strip. She let the wind blow her hair and her thoughts drift to the man from lunch.

For so many years, avoiding being discovered or revealed for who she really was commanded every one of her actions. She must have reached some breaking point, spurring her to fall for Carson. She was spiraling out of control and had no idea how to stop it, nor did she want to.

But she had to.

Sure, there were other men over the years who had watched her and gave signals they wanted to know more about the stripper onstage. She just avoided any real eye contact. Scanning the audience as she blew kisses to the crowd, her signature farewell each evening, she took in the smiles and pleased expressions, but gave nothing more.

Sienna never really interpreted any of the looks to be anything greater than wanting a good time, and she certainly never pursued any of the men like she had Carson.

Now she was deep in a situation that could prove to be disastrous.

electrified

So, her mission to the Cat's Meow was twofold.

She actually did need a wax in order to wear what she wore every night at the club, and she knew she could turn to Penelope, the always sassy, up-for-anything owner, for man advice. As usual, Sienna parked in the back of the Cat's Meow and called the front desk for someone to let her in. She knew a little talk with the bikini waxer to the stars of Las Vegas was just what the doctor ordered.

Penelope certainly had her fair share of men, but she never committed to one for a long time. She was a lover of life and all flavors of men, and had been around the block. A Vegas native, her mother a longtime showgirl, and her dad a casino host back in the good old days, she was a bit of a mother hen to a select group despite her sultry vixen appearance. With natural red curls that hung down her back and her sea-foam-green eyes, creamy skin, and always sexy, incredibly hoarse voice, she didn't make it easy for men to look the other way.

Plus, she was smart. Penelope took full advantage of living in Vegas and looking the way she did. She would advise Sienna on how to take what she wanted from Carson and move on.

But did she even want that?

Inside the Cat's Meow, she went straight to Penelope's treatment room. Penelope no longer took appointments through the front desk, choosing instead to work exclusively with a small clientele who contacted her directly for both privacy and immediate service. When Sienna texted her earlier, Penelope gave her the green light to head in during the afternoon.

Sienna took a deep breath as she undressed and lay down completely naked on Penelope's table. She needed the works—a Brazilian bikini, her eyebrows, and the small trail of peach fuzz from her stomach to the area that Carson had recently lit on fire. It would give her plenty of time to discuss the issue with Penelope.

"Hi, Sie. How are you doing, honey?"

Sienna relaxed at the sound of Penelope's soothing, inviting voice. "Good, it's been packed at the club. Asher's happy, so I'm happy. Syd and Petal are lighting up the stage, which is great for them. And I like a guy." She had no clue why her usually guarded self just spit that right out. There she was talking about guys like it was a normal, everyday thing for her.

She lay still, purposefully taking long breaths in and out. They were more about her sudden talkative mouth and less about the hair

109

about to be ripped from her most sensitive areas.

"Well, good for Syd and Petal, but even better for you," Penelope said warmly. Then she got to work, providing Sienna with just the right amount of distance to continue. She might have been lying there naked, but to bare her thoughts, Sienna needed a distraction. She couldn't have said what she wanted to say while looking Penelope in the face.

"So, this guy, Carson, has been coming to the club and staying for just my act. He's good-looking…well, gorgeous, and it seems that he likes me and I think I may like him. He's tall and dark, and he has this funky tattoo that just adds to his mystery. Short black hair like mink, curling around his ears, and a scruffy five o'clock shadow speckled with a little gray. It makes him classy and distinguished." She paused for a second, then said, "He's tough and strong, but you can tell he's got a gentle soul. I've fallen for this one."

Penelope only nodded her head and murmured a soft "Mmm-hmm" to show she was listening.

As she stared at the ceiling, Sienna went on. "You know I've never really been involved, but I may want to test the waters with this one. It's a good way to get my feet wet because he doesn't live here, so no real fear of a big commitment."

Rip. *Rip*. Penelope's gaze was totally focused on Sienna's inner thighs, but she was all ears. "Go on."

She tried to remain cool and noncommittal. "I feel a connection. Like maybe we could get together a little bit…together-together, you know? But there's something else. I'm a little inexperienced in intimate relations. I'm not sure how to act or what to do."

Penelope sighed. "Aw, sweetie, you don't have to do anything but be your lovable self. If this man is all that you describe him to be, he's an alpha and he'll lead the way. That's it. Nothing to worry about."

Sienna lifted her head and caught Penelope's gaze. "Are you sure? Do I need to be sending out some kind of signal?"

More ripping. Penelope moved Sienna's legs up and in, making sure she could wear a thong and reveal nothing but a bare bum.

"Oh, I'm sure, Sienna. Besides the fact that you've got a killer bod, you're the hottest stripper in Vegas with the most spectacular smile and personality of anyone I know. Just be you. Let your inner and outer beauty shine."

"Hmm, okay." Sienna was unsure about that being true, but she had no other reference point, so she'd run with it. "What if I don't want to get too attached? I don't think he's that type, but just in case?"

Done with the waxing, Penelope began applying an exfoliant to her stomach, making it smooth and glowing. She bit her lip, then looked at Sienna and said, "No protection from that, honey. Maybe for a woman like me who can keep her heart distanced, but not for someone as kind and lovable as you."

She gave Sienna a smile and said, "No man in his right mind would let you get away."

twelve

Sunday night

THE CLUB was definitely buzzing on the evening following her lunch date with Carson. They called it the Electric Tunnel for a reason, and tonight, the place was electrified with sexual energy, pulsing curiosity, and the sheer force of several hundred people seeking out a sensually charged good time. It was like a live wire inside the four walls of the club.

Tonight only more so for Sienna.

Even though it was Sunday, Sienna stayed back in her dressing room until she went onstage. Tonight was busier than usual, more like a Saturday than a Sunday, so Asher had put his foot down and insisted there would be no walking the club, definitely no peeking out in the crowd. She needed to level her emotions over Carson being out there somewhere, not heighten them, so she gave in without an argument.

Petal stopped by and mentioned the floor was packed. "Wall-to-wall people out there. Men, couples, and even a bachelorette party."

Asher came by and said the dude in the cowboy hat was back, but they didn't let him past the rope outside the door. In fact, they told him he wasn't welcome anymore. Ever.

Sienna wasn't sure if that was a relief or an omen. Why would he come back if he was asked to leave? Why did he want to find her so badly?

She didn't have time for it.

Not going to ruin my night.

Asher also casually mentioned the guy she had asked him about a few days ago was back. "The one who sat front and center, came and went before and after your show with the black hair? Come to think of it…I think he's the same man who spoke to you when you broke your own damn protocol and walked the club on Friday? I got an eye on him, but don't have any details yet, doll. You okay with him being out there?"

She began to twirl a stray strand of hair and focused her attention on the floor. "Uh, Ash, I should probably tell you this now. I went on a date with him. Before you get mad, that's what I came to chat with you about when I found Nat in your kitchen." She didn't dare raise her eyes.

"What? What the fuck? You went on a date and didn't tell me? Jesus Christ, he could've been a scumbag, attacked you, or hurt you. You don't know anything about this guy." Asher paced the length of the room, anger pouring off of him, definitely making Sienna regret waiting to tell him about Carson.

"No, no. He's not like that, but I took Mike with me both times I saw him." She risked lifting her face.

"Both?" He stopped moving and stood over her, his hands at his waist, his expression ominous.

"Y-y-yes. Once for coffee, and earlier today for lunch. Mike tailed me, had his eyes on me the whole time. It's all fine now. Don't freak out! I was curious. I don't think it's going to be anything." She tried a smile on him and it worked like a charm; the tension melted from his body. She knew Asher couldn't bear to be mad at her for long.

Asher pulled Sienna in for a hug. "Oh, babe, I wish you would've told me. I could've stepped away from Natalie for a minute. But now I'm so glad you went. Making a life for yourself, that's what you have to do."

She breathed into his chest. "Ash, I don't think so. I'm not ready, but this little thing was fun. Now I'm going back to life as I know it. Don't worry, I'm going to be fine."

"Whatever you say, missie, but we're going to discuss this more this week when we go out of town," Asher said with a wink. "This is a step in the right direction. Time to branch out, but that doesn't mean I'm still not pissed and you don't have to be cautious. I don't like being kept in the dark."

We are so not discussing this when we're away because I'm going to be forgetting Carson.

Sienna's time to head out to the stage was up. She went with a cat suit again tonight. Her hair was still down like earlier, soft waves rippling through the golden-hued lengths. Her suit, a white opalescent second skin on her curves, a zipper running the entire length of the bodice, only exposed a tiny bit of her neck and chest at the moment, and she'd chosen sparkly gold platforms for her feet. Her makeup much heavier than usual, with cat eyes formed from her dark midnight-blue eyeliner and smoky-gray lids. Once she'd finished off her makeup with gold lip gloss, then smoothed shimmery lotion over every inch of her skin, Sienna was ready to titillate.

Heading up the braided ropes dangling from the ceiling, Sienna planned to start swaying from the rafters before moving around the stage, lingering more toward the pole, avoiding the front. She didn't want to get caught up in Carson's smile or dimples. She shouldn't be so intrigued by him. He was just a man lusting after a stripper, and she was a young girl trapped in a stripper's body trying to live her life. A life without conflict and definitely no love affairs.

Sienna was trying to convince herself to pull back, but she kept stepping forward. The little break away with Asher would be good. She needed space, air to breathe, and time to reaffirm her resolve.

This was what she told herself as she inched toward the edge of the stage, slowly unzipping her cat suit, revealing her glimmering skin and cleavage, the flaps opening right to the edge of her nipples, exposing the firmness of her side cleavage. With her teeth nipping her bottom lip, her gaze somewhat down, her lashes covering her eyes, she gave one more zipper pull and her suit was now all the way open.

There was nothing left to the imagination when she flipped her head straight up, her hair whispering through the air and landing back down her back, her sculpted breasts and a tiny see-through thong peeking out from the cat suit left dangling open. Her eyes were open now. Open and staring right into warm brown eyes trained on her. Carson wasn't taking his gaze off her, and she wasn't able to move hers from his either.

With their eyes locked, Sienna strutted backward, never taking her sights off the man who was making her body boil with lust and her brain want to seek flight. She kept her baby blues homed in on him as she finished on the pole and the stage went dark.

Sadness swept over Sienna as the darkness stole Carson's warm expression from her. She was in trouble, big trouble. She had to get away for more than a day. There was a rogue cowboy out there looking for her, and she was falling quickly down the rabbit hole when it came to Carson.

Her trouble was bigger than she thought as she headed backstage. This was a time to be clear-headed, not in a Carson-induced fog.

"Hey, Sie. Wait up!" Mike said as she zipped her cat suit back up and headed straight toward her dressing room.

"Hey, Mike, what's up?"

Mike frowned, and hung his head. "Listen, your guy wants to come back and see you. He came and found me because he saw me watching you, and he asked me to bring him back after your dance. Shit, I'm sorry to even bug you with this, but I thought you'd want to know after you went to lunch with him."

"No, that's cool. I just don't know what to do. I sort of like him, but I don't know what he sees in me other than what he just saw onstage. Plus, I don't really want to be involved with someone right now."

"Sienna, honey," Mike rumbled in a low voice. "If he only liked what he saw in the show, he wouldn't want to come back and visit. He would be hightailing it out of here to jerk one off. Let him come back and chat…that is, if you like him. Nothing wrong with that." His tough-guy expression lightened up and he placed a hand gently on her shoulder, turning her to face him directly.

She gave it a moment's thought, then said, "Sure. Give me fifteen and bring him back. You can post Billy at the door. Tell him I'll knock if I need him."

"Sure thing, Sie." Mike grinned big-time.

Sienna was panting by the time she made it the few paces back to her dressing room, and it wasn't from dancing. She was out of breath thinking about Carson and his sexy forearms.

Forearms, really?

His forearms and his eyes and his big muscles and the dimple. She shouldn't see him, but she wanted to more than anything in her life. So she was going to take the risk and see him because she couldn't battle her heart anymore. She wasn't strong enough, had never felt anything close to this, and by God, she wanted to experience it.

While tossing off her shoes and changing into yoga pants and a white tank, Sienna heard a knock on her door. She looked out and found Billy standing there with Carson. Something heavy hit her chest. Nothing exactly tangible, and definitely not a feeling she'd ever felt before, but it was strong nonetheless. It was a mixture of excitement, anxiety, bottomless lust, and most of all, an enormous gutting sense of being overwhelmed.

She put up a finger and motioned for them to wait a minute, then shut her door. Leaning back against the door once it was closed, allowing the hard wood to cool her off while taking deep breaths, Sienna told herself everything was going to be just fine. She was in charge, and although she obviously was having trouble controlling her emotions, ultimately, she had this. This was good, despite feeling like her heart was about to crash head-on with who was standing outside her door.

She took a sip of water to calm herself, then reopened the door and motioned for Carson to step inside.

"I'll be out here if you need me, Sienna," Billy said and nodded.

"Thanks, Billy," she said while shutting the door.

"Hi. Sorry I asked someone to be at the door, but Mike and Asher wouldn't allow it otherwise, and I didn't feel like arguing," she said very softly to Carson. Overcome with shyness all of a sudden, Sienna didn't know what to say next.

"Can I sit here?" Carson asked while pointing to the chaise.

"Yes, of course. I'm being rude. Come in and make yourself comfortable. Would you like a bottle of water? I don't have anything stronger back here." She moved around the small dressing room, unsure of where or how to settle.

Carson fixed his calm gaze on her. "You don't have to entertain me, you're working. I just wanted to come back and say hi. You were great tonight, better than great. I don't know how to explain what watching you does to me."

She somewhat relaxed, stilled her movement, settled on the small stool at her vanity, bracing herself against what she had to say. "It's what I do for a living, but I'm afraid you have that part of me mixed up with who I am. Actually, forget that, because outside this club, I don't know who or what I am either. I'm always working. I guess you could say I'm a workaholic, so when it comes to living life, I'm inexperienced."

Sienna wasn't sure where this was coming from, but she was going with it. She needed some way to explain her naïveté when it came to relationships. She didn't want to look foolish when it came to men, although she was incredibly so.

"Fuck," Carson said, rubbing his hands back through his hair and down his neck, then leaning his head back into the cradle his hands made. "I didn't mean to minimize you and make you think I was just after you for your stripping, I mean, dancing. Shit, I'm screwing this up and now I'm swearing and stumbling over myself."

"It's okay. I get it. I'm as unnerved as you." She looked down at her bare feet.

Still keeping distance between the two of them, Sienna remained seated at her vanity table while Carson sat somewhat uncomfortably on her purple velour chaise, obviously searching for something to say.

"I admit I was initially smitten with 'Sienna,' the adult dancer. But now after coffee and lunch, I like *you* even more. Sienna in a ball cap, without makeup, dressed for the grocery store. That Sienna. The real version."

Who is the real Sienna?

"I'm sure it's hard to separate the two," she said. "Sienna from the stage and this Sienna sitting here in front of you, because it's hard to distinguish the two, even for me. I don't have a ton of practice."

Carson nodded. "I get it. It's like when I was in the FBI, and I tried so hard not to let the agency define me. Either way, I'm glad you let me come back. I wanted to hang out a little more with you since I'm leaving in the morning." He let out a long breath and tried to fit his large body more comfortably on the suddenly fragile-looking chaise.

Sienna felt the thing, the one she couldn't name or describe, tighten in her chest when he mentioned leaving, but there was no way she was going to address it. She only said "Thanks" for the millionth time. "Thanks for coming tonight, too. What are your plans back east?" she asked, trying to keep her disappointment from her tone, but failing.

The pair made small talk for a while, ignoring the obvious tension over their weekend coming to a close. Carson explained he'd be mostly working over the next few days, and would probably catch dinner with a friend one night.

Then he admitted to wanting to know something altogether different, forcing the conversation into a direction they had obviously been avoiding.

"I plan to be back to Vegas a lot in the next few weeks," he said. "Can we see each other again?" He offered an overly hopeful grin.

"That would be fun, you have my number." Realizing she was giving in to her heart, Sienna started to backpedal on her original excitement. "Actually, I'm going away for a night or two this week for some R&R, so next weekend will be jammed for me, making up for lost time and stuff. So can we play it by ear?"

Stop protecting yourself. You want to see him.

Carson frowned. "Not sure if I'll be here next week or the week after, because I have to go back east for a day or so and straighten out my schedule. We'll figure it out. I'll make it all happen, even if you're busy."

"Okay," she said in a hushed voice.

Shifting subjects, Carson asked, "So, what do you do now? Now that your dancing is over for the week?" He finally gave up on getting comfortable and leaned forward, placing his elbows on his knees.

Sienna shrugged. "I go home, unwind, and get ready to enjoy my day off."

"Can I walk you to your car?"

She winced and said, "I don't drive myself here. I take a club town car to and from work. Asher insists." Then she threw her hands in the air, feigning defeat.

"Would it be too forward of me to offer to drive you?" Carson stood and stepped toward her.

Sienna was stunned. She'd never been faced with this type of decision before, and she was speechless. Asher and Mike would pitch a fit. She'd be risking something, everything, or nothing.

"Umm, I think so, but it would have to be cool with Asher and Mike. They take my safety very seriously." She tilted her head to look up at the man looming over her.

"I'm down with that. You're a well-protected commodity," Carson said jokingly.

She thought so. Or at least hoped so.

Sienna joined him, standing up in the middle of her treasured private space, nervous about him seeing an even more protected spot. Her house or her heart; she wasn't sure. "Let me just get ready and we can walk out and tell them," she said as she wrapped a little purple scarf around her neck, then threw on a lightweight gray cashmere cardigan over her tank. Slipping her feet into black boots, she grabbed her tote and blew out the candle burning in the corner.

"Come on." She started out the door because if she didn't get a move on, she was going to either implode or chicken out.

Carson placed his hand on the small of her back for the second time in one day, and her skin burned just as it had earlier under his light touch. A fire was scorching her entire body from just the light trace of his fingers on her back, and she couldn't help but to rush a little toward Asher's office.

She wasn't sure whether she was hurrying to catch more of Carson's warmth, or relieve herself of his hand. But Sienna didn't have time to dwell on it because she found Asher pacing when they entered his office. Obviously he'd learned that Carson had been in her dressing room.

With Asher's protective instincts on high alert, Sienna knew she had to tread lightly. "Ash, hey. This is Carson. Carson, this is Asher," she said warily, motioning between them.

The men eyed each other, obviously sizing each other up in that uniquely male way that made her want to roll her eyes. Carson held out his hand, and after a moment's hesitation, Asher took it, shaking his hand firmly.

"Ash…Carson is going to drive me home instead of the town car."

Asher's head snapped toward her. "What? Really? Excuse me, Carson, can you give us a minute," he asked as he motioned for Carson to wait outside the office.

Carson looked to her, silently asking what she wanted him to do. If he didn't, Asher would combust, and she wasn't in the mood for one of his overprotective tirades. So she nodded, and he stepped outside the office to wait.

As soon as Carson was out of earshot, Asher started in on her. "Are you certain, doll? Do you feel comfortable? This is a big step for you, the girl who said she didn't want to date." He raised an eyebrow.

"Yes. He can be trusted. I like him. Plus, he's former FBI. I'm sure he's capable. It's just a drive."

"What if he wants to come in?"

Oh shit. She steadied herself by holding on to the back of Asher's enormous desk chair, then said, "I don't think he will."

Asher shook his head. "I wouldn't be so sure of that, Sie, he is a male. One who's been watching you strip onstage all night."

Sienna squeezed the back of the chair tightly and pasted on a neutral face. Then she shook her head firmly and frowned, silently disagreeing with Asher.

He pressed his lips tightly together, then sighed. "I'll trust you, but either way I'm going to be five minutes behind you. I'll be home, just footsteps away, in case you need me." Then he grabbed her, kissed her forehead, and murmured, "Be careful."

Asher then opened the door and glared at Carson, warning him with his eyes just what a responsibility he had been tasked with in driving Sienna home.

Luckily, Mike was at the back door, so Sienna was able to let him know the plan. He whispered in her ear, "Want a tail?"

Sienna put on a brave face once more and shook her head. She seemed to be doing a lot of that lately, she realized—denying her feelings.

Mike turned to Carson, no longer whispering or being gentle, and said, "Hey, man, go get your car. We can't have Sie walking around front and getting in a car with a customer. The crowd would go nuts, the media would be alerted, and it would be bad for so many reasons."

Carson couldn't argue with that, so he pulled his vehicle around back to pick up Sienna. As he grasped her fingers to help her into the low-slung car, Sienna felt a small shiver travel up her spine, wondering if letting Carson take her home was a very, very bad idea.

And she realized that at the moment, she really didn't give a damn.

ONCE THEY were on the road in his small black sports car, Sienna remembered Carson didn't know where she lived, so she gave him directions. It only took them about fifteen minutes to get to her place this time of night, with Carson shifting and driving like a bat out of hell through very little traffic. They turned in front of Asher's house and pulled down the driveway toward the back, where Sienna's small carriage house was located.

When Carson pulled the car to a stop and cut the engine, the air grew heavy with silence.

Sienna didn't know what to do. Say good night? Wait for Carson to say it? Was he going to kiss her? It was as though they had been on an epic date since lunch, but she had actually worked a shift in between.

"May I walk you in?" was all Carson asked.

"Yes." She said it so softly, she wasn't even certain she heard herself. Sienna forced herself out of the car, wary of what would happen next.

The two of them walked up the tiny path leading to her house. She opened the door and switched on the light, flooding the entryway in an amber hue. She put her bag down on the bench to the left of the door and turned around, meaning to thank him for the ride, when Carson pulled her in for a kiss.

Feather-light and closed-mouthed at first, Carson broke away for a second, smoothing the hair down Sienna's back while looking straight into her eyes and asking, "Is this okay?" before moving forward.

Sienna didn't answer with words. She couldn't. She just nodded once and leaned back in for more.

This time, Carson deepened the kiss. He parted her lips, slid his tongue inside, and took her to a place she had never been with his mouth, his hands, his body, and everything else. The pair stood in the middle of the entry, the golden light shining down on them, the rest of the house pitch-black, and the real world falling into oblivion.

The kiss went on and on, no end in sight, and Sienna was more than fine with it never ending. Carson held her tightly, almost supporting her weight, which was a good thing. Her body felt boneless, she was so shamefully overpowered by the kiss.

Carson kept Sienna steady as they explored each other's mouths, and she thought to herself with some amazement that this was her first real kiss. There were a few chaste ones on her honeymoon night with Elon, but that was it for kissing during her marriage.

Disturbed by the direction her thoughts were taking, Sienna shoved them from her mind. She was consumed with Carson at the moment, and she wanted him to take over all her brain space, devour her body, and inhabit her soul.

Carson's mouth was warm and soft, and he kept nibbling at her lower lip like he could do it all night. And she wanted him to.

After a few moments, Sienna talked herself into pulling away so she could invite Carson inside her place.

And my heart?

"I guess I should ask you to come in and offer you a drink, but we got sidetracked."

"Not sidetracked," Carson said as he traced her lips with his thumb.

They were eye to eye, and he didn't take his gaze off her, as if they were having a silent conversation. It seemed he was allowing her time to digest what just happened. Somehow he seemed to know that it was more than just a kiss to her, and that perhaps they were both trying to figure out what it was.

Finally, Carson asked, "Can I stay and make you a cocktail? If I'm totally honest, I don't want to leave you yet."

She bought herself a few seconds by stepping away and turning on the lights, shining a glow on the rest of her own personal safe house. "Yes." It was all Sienna could get out. It appeared "yes" was the only answer she knew when it came to Carson.

"Why don't you sit down and tell me what you want, where you keep it, and let me do the work." He gently nudged her toward the navy sofa, right next to the chair Petal had occupied earlier in the day, which somehow felt like a lifetime ago.

"Umm, just a club soda with a splash of cranberry for me. Everything is in the fridge. If you want something stronger, I have a little bar behind that table," she said, pointing to the far end of the room as though she had male company over all the time.

Sienna sank a little deeper into the couch and closed her eyes, willing herself not to obsess over the kiss while Carson poured the drinks. She still had her eyes shut when she felt the couch dip as he sat down next to her. She would have known he was near even if the couch didn't dip, because tiny electric sparks were set off in her body whenever he got close.

Logically, she knew this was a bad idea. Lila had a plan. The same Lila who never had been fully kissed, hadn't once had a man's mouth make love to her, but oh she wanted that more than a little bit. She actually craved that and more like a hot shower after a long day.

Lila wanted it all…fun, sex, bedroom talking, hand-holding, kissing, and she was already starting to push down the barriers set up around Sienna.

She felt like she had a split personality, as if her life were one big role. She played Sienna, adult dancer, stripper, the face of the Las Vegas underground, all the time. Yet Lila was simmering just below the surface, bubbling to come out a little bit. Lila wanted a full, sweet, good life. Sienna accepted what she had—a few friends, house, car, business—and made the best of it.

The Lila who had run away from an awful existence, looking for safety, security, and just a little bit of sweetness, needed to be tucked away, protected, and not be let out. For her own good.

But can I have just a tiny bit of fun?

Sienna took her drink from Carson and sipped slowly. She decided to take it down a notch and try for some conversation. "Cheers," she said as she clinked glasses with Carson. He'd poured himself a scotch, which amused her. That was what Asher drank when he popped over.

Carson gave a little nod, concurring with the sentiment, and knocked back his whole drink.

"You're welcome to have another one."

"No thanks. I just needed a little something to cool me down after that kiss," he replied as he pushed a few stray hairs behind her ear, caressing her cheek when he was finished.

"I don't drink much. Being lucid is better for my occupation, so my body isn't used to it. But it doesn't bother me if you do."

"I'm good. Are you good? Is this okay? Because I want to kiss you again." His eyes darkened, waiting for her reaction.

Sienna looked down. "It's all good. I've been honest so far, so I should tell you that I've never had a kiss like that before." She ran circles on her thigh with her free hand, staring at her action as though it was fascinating. She looked up at him when he started talking again.

"Let me be honest, too. I haven't either," Carson said, right before he went in for the kill. Or the kiss, depending on how one looked at it.

This time, he didn't start slow. The kiss was demanding, seeking, and punishing in a good, marvelously good way. Carson slid his hands down Sienna's back and up again, massaging her muscles, finally sliding one hand to her side. He caressed the side of her breast with his thumb, gentle strokes up and down, round and round, then more up and down while holding her tight against him with his other arm still curved around her back.

Sienna felt a carnal need she had no idea even existed within her. She was flush with want and wet between her legs, yet had no idea what to do next. Did she want to encourage Carson to move faster? Slow down? She had no idea.

Natural instinct propelled her to push her hands through the hair at the nape of Carson's neck, pulling him closer, indulging further in the kissing, and letting him lead the way.

Carson pulled away and took her drink, which was somewhat precariously resting against her leg on the couch, and set it on the coffee table. Then he gently nudged Sienna back into the couch, sliding next to her, not quite on top of her, but as near as they could get to each other. He lay down on his side, propped up on his elbow, bicep bulging and beckoning her to touch or lick, and ran his hand gloriously along her body, his assault continuing on her back, side, and breasts. He touched her lightly all over, setting little burning fires along the way.

His hand didn't stop at Sienna's breast on his latest lap over her body. Instead it dipped down farther, gliding over her stomach, settling right between her legs. Sienna was still fully clothed, but just feeling his hand on top of her heat through her pants nearly set her off.

Set her off for what? She didn't know. She'd never had an orgasm with a man, but she was pretty sure she was about to have one from a little heavy petting.

Sienna gave a tiny moan, something else she'd never experienced before. It escaped without warning. Immediately, she clapped her hand over her mouth, trying to stifle the sound.

Weren't girls supposed to play hard to get? Here she was giving away all her secrets, letting Carson know precisely how excited she was by his touch, his presence, his kiss.

As if he knew she was becoming uncomfortable, Carson stopped and locked eyes with Sienna. He moved his hand back up, leaving her cold and lonely.

"I don't want to go too fast, but I really want to touch you all over at the same time. My heart is pounding and my mind is racing, and all I want to do is please you."

Confused, Sienna said, "But you were touching me."

"No, touch you. Touch you underneath this. I want to please you, let this be all about you," he said while stroking her on top of her layers of clothing.

In a moment of sheer and utter weakness, Sienna said, "I've never had that, had someone do that to me." There had never been a man wanting only to please her, feel her inside out, and make her scream with passion.

"Can I?"

Embarrassed, she nodded her head, but kept her eyes lowered, not wanting him to see the heat in them.

Carson didn't wait for her to reconsider. His hand was back roaming her body, this time against her bare skin. He dipped under her tank, and as he was fervently kissing Sienna, nibbling on her neck and ear, and pushing his hardness into her side, she was electrified.

It was like a little sparkler crackling in the wind and setting off sparks. A firefly zooming in the dark and lighting up the sky. A wire cut loose and sparking from each and every touch.

His hand slid deeper inside her yoga pants, brushing past her totally bald mound, right to where she was throbbing and pulsating with energy.

Oh God, his thumb was softly teasing her most sensitive spot, at the front of her core while his other finger slipped deep inside her. She'd never felt anything like this, and she was pretty sure she was going to combust. At the very least, she was going to have an orgasm within two minutes of him touching her, and that was flat-out sad.

She couldn't let him know how desperate she was for his touch.

Sienna did her best to control her reactions. She kept her eyes closed, partly shy about what was happening, but mostly afraid to wake up from this dream.

"Open your eyes so I can see how beautiful you look when you come," was all Carson had to say, and Sienna obliged him on both accounts.

It was as though he could sense she was holding back, so he kept plunging forward, taking her pleasure higher, strumming her inside, playing her nub, taking her to the brink, and then Sienna exploded. She let out a moan while her body shivered hot and cold everywhere. An unknown yet intimate feeling rushed through her spine, seeping out into her whole body, leaving little tingles everywhere it touched.

From just his hand. She thought she wouldn't be able to have real sex with Carson, or she'd pass out.

Should I touch him now?

Sienna's thoughts were all over the place when Carson moved back up to gently kiss her. "Nothing more beautiful than watching you do that for me, and know you never did it for anyone else." He flashed the most panty-melting smile.

Was it that obvious?

Sienna had no idea how to respond. Shouldn't she return the favor? Pleasure him with her hand or mouth? She was thankful when Carson kept talking.

"Let's get you tucked in. I've got an early morning, and as much as I don't want to leave, I have to. Otherwise, I won't be a gentleman for too much longer." This time, his smile was a touch more devilish.

"Oh. Are you sure? Did I do something wrong?" Sienna wasn't sure whether to be appreciative with his sudden gentlemanly departure, or sadly disappointed.

"No, honey. Nothing wrong. I'm having a hard time cooling my jets, and I don't want to rush this. Or you." Carson's smile softened, and he brushed a lock of hair out of her face.

"Okay. I'm going to lock up after you go and get ready for bed," she said, still wondering if this was normal or unusual, although it wasn't like he'd fucked her and left.

Was he being kind, or does he really not want to get involved with such an inexperienced woman? He didn't even get any pleasure himself. What the hell do I know?

Reading her mind, he said, "Sienna, don't think I didn't enjoy tonight, a little too much. I want to go before I can't, before my desires get the best of me."

Sienna decided to act nonchalant when she was anything but that. She lowered her lashes and said, "Good night. Have a safe trip back east and a good work week."

Carson lifted her chin, and the electricity running between the two of them was like lightning in the sky. Staring straight into each other's faces, there was absolutely nothing nonchalant about it. Instead there was an intensity and attraction that Sienna had never experienced before. She'd heard about it, but never believed it existed.

"Can I call you?" he asked. "Keep you up-to-date on when I'll be back?"

With a small breath of relief, she answered, "Yes," for the millionth time that evening.

Yes, Carson. Lead me to my death.

What was she agreeing to? A convenient hookup, bragging rights to have slept with Sienna Flower, or something more? No. The powerful pull between them was palpable, alive, moving at its own speed. It was nothing close to convenient.

"Good night, then," she said again, trying to avoid her thoughts while walking toward the door. Carson swept her hair behind her neck one more time and landed a bonus kiss on her lips. Not open-mouthed, but just as decadent.

This time, Sienna held on to Carson's shirt as he romanced her with his lips, afraid to let him go. She knew this was her one and only chance at intimacy. He might or might not call, but this was it.

She had to protect Lila. With that thought in mind, she felt Carson kiss her forehead, whisper good night, and walk out the door.

electrified

SIENNA FELT chilled and lonely as soon as Carson left. Knowing sleep wouldn't be a reality, she made hot tea and slipped into the tub. Her tub was her biggest pleasure. At least it was until she'd met Carson, and he'd made her feel something indescribable. A feeling she had no right to experience.

She had to get back to a place where she appreciated the little things, like her tub, and wasn't chasing dreams. Dreams that weren't hers to have and hold.

When she'd first moved out of the seedy extended-stay motel she found when she'd first arrived in Vegas, she thought Asher's carriage house was a palace. It still was her very own palace. It might be small and cozy compared to the rest of the upscale neighborhood, but it was the best she'd ever had. It was so distinctly different from the house she grew up in, and the small apartment she'd shared with her husband, Elon, but it suited her perfectly.

Her family lived in a tiny brownstone, a walk-up in Brooklyn. That was where she grew up. Not knowing anything different, she loved it. Her dad worked hard to be able to afford the small house. Her three brothers shared a bedroom, her parents had one to themselves, and Lila slept in the sitting room on a daybed. Her room was small, but had a large window where she would sit for hours and watch the bustling neighborhood. She had always been a people-watcher.

Her mom would come in to sew in the corner of the room, and a couple of days a month, her mom would sleep on the trundle from the daybed with Lila. As a young girl, this made her feel close to her mom. She once thought they'd always share that closeness.

It wasn't until she became a woman herself that she fully understood why her mother didn't stay with her father when she was "unclean," or having her period. Most religious couples had twin beds to facilitate this, but her parents were always a little more extreme.

Not as extreme as my husband.

Back then, Lila accepted this separation as part of life, although she didn't know it would be a sentence to a cold, distant life with her own husband. She was taught as a young girl that when she married, following this custom would be expected of her, but had no idea what it really meant when she was promised to Elon.

With Elon, there were no relations when she was unclean, but there was also no touching, embracing, or caressing when she was. Well, no touching unless Elon was putting his strong and violent hands all over her.

Sex was no different with Elon. It was mechanical, rough, and devoid of anything intimate. He'd take her without any preparation, slamming into her with force, tearing and squeezing her dry skin. He never took her shirt or bra off to worship her beauty. He just lifted her skirt, pushed her underwear to the side, and entered at his own whim. It was all about him.

She had no idea how it was enjoyable for Elon, but he obviously was turned on by roughness.

Lila's father, on the other hand, wasn't a violent and cruel man. Austere, old-fashioned, caught up in customs that bore no meaning in the modern day, but he wasn't mean. Her parents shared occasional soft looks and warm hugs. At least, she thought so from her childhood memories, but the life they subscribed her to wasn't indicative of caring people.

Lila tried to accept she was doomed to live a life without a gentle, caring, or sensitive touch, but after some time of being battered and beaten, she'd decided she wouldn't accept it. So she ran and never looked back. It was easier swallowing a fate to live alone over staying in a loveless marriage ruled by a heavy hand.

It took her months to craft her escape while still enduring the mess of her home life, all the while hoping and praying she didn't get pregnant. Siphoning off a little money here and there by skimping at the butcher's or the bakery permitted her to pick up a few real-world clothes for her journey when she was supposedly running errands for the house. As a young woman, she babysat a number of the neighborhood kids, and she had kept a good bit of the money in a change purse over the years. Betrothed to Elon straight from her family home, she'd never needed it. This was how she afforded her bus tickets west and the hole-in-the-wall motel. Other than that, her journey to freedom was the biggest gamble she ever took.

It was all behind her now. She hoped she'd won that bet.

When Sienna let herself think about her family, she missed them. Especially her brothers, so she tried hard not to go there. Thinking of the three of them always made her heart heavy with loneliness and regret. She hoped they were all still happily married, and that they were kind to their wives. If she could reach out to them, she would in a heartbeat, but she knew they'd tell her parents, and she couldn't risk that.

Her mom and dad were good people, but firm believers that Lila was in a match that was meant to be. A match, ironically enough, that was very good for their standing in the community, yet devastating for her.

Elon, a boy from a rich and pious family, one with resources and a good reputation in their Brooklyn neighborhood, was a son-in-law her parents were thrilled to call their own. There was nothing that Lila could say to persuade them differently. Once, right after being married, Lila tried to mention Elon's temper to her parents over tea. Neither of them would hear anything about it. They were in love with the idea of their new in-laws, who owned a large publishing house and were among the wealthiest in their community. Her in-laws donated large sums of money to many of the religious causes in their neighborhood, which only increased their stature.

Her parents couldn't even begin to believe Elon was anything but righteous and good like his family, but Lila knew differently. Elon wasn't good, kind, gentle, or pious. He was mean to the core. He'd been spoiled by his parents, never told he was wrong, and given the family business to run without ever finding his own way. He wanted Lila to fall in line with his ideas, no matter what he had to do in order to exact results.

Lila always wondered what his childhood was like, or if his dad had a temper like Elon. Elon's mother didn't work. She took care of the house, her husband, and children, and was always docile. Lila questioned whether her obedience was her natural temperament, or if it had been beaten into her.

While growing up, Lila had always wanted to work at the school library. She loved kids and reading. Elon made it clear that wasn't going to happen. She was going to stay home, keep a perfect house, prepare food for every holiday, and make him babies. If she dared read at story time or go visit the school to volunteer in the little library, Elon lost it. Eventually, she stopped trying to sneak over there.

Thank God or whoever might be in charge, the baby thing didn't happen, which only angered Elon further. So once a month not only would she bleed from her period, but as a result of Elon's heavy fist.

Elon never struck her face, but everywhere else on her body was fair game. In her culture, women didn't show skin other than their hands or faces, so her clothing and heavy tights covered every inch of her. They also covered the bruises. When she went to religious services,

129

no one could tell what a hell she was living in at home. Elon would be full of himself, praying like he had a direct line to God, when in fact he was nothing more than the devil.

Sometimes, Lila was sad that she no longer believed in God. It was such a part of her growing up, she didn't like when her original doubt surfaced. She was a nonbeliever now, though, beyond a shadow of a doubt. If God existed, he wouldn't allow a man to do what Elon did to her.

From the time she was old enough to understand, her parents led her to believe it was a sin not to believe, and an even greater misdeed to not marry a religious man, one she could raise a righteous and believing family with. Now that she'd had her first sincere and loving affection from a nonbeliever, a man of a different faith, she was fine with that.

Actually, she didn't even know Carson's religion. It wasn't the same as the one she was raised in, and she couldn't have cared less. It was a whole new mentality, a breath of fresh air to be attracted to someone, rather than be promised like a piece of property. There was no way she could ever go back to having a firm faith, let alone think she would live a life of lies and deceit because her parents expected "believing" grandchildren. She was never going back, even if she thought for a minute her family would welcome her with her newfound ideas.

She hated every minute of running away from her family and friends, but she'd run out of options. If she'd stayed, Elon would have killed her someday. Either that, or eventually she'd get pregnant and he'd kill both of them, Lila and an innocent baby.

It was ironic that Lila had found solace and safety in one of the dirtiest, naughtiest cities in the country. Living in Sin City with a makeshift family of adult entertainment people and bouncers, she'd felt safer than she ever did in Brooklyn. Her new family protected and guarded Sienna, and that was all that mattered. Certainly what they did for a living didn't matter.

The people she now called family were good and decent, despite the general opinion that anyone who worked in the adult industry was evil. She knew from her marriage, evil often disguised itself as good.

Sienna had dwelled on the past for so long, her bath turned cold. She dried off, slipped on satin pajamas, and curled into her bed where she thought about something way more pleasant. Carson and her first orgasm with a man.

She liked him. He was her first crush. How ridiculous was that? Her marriage was a setup and a sham, and she hadn't allowed herself to be attracted to anyone since leaving Brooklyn. Now, she liked someone.

A dark tough guy who was rough on the outside and gentle on the inside. Good disguised as bad.

She knew as many times as she told herself not to see Carson again, she'd see him as soon as he called.

Sienna fell asleep thinking naughty but oh-so-nice thoughts, dreaming of his tattoos, and all that was Carson. It was becoming a nightly habit.

CARSON KNEW he had to leave Sienna's place. He wanted the woman so badly. Not just for a quick fuck; he wanted the whole woman. He wanted to know all of her—her secrets, her past, and what she wanted for the future. Jesus, fuck, he usually wasn't a sentimental little shit. He had to get a handle on himself.

He had tried to talk himself into turning the evening into a night of no-strings-attached sex with the stripper.

But she's more than a stripper. So much more.

When Carson took her home and saw her dainty place, tastefully decorated, all homey, he knew she wasn't only a dancer. She was a million different parts, the sum of them being the best, and that could be bad, a fucking disaster, because he could really start to fall for her. *More than I already have?*

And he didn't believe in all that, or did he?

He liked Sienna, all of her. Her eyes were just the beginning of what he found enticing, and the stripping was only a small part of that. His body seem to seek her out, and like an idiot, he started to think about crazy stuff like making a life with her.

Christ, she's so fucking fabulous on the stage.

Her comfy home, the little wet bar stocked with excellent scotch, the taste and smell of her tight pussy, and the way she said his name while taking in her breath, making it come out all hoarse when she came. Her voice, the way her whole body quivered, the beckoning in her eyes, and the hesitancy she tried to disguise over what to do next told him her orgasm was all for him. It was a first for her, he knew it, and he got to claim it all. It made his head swim with thoughts and ideas he'd never dreamed of before.

She was a woman he wanted to know. Period. Now he had to get back east, work fast, and mostly figure out how to get the hell back to Vegas to pursue this woman.

Carson knew the window of opportunity was narrow, and he had one foot in the door. He wanted to crawl all the way the fuck in and stay a while. Not forever; he knew that didn't work.

Or maybe it did?

Take a look at his own hellish situation with his parents. His mom had walked out when he was in kindergarten. She didn't like having a kid; said it cramped her lifestyle. A lifestyle made up of her going out and having fun without any cares, especially not a son who needed to eat, sleep, and get to school on time.

Did it have to be that way?

He remembered sitting there, eating a bowl of macaroni and cheese with a neighbor, not at all worried his mom didn't make it home for dinner again. The evening was burned into his memory after Carson learned she wasn't coming back. Ever. His own mom, whether she was adequate or not, didn't value the meaning of forever.

Could I?

His dad did the best he could raising a boy all on his own. He worked, put food on the table, made sure Carson went to the doctor and the dentist, that he wore his winter coat and did his homework. Eventually his dad started dating again, but he'd never remarried. When his father was diagnosed with cancer and died during Carson's senior year of high school, he found himself alone.

At least his dad died knowing Carson was going to college. He'd already been accepted to Brown University before he passed. He hoped that gave his dad some sort of satisfaction that he did at least one thing right.

Carson lived out his last year of high school with his friend, Alex, and his family. He graduated, went to Brown on a full scholarship, and rarely allowed himself to think about the old days.

After graduating, Carson was already a very big, daunting man; he could take care of himself. His physique, brains, and educational background made him an ideal recruit for the FBI. Political science and history major, no relationships, no known family except for an estranged mother, built well, strong, unbreakable, and off-the-charts smart. They asked him to join and he jumped at the opportunity. Carson spent the better part of a decade solving high-profile crimes, making decent money with lots of government perks, and a long list of beautiful conquests.

He made even better money now that he was on his own. He charged astronomical rates, traveled when he wanted, lived life, and indulged in his desires.

But now he desired spending a little time in Sienna's life, which was something completely new. Her house was so welcoming and comfortable. And the little moans she made when he slipped his finger inside her weren't bad either.

Carson imagined taking her to bed in her place, where she would say his name all breathy and hoarse while he fucked her, and then she'd get up and make coffee or some shit.

It was a stupid fucking idea, but he'd never had anything like that. Maybe a little dose would be good.

Then he could go on vacation.

thirteen

Monday

As Sienna packed for her overnight getaway with Asher, she knew Carson was boarding a plane to head back east. A wave of melancholy washed over her, blanketing her with a loneliness she couldn't quite fathom. She didn't know why. She'd known the man for a weekend and he seemed to unlock every closed door of hers in the space of those forty-eight hours. It was a freedom she hadn't felt in her whole life.

Now it was Monday and the feeling of being free was gone. Gone on a plane, and Sienna was mourning the loss of it. She took some time to unwind, straighten up her place, and check on her garden like she did every Monday, except this one felt markedly different.

She felt an unknown sensation crackling in her nerve endings, more alive, ready to catch life, but withdrawn at the same time because her source of energy wasn't with her.

Was it just the orgasm? No, it was the coffee, lunch, having Carson in her dressing room, in her house, and the orgasm he gave her there. She had never experienced any single one of those before in life—okay, so she'd had an orgasm, but only by herself—but she'd never had all of them with one man and in such a short time. It was overwhelming.

Even prepping to head to the desert, she felt as though everything she did was brand new, seen through a new light, brighter, more exuberant in its color, but missing something or someone. Carson.

She and Asher were going to spend a night in the Red Rock Desert at one of the spa resorts. Their plan was to get spa treatments and be pampered, enjoy a decadent, relaxing meal, and let the stress roll off of them. Sienna was fine with going away with Asher; she was absolutely certain there wouldn't be any lines crossed.

In fact, she reminded herself to ask him about Natalie while they were away. She wanted to concentrate on his love life rather than her ridiculous crush. If she opened the floodgates to discuss Carson, Sienna wasn't sure she would be able to close them.

Around two o'clock, Asher popped over to see if she was ready. The two of them loaded their overnight bags into Asher's large SUV with blacked-out windows, and rolled down the driveway. Before turning onto the street, Asher noticed the guy sitting across the way in the black sedan moments before she did.

The cowboy.

"Fucking Christ, do you see him, Sie?" Asher yelled.

Sienna jumped in her seat. "Yes, what does he want? Are you thinking what I'm thinking? Is my past catching up with me, Ash?" she said, turning to face Asher as he threw the car in reverse.

"No fucking way. I won't let it," Asher said as he punched the gas and the car sped backward. He then called Mike.

"Mike, we got that cowboy yahoo sitting outside my place, waiting to catch a glimpse of Sie like some crazy fucking fan. Get over here and escort him out of town, *way* out of town." Asher then disconnected the call and threw the phone into the center console, cursing loudly as he parked the vehicle in front of his garage, where they'd started.

"Oh my God, Asher. I never meant to cause you so much trouble." Sienna shuddered with a full-body shiver. She felt ice running through her veins, numbing her every feeling and sensation, invoking fear, not just for herself but for her friends.

Asher glanced over, then turned off the engine. "It's not, love. This guy is just an insane Sienna fan. Don't let your mind get the best of you. We'll get rid of him and go away."

"I'm not sure," Sienna said while rubbing her temple, massaging the growing ache in her forehead. She wanted to believe Asher, but she thought it was so creepy the way this guy kept popping up. Was Elon looking for her? Would he send this amateur? Would Elon even know how to hire someone competent?

The cowboy was an idiot, but it didn't mean he'd told Elon where she was. Yet.

Asher insisted they go back inside and wait, and Sienna was in a full-blown panic by the time Mike arrived. From the big bay window at Asher's, Sienna watched him approach the car, where she had no idea what he said. Then Mike got in his own car and followed the sedan out of the neighborhood.

"Okay, Sienna," Asher said, interrupting her thoughts. "I see the worry all over your face. We're still going to Red Rock. We're going to do what we said and relax and have fun. We're not going to let this ruin our adventure." Loosening his jaw and cracking his neck back and forth, he grabbed his car keys.

Sienna had no idea how she was going to control her runaway imagination, but she knew there was no arguing. "Okay, Ash. Give me a minute to use the bathroom and have a drink of water." She turned on the water and stared at herself long and hard in the mirror once she'd locked herself behind the powder room door. She slowed her breathing, taking deep breaths in and holding them for a moment before slowly releasing them. Talking to herself softly, the water drowning out her words, she calmed her nerves and prepped for the worst.

Before long, Sienna and Asher were making the same trek down the driveway as earlier to their destination, but Sienna knew that guy would be back. She had lots of fans. Fans who watched her all the time, came to the club as much as possible, even tried to get their picture snapped with her.

But no one ever came to her house. Actually, no one knew where she lived because the property was legally titled to Asher. The only way this guy would know that she lived with Asher was if he tracked her down, and not because he was a fan. He was something else. Something sinister.

For the very first time, Sienna faced the prospect that she might have to give up the little slice of happiness she'd created for herself. She wouldn't drag the few people she'd come to care for into her mess of a past. They didn't deserve the wrath of her old life.

She'd go on this trip with Asher and as soon as she got back, she'd figure out a new and revised plan, and get out of town for good.

fourteen

Wednesday

CARSON SHIFTED in his first-class seat, put on his noise-cancellation headphones, and motioned for the airline attendant. A good scotch was in order. It had been a long day, and it was time to block everything out and get straight back to work. He'd spent the last couple of nights in his place in Philly, exercised his very neglected motorcycle, allowing the engine to roar all the way to and from dinner with a buddy. This morning he woke up and took a long run along the Schuylkill to clear his head before traveling to meet with his client, then jumped on the last flight out for the day.

Now he needed to find this damn person and close the case. He wanted to be done with the job and those godforsaken clients even more. He never should have accepted the job, but it played on his heartstrings for some weird reason. He didn't care if it meant he was a cocksucker; he hated this case. Those people rubbed him wrong every which way, and for fuck's sake, he only wanted to be rubbed in one way, by one woman. One who was about five foot nine and curvy, with perky and voluptuous breasts, a brilliant smile, and scintillating eyes when she was on the pole, that turned caring when she was at home.

Stripper or not, I want her.

After meeting with his most recent clients, Carson had little more to go on in the case. He was heading back to the West Coast to do more of what he'd already been doing—looking for someone who had disappeared without a trace, who clearly didn't want to be found, and who obviously was hugely misunderstood by their family.

The only additional information Carson gained on this trip was the victim was married.

Married?

Originally contracted by the immediate family, he thought he was looking for someone unconnected. The parents never brought up a spouse, and the victim was young enough for him not to assume there was one. He never would have guessed they would have left out such a pertinent detail. He didn't ask because he assumed the family gave him all necessary personal information when he requested it, since they should want to give him everything possible to find their kin.

For a while, he considered childhood abuse of some sort, with the victim hitting the road in early adulthood, but this was something altogether different. A spouse who hadn't been revealed at his initial meeting was now in the picture, and clearly played a larger role than anyone wanted to admit.

Why didn't he learn about this earlier?

The spouse was "in denial," the family said. After seven years? Really? Why didn't the spouse initiate the case? All of them, the whole damn lot, were hiding something. He had to figure out what, and he wanted to do it fast.

Knocking back a bottle of water and two ibuprofen before ordering a mini bottle of scotch, Carson tried to unwind and clear his mind. If he wasn't thinking about the case, he was fantasizing about Sienna. He wanted to bypass this little operation in Los Angeles this coming week and head straight to Vegas, but she wouldn't be there.

That was the only thing stopping him. The only thing.

When he had texted Sienna the night before, she texted back that she left on her spa getaway. He didn't want to disappear into thin air after the weekend they shared, so he thought a text or two was appropriate. Unfortunately, Sienna was short in her replies because she was with Asher, and he was working. He tried not to be resentful or question the whole scenario.

He had no right. He didn't fucking own Sienna Flower.

Do I want to? No, she's a small obsession.

The only thing left to do was try to get some shut-eye before landing. Carson closed his eyes, leaned back, and started going over a plan of action for LA, based on where the family thought their missing relative could be hiding out with a similar God-fearing cult as the one back east.

As he made his plan, his mental checklist went something like this: Rent a car, check into a hotel, hit the streets, scout out a few predetermined neighborhoods, Sienna's tits.

Shit. He was so screwed.

fifteen

Thursday

THE ENTIRE week so far had proven to be largely nonproductive for Carson. He was barking up the wrong tree when it came to this case. He needed to clear his head. But which one?

His need to see Sienna was interfering with everything else in his life, and for what? This would be his last weekend in Vegas. He'd spend some time with her, going as far as she would go, get as much of her body and mind and eyes out of his system, and move on.

He couldn't let his personal life screw with his work anymore. He'd kissed ass long enough at the Bureau and now he was his own boss, but that didn't mean he could keep fucking up and not solve cases. He made up his mind to spend the next seventy-two hours with Sienna, and hoped to spend a number of them deep inside her.

Carson was itching to go to the Tunnel as soon as he pulled into his home away from home, his hotel on the Strip, even though he knew Sienna wouldn't be onstage for hours. He also knew she was already there. Maybe she would let him come back and see her? He wanted to text her and ask, but he didn't want to look as incredibly desperate as he was.

140

He decided on a quick workout, steam, shower, bite to eat, and then the club for Sienna's dance. He was going to ask if he could go back to her dressing room afterward. No doubt.

DESPITE THE rocky start, Sienna had made an effort to relax on the trip to the desert earlier in the week. It was nice to be away with Asher, the only person she could truly be herself around. Except these days, Asher always called her Sienna in public. Way back then when the two of them would get together, she was still Lila to Asher.

Sienna was pretty sure everyone at the hotel had thought the two of them were a couple. They'd shared a room, and had lain next to each other in a little cabana by the pool and indulged in a couple's massage. The two simply enjoyed each other's company, and there was a lightness of spirit when they were together.

There was no denying Asher was on high alert for Sienna's safety, evidenced by his insisting on staying attached to her hip even more than usual.

This actually worked in her favor, because he couldn't escape Sienna when she asked about Natalie. With a lot of prying, Asher finally opened up about what was really going on with the couple, and now Sienna regretted asking. The situation was so complex, she had no idea how to fix it for Asher.

With little to no experience in relationships, Sienna could only listen to Asher and his crazy story. It was all new to Asher, his life was about to be completely upturned when everything came out in the open, and he begged her for some time to digest it himself before they figured out how to solve it. Good, Sienna thought, because she didn't even know where to begin.

To say it was complicated was putting it mildly. Sienna's head throbbed while trying to tie all the loose ends together. It was a sordid tale even for Vegas standards, and she wished the whole situation would end favorably for all those involved, although it seemed unlikely. In the end, Asher promised that he would come to her when he was ready to make any decisions. That worked for her.

Now that the little getaway was over and they were back in the city limits of Las Vegas, Sienna was completely on edge when it came to her own affairs of the heart. She'd been massaged, her pores cleared from a facial and the steam room, and she wasn't one bit relaxed. Between the cowboy—who they now knew was named Sam Charles, thanks to Mike calling in a favor with the police—and anticipating Carson's return, she was unraveling.

As for Sam Charles, all Mike's police buddy needed was one security camera image and a fingerprint from his glass at the club, and he pulled up a file. Sam Charles had been born and bred in New Jersey, and certainly had no reason to sport a cowboy hat. Sienna was convinced he was after her, thinking he could throw everyone off with his stupid hat and Southern bullshit.

Sienna's nerves were unraveling, the worry threatening to tear her apart over this guy, Sam. What was he doing in Vegas? When did he get there? What did he want?

Her, of course!

Mike had been keeping a close eye on the Tunnel and other strip joints in Vegas. Sam hadn't been seen in days. Mike felt confident that he ran him out of town, but Sienna wasn't so certain. She didn't know why, but she was convinced he would be coming back to get her.

On top of Sam Charles, Carson was officially back. He'd texted her the night before to say he was wrapping up his work week in Los Angeles after a fast turnaround back east, and he would be at the club to see her show tonight.

As she put on her makeup, Sienna wondered if Carson was out there already. Should she invite him backstage? No, absolutely not. She had too much on her mind and needed time to get herself straight.

She was royally screwed up between Sam Charles, who had tracked down where she lived, and the impending sexual tension with Carson. One man was going to mess with her heart, and the other was going to mess up her whole life.

Her whole life, which she had carefully crafted to stay alive, could be blown to bits by an imposter in a cowboy getup. It could all come crumbling down, and yet the only thing on her mind was kissing Carson. She wanted to do it so badly, she was willing to risk everything.

She wasn't as smart and strong as she thought she was, because she was ready to throw it all away for one man. A beautiful man.

Sienna mentally shook herself and made a firm plan. She would dance, invite Carson back for a drink, feign exhaustion, and go home. Period.

Lost in deep thought, she sat in her dressing room already wearing her college-girl look for tonight's performance—a cherry-red thong, royal-blue knee socks, a too-small Superwoman T-shirt tied tightly in a knot at her navel, with her hair down and lightly curled. Mike knocked, interrupting her thoughts, to escort Sienna out to the stage.

She might be dressed like a coed, but she needed to channel all the strength she could from the T-shirt. She'd played the role of Superwoman for so long, being strong for herself because she had no one, yet now she could barely dredge up any strength.

Unbreakable, fearless, tough. Sienna had been all of those. And one dumb idiot from New Jersey, of all places, wasn't going to take that away from her. Neither was she going to be afraid of Carson and what he might expect from her this week.

She had superpowers.

Sienna opened tonight's act flat on her back onstage. When the lights went up, she rolled over, propped up on her elbows like a schoolgirl, and swung her feet back and forth. The crowd was already clapping and screaming, and she'd done nothing. She pushed up to her feet and swung up on the pole, turning upside down and giving the audience a spectacular view of her behind.

Out of the corner of her eye, she saw Carson. He was holding a lowball glass with amber liquid, probably scotch, and he wasn't taking his eyes off her. His were heated, very heated, pooling with desire as she turned right side up and slid to the floor.

She lifted the Superwoman tee over her head to reveal a skimpier-than-skimpy red lace bra. She was teasing him, she knew it, but couldn't help it. His slight smile and dimple had come out to play, and she wanted to make them stay.

This she could do. Twirling and taunting from her stage, her pole, that she could do. Being intimate one-on-one was a whole different story.

The song was an pulsing alternative number. Sienna swayed from side to side to the drumbeat, her perfectly rounded butt on display with her thong creeping up between the cheeks, making the music an afterthought.

To end the number, Sienna went back up the pole and flipped out her hair while she held herself up with her legs twisted around the cylinder. Then she dismounted and blew kisses as she strutted offstage, walking straight into Asher.

"He wants to come back," Asher said without any further explanation. She knew who he meant. She'd been thinking about him all night, a piece of her hoping he came earlier in the evening before she went out, and the other half wishing he didn't come back at all.

"Okay."

"Sienna, honey, I love seeing you get a life, but are you sure? I never thought you'd like someone from the club, a customer. Don't get me wrong, doll, I'm thrilled and he seems decent, but—"

"I'm good, Ash. It's just an innocent crush. All I want is a little fun, nothing more. I do love you for caring. What would I do without you?" She placed a hand on his cheek and rubbed her thumb back and forth, showing what she couldn't express.

Asher's eyes hardened, then he said, "I'm going to be in my office if you need me. I'll have Petey walk the guy back." Then he walked away.

What's bugging him?

Sipping a bottle of water in her dressing room, Sienna answered the door as soon as there was a light knock. No need to ask who was there; she already knew. She could feel the sexual current when he was coming down the hall.

Sienna was wearing yoga pants and a tiny lilac camisole when Carson arrived. He didn't say one word, he simply hooked one finger into the flimsy strap of the cami and pulled her in for a kiss. It was a soft kiss, gentle and closed mouth, but spectacular nonetheless. It spoke volumes. With each brush of his lips, she realized how much he missed her, felt somewhere deep that he couldn't wait to get back to her, and that he was so happy to be exactly where he was.

She had no clue how she deduced all this from a kiss, but she did. It was like her feminine senses were coming to full bloom with Carson.

He released Sienna's mouth before she was ready. A small sigh escaped from her before she could get herself in check.

Obviously, I have no idea how to play hard to get.

So she simply said, "Hello."

"Hi. I was hoping to see more of the Superwoman tee. You're one hot superhero."

Sienna smiled gently, the tenderness making its way to the slight creases at the corner of her eyes, and tried to quickly gather her thoughts. "This is truly me, comfy."

Carson grinned down at her. "I think that's what I like the most. You're so different from the role you play onstage. Of course, like I told you last week, seeing you up there was the original attraction, but knowing you offstage is so much better. And the more I know, the more I want to learn." He gathered her in his arms and dragged her toward him, filling the gap that had unfortunately opened between them, kissing her one more time before he moved comfortably around her personal dressing room.

The air whooshed from Sienna's lungs. How was she ever going to control her feelings if Carson kept saying stuff like that to her? She knew she was blushing, and had no idea how to reply, so she didn't. She stumbled over to her vanity and sat on the edge of the stool, observing the man roaming her space.

Carson made himself comfortable in her dressing room. He walked over to the little fridge that had been replenished and mixed Sienna a club soda and cranberry.

He remembers?

"Do you have much longer here tonight?" he asked after finding a spot for himself on the chaise. This time he lay fully back with his head on one end and extended his feet toward the other. He looked so adorable stretched out on the feminine piece of furniture. He also looked to be something else. Stretched out along the plum-colored velour, he appeared to be every bit as durable and strong as he was, and while Sienna didn't fear for her body physically, her heart was a whole different matter.

Shoving any worries about her heart to the back of her mind, she answered, "I'm going to visit a little out on the floor before the weekend starts tomorrow. I promised some of the girls I would show my face. Then I'll be done for the night."

"I forgot you make rounds. I should go back out and grab a table and keep my eyes on you, make sure you don't escape with anyone else. I was hoping to be your ride home tonight. I don't want to lose that privilege."

Sienna chuckled. As if she went home with anyone else, other than the one time she went with Carson. "You're silly. You have to know by now I'm not looking for a ride home. I'm not even sure if I'm going to go with you. I have a routine, you know," she said with a smile, teasing him, pleased that she was finally getting the hang of flirting.

Carson stood as she said this and pulled her in close. With one hand tight around her waist and the other threading through her hair, he stared straight into her eyes and spoke with authority. "I'm definitely driving you home tonight."

That was all he said before laying a kiss on her. A long one. He pushed his tongue inside and made love to her mouth, plunging deep, feeling her from the inside out, and drawing her tongue out to play.

Sienna couldn't help but return the favor, taking the chance to slip her much more delicate tongue into his mouth, exploring, encouraging, and wanting all he could give her.

I am so letting him take me home.

Carson was the first to pull away from the kiss, framing her face with his big, sturdy hands. "So, let's get the show on the road. I'm heading out for a cocktail while you work your magic out in the club, but save something special for me."

She walked him toward the door, speaking quietly, not facing him as she did. "I have to change my clothes, and I need to be out there for about forty-five minutes. Do you mind having your drink at the back bar? I don't think I'll be able to focus with you front and center," she said while blushing once again. A stripper who constantly blushed… that was crazy.

Carson didn't respond right away. Sienna worried he wasn't going to sit in the back, and she really had no idea how she would entertain patrons with him in the same vicinity, let alone within eyesight. Then he pulled her around to face him, scanned her face, and said, "If that's what you want, you got it. Should I pick you up out back in an hour?"

"Great. I'll have Mike or Petey walk me out."

Simple.

SHE WAS so goddamn striking as she moved among the tables, captivating the crowd, that Carson was having a hard time staying in his seat. Part of him, rather all of him, wanted to go complete caveman, pick Sienna up, carry her out, and keep her away from every other man in the room.

Keep her for what?

That was the one thing stopping him. He had never wanted to keep anybody around, let alone a woman. A woman who lived several thousand miles away from where he called home. A woman who commanded the attention of every man who crossed her path, who obviously drove her boss crazy, and had every bouncer in love with her. This was the woman he wanted to "keep."

He swirled his scotch in his glass and stared at the brown liquid swishing around the tumbler.

You couldn't hold on to a woman like that even if you wanted to. He didn't really know, but he assumed from what he heard about the

electrified

type. Yet this woman, Sienna, didn't exactly fit the mold.

She seemed genuinely intrigued by him, almost scared of him. Scared of falling for him and liking him more than just the average Joe; she made him feel like she didn't care about the other million men wanting to keep her.

How could she spark sexual thoughts like she did night in and night out, and seem so hesitant when it came to intimacy? Christ, she was a mystery, a paradox, and one he wanted even more so because of it. He wanted to crack the code. Only him. He wanted to be the only one to do it.

He just needed to make sure the wanting eventually went away, because he wasn't making a permanent thing with anyone.

He knocked back the rest of his drink, letting the burn take his attention for a brief moment.

Damn, that fucking jerk over in the corner. The dude was fucking running his eyes up and down what Carson wanted all for himself.

sixteen

SIENNA WORKED the floor with her usual healthy dose of pure innocence and sexual tension that evening. It was her calling card. The glossy *Inside Vegas* magazine recently wrote that she had:

> *…the moves and body of a sexual tigress, yet the grace of a virtuous lady.*

The reporters, the audience, everyone thought she was acting. What they didn't know was that no one could fake it that well. The contradiction between naughty and nice, good and bad, devious and straight, was exactly who she was. She pretended to know her baser side, but couldn't keep her sweetness from shining through.

The stripper in her roamed the room, giving the impression she was a predator on the loose that was looking for willing prey, adding a little spice to the bachelor party in progress. She might not work the floor herself, giving lap dances, but a quick visit with her definitely padded her girls' pockets.

The whole crew was drinking and enjoying lap dances. Her girls were raking in the cash, and that was better than good. Hope they put it away like I tell them to, she thought. In the bank for the future.

electrified

She didn't stay long with the party. They were quite happy with Petal and Sydney, which made Sienna proud as any big sister would be. After leaving the men to savor her protégées, she moved around the room, stopping to say hello to a few regulars and new customers. No pictures, as usual, but she did sign a few napkins, not just with her signature but also an imprint of her lipstick.

As she moved from table to table, she saw the phones come out. No doubt tweeting something about seeing Sienna Flower in the flesh. Petey had both eyes on her every movement and he was making sure that no flashes went off, no one snapped a pic, and definitely no hands reached out.

Sienna also felt Carson's warm stare on her, searing her skin, heating her, and making her wet in places she'd never experienced. She could almost sense his breath tickling her skin. It would smell like mint and scotch, cooling and heating her flesh at the same time, and leave her panting for more.

As she drifted around the room, her thoughts did laps in her head. What did he want tonight? Did she want the same? What could she possibly do with him that he couldn't get better elsewhere?

Forty-five minutes had come and gone, and Sienna knew she was avoiding being with Carson. It was one thing to be an adult performer, giving off the essence of every man's sexual fantasy, it was another to actually be who she played. She was pretty sure Carson didn't fully understand how absolutely naive she was, not to mention scared.

Avoidance was her only tactic at the moment.

Unfortunately, she caught Carson walking across the room, motioning to Petey that he was going to get his car and meet Sienna out back. She was on borrowed time. The guys wanted Sienna to date, had obviously decided they liked Carson, and they were taking his side.

"Your ride is ready, Sie," Petey said when he approached her.

Yep, they were on Carson's side all the way.

She waved toward the stage entrance and held up one finger, signaling she would be just a minute. "Sure, Pete. I need to change first." She wasn't really stalling. She couldn't go out to the car in the gold jumpsuit she was currently wearing. First of all, she was trying to defuse the sexual tension between her and Carson, and the jumpsuit screamed sex. Secondly, it was uncomfortable.

Okay, I need a little more time, too.

Once she felt secure in her leggings and comfy, heather-gray off-the-shoulder sweatshirt, she grabbed Petey to take her out back. Carson was waiting in his rental sports car as she exited the rear door, her arm looped around the bouncer's arm. It didn't mean anything, and she let go as soon as she hit the night air and walked briskly toward the little black coupe.

In the short time she knew him, she'd learned Carson liked speed. It occurred to her that he probably liked everything fast in life, not just his cars.

She took a deep breath as the man in question came around the car to help her into the passenger seat. Petey simply gave him a nod and turned to go back inside the club, which allowed Carson to slip his hand underneath Sienna's hair, his warmth tingling the nape of her neck.

He pulled her in for a kiss, sucking on her lower lip, then moved his other hand around her waist and took his time with her, letting her feel his erection against her when he pulled her closer.

Just when she couldn't breathe anymore, Carson stepped back the tiniest bit and said, "Sorry I didn't let you up for air, but I've been waiting all night to have you to myself. It's not easy watching all those other men feast their eyes on you."

He landed another tiny kiss to the spot on her neck underneath her ear, took a deep breath, pulling in her scent, and whispered, "Let's go."

Sienna let out a little sigh, glad that her long sweatshirt covered up where she was undoubtedly soaking through her yoga pants with want and desire.

Carson took her tote, helped her slide in the car, jumped in the driver's seat, and sped out of the lot.

Sienna's head whipped back from the acceleration and she immediately gripped her seat. Although she wasn't sure if it was because of the speed Carson was driving, or what they were speeding toward. The air in the car was thick with want.

She wasn't a virgin; she really needed to calm herself. She was a stripper, for goodness' sake. She should be able to at least fake some sexual knowledge.

"You tired?" Carson asked, interrupting her thoughts.

"A little, but it usually takes me a while to settle down when I get home. I'm used to it by now. I go to bed late, but sleep a little later in the morning."

Changing gears and subjects, Carson said, "Just about there. May I come in for a drink? Help you unwind a little?"

I should've gotten that dog. Then I would've had someone to come home to.

"That would be nice," Sienna answered as they pulled up to her house, nervous from the tingles running through her entire body.

Carson carried Sienna's tote to the door, and turned on the lights when she opened the door. "Sit, I know what to make you and where to get it," he ordered.

She did as he asked, sinking into the couch to wait for him as if they were a longtime couple who did this every evening. The truth was that she was flat-out exhausted with all the emotions from the week. Her head was like a roller coaster. Up and down, and down and up, worrying over Sam Charles, catching Natalie over at Asher's, Carson, and what was about to happen.

Before she could get carried away in her head again, Carson sat down next to her with her club soda and cranberry. He had poured himself one finger of something stronger. Having drinks together at the end of the night was beginning to feel as comfortable as a worn-in old sweater.

"Thanks," she said. "It's been a long time since I had anyone take care of me."

"Is that so? I like it. It's nice seeing you at the club and knowing that I'm taking you home, if not for anything other than to have a drink with you."

They sat staring at each other, the silence building as thick as the sexually charged air.

Despite his words, his eyes said he wanted much more than a drink. Their usual light brown had darkened with lust. Sienna tried not to stare into their depths, but she couldn't help herself any more than the way she was damp down below.

"Well, I don't know how great company I am at this time of night." She leaned her head back against the cushions of the soft overstuffed couch, and closed her eyes for a second.

"Perfect, you're just perfect. Did you have a good week?" he asked as he leaned in and brushed a wisp of hair from her brow. His hand started lightly touching her face, rounding her cheek, moving down and massaging her neck, finally landing on her tiny tattoo peeking out from her tank top.

His finger traced the shape delicately, as if he was trying to interpret the meaning. Her flower, trying to survive while being choked by its very own stem, was anything but delicate. It was strong and hearty like she was. Or at least, how she tried to be.

She lifted her head and nodded before taking a quick sip of her drink. "Yes. Asher and I went to Red Rock so I took an extra day off, something I haven't done in a long time. How was your trip back east? Are you any closer to being finished with whatever you're working on?"

She watched him, taking in his features, the way his mouth moved when he talked and how expressive his eyes were when he was invested in a conversation. And she liked all of it.

"Unfortunately, no. I'm working a case that's hard to crack, even for me. I don't want to ruin the evening talking about work, though." He leaned closer and inhaled her scent without trying to hide it.

Sienna waited for him to inch closer, leaving no empty space between them. He was searching for someone, just like Sam Charles was looking for her. Carson was someone she should be careful around, perhaps even afraid of, but her mind and body wouldn't allow that.

He moved in with his lips, feathering them lightly along her cheek as he lifted her hair and tucked it over her shoulder, and then he looked at her with want.

She licked her lips, not sure how to act on her mutual desire, so she stalled. "Have you ever been to Red Rock? It's so nice. Quiet with the mountains in the background, the desert spread out all around it. Ash and I love it."

"Hey, I thought you said I didn't have to worry about Asher being competition," he teased, smiling while weaving the large fingers of one hand through her smaller ones, his other hand caressing her collarbone and neck, lulling her into relaxation. He knew exactly how to put her at ease.

"Ha, no. Ash is like a brother to me." Then she laughed, smiling like someone who just won the jackpot, yet she had no idea why she was so deliriously happy. Other than Carson.

"Good," he said while bringing her hand to his mouth, placing kisses along her petite knuckles, moving up, and making good on the promise in his eyes to please her while gliding his tongue along her wrist.

Sienna closed her eyes for fear she couldn't extinguish the blaze he was starting in her. She sucked in a deep breath, and let herself adjust to the moment. He took advantage of her relaxing and moved in for a real kiss. A heavy, passionate kiss.

There was nothing slow about the moment anymore. Carson was on top of Sienna within seconds, not putting all his weight on her, but he was definitely making a move. He leaned over her with his weight resting on one arm, the other reaching around Sienna's slight body, and pulled her against him, showing her how much he wanted her.

Without breaking the insanely deep kiss, he slid his hand from her waist and up her back, all along her spine, then around front, urging her gently to lie back on the couch as he set more fire along the way. She wasn't wearing a bra, so his hand met nothing but skin when it slipped beneath her sweatshirt, his finger tracing along her nipple.

He slowly massaged one breast, teasing the tender skin, rounding and hardening the tiny bud, and stoking the burn between her legs. He pinched a little harder, making Sienna gasp and gush down below before he went back to slowly teasing again.

Still kissing her, exploring her mouth with his tongue, silently telling her of something much better, Carson moved his hand to her other nipple, giving it the same attention he had just given the first.

Finally, he broke the kiss and looked at Sienna for a sign that this was all right with her, begging her with his eyes to say it was. She couldn't find the right words, so she just started unbuttoning his shirt as fast as she could before she lost the confidence.

When he was bare-chested, her hands had a mind of their own. She was drawn to his masculine, smooth nipples like a magnet. She didn't need permission to touch. Everything she needed to know was right there in Carson's face and the way he was looking at her in a sexual haze. She slowly brought her hands up to his nipples, running small circles around each one before moving down to his smooth, hard abs and back up again, when she pulled him in for another kiss.

He granted her a small kiss before he stopped to take off her sweatshirt. Once they were skin to skin, Sienna thought she might disintegrate from the feelings that overwhelmed her. Her skin broke into huge forest fires everywhere they made contact. She was coming undone from the inside out, and had the fleeting thought that she couldn't stop what was happening if she wanted to.

She wanted this intimacy in the worst possible way. Every inch of her desired Carson, and now that their bodies were gliding along each other, still half-clothed, she wanted it all.

It didn't matter that she barely knew him, or that he represented something she was coming to loathe, men who look for missing persons, like Sam Charles. His smile, which seemed to only appear for her, that dimple, the tattoo on his arm that she knew nothing about, and the power when their eyes locked was enough.

It was a raw need, but it must mean something.

There were the little things, too. His fast-driving, enigmatic personality, and the way he made her club soda and cranberry after only knowing her a week. He represented all the sweetness and tenderness she didn't think she'd ever have in life. She was going to take a little taste of life's finer things, whether it was good for her or not.

Just a taste, and then she was going to make a new plan on how to survive.

For now, she was going to take it all in. Especially since at the moment, Carson had her tucked into his side and was planting kisses along her neck while his hands made their way down her body. Way down.

He slipped his hands into her pants, roaming her ass, pulling her against his hardness, and showing her his own body's response. She wanted to be even closer, naked, touching in every way possible, a brand new want and desire for her.

She was practically naked every night at work, but for the first time she really wanted to be truly naked, stripped of any pretense with everything off, all the way down to her soul. She lifted herself a few inches and whispered, "Let's go to my room."

Carson stopped what he was doing and took a long, hard look at her. He scanned her face as if trying to determine if she really meant it, making her want it, whatever *it* was, even more. She gave a little nod, encouraging him to move from making out on the couch to the unknown in her bedroom.

He stood up and bent over, holding out his hand for Sienna's, then he paused and allowed her to lead him down the hall to her room, where she'd never brought a man.

When Carson got to the threshold, he stopped for a moment and pulled her close, searching for clues, gauging her feelings, making sure she wasn't second-guessing asking him to her bedroom. He smoothed her hair, massaging her temple with his thumb, and delved deep into what felt like her mind, body, and soul to be sure she was truly okay with this decision.

WHAT THE *fuck am I doing?* I should be through her bedroom door and deep inside her already, Carson thought. Balls deep inside her, yet here I am staring at her and checking in, making sure she's okay with moving forward.

Since Carson picked Sienna up at the club, his plans to get inside her and get her the hell out of his system were out the window. Rational thinking had left the building, and he knew one thing for sure—this was bad. Not bad in the sense that he was finally going to take his time and savor the woman who had been the one and only focus of his fantasies for weeks, but not good because he wasn't a get-involved type.

But there was such a difference between the Sienna who roamed the club making guys practically cream in their pants, and the Sienna who showed up at the back door waiting for him. The fantasy Sienna was just that. A fantasy.

This Sienna was a whole different kind of dream. The real Sienna was passionate and hesitant all at the same time. She had such flavor for fantasy and all things sexual onstage, yet she had this innocence in real life when she was stripped of the glittery thongs.

Fucking Christ.

He wanted her in the worst possible way, but also wanted it to be good for her. He didn't want it to ever end for him. He should stop, leave, go back east and never look back, but he knew as sure as his dick was rock hard, he couldn't do that.

With a quick glance at her face, taking the time to massage her temple, touching the smoothness of her hair, and checking in, he moved toward the bed. He set her down gently, even though his instinct was to take her hard and fast.

Her hair fanned out around her on the pillow as he laid her down, a blanket of soft, silky golden locks that he wanted to rub all over his body. She was a sight. He pulled off her yoga pants, revealing nothing underneath. Just beautiful, soft skin still shimmering from her special lotion, and between her legs, where she was completely waxed smooth, glowed with wetness for him.

Carson knew her core would be tight and would invariably hold him captive. Not just his dick, but his mind. He wanted in there, to stay, but first he wanted a taste. The way Sienna stared up at him with starry blue eyes, he got the sense this was a new experience for her.

He liked that, but he couldn't understand it. She was a stripper. He had to keep reminding himself of that fact. She seemed so real, vibrant, and alive in the moment, as if everything was fresh to her.

For the second time in minutes, Carson had to drag himself away from his contradicting thoughts and focus on what was in front of him. Sienna naked, glistening everywhere, and ready for him.

He left his pants on and lay down next to her, massaging her breast with one hand, the other turning her head toward him for a kiss. He didn't kiss her for long. He couldn't wait. He swirled his tongue one last time in her mouth, pulling the softest, most feminine moan from her before breaking away.

His other hand, which had been back to softly rounding her nipple, moved down between her thighs where his mouth wanted to be, soaking in the wetness he craved to taste. He slowly lowered himself that way. Peeking up at Sienna, he saw that her head was tilted back against the pillow, her eyes closed, and fuck, she was stunning like that.

She was completely open to him, and somehow he had become entirely convinced she'd never done this before. After the other night and her earth-shattering orgasm, he knew he must be right. This was all brand spanking new to her, and it was his to own. He felt a primal need to roar, as if he were some fucking king of the jungle, but suppressed it.

Carson finally landed where he'd wanted to be all night, between her legs. His dick throbbed inside his jeans, but it was worth it. He'd never wanted to savor something so badly. He pressed his mouth to her, and immediately another soft moan escaped from above on the pillow.

He kissed and lapped her skin at a leisurely pace at first, allowing his tongue long licks and time to linger on her most sensitive bundle of nerves, learning his way around what made her squirm more. Sienna's soft moans turned into something altogether more husky, and had his cock throbbing.

Finally, picking up speed and staying focused on her hottest area, he slipped his finger inside her, finding just the right pace and spot. Within seconds, Sienna was writhing underneath him.

It absolutely was a first for her. No denying it. The way she let go with reckless abandon, the flush that spread across her entire body, he couldn't help but feel the newness of all this for Sienna.

He didn't let up until she calmed, allowing all the little tremors to flow through her body while he softly caressed her with his tongue through all the aftershocks. He wanted this to be the best first ever.

Carson shifted his body back up to meet her face to face. He nuzzled her neck, pressing small kisses around her ear while gently pushing his hardness against her. His jeans were strangling him, but he needed to know she wanted him before he took the next leap.

"I want you so bad, Sienna." He paused, breathing deep and steady, and waited for her response.

He suspected she might retreat into her brain for a minute while weighing the pros and cons, but she surprised him by saying, "I've never felt so good. I want you, too. Now." She was so firm in her choice, she didn't even flinch a muscle.

Carson didn't need any more convincing. He reached down and pulled his jeans off. Sienna looked so fucking inviting, lying there on the bed, flushed from her orgasm, he was ready to delve right in, but he forced himself to stop and fish protection out of his pants pocket. He tore his boxer briefs off, slid the condom on, and was slowly sliding inside her before anything could change.

He angled over her body with one arm holding his weight up on the bed, the other gripping Sienna's hip, giving him purchase to rock deep inside her. His thumb moved across a long scar, hidden in the sparkles of her body lotion, but he rubbed it a few times to make certain it was there. The detective in him wondered what it was from, but the man in him won over his thoughts. He could do nothing but think about how he was sliding in and out of the best woman he'd ever had.

Something was immediately clear—there was no way one time with this woman was going to cure him of his Sienna addiction.

After slowly settling inside her, he steadied his mind, wanting to make this good for her and not come too soon. Problem was, he was so fucking taken with her, he couldn't even think of a topic to take his mind off her. He felt her arm slip behind his head, drawing him in for a kiss and further into the moment. She wasn't even turned off by her taste all over his mouth. She wanted everything that was happening with a fervor he had never experienced with a woman before Sienna.

He shifted his weight a little, pushing deep, quickening his pace, and Sienna's leg wrapped around his ass.

"Oh God," she said in a breathy voice.

"Is this good, Sienna? You fucking feel amazing," he whispered along her neck.

"More than good," she said, and then moaned again. He pushed deeper.

Her foot dug into his ass as he kept sliding in and out of her. His hand traveled south, spending a little time on the side of her breast, finally landing in between them, where they were joined. Feeling himself going in and out of her only ratcheted his desire, if that was even possible. His finger found her most sensitive spot and swirled around it, leaving her panting and breathless.

With one more swift pass and press of his finger, Sienna came. She came hard and the vibrations of her clenching his dick traveled all the way up his spine, causing him to release right with her. He stayed deep, allowing her waves to subside, letting her milk him for everything he had.

After begrudgingly pulling out and removing the condom, Carson settled right beside Sienna, one leg lightly resting over hers while he smoothed her hair behind her ear. They were silent.

Carson could feel her uncertainty surfacing, her anxiety over what just happened. He didn't know what to say to make it go away. This was uncharted territory for him. He did good times, drinks, and sex. He had no idea how to comfort and reassure in bed.

So he said, "You all right?" when what he really wanted to ask was if it was good for her. He wanted to take away her fears and tell her that he quite possibly wanted to do this for a long time. But he didn't.

First, he had no idea where those thoughts were coming from, and second, he had no idea how make those words come out of his mouth.

"Yes, I'm fine," she replied. "Thank you for being gentle with me. It was clear you knew how new this type of thing was to me. I'm kind of embarrassed, but it was so decadent." She hid her head in the pillow.

"Don't be." He lingered with his fingers in her blonde locks and allowed her to hide, desperately trying to figure out how to wrap this whole thing up, despite wanting to pull her tight against him and stay there for days.

He had to leave before he was stuck. Not just physically stuck, but mentally.

Cocksucker.

Then she let him off the hook. Pulling her face out of the pillow, she looked at him with softened yet unsure eyes and said, "I've never had anyone sleep over, and I don't feel comfortable with it. Let's say good night. I'm going to shower and go to bed."

That was it. She dismissed him. His stripper—who was anything but experienced when it came to intimacy, which he liked a lot—was asking him to leave after sex.

He didn't even have to try to slip out. She gave him an easy out, and although it was what he thought he wanted, Carson suddenly realized he really didn't fucking like that. Not one damn bit.

"I understand," he answered nonetheless, and slowly moved to get up.

Not being able to control what happened next, he asked, "Can we see each other tomorrow? I know you work, but a late lunch or coffee?" Somehow, he didn't want to ask for a nightcap and have this just be about sex.

"I have to help a little early at the club tomorrow. We have a VIP party coming in, and I have to make sure the girls are all set. Perhaps a quick coffee, but honestly, I don't want this to be about guilt over what just happened. I'm a big girl."

Carson tilted his head to the side, trying to understand and make sense of where this sudden change in personality was coming from. "That's not what this is about. I'd like to get together, have coffee, talk. I could pick you up around three and then drop you off at the club, so you wouldn't have to take the town car."

Shit, I'm eager to spend time with her and prove her wrong.

"Okay," was all she said in response.

He wasn't going to argue. As he finished putting on his pants and shirt, he said, "It's a plan," then leaned over and placed a soft kiss on her lips. He tasted like her, smelled like the two of them, and he was leaving when all he wanted to do was stay.

Fuck, what's wrong with me? Go!

Sienna got up and wrapped herself in a robe, then walked him to the door. With weariness in her eyes, she said good-bye, then locked the door behind him.

AFTER SAYING good night to Carson, Sienna wasn't in the mood for her usual nightly bath. She didn't want to be alone with her thoughts bubbling in her head. Despite desperately wanting to keep his scent all over her body and hair, she showered like she said she was going to when he left. As the water poured down from the rain head, she could only think one thought: My first time with a man who actually cared about pleasing me, and I ask him to go.

She had no other choice but to ask him to leave; she was going to drown in emotion if she didn't. It was one thing to be made love to gently for the first time at twenty-eight years old, it was another to sleep next to the man involved and keep her emotions at bay.

It would be undeniably impossible to keep her feelings wrapped up nice and neat if he stayed, lingered in her bed, whispering sweet nothings and false promises, and then fell asleep next to her. This was the same reason why Sienna begrudgingly washed their mixed scents off her in a hot shower and slipped into a fresh robe. She needed fewer reminders of all that she wanted in life, yet couldn't begin to allow herself to have. All that was Carson.

She couldn't bring herself to change her sheets, so when she climbed back into bed, it smelled like Carson and her orgasm intermingled with his. She couldn't help but to breathe deeply everywhere she could. She wrapped herself tight around her pillows, sheets, and blanket, chasing her drug of choice, inhaling deeply of every last scent of Carson and the two of them together from her bed.

Then she cried. She cried for her first orgasm while making love to a man and how beautiful it was. She shed tears for the only time she was with a man who took his time with her, wanted to make her feel good and loved, even though she knew that wasn't what this was about.

She called what happened making love because she couldn't bring herself to call it fucking. Sienna wasn't sure whether Carson thought it was fucking, but she couldn't tarnish her memories. In her mind, she wanted to put what just happened on a pedestal and leave it there forever.

Yet another reason why Carson had to leave. If he stayed, she risked not being able to remember this special night, and she wanted desperately to memorize it. She needed to save it, bank it away for a cold and lonely night.

What made her cry even harder was the thought of living a life devoid of love, romance, and spending her days with someone to hold her. She might never have any of that, but she had this night. A night where she felt everything there was to feel at its greatest heights. A night where she felt safe and warm, adored, and satiated in the best way.

This evening also stood as a reminder of what she was missing, what she had to give up when she ran from all she ever knew. More tears began to flow for the partner, the forever someone, that she would never call her own.

As her sobs began to lessen, Sienna forced herself not to think about what she had to live without, and concentrated on how she was going to stay alive. She would keep this delicious memory with her, but she had to run again. Having to leave the small little cocoon she'd created for herself in Vegas with a few friends, a career, money, and a house was almost enough to break her, but she loved life too much. She also adored her new family, and with this crazy Sam guy chasing her around, she couldn't risk any of them getting hurt. Who knew what Sam Charles was really up to?

The idea of saying good-bye to Asher, Petal, and Mike made her cry the biggest and hardest tears. Did she owe them the truth? Could they take it? Would they want to make it right with Elon and expose her?

Finally exhausted, Sienna cried herself to sleep.

seventeen

Friday

WHEN SIENNA woke up the next day puffy-eyed, she wanted someone to talk to. She didn't want to lie there by herself and cry some more. She really only had two choices, Asher or Petal. After interrupting Asher and Natalie earlier in the week, she chose Petal.

Within a half hour of her text, Petal let herself into Sienna's place and crawled into bed with her, holding a mug of warm chamomile tea.

How had their roles become reversed? Sienna was supposed to be the one mentoring Petal, yet she was so inexperienced in relationships, she had to turn to someone younger for comfort.

Petal smoothed Sienna's hair, and all that did was make her think of Carson's soft touch, the way he caressed her hair behind her ear the night before, and how she'd washed his smell off her whole body and shampooed it out of her hair.

Soon Sienna was crying again, and Petal kept repeating, "Shh, don't cry." After a few minutes of letting her tears run their course, Petal asked, "What happened, Sie? Did someone hurt you?"

Oh God, Sienna thought to herself. She couldn't deal with anyone thinking Carson hurt her. She straightened up and firmly said, "No, nobody hurt me."

Then she sighed and fell back into the pillows. "Actually, the opposite. This someone, Carson, made me feel so good, and I've never had that before, ever. Isn't that so sad?"

Once she started opening up, she couldn't stop. After wrapping herself back in her Carson-scented comforter, she said, "He treated me so delicately, and took his time making me feel things I never felt before. Like never, Petal. It felt like he cared for me, more than just the stripper he was smitten with. I never had any of that in my life. Then I asked him to leave. I didn't want him to stay. I was so scared of getting even more attached in one night, if that's possible. Is that normal? Ugh, I know it's not. I'm not normal. I'm a sex symbol who doesn't know how to spend a night with a man."

Petal listened. Somehow she knew Sienna needed a friend to hear her out, which was probably why she approached Petal instead of Asher. Being a man, Asher would have tried to fix everything, and she just needed to talk, cry, and talk some more. After an hour of quietly listening to Sienna unburden herself about the night before, Petal encouraged her to take a bubble bath with some cold compresses on her eyes.

After helping her get settled, Petal stayed in the bathroom with Sienna. With her eyes covered with cold cucumber slices and her body submerged in bubbles, it made Petal's next statement a lot easier for Sienna to digest.

"I know you didn't come from an easy life to Vegas, Sienna, and if you don't want to go into details, well, I get that, too. But how is it that you, someone so kind and giving, was never given anything good? Why is this the first time you felt something decent from a man? There's something wrong in and of itself with that. You not only deserve good, you should have better than good. Do you understand?" With her eyes fixed on Sienna, her friend waited for an answer.

"I understand what you mean," Sienna murmured from the tub, "and I know that I should allow myself to have the sweet part of life, but I just can't. A long time ago, I had the worst of the worst. I don't want to talk about it. Even though I want it all right now, I can't have it. My life is a whole lot of wants that aren't possible, my past won't allow it. That's all I can say."

Petal sighed. "Look, we all come from checkered pasts, Sie. Like I said, I'm not going to pressure you. I'd never do that. Just know that you more so than anyone, it's only fair you get a good life. You take care of all of us at the club. You need to give in to yourself one day and go after what you deserve."

Sienna looked away. "Petal, I love you, and one day I want to explain it all to you, but right now, this is all whatever this is can be with Carson, a memory of the best night of my life. We're going to have coffee this afternoon, and then he'll go back on assignment wherever he should be. And that's it." She released a long sigh that almost sounded like a whimper, then closed her eyes before sinking further into the bubbles.

"I'm not going to argue with you," Petal said softly, "and I'll support you in all your choices, whether I think they're crazy or not. I love you, too, and one day, I hope you'll confide in me so we can figure out how to make sure you get it all." She brought her hand to Sienna's forehead and pushed a few loose hairs back before placing a single kiss on her forehead. Then, to give Sienna some space, she was sure, she moved to the makeup table and started looking through Sienna's lip glosses.

With that, Sienna knew she had to change the subject to something less invasive than her past. She could only hold it in for so long, and the way her emotions were going up and down and around like a roller coaster, she was close to breaking down and spilling everything. She needed to move on to safer territory.

She opened her eyes and reached for a towel, then slipped out of the tub and dried off. While she dressed in loungewear, she said, "Thanks, love. I'm feeling better after talking with you, and the bath. Now tell me all about the bachelor party coming in tonight. How many men? Rooms? Which girls are working the party?"

She laughed about how much money Petal said she expected to make that night. Her "little sis" shot right back with reminding Sienna to eat, get dressed pretty, and be ready for coffee.

Petal didn't wait for Sienna to come back with any arguments. She left Sienna to her thoughts after mentioning the coffee date.

A T PRECISELY three o'clock, Sienna heard a knock on her door and knew it was Carson. Steeling against flinging herself into his arms, she smoothed the front of her midnight-blue cashmere sweater, making sure it lay flat against her skinny jeans, brushed a lock of hair from her face, since it was down and set in light waves, and opened the door. Carson looked his normal casual, masculine self, dressed in a gray thermal pullover pushed up to his elbows, worn-in jeans, heavy boots, his black hair mussed up, and his little dimple in his cheek.

Under other circumstances, they would look like the perfect yuppie couple heading out on a brisk Vegas winter day. Sienna wanted to run her finger along Carson's ear where his hair was slightly turning gray and curling up, obviously still wet and fresh from a shower. She was dying to reach up and kiss him intimately and whisper hello in his ear, something she always dreamed about doing when her husband came home, but they weren't the idyllic yuppie pair. They were a stripper and her fan from out of town.

Instead, she clasped her hands behind her back, and said hi sheepishly.

"Hi to you. How was your morning?" He moved confidently through the door.

"Good. Relaxing, actually." She wasn't going to tell him about her meltdown.

"Nice. I kind of hoped you were going to say you counted the minutes until you saw me again," he teased. "Are you ready to go, or do you need some time?" He then stepped in to brush a kiss across her lips.

A lump formed in her throat over the night before and asking him to leave. Did he not mind at all?

"I'm ready, let me grab my tote. Oh, wait, I have to text Mike and tell him I don't need a ride to the club tonight."

Carson waited for Sienna. When she was ready to leave, he held the door for her to leave her house and walked her to the car with his hand on the small of her back. Even with it being the third time he did this, she was already burning with desire by the time she got in the passenger seat. She wondered how she had ever walked without his hand there.

When they started down the driveway, Carson asked if she might like to go to the bakery and coffee place inside the new hotel on the Strip, or back to Canyon Coffee.

"You mentioned you never get to venture to the Strip for fun stuff, so I thought it would be a change of pace," he said as he glanced at her, selling her on the idea with an ear-to-ear grin.

Considering this dating thing was all new to her, she'd never been on a date to the Strip. She had a ball cap in her tote and she was wearing her giant white sunglasses, so why the hell not?

"That works, as long as you don't mind me putting on my hat."

"I only mind because I love looking at you with your hair flowing all around, but I guess it will have to do," Carson said jokingly.

It was entirely too comfortable between the two of them. She thought she'd feel awkward after the night before, but with one look and a single smile, Carson had put her completely at ease. Even the elephant in the car—their night spent apart when it could have been spent together—had now dissipated into thin air.

Most women would think this was great, but not Sienna. This being so at ease with Carson was bad, really bad, because with her defenses down, she was going to get attached and run the risk of slipping up with her story. She had already revealed far too much to Petal earlier today.

As much as she tried to rein herself in, she couldn't. She was too happy and enjoying herself for the first time in her entire life. Was this what happened when you had an orgasm? Did everything else stop mattering and all worries fell into the abyss?

The pair made small talk on their way to the Strip. Sienna pointed out a few hotels and fun facts as they drove to the new mega hotel/casino. As they pulled up front, Sienna put on her cap and pulled it low before she got out of the car when the valet opened up the door.

"Sienna Flower! Welcome to the Palace on the Strip," the parking attendant said in what was meant to be a whisper, but came out much louder. So much for the disguise.

A manager who had been chatting with guests nearby looked up in fear when he realized the young valet's mistake and came over to apologize. Unfortunately, the valet had already caused a stir with the local paparazzi camped out at the hotel, and a few of them ran over to Sienna, bombarding her with questions about the club, her private life, and what brought her to the Palace.

This is what an orgasm gets me.

Sienna felt Carson's hand on her back again and heard him saying, "Move along. Miss Flower is out on a personal errand. She's not taking questions." His firm tone combined with his imposing six-foot-plus frame convinced them to move away. Carson continued to escort Sienna into the hotel as if he were one of the bouncers from the club.

As soon as they went through the double doors, a VIP host was there to greet them, apologizing for the misunderstanding at the valet.

Carson stated matter-of-factly, "We were going to have coffee and something to eat at Le Mirage Bakery. Perhaps there's a private room where we can enjoy something from there?" He held his posture straight and rigid, letting his eyes roam the casino lobby before coming right back to bore down on the host.

"Yes. How about we set you up in a private gaming room and bring you a menu from Le Mirage?"

"Good, lead the way," Carson said tersely.

Sienna felt like she should apologize. She leaned close and said, "Sorry, Carson. We should've just stuck with the coffee place by my house."

"Don't you dare apologize. That valet had no right to shout your name and alert those photographers. At least now I get to see you with your hair down." He set her at ease with one of his sexy winks.

Sienna gave him a small smile in response. She hoped no one was tweeting that she was on the Strip; she really wanted a quiet afternoon without crazy fans. On a good note, this always made for extra-heavy crowds at the club when she was spotted. All the chatter made even more people want to see her live. Asher would be pissed she was on the Strip without letting him know, but the Tunnel would benefit.

Finally, the host opened the door to a private gaming room, where Carson pulled out a chair at a small table by the observation window, then pulled open the heavy drapes so she could look out. A waiter rushed in with menus for Le Mirage, and opened a bottle of sparkling water for the couple. They took a minute and ordered coffee and pastries, then were left to their own devices.

Sienna took in the man-made beauty outside the window, her eyes wandering over the neighboring hotels and their opulent, perhaps ostentatious, displays. Taken with the water shooting into the air from the fountain directly across from their window seat, the stillness of the room caught up with her, and she suddenly felt nervous. Should she bring up last night? As it turned out, she didn't have to.

Carson took her hand in his, turning it over and running a finger around her palm. "Listen, I never really like spending the night with anyone, so when you asked me to leave last night, I did. Then I got back to my hotel, and I realized I made a mistake. I wanted to stay with you even if I didn't want to admit it to myself. I should've insisted on staying, Sienna. I don't think it was very considerate of me to leave, especially after what we shared, and I was a fool. I'm sorry." He brought his other hand up to wrap her delicate hand in both of his.

She shook her head. "You don't need to apologize. I understand. I wasn't sure what to do when we were done, and so I chose the easy way out. I felt a little lonely with you gone. Actually, a lot. You and I both know it was for the best, though, right? Where can all this go? Last night was really great, but I don't think it's wise for us to get too attached," she said, no clue where the false confidence was coming from.

"I disagree. I went along with you asking me to go last night. I thought maybe that was what I wanted, too. But what I'm saying is that felt all wrong after what I did. You may be inexperienced, Sienna, but I'm figuring out things just like you are. Now I realize that leaving was wrong, and the truth is, I want to get a little attached. Know you. The real you."

Red flag, red flag!

Sienna wanted to run, but she didn't move. She only stared at the man across from her. "But my life is crazy. I'm a stripper. I dance all night, get caught up during the day, and do it all over again. You don't live here, and I really don't like to travel. I just don't see how this can go far," she said, trying to gently salvage her precious memory from the night before.

Carson gave her a half smile. "Well, lucky for you, I travel, don't require much sleep, and enjoy watching you dance. And I like spending time alone with you even more."

I'm completely and royally screwed.

CARSON HAD no idea where all the sincerity was coming from. He'd literally never spoken words like those before in his whole life.

Boy, I changed my tune since the last time we had coffee.

Even worse, he could detect a small amount of panic in Sienna's face as he kept sharing his thoughts of their making a go of whatever this was. He knew she liked him, so what the hell was with the little look of fear? Was it leftover embarrassment from the night before? Perhaps, the paparazzi scaring her off? Or something altogether different, as in someone else?

He didn't fucking know, but he did want to know why. And he wanted to know her, all of her, and he was going to no matter what. His head and dick were in agreement at the moment, and they both wanted more now. It was a heady combination he'd never experienced before, yet for some reason, he was going to run with it.

Sienna had barriers, obviously, but he was going to break them down. He was in the middle of telling her how he would make this work, how he would do the work and it would fall on him, all while her phone kept dinging with text messages.

In his experience, that was never a good thing. It must be urgent the way the phone kept dinging repeatedly.

"Go ahead. Get it," he said to a shell-shocked Sienna, who currently had both of her hands in his, her fingernails digging into his flesh. He knew she didn't realize how tight she was gripping him.

She pulled her hands away to reach for her phone, and swept her delicate finger across the screen. Without realizing it, Sienna read the texts aloud as she went down the list of missed ones.

Asher: YOU spotted in parking area of Palace?!?!? WTF, Sie? I'm sick.
Mike: 25 different people tweeted & posted about you being on Strip. Were you going to tell me? Is your man with you?
Asher: Paps posted exactly where you are! Mike's been eyeing Cowboy Sam. He's staying down the Strip. Heading your way. Do not move. Wait for Mike.
Mike: Stay put, Sienna. Trailing the cowboy. Wait for instructions to meet Petey out back.

Carson's thoughts whirled. Who was Cowboy Sam? The reason why Sienna wouldn't get close? He rubbed his palms over each other, feeling the tiny nail marks his woman had left there. Shoving jealous thoughts to the back of his head, he reached across and held Sienna's hand while she read through the texts one more time.

Geez. What the fuck was going on? He was pretty sure he just got himself involved in a situation, and not the good kind.

Just as Carson was about to ask Sienna exactly what he could do, the damn waiter walked in with their coffee. Carson gave him a quick nod and word of thanks, and made it clear they wanted their privacy.

"Sienna, what's going on, babe? I imagine you deal with paparazzi from time to time. This can't be unusual, but who is this Sam guy you keep mentioning? Is he bad? Did he hurt you?" He slid his chair catty-corner to hers, and moved his entire body closer so he could absorb the nerves and anxiety rolling off her.

Sienna was visibly flustered, obviously not wanting to answer. She waved a dismissive hand and said, "He's no big deal, some crazy fan or something. He's the guy who rushed the stage last week. Mike has it under control."

Carson could tell it was all a put-on, an act. He was ex-FBI; did she really think she could fool him? He didn't want to stress her out any more than she already was, so he let her think he bought the nonchalant act. He motioned to pay the tab, so he'd be ready to let some other dude come and rescue them.

He was capable of watching over Sienna and getting her out of there safely, if she'd only told him what the hell was going on, but he was stuck waiting on Petey. He knew without a doubt that Sienna wouldn't ignore Mike and Asher's instructions.

Sienna went quiet, obviously in her head, so Carson let her stay there while keeping a hold of her hand and rubbing her thigh up and down with his free one. She didn't even notice he was touching her. How could she?

After all, he was in his own head, devising a plan for him to gain control. He thought those guys were nice enough, but if he was going to date Sienna, he was quite capable of being in charge of keeping her safe.

He was a big, bad boy, too. No one was going to outsmart Carson in taking care of Sienna, once he had all the facts. He knew better than to ask Sienna for more details. She was totally clammed up at the moment.

But he had an idea, though. Carson decided to pal up to Mike later at the club under the premise of thanking him for taking such good care of Sienna. Just two guys sharing a beer, and he would make Mike tell him what he needed to know. He didn't leave his interrogation skills along with his badge when he left the Bureau.

Carson continued to caress Sienna's leg, warming the goose bumps that kept rising to the surface, while he worked this all out in his mind. Sienna, he was certain, was crafting all kinds of excuses for what was actually happening.

That's okay, I'm going to circumvent all this bullshit.

Within ten minutes, Petey texted to let Sienna know he was out back. Carson didn't let go of Sienna's hand as they walked out of the private gaming room and straight to the emergency exit at the far end of the casino. He took notice she didn't even try to let go, either. She was scared.

He didn't need to feel her pulse racing to know she was fighting a fight-versus-flight reflex, he could see it in her eyes, and feel it in the way she alternated gripping his hand in a death grip and fully releasing his fingers.

He wished he could let her know that staying close to him was the smart choice, but then Petey was there as promised in a black SUV with blacked-out windows. Carson opened the back door for Sienna and she got in, then slid over, making room for him to get into the seat next to her.

As soon as he was in the backseat, Carson made a point of staring Petey down in the rearview mirror. This was his date with his woman, and he was going to see her through this, no matter who was driving the damn car. Petey might have picked Carson and Sienna up, but she was on a date with Carson. End of story. He'd pick his car up later.

With traffic, they were at the Tunnel within fifteen minutes. Sienna was in her dressing room approximately two minutes later with her door locked.

It looked like he wasn't going to have to wait until later to feel out Mike, since they were both standing like two chumps outside her door, effectively locked out.

Carson leaned one shoulder into her door in feigned defeat. "Hey, want to go grab a drink and let her shake the mood off?" he asked Mike. "I could stand to unwind a little after that scene. It would be a load off if you joined me." He held his hand out to the club, motioning for the big dude to lead the way, surrendering control and already playing his part.

Mike shrugged. "Yeah, all right, man. One beer, because I got to work tonight."

"I got ya," Carson answered. He spoke bouncer.

Taking a sip of his draft beer at the bar a few minutes later, Carson said, "Shit, that was something today. When the paps saw us, I didn't think it would be such a big deal."

"Man, it normally isn't," Mike said as he stared into his beer. "Then again, I usually go to the Strip with Sie. I know most of the valets and casino hosts, so I'm able to get her in and out relatively unnoticed. Pulling up front with you like a tourist got her busted."

Dude isn't going to be as easy as I thought to crack.

"Fuck, that was all me, man. I wanted to show her a nice afternoon."

He fell on his sword when he lowered his head and stared into his beer. Boy, he could act.

Mike slid him a sideways glance. "Look, I like you, dude. I love Sienna, though. She's got no one but us here at the club, and we got to keep her safe. We've been wanting her to branch out, make a life for herself, so I was fucking all for her getting to know you. But you gotta know, she comes from something bad. We're not going to let that touch her ever again. You gotta respect the protocols we have in place for her, my friend." Mike leaned back and stretched his arms overhead, trying to intimidate. Obviously, the young bouncer could act, too.

Carson nodded, feeling appropriately chastised. "I got ya. I like her. At first, I wasn't sure it was anything more than a little lust, you gotta know what I mean, with her on that stage every night. Now I'm into her onstage and off. Fuck, listen to me, talking like I have a pussy. I get you have rules, but I don't know anything about what Sienna comes from. What do you mean, bad?"

Mike lowered his massive arms and crossed them in front of his chest. "Buddy, I don't know much, that's Sie's story to tell. She just showed up here about seven years ago, and Asher took her under his wing. He helped her make a new life. It was clear she was never going back to wherever she came from, no fucking way, but that's all I know. We take care of her, and we'll never stop."

Carson nodded. "I get it. She's precious. What's with this Sam dude? Could he be an ex or someone from her past? Or is he just a crazy fan? Have you checked him out?" He fired off questions as he made a mental note to look into Sienna's past. He could call in a favor for that.

Mike took a swig of his beer, then shook his head. "We don't know what the deal is with this Sam guy. Sam Charles, from Jersey. He rushed the stage last week, then showed up outside Asher's house before he and Sienna left for Red Rock."

"What?" Carson was raging with jealousy, which he knew was unfounded, and anger, which was unwarranted. "She didn't say that to me. What did he want?" He stood up, his back against the bar and mimicked Mike's posture, crossing his arms over his chest.

"Yeah. He was parked a couple houses down with eyeballs on the two of them. Ash clocked him right away, and I ran him out of town. Been watching the asshole since he got back in last night. He's staying on the Strip. The dude even had the nerve to ask the concierge to call and get a Samuel Smith on the list here. I was gonna question him tonight when he tried to get in under a different name, but then Sienna turned up on the Strip, bringing him out to see her. I had to shut him down. I'm not sure whether he'll show tonight."

"Where's he staying?" Carson spit out. "I want to check him out. What could he want?"

"We don't know," Mike admitted as he tugged at the corner of the damp label on his beer bottle. "Sienna mentioned it was her past catching up with her, but I think he's a fan. A crazy fucking one." Then he shook his head in disgust, lifted the bottle, and downed the last of his beer.

Carson's instincts were screaming at him. "You want me to look into the guy? I could call my buddies over at the Bureau and do a little scouting myself." He didn't really need permission. He'd already decided his next move would be to step outside for privacy and make some calls.

"Nah," Mike said. "My guess is this guy isn't worth the trouble of calling the Feds. Sienna is just all panicked, but this yahoo is a fan gone wrong. We're gonna deal with him." Then he got up, slapped Carson on the back, and headed back to work.

Carson nodded, but he had no intention of letting this go. It was in his DNA to get to the bottom of things.

Since he solved his first case, finding his own runaway mom when he was nineteen years old, he did nothing but make sure to tie up loose ends on every job. When he uncovered his mother, he didn't even go talk to her. He knew all he needed to know from his investigation. She'd been remarried for a decade to a wealthy slumlord. They had two kids she drove to extracurricular activities, and spent time volunteering at their schools. None of her friends or neighbors knew about her past. It was an open-and-shut case. She wanted a life with more money and no responsibility other than bake sales. She left him and his blue-collar dad, and never looked back.

With that information in hand, Carson had returned to college after the spring break he'd spent on his investigation, and added forensic psychology to his course load. He knew then and there he was heading to the FBI. Finding missing people, uncovering the facts surrounding their disappearance, allowing others to close chapters of their lives, this was his greatest mission in life.

He solved some of the biggest missing-person cases for the FBI, from the missing sixteen-year-old girl in the Midwest, to the one right before he got out, where he found and turned in the biggest white-collar criminal to date, the one who'd stolen billions from his clients.

This was who he was, and he wasn't going to let a little slime-ball fan torture Sienna, nor was he going to walk around with his thumb up his ass not knowing what her fucking deal was.

Carson ran his hand through his hair and stopped at his neck, massaging to ease the tension a notch. Of all the women in the world, he had to make a run for one who needed FBI vetting. Christ, he was a dumb fuck.

That was what he told himself as he walked out to his car to make a few calls before going back into the club for the night.

eighteen

SIENNA LOCKED her dressing room door as soon as she got back to the club. *So what if Carson or Mike or Ash are mad? Let them be mad all they want.*

She knew they were all going to argue with her over being out on the Strip without a security detail, but Carson was able to do that, right? Carson didn't know all the facts, but that shouldn't make a difference. He could keep the crazies away.

She was never going to tell Carson the truth, so it was a worthless argument. Actually, Mike was in the dark, and he loved her unconditionally without knowing every detail of her past. He'd never let anything happen to her, so it was safe to assume she could be safe with Carson without him being completely in the know.

Yet she didn't have time to dwell on all the men in her life because one man, Sam Charles, was insistent on turning her life upside down. She'd made such a great life as Sienna Flower, and now she had to consider her options all over again. She was fairly certain she'd been discovered and revealed to Elon, so she needed a new plan. A new life, which was hard to digest because she loved her life as a stripper.

She might not have much, but she adored the little circle she had created in the underbelly of Vegas. She even loved her fans at the club.

They showed her more affection and praise than her husband ever had.

Ugh, and Asher. *Asher, my beacon of light, my sword of strength.*

How could she leave him? She was in a bad position, no matter how she looked at it. She was in deep with Carson, but not deep enough to exorcise demons from her past.

Sienna decided to burn through her nerves with cleaning her dressing room, except she knocked over more makeup than she straightened when she went to organize her vanity. Her shaking hands could barely line up the perfume bottles.

With her door locked and no one to witness her meltdown, she secretly considered going back home, seeking a divorce, and losing herself in Carson. That was a fairy tale, though, because there was no happy ending for Lila. If she went back, Elon would never grant her a divorce.

Oh, she could get a civil one, but the religious leaders wouldn't accept it. All this was best-case scenario because she knew damn well if she went back, Elon would beat her to a pulp. She might not even make it out alive to ask for a divorce if she showed her face back there again. Their community would surround the wagons, cover it all up, and no one would know what really happened to her. The culture she came from didn't need any more bad publicity. They were already viewed as strange since they refused to conform to societal norms. They would never allow anything negative to go public about their community.

Furthermore, she knew her family and neighbors would never suspect what kind of person Elon actually was. Even worse, she was sure her family wouldn't back her up either. Her mom and dad would never risk being disgraced in front of the community, the church, and their friends. They were devout, followed every commandment, and turned a blind eye to anything that would tarnish their reputation among their fellow worshippers.

She whipped through her clothing rack, pulling hangers out like they were the enemy and shoving them around, color-coordinating her clothes in an OCD fashion.

Stop. This was all dependent on the notion Carson actually wanted more from her. Lots more. Not just more sex.

Sienna only allowed herself to indulge in a few minutes of this kind of happily-ever-after thinking. She wasn't going to have one. Not that she didn't believe she deserved one, but she needed to put staying alive over a fairy-tale ending.

She flopped herself onto the chaise in defeat and covered her face with her hands, hiding her tears from the sheer emptiness and isolation of her dressing room.

Deserting any dreams she was having about walking off into the sunset with Carson, Sienna got her head together, dried her wet cheeks, remade her face, and dressed to dance and meet with the girls before the VIP party. She would play her part. Sienna Flower. Sienna was safe at the moment, and she wasn't giving that up.

With Mike, Asher, and Carson at the club all weekend, she'd be protected, and then when the weekend came to a close, she'd plan to leave.

Sienna pulled out her black lace cat suit for extra courage. She exuded sex and confidence in the second skin made of lace with the tiny little zipper up the front. She made sure to leave the zipper open all the way to the bottom of her cleavage, revealing a luscious valley between her breasts. Her nipples showed faintly through the lace, and peeking out between her thighs was an emerald-green thong covering her special spot. The place Carson had set fire to recently.

Carson, the only man she'd ever bared herself to, either physically and emotionally. For however long it lasted, it was amazing.

After unlocking the dressing room door, Sienna strutted past Petey and out to the main floor where the girls were sitting, looking like a sensual explosion of lace, sequins, color, and skin. They were dressed to kill for the party, and Sienna wasn't going to let them down. She gave them their instructions on dance rotations, lap dance protocol, and then made a huge announcement.

She strutted over to the group and threw her hands in the air, signaling she had big news. "I'm opening up the club tonight and joining Syd in the first performance!"

Dancing was the kindling to her flame. She would find her strength out on the stage tonight, and would burn bright for the audience.

Sienna wasn't going to stand still while the rug was pulled out from under her. She didn't fight so hard to escape and build a new life to allow it to be stolen so easily from her grasp. She was going to have a bang-up, courage-building weekend, and figure everything out on Monday.

She always did. She had climbed through that window so many years ago with only the desire to live her life. That was exactly what she was going to do; otherwise, her escape was all in vain.

CARSON WALKED back into the club after speaking with two of his old partners at the Bureau. They were running background checks on the names or aliases, Sienna Flower and Sam Charles. He didn't really want to do this with Sienna. He'd hoped to get to know her, but after talking with Mike, he realized there were too many unknowns.

He immediately found Sienna finishing up her meeting with the other dancers, and played it cool. One thing was for sure, she would freak the fuck out if she knew he was looking into anything, let alone her past.

If Carson was going to take a stand in helping to protect her from this Sam dude, he needed to know all the facts. There was something missing as to why the whole lot of them—Asher, Mike, and Sienna— were so freaked by Sam. They kept calling him a stalker, but if that were so, they wouldn't be delving so deep.

Carson was sure there was more, and he would bet it was rooted in Sienna's past. The stuff she hadn't told him, and that Mike had alluded to but wouldn't share with him. He couldn't decide if he believed Mike or not about whether he really didn't know all the details.

Either way, he'd put money on it being a complicated web. One that he was now strung up in, which is exactly why he didn't do relationships.

Too late now, fucker.

This was the thought running through his head as he walked very nonchalantly toward Sienna, even though her black lace bodysuit had his dick hard and his brain screaming to take her to her dressing room and bend her over the couch.

"Hey, babe, you all right?" Carson wrapped his arm around her waist and whispered in her ear.

She leaned into him and very quietly said, "Thanks for giving me a minute. You didn't have to stay."

"Yeah, I did. I had to make sure you were okay and see you before you went onstage. Want to go back and start our date over in your dressing room?" he said jokingly, trying to defuse the tension. He looked her up and down, knowing his eyes were filled with want, telling her exactly what he wanted to do, betraying every single one of his very secret naughty thoughts.

Sienna shook her head. "I'd love to, but I can't. I'm going to open up the club in a half hour with Sydney. I feel like getting onstage early tonight, so she and I need a few minutes to make a plan."

"Well, it's good thing I stayed. I wouldn't want to miss that. And to be honest, I don't think I could be alone with you in that outfit. Wow, stunning doesn't even begin to cut it." His eyes continued to roam, finally settling on her gorgeous face.

He needed to keep the status quo until he could figure out what was really happening here. Fucking hell, he knew damn well he wasn't going to leave anything as it was. He'd fallen for the stripper all those weeks ago silently watching her, and now after a few dates and one time deep inside her, he was willing to chuck it all. Toss all his beliefs and notions into the garbage can.

Carson grabbed a seat at the back bar. There was no way he could be up front tonight with Sienna in that outfit. He didn't know what it was called, but his cock was like a rock just from the little glint of her green panties through the black lace.

Knowing she was totally bald down there as he watched her gyrate and climb the pole, and wanting to inhale her all the while, would surely have him close to coming in his pants. Something he hadn't done since he was fifteen, and he wasn't about to start now. Plus, he wanted to make sure he was able to duck out and take any calls that might come through regarding what he now considered his own personal case.

The bartender had just fixed him a scotch when Sienna hit the stage. She and Sydney moved in perfect unison on the two poles at the front, as though they had rehearsed it a million times.

The luscious women onstage made the hard-core rap mash-up with an eighties dance number an afterthought. Of course, the music was fucking perfect, providing just the right amount of sensuality and dance beat as they worked the crowd into a sensual haze.

Carson sipped his scotch, but kept his eyes on the prize. Sienna inched the zipper a tad lower on her suit, swinging her gorgeous, fuckable body from side to side. He wanted to tear the whole damn zipper with his mouth and run his tongue all over her, every inch of shiny and smooth skin, marking her as his.

Sienna's hair moved with her, and all he could think about was her underneath him, all lush and on the verge of orgasm. He was pretty sure the rest of the men, and probably some of the women, in the room were thinking the same thoughts, but he'd already had her once and he didn't plan on sharing.

He wanted her again and again until he couldn't move. He could die doing her. It would be a good way to go, wrapped in sheer perfection.

What the hell is going on with this woman? All I can think about is being inside in her, body and mind.

He had to get himself in check. There was a lot he didn't know, and he couldn't allow the lure of Sienna's curves to distract him.

Yeah, right.

About twenty seconds into the performance, Carson totally forgot Sydney was on the stage. He was so deep into Sienna's moves and his own personal fantasies, he didn't feel his phone vibrating in his pocket. The music was hitting a crescendo and Sienna was back up the pole, giving the entire audience the most amazing view of her cleavage as she leaned to the side of the pole and wrapped herself farther down its the length. Her cleavage was only for him, he told himself.

Her legs were twisted around the metal pole, and he could only think about how they were wrapped tight around him the night before, and how they would be again in a few hours if he had anything to do with it.

As the number came to an end, Carson couldn't think of anything else other than the pole being his cock rubbing up and down Sienna's body.

The dance ended and Sienna blew her usual kisses at the crowd. Then at the very end, she looked directly at Carson and winked while blowing one kiss his way. That was his cue. He was up and out of his seat, heading to her dressing room. God help anyone who tried to stop him. They better know the score by now, and let him make his way back to his woman.

Christ, his dick ached. He felt even worse for the dumb idiots who had to go home sporting that wood. He got the prize at the end of the night.

He felt on top of the world moving toward the other end of the club when his phone started to vibrate again. He pulled it out and realized he'd missed a call while Sienna was dancing. Good thing his old partner, Ray, called him back.

Sadly, he had to pick up, but he figured Sienna would need a few minutes to cool down and change her clothes. He nodded at Petey, motioning to his phone while he ducked out the back door.

"Hey, Ray, what you got, man?" He leaned up against the building, propping one bent leg behind him to provide him some leverage. For what, he didn't know.

"Well, the Sam Charles guy is simple. Amateur porn maker from

Jersey, been making the rounds around the country stalking a few of the big adult clubs and recruiting dancers to make it big in his films. For the most part, all of the club owners have thrown him out on his ass. Now, he's decided to set his sights on Sienna. Figures if she signs on, the others will follow."

Carson grunted and strummed his empty, idle fingers against the wall behind him. "Hmm, that's interesting, but I doubt Sienna is going to do that. She doesn't even do lap dances, so I'm pretty sure she isn't going to star in a film featuring her having sex. At the end of the day, it sounds crazy, but she's kind of innocent, untouched—"

Ray cut him off, which was a relief considering he really didn't want to reveal his true feelings to himself, let alone to Ray. "Yeah, that's the thing, Carson. Sienna is a bit of a mystery. I don't know what's going on with her. Sienna Flower didn't exist until she arrived on the scene about seven years ago. I know that's not such a red flag. A lot of these dancers use stage names, but Sienna Flower is the name Asher lists on an unofficial partnership agreement I dug up from his files. Why would he put Sienna Flower and not her real name for legal tax purposes? The only explanation would be that Sienna files under that name, but Sienna Flower hasn't filed taxes. Ever." He released an audible sigh.

Carson listened, tightening his grip on the phone as Ray revealed more of what he'd learned.

"There's no paper trail for Sienna," Ray went on. "No registration as an LLC or assumed name paperwork, no tax returns, or even a driver's license. Which again, wouldn't be a big deal except for the fact that Asher had put the name Sienna Flower on the agreement. I would think he would put her real name or the one she uses for financial filings on that; legally that makes sense. I did notice Asher has a small corporation named SF, LLC, listed for talent appraisal, to which he pays a pretty big sum each month and then fairly quickly cashes out. My hackles are up on this one, Carson, but I'm going to need some time."

Carson's head was swimming with possibilities, but he didn't want Ray fishing around and mucking it up. He was certain Ray was thinking there was something big-time illegal going on, but Carson had only one nagging feeling in his gut.

The dates. The timeline of Sienna's appearance coincided with the case he was working, but there was no way. No fucking way these two people could intersect.

"Let me work on it a bit, Ray. I may be able to connect a few dots, buddy, and not call in every favor you owe me just yet. I'll give you an update in a few days. Thanks, man." He pried himself from the wall and turned back toward the door.

Until he made certain that the two cases were absolutely not related, Carson didn't want anyone near the facts. Now he was sorry he'd called Ray. He hoped the little shit didn't get nosy, because his clients were under his privacy policy.

Forget them. He really hoped Sienna wasn't who he was beginning to think she was. There was no way it was possible. The woman he was looking for was a devout religious fanatic, and Sienna was a stripper. She took her clothes off for money, and never filed a tax return.

Carson let out a long breath as he went back inside the club and made his way back to Sienna's dressing room. He had to push the call to the back of his mind and think on it later, because as soon as he got close to Sienna, he started getting hard again. He couldn't think now, nor did he want to. If this all ended up being related, he was in deep shit.

He didn't know Sienna well, but he was pretty sure if she and the woman he was looking for were one and the same, there was a good reason. And he was pretty sure that reason wouldn't make him happy to return her to her family.

S IENNA WAS in a great mood after dancing. She felt in control again; commanding the crowd did that to her. She hoped Carson would come back after her performance, but he seemed to still be giving her space. Did she make a mistake in shutting him out earlier?

Lost in her head over why he wasn't back to see her yet, Sienna heard a little knock on the door. *Thank God.*

Carson walked in confidently, as always, and immediately swept her in his arms, brushed his lips across her cheek, finally coming to rest on her own. He landed a deep, passionate kiss on her, only breaking away to say, "You looked fucking fabulous out there. I couldn't help but think how envious every other dude would be of me if they knew I was the one taking you home."

Sienna kept telling herself to let this whole thing go between them, but then he said something like what he just did, and her plans were out the window. Even though his words were lust filled and fueled from her dancing, there was something underneath them. A feeling that said they were more than dirty talk, they were words of promise. A promise she could never make good on.

She couldn't be weak at the moment, or could she? With Sam Charles in the picture, she needed to assess her plan and safety, but for the moment, she let herself feel good in Carson's arms.

Of course she would let him take her home. Nothing wrong with making a few more lasting memories, especially since she was moving on. And soon.

Sienna had one more dance at her regular time, and then she could leave. After a little quiet time kissing, touching, and taking in Carson, she needed to get ready to go back onstage.

She assumed Carson would stay and watch her dance, but he said he needed to go make a few calls related to work. Strange. He never did that before, but she figured she had been occupying a lot of his time, so he must be a bit behind.

After devouring her mouth again, Carson promised he'd be back to pick her up. His hand slipped alongside her breast, his thumb lightly rubbing her nipple with the promise of more later.

Instantly, Sienna was out of breath, and any thought of something being off with Carson was long gone.

"See you soon," was all she could get out before Carson walked down the hall.

He's so hot. Smoking hot.

nineteen

CARSON HATED to leave Sienna. Only the present mission could sway him from staying and watching Sienna play out all his sexual desires and urges onstage. If he didn't need to prove himself wrong, assure himself Sienna and the woman he'd been fruitlessly searching for weren't the same, he would be at the Tunnel.

But first, he had to attend to a few details. Namely, he had to put his mind to rest and get back to the club, so he could take Sienna home and fuck her. Not fuck her, bury himself deep inside her, be one with her, take everything she had to give, and fulfill his every want with her goodness.

He was in a hurry to get back to pleasure, so his current business was going to be quick. Real quick.

Carson wasn't as worried about Sam Charles anymore. He was thinking the yokel was just an idiot. Good thing Mike and Asher wouldn't let Charles get close to Sienna, because this pursuit required his full attention.

Their protection of Sienna allowed Carson to put his worry over Charles on the back burner, since the possibility of Sienna agreeing to be in his movies was slim to none.

This left Carson hurrying, strumming the steering wheel, and grinding the clutch all the way to his hotel. For once in his life, the speed didn't take him away.

If what he feared most was true—that Sienna was the woman he'd been chasing around looking for—he realized Sam Charles would make a good decoy. The asshole would throw everyone off of him. At least until he figured out what he wanted to do, or needed to do to keep Sienna safe.

Carson took the turns faster than he should, going over what Sienna had told him about herself in his head. He was rolling over her words in his mind. Military kid. But military brats were usually pretty rule-oriented; they didn't typically avoid paying taxes.

Mike and Asher knew Sienna about seven years, which was around the time she slowly started making it onto the scene. Around the same time period his current client told him their daughter went missing.

He banged the steering wheel with his hand. Luck of the fucking draw. He'd been on a wild-goose chase around the west, and he might have just fallen for the victim.

Carson concentrated on breathing. He needed to be pragmatic, like they taught him to be when he was in training. He couldn't let emotions rule his thought process. He had about ninety minutes, tops, at the moment. He needed to go back and review his notes in the quiet of his hotel room before he jumped to any conclusions.

Once back at the hotel, he punched the elevator button like it was the enemy. He needed to get back to his room before he put his fist through the wall. His thoughts were moving as fast as he liked to drive.

How could he fall for a stripper? Did he really believe he could have a future with a woman who took her clothes off for hundreds of men every night? One of those fucking men could be trying to take her home at the moment.

Was Sienna a person of interest? Did he even care? Would he turn her in, or help hide her?

What happened to years of service with the government, and the number one rule to never get involved with someone on a case?

Well, he didn't know.

Life was a bitch.

He dwarfed the miniscule hotel room workspace as he sat down. He crouched down to fit his legs under the desk. Fuck it. Now wasn't the time to be comfortable. With a bottle of water cracked open since it wouldn't be smart to have another drink that might further cloud his instincts, Carson opened his laptop and waited for his notes to load. This was such bullshit. He knew this current job was taking much longer than he expected. He was looking for a young woman, twenty-eight years old, who just up and disappeared about seven years ago. There wasn't even the smallest trace of her. She was good.

When he took the case, he had never expected her to be able to disappear so completely. Her young age combined with the less-than-worldly family who hired him didn't exactly say "criminal mind."

Her family appeared to be clueless when it came to the real world, so he was unsure how she planned such a clean escape since she'd grown up in such a sheltered environment. They were like a cult or something. "Religious freaks" was putting it lightly. He wasn't sure they even associated with anyone in the outside world.

In fact, he had no idea how they knew his friend, Alex, who referred them to him as clients. Oh right, he had a relative who lived in their area, but Alex wasn't one of those religious freaks.

Maybe Carson could talk to Alex and get some insight?

Nah, that would mean I'd have to reveal this pitiful mistake of falling for the wrong woman.

All the evidence aside, Carson got why the woman wanted to get the hell out. Her family was downright fucked up, in his opinion.

He hated cults. How the hell anyone survived such closeness, scrutiny, and judgment among family members and community, he didn't know. He would hightail it out of there if he'd been born into such a group.

What if there was more of a reason why this girl fled? Could it be the husband who recently crawled out of the woodwork?

Her family had him running all over. Although she grew up in an urban setting in Brooklyn, New York, her relatives decided it was likely she was hiding in a small rural town as far away from New York as she could get. Why would they say that?

Setting me off course on purpose? Why hire me in the first place?

"Why? How do you figure a rural area? What is she running from?" he remembered asking the parents. He had scanned their faces for any signs of emotion, but had seen none.

"She wanted to live differently, abandon our customs," her family had told him. "She wanted to experience something different from what she grew up with, so we think a rural community is logical."

Logical, my ass.

electrified

The family's innocent act didn't match how desperate they were to find her. He knew it all along, but he became a little too occupied with watching a stripper, who he was now smitten with more than he cared to admit. She had come to represent so much more, and had diverted his focus from his case.

Now, he had several problems on his hands. First, he had let himself fall for an adult dancer. Second, he'd never lost his grip on a case before. Third, how was he going to fix this if Sienna was who he was afraid she was? And did he want to fix it?

If the woman wanted to go her own way, why wouldn't her family let her? She was an adult at the time she left. Carson couldn't stop all the scenarios and questions running through his head when his notes finally opened on the screen.

His original notes were about as bare as a cue ball. This should have sent up a number of red flags, but at the time, Carson was determined to do a favor for his friend Alex. After all, Alex's family had taken him in when he had no one.

Glancing over the notes from his initial meeting, he was starting to doubt his decision.

Female, disappeared, early twenties.

Name: Lilach Dasher

Current Age: 28

Hair: brown

Eyes: green

Weight: 120 lbs.

Height: 5'9"

Parents spent the last six years looking on their own by reaching out to family while saving funds. Why wasn't the situation more urgent to them?

Didn't contact authorities? "No, we don't do things like

that in our community." Small religious community governs itself???? (Need to research.)

Carson banged his fist into the small hotel desk, making the whole damn thing shake. Then went back to reading his notes.

Young woman was just gone. All her clothes and personal belongings were still in the house, including her purse. Purse was missing cash, but credit card and license still there.

Both first and second meetings, family reiterated, "Prefer not to bring outsiders into our lives. Not our way."

Initially, parents told community their daughter was "visiting sick relative" in anticipation of her returning, when she realized couldn't make it on her own. ALMOST SEVEN YEARS AGO?

He downed the rest of his water bottle, wishing it was something stronger, and then chucked it across the room. It did nothing to alleviate the anger that gripped him.

When she didn't come back, community spread many rumors. She was sick. She ran away to a new religion. Family assured everyone she was now "volunteering at military base."

Why so much covering up? Lies.

Christ, he could chuck a grenade across the entire hotel and it wouldn't dispel his fury.

Carson scrolled down the screen to the part where the bombshell dropped. After working the case for almost a month, he had flown back to New York for a periodic reporting meeting with the family when he was unexpectedly introduced to the young woman's husband.

Husband. If he'd had any inkling there was something wrong with the case before this monkey wrench had been thrown into the works, it was certainly confirmed afterward. The case was now gnawing a hole in his gut.

***Edited to add after MEETING HUSBAND, Elon Finder:

Married name is Lilach Finder.

Husband went to bed at night (husband and wife slept in separate bedrooms during wife's menstrual cycle?—need to learn more about this). He woke to wife missing. Husband usually went to bed late, around one a.m., and woke by six a.m. daily, so wife escaped during small window of time. There was no sign of foul play. No forced entry.

Carson sat on his hands, tucking them underneath his legs to avoid punching a hole straight through the wall. If Sienna was actually Lilach Finder, then she had a husband she'd neglected to tell him about.

THIS IS ALL NEWS. Woman ran from apartment shared with husband, not family home? More lies.

In-laws' opinion and status extremely important to these people; son-in-law very involved with offering theories now that he's alerted to investigation.

Family tells son-in-law, they "set out to find daughter to surprise him, please him when they brought her back."

Bringing her back would restore the relations between his family and their own. FOR REAL—what about their daughter? SOMETHING IS OFF. Don't they want to find her?

He stood up and stretched his legs, looking for somewhere to escape the ugliness glaring in front of him, and realized there was absolutely nowhere. He had to finish.

"Small personal crisis," they told neighbors, and "wanted

to commit herself to something noble."

When pushed, family feigned ignorance on why she left. Continued to claim personal identity crisis.

Feel certain she's living in some tight-knit community out west, but not urban. That was where she would feel comfortable.

Their friends have been saving for five years to hire someone.

Almost a sense of desperation in finding her, but not because they miss her? In-laws, in-laws, in-laws—all they talk about.

Missing piece to the puzzle: Did woman have money? [no]

Did woman hold key to money, secrets? [Maybe with in-laws?]

Carson hung his head. He had obviously failed this young woman, wherever she was. That was all the information he had. All of it.

He ran a hand through his hair, contemplating the facts he knew and compared them to everything he learned today.

Lilach Finder had green eyes and brown hair. Sienna was completely bare down there, so no knowing her true hair color. And her eyes were blue. Right?

No way they're the same person.

Sienna had showed up out of nowhere in Vegas about seven years ago and joined a mostly all-cash business. The woman he was looking for being missing the same amount of time was an unusual coincidence, that was all.

He had one picture he'd been given of Lilach. She was teaching a lesson to a group of children, and was pictured lighting some religious-type candles. Her hands were cupped loosely around her face, leaving a slight shadow to fall on her features. There was a clear beauty to her, but her hair was definitely brown and her nose wasn't perfect like the woman he had come to care too much about.

The woman performing a blessing and praying to a god he didn't even believe in wasn't Sienna. How could it be? Sienna provoked the most impure thoughts in men and women. She wasn't the type to cook dinner, set the table, and observe an age-old custom every week while hosting neighborhood children.

He paced the carpet in the hotel room, walking back and forth, leaving a distinct trail of his footprints crossing the room.

Yet, there was something to this strange woman in the picture. An uncanny and untainted innocence, the same quality he immediately was attracted to in Sienna. Even with a few slight imperfections, there was an inexplicable beauty to the woman guarding her face with her hands. As if she had a spark waiting to be released, untapped purity and goodness.

Carson thought back to Sienna's innocence, which drew him further to her, how it was a bit strange for the industry she worked in, but there could be other reasons. Like her saying she was a military brat. Her family might not have laid down roots long enough for her to form a relationship as a younger woman, although that didn't fit the path she had chosen now. Still a possibility, though.

Typically, women in the adult entertainment industry came from a hard life and looked for a way to make good money. Lots of it. Many of them had sordid stories. Stripping made them a lot of cash, so the money went a long way for a woman who never finished school, a commonality among strippers.

He knew he was generalizing in his head, but he was trying to figure out Sienna. He was desperate to prove she wasn't Lilach, yet a military background wasn't standard issue for adults-only nightclub work.

There definitely was something else at play, but Sienna couldn't have run from a highly religious sect to be a stripper only out of fear of God?

Exhausted from going nowhere either physically or mentally, Carson sat on the edge of the bed.

Maybe it wasn't the religion. Was it the husband who popped out of nowhere a week ago? Had Sienna been in a violent relationship and run to Vegas to escape it?

The answers to all those questions could be yes, and she still might not be Lilach. It might be only an awful joke. All he had to go on were the similar time frames, and the look set deep in both women's eyes.

Well, and Sam Charles, who had Sienna pretty spooked. Was she afraid her past was catching up with her?

The pieces were all falling into place, but Carson needed to be one hundred percent certain.

He formulated a quick plan so he could get back to the Tunnel before Sienna started to wonder where he was. Obviously, he wasn't going to breathe a word of this to anyone. He would head back to Brooklyn next week, even though he really didn't want to, especially now that he and Sienna were becoming so close, crossing a chasm and entering a new phase in their relationship.

First, he would question the husband and get more pictures. Her family needed to provide more information and stop being so damn outlandish about their customs. Fucking weirdos. He knew he hated this case for a reason.

Carson definitely wasn't going to share what he knew about Sam Charles. He would let the man provide a great distraction while he did his own work in the background.

All he could think about was the fact that he was all-in with Sienna now. His first priority was to put his suspicions to bed about Sienna being the runaway he'd been looking for, so he could move forward with her. There was no denying it, he was in deep. And it was way more than physical.

This was the price he paid for never getting involved and falling hard for the first woman who twisted his head up.

Grabbing his valet ticket and room key, Carson ran for the door. Now he wanted to find Lilach more than ever, to prove himself wrong and get back to convincing Sienna to take a chance on him.

Somewhere deep down, Carson knew that wasn't going to be the case.

SIENNA FINISHED her second act of the night and headed straight to her dressing room. She was surprised how much she missed Carson being in the crowd. Looking out, finding his gaze hot on her, had become part of her routine. It didn't matter whether he was front and center or sitting at the back bar, she felt more alone than ever before without being able to make eye contact with him.

She was done fooling herself how much she was drawn to the man. She was going to enjoy this with him, whatever this was, until she came up with a new fallback plan.

Sienna wasn't in a hurry to run, although she probably should have been. She was being selfish and wanted to soak up every last ounce of perfection, goodness, and sweetness she could, which she was ready to indulge in now that she was finished dancing for the evening.

After changing quickly and settling in to unwind on her couch, she heard a heavy knock on her door. She sighed out loud. The person behind the knock wasn't the source of everything ripe and delicious in her life at the moment, she could tell even before opening the door.

Opening the door a crack, she found Mike filling up the doorway with his huge bulk, wearing his usual high-tops, jeans, and black warm-up jacket. Missing his usual smile, his face was grim.

"Hey, Sie. You did great tonight. You feeling good?" he asked as Asher followed behind him into her dressing room.

Ugh. Asher is going to be pissed.

Sienna pasted a smile on her face. "I'm good. I swear. I was a little spooked earlier, but I know you guys have it under control."

"Sie, doll, you can't go off to the Strip or public places without us knowing. I know you trust Carson, and strangely, I do, too. But I can't protect you without knowing all the details."

This, from Asher, wasn't as bad as she thought, and Mike nodded in agreement. Both men wore the same serious expression.

Time for a little damage control.

"I know. I was swept up in the moment with Carson picking me up and wanting to go somewhere new. I'll check in from now on," she promised.

Sienna knew she had to give them the words they wanted to hear, despite what she might be planning. There was no way she could let them catch on to her line of thinking. Her Tunnel family wanted her to make promises, so she did, yet she felt guilty that they were empty ones.

"Okay, baby," Asher said while pulling her in for a hug, then placed a kiss on her forehead. "You're my family, you know that, right? If something happens to you, I have no clue what I would do." His lips turned up into a tiny smile.

Carson knocked lightly, then walked in right as Asher was hugging Sienna. He stiffened and shot a quick look of possessiveness Asher's way, but softened when he saw the look in her eyes. It was clear Asher was holding Sienna like a sister, which apparently was cool with him, and let her relax.

"What's up? Did you guys find out anything new?" Carson asked while wrapping his arm around Sienna's waist, pulling her close to him as Asher moved away.

When did Carson become such an integral part of everything?

"Not much, man," Mike said. "Looking into Sam Charles. He's from back east. We're going to head over to see him at his hotel now. See what the hell he wants."

Carson nodded. "That's good. I'm going to take Sienna home. Make sure she's safe, let her relax." He didn't let up his hold on her. She was tucked tight inside his arm with no chance of escape.

Sienna couldn't make sense of all the men in her life currently making decisions for her well-being. She sort of liked it, even though she told herself when she ran from Brooklyn, she would never allow anyone to make decisions for her again.

This was new. Men being worried if she was all right, touching her in a compassionate way, and making her feel safe and warm.

Not letting her mind get the better of her, but following her heart, Sienna said good night to Asher and Mike, and headed toward the back door with Carson.

As he was helping her in the car, Carson ran his hand down Sienna's side, settling on her hip, moving on and giving a little squeeze to her thigh. It was so primitive, yet endearing all the same.

She might have even sighed before Carson jumped in the driver's seat and sped them into the dark Vegas night toward her home.

After parking in her driveway, it was obvious Carson assumed he was coming inside and not just walking her to the door. She couldn't blame him; she made the same assumption. She couldn't go to his room on the Strip where he was staying, and their date was cut short earlier. They both obviously wanted more time together.

The difference was time together in Sienna's home was way more intimate than in a coffee shop, a restaurant, or a private gaming room. Scary in ways Sienna wasn't ready to admit.

As much as she wanted to deny it, Sienna wanted Carson to come in and be very intimate. Just a few more days; that was all she wanted. She'd been celibate for so long, but now she wanted to experience it all: love, lust, touching both soft and rough, sex, making love, and whatever else Carson brought her way.

Sienna poured Carson a drink from her bar while she let a pot of decaffeinated coffee brew. She needed something warm to relax her, and her inhibitions were already wild with abandon so much so that she didn't need alcohol.

When she handed Carson the tumbler of scotch, he took a sip and set it down, pulling Sienna in for a long kiss while holding her tight to his strong frame. His arms wrapped all the way around her, pulling her into his strength, heating her, and making her feel secure.

His mouth began to explore hers, compelling her to take, and teasing her to give back. He tasted like his usual, a combination of scotch and mint. It was the strangest, sexiest, and most divine mix of hot and cold as his tongue delved into her mouth, pulling hers out to play. All of Carson's wants and desires ran through her body straight from his tongue teasing hers. She could feel a current running between them, pulling their bodies together, and stretching her imagination with the possibilities.

Sienna leaned away and simply looked at Carson, running her hand down the back of his hair, and trying to gauge if he felt it, too. She bit her lower lip as she took him in, trying to determine what he ultimately wanted. Finally, she lowered her head to his chest and rested it above his heart, listening to its even beat. She was quiet because she was afraid if she spoke, she would spill her heart out, tell him everything, and reveal her whole sordid story.

She was so overwhelmed with feelings, both physical and emotional, Sienna needed a moment to gather herself. It appeared Carson understood this and was willing to give it to her. He just stood there quietly while rubbing her back, smoothing her hair while she collected her thoughts.

They were so in sync, it was hard to believe there were so many lies on her part. She had never felt more connected to someone. Imagine what it would feel like if he could really know her. Know Lila. Would their relationship be even stronger? Or would the revelations shatter anything they had?

Somewhere in her mind, she had the fleeting thought that Carson knew she was hiding something big, but he liked her anyway. Maybe his detective skills picked up on her abusive background and he was letting her keep that to herself?

She doubted it. Carson seemed like the type of man who met a conflict head-on without thinking twice. She didn't see him as the type to allow her to bottle that inside her if he thought for a second it existed.

Never before had she wished she could be Lila, put her whole past behind her, and move on with this man for however long it lasted as her real self.

Carson only granted her a brief silent reprieve before he held her hand and walked her directly to the bedroom, leaving his drink and her coffee waiting. Once inside her room, Carson didn't move toward the bed, but to the bathroom where he started drawing a bath.

"You've had a long, stressful day, Sie. Why don't you unwind a little."

She loved the way he'd started using Asher's nickname for her, Sie. It might not be her real name, but it was endearing, and felt comfortable and more real to hear him use the abbreviated version of the name she'd chosen for herself.

Hearing Carson refer to her in such a comforting way made her want to hear "Lila" come from his lips. She wondered if he would think it was a pretty name? A fitting one? Would he shorten it, too? Years ago, Asher used to call her "Li."

Lost inside her head, Sienna allowed Carson to pull her to sit with him on the side of the tub. He proceeded to take her clothing off one piece at a time, touching and stroking her entire body along the way, bringing little shivers and goose bumps to the surface.

He slid her tank top off in one swift motion, pulling it straight up and off, revealing her lack of a bra. Her breasts sprang to life, reaching for only his touch. Kneeling in front of her, Carson's hands were magic as they slid down her body, rounding her butt and making their way back up to spend time tracing her rosebud tattoo, causing her nipples to pucker while waiting for him to come back to them.

She thought back to the day she got the tattoo. It was a reminder of how the life could literally be squeezed out of her. A flower wasn't only symbolic of her stage name, but her life, and the actual meaning of her god-given name.

Sienna was a bloom, a botanical representation of life, just like Lila had once been. A flower could be strangled by its very own roots, and Lila was almost squeezed to death. She was a firm believer in God back in the day, but no more. Her parents and her marriage all in good faith took it all out of her. Being battered, hiding it, and having no one to turn to almost sucked her dry of life.

These days her tiny tattoo, the rose strangled by its own stem, was a constant reminder of how precious life was. She was a tiny bloom and every breath she took, each living moment, wasn't to be taken for granted. It was up to her to stay alive. Belief in God didn't save her once before.

She wouldn't rely on God, or anyone else, ever again.

Carson still swirled his finger along the tattoo. "Does it mean anything special?" he asked while staring straight into her eyes, without stopping from tracing the design.

She couldn't divulge everything that just went through her mind, but she owed him some truth. "It means life to me. How sweet and pure life can be when it blooms, it becomes something magnificent. I don't know. When I was younger, I found beauty and some crazy meaning in the delicate flower design."

Her hand reached out on its own volition and traced Carson's markings on his forearm. Just the heat from touching his skin scorched Sienna. Their skin coming together was like a wildfire spreading through a wooded area.

"And this?"

"It's ancient Arabic for *alone*. I, too, was much younger and feeling sorry for myself. No siblings, my mom up and gone since I was little, and I was the new guy in the FBI. I felt alone, and on one of my solo trips, I got this. Now it reminds me not to go back to that place of despair. To enjoy life. I guess our tattoos are pretty similar."

Sienna nodded. "It's hard to feel alone. I know, but we make the most of what we have. Like Asher made a family at the club for all of us. He, too, didn't have a mom or dad to speak of, so he created a life for himself. I guess we all found one another for a reason. Like you and me."

Feeling relaxed and sentimental was dangerous, Sienna realized. Too many truths were rolling from her mouth. She stiffened, determined not to reveal any more.

Then Carson reached over and kissed Sienna with a force and power that was both beautiful and aggressive, which brought a headier problem for her. They were in unknown territory, and she was trying to avoid emotional land mines as they rushed to each other.

It just didn't seem possible.

Steam from the hot bath hung like a cloud of want and desire, waiting to burst all around them as Carson rubbed her arms, massaging her tired limbs, stopping to caress her breasts, his fingers giving a small squeeze to her nipples. He finally licked softly around one nipple, and then the other. He pinched each nipple again and soothed the slight but decadent pain with the warm heat of his tongue. The mixing of hot and cold on her breasts drove a little moan from Sienna's throat.

Finally, he leaned her slightly back, keeping an arm wrapped around her back for support, and slid her yoga pants down her legs. She was totally bare underneath, and he took his time running his strong, rough hands down her smooth legs, coming back up again, slipping one finger inside her most sensitive area where her thighs met.

He had her breathless within seconds with just a little flick of his thumb while his other finger remained deep inside her, finding and rubbing her pulsing need. The sound of the water running, filling the tub, drowned out Sienna's moans and gasps for air, but her reflection in the mirror showed the growing pleasure clear as day.

Carson's eyes were directly on the real thing, not the mirror, staring her straight in the face, devouring her pleasure. He moved slowly, teasing her to the edge, softening his stroke even further, then finally picking up the pace, drawing her climax in a rush.

Sienna thought he must think she was so stupidly innocent and young when she went off like a rocket from just a few touches and twitches to her core. On the edge of a bathtub, no less.

No one had ever really spent time exploring her body, adoring it the way he just did. He worked her as if he had known her for years. Carson knew exactly what to do, how much pressure, where to touch a little rougher or a little softer, until she screamed his name in ecstasy. Although she wasn't sure if it was the intimate touch or the adoration she saw in Carson's expression that put her over the edge.

Sienna was once again ashamed of her lack of experience and lowered her gaze to the bathroom tile. Carson, always appearing to be in tune with her thoughts, seemed to understand. He didn't give her a free minute to try to talk or explain. Not allowing her any time to be ashamed in the guilty pleasure he gave her, he helped Sienna into the tub so that the soft bubbles and warm water could envelop her. He tipped her face to his with a gentle hand on her chin, and said, "Just relax."

With those two words, he stood up and disappeared down the hall to retrieve a cup of coffee for her. He already knew how she took it, with one sugar and a drop of cream, from their botched casino trip. He was the first man to know. Except for Asher, but he didn't count.

Sienna sank into the water, closing her eyes and breathing in her own arousal and orgasm. The scent permeated the bathroom. It smelled like heaven to her, to take in her own sensual scent. It reminded her she was alive, experiencing some of the best parts of life for the first time.

Carson came back and sat on the side of the tub with their drinks. He pulled his shirt off, reached over for the soap, and started lathering Sienna. Another first. Ever.

Sienna could no longer think about anything except for Carson. He was everywhere, surrounding her with his masculine musk, touching, feeling, caressing, and commanding every emotion she had hidden deep within her. She never wanted to leave the tub.

She was in a dreamlike state when he whispered, "You're so beautiful inside and out, Sienna."

"I don't know what I'm supposed to say," she admitted. "You're so beautiful to me, too, but I don't think you say that to a man."

Carson smiled, his dimple making an appearance just for her, warming her heart. "I don't know whether it's right or wrong, because connecting with someone on this level is not something I've done, but I like hearing it, feminine or not."

She sank deeper in the tub, wishing she could hide. "We're sort of connecting pretty fast. At least, I think this is fast, and I guess I'm sort of embarrassed by it all," she said as he continued to soap her whole body, massaging down the front of her chest, paying close attention to her breasts.

When did I become close enough to someone to allow them to do this?

The way Carson was washing her while speaking hushed words and declarations was the most intimate experience she ever had.

Carson gave her a speculative look, then murmured, "Yes, pretty fast. It feels right, though. Nothing to be embarrassed or ashamed about, and the fact that this is new for you makes it even better for me." He dropped the soap and leaned in for a kiss. When she felt his hands weave through her damp hair, she placed hers around his neck, and rubbed a thumb along his hairline.

He moaned.

Lost in the sound of his desire for her, Sienna didn't immediately notice Carson was rinsing her, helping her out of the tub, drying and bundling her in a towel, and carrying her to the bed, where he ravaged her with his hands, mouth, and tongue all over again.

It was like nothing she had ever experienced before; no part of her body was left undiscovered. Carson's mouth started on her breasts, licking, lightly teasing with his tongue, and mapping them with his feathery breath before traveling below. Completely dedicated to pleasing her until his name was the only word her mouth could form, and she was pulling his hair with reckless abandon.

When it was all over and she was coming down from her second high of the night, Sienna lay perfectly still with tremors quaking through her spine, unsure how she was going to escape. The notion of leaving whatever this was between the two of them became even more removed as Carson pulled a condom out of his pocket while seeking silent approval that she was ready for that step.

He looked straight into her eyes and she couldn't avoid looking right back into his. They were like a molten chocolate abyss, inviting her, beckoning her to be one with him. She smiled, nodded her head, and pulled him toward her. That was all it took before he was sinking deep inside her.

There was no question in her mind, Carson was making love to her. Each thrust was even, smooth, drawn out as the two of them locked eyes and mouths. He gently rocked into her, coaxing her third orgasm of the night from her by delving in slowly, pulling his full length in and out at a torturous crawl, letting her feel the full length of him, hitting every nerve, and making her entire body vibrate with pleasure.

He brought Sienna's hand down to feel the connection between the two of them. She felt the place where they became one and let her fingers linger there for a few thrusts before he lifted her hands over her head, picked up his speed, and brought them to an altogether new plateau.

Carson was equally deep inside her mind as her body. She could barely breathe from the fireworks happening throughout herself, yet she felt more alive than any other moment in her life with thoughts of Carson drifting through her head. He was a good one. He might be big and tough, drive fast, and indulge in a bit of scotch, but he was a decent man. And he was inside of her.

With one more deep push, Carson reached his own climax. Sienna savored the way he pulsed inside her, wrapping his arms tight around her as he did, whispering how incredibly wonderful she felt.

This wasn't just sex or a one-night stand; they had moved way beyond that. She made a placeholder in her mind for each nuance of this moment. She had to go soon, but she wouldn't shut out these memories like she did the ones of her marriage.

He removed the condom and collapsed next to her, draping his leg lightly over hers, and making circles on her stomach with his hand. She was exhausted after the events of the day, dancing at the Tunnel, and especially after Carson making love to her. She had no brain power left to give at the moment, yet she was completely unsure about what to do.

Should she let herself fall asleep with him right there next to her, or ask him to leave again? Leaving didn't seem to agree with him the evening before.

"You must be so tired," he said quietly, as if confirming her thoughts. "I'm wiped, too, but if you want me to go, I will. I really want to stay, though."

Once again, she didn't have to ask or say anything first, because Carson was so in sync with her.

"No, I think I'd like it if you stayed. Do you want me to get you anything? Extra pillows?" It came out as a whisper, barely audible, but this was about to be the first time she spent the night sleeping next to a man.

"Uh-uh, I'm good right here with you all wrapped up in me. I don't want you to move an inch, even for a second," Carson said as he tucked her underneath his arm, yawned, and drifted off to sleep.

She slid her leg even deeper next to his, entangling their feet and toes.

With that, it only took minutes for Sienna to fall asleep nestled against the side of a man. A first she never believed would be hers to have.

And she slept sounder than ever before.

twenty

Saturday

THE WEEKEND went by in a blur as Sienna lost herself further in Carson. He made her breakfast in bed on Saturday after he spent the night. A completely mundane act to anyone else, but all new for Sienna, making it close to impossible to maintain any distance.

She liked it all.

After Carson cleared the tray from bed, he proceeded to make love to her again and again, keeping her captive in bed for the rest of the day until it was time for her to go to work. A day unlike any other she had ever had, topped off with Carson in his most recent preferred spot at the back bar while she danced at the Tunnel.

Mike, Asher, and Petey allowed Carson free rein in walking around the club, going in and out of backstage to visit with Sienna without an escort, making his way from the back toward the stage entrance without any hindrance.

In just a few days, Sienna's life had been totally turned upside down, and she was quite afraid that she was getting used to it.

How am I going to leave?

Carson powwowed with Asher and Mike on Sam Charles. When

Asher and Mike visited the cowboy-hat-wearing guy from Jersey, he admitted to wanting to cast Sienna in his latest porno films.

"We told him it was a firm 'no' in not so many words," according to Mike. Sienna was afraid to know what that meant, but she let it go because she was so absolutely smitten with Carson, and everything fresh and new she was experiencing.

A few times on Saturday, Sienna found Asher and Natalie talking, almost fighting, and she caught one moment when Carson was giving Asher what sounded like a pep talk. She still hadn't found the best time to ask Asher more about his situation, but he said he'd find her when the time was right for them to chat.

She felt bad because Asher had given her everything, and he was still busy with her problems. She should be dedicating time to him, but instead she was wrapped up in her own worries. And now Carson was involved with her troubles, and possibly Asher's love life.

She needed to leave soon; she knew it somewhere deep in her gut.

Sienna didn't know whether Sam was a big threat or not, but if not him, there would be someone else. She had to protect those around her, the people she'd come to love. They deserved that.

It didn't mean it hurt any less. It pained her beyond belief to say good-bye to the crazy gang she had come to call family. The pull to stay in her little nest in Las Vegas was omnipresent, but she had to admit to herself, if she stayed she would only endanger her loved ones.

More so, she felt like an ungrateful bitch because she would be gone before she could talk to Asher about his happiness and see him make a life. Not just him, but everyone else. How would the girls do without her? Would they be smart and save money? Did Mike think his relationship was going to last forever? Why wasn't he making a move to take it to the next level?

And Carson. Leaving Carson was going to break her. She'd been broken before, so she knew she'd be able to pull herself back together, but this time around it wouldn't be as easy. She was already a shell of who she was. What could she expect after being forced to give up Carson?

There was one difference. This time around, she'd hold on to the memories of what happened before she came undone. Unlike her life with Elon, these memories were good ones, and she was going to suck up every last one of them, hide them deep in the recesses of her brain, and pull them out whenever she needed one.

Heading onto the stage, she put her heart and soul into dancing, as if it could be one of her last times. She was wearing too-tight bright-blue boy shorts and her Superwoman T-shirt from a couple of days ago; she knew Carson liked it. With her ass cheeks peeking out from her shorts and the T-shirt secured tightly in a knot under her breasts, baring her whole midriff, Sienna left her bra and nipples a mystery that night.

She knew Carson was wondering what was underneath the shirt, and she wanted to keep him guessing, along with everyone else in the crowd. But when she invited Carson back to her dressing room afterward, she could show him. Just him.

The crowd couldn't have cared less if Sienna stayed covered up, her moves were tantalizing enough. She had the entire club buzzing with sexual heat. For the first time in her dancing career, Sienna felt like she knew the meaning behind all the lust and desire floating around the Tunnel as she ran her hands up and down her very own body.

Unlike every other night onstage, she didn't have to fake her own passion and urges; they were right underneath the surface, dying to come out and tackle Carson.

Which was exactly what she did when Carson made his way into her dressing room after her performance. She could tell he was heady with lust, even though they'd indulged in each other all day.

He turned the lock on the door, walked toward her with one eyebrow cocked, and said with a wink, "So, were you waiting to take your shirt off just for me?"

With those words, Sienna was a dripping mess of desire. Yet another first to add to the very long list accumulated over the last twenty-four hours.

"Uh-huh," was all she could make out.

"You were fantastic and, well, so absolutely gorgeous tonight. I was pretending I was the only man out there." Carson lifted her shirt, exposing the cobalt-blue demi-bra she had on underneath, and his breathing hitched as he smoothed his hand along the satin.

Sienna's breasts spilled out of the cups, urging Carson to touch them, do whatever he wanted to them. Which he did, much to her satisfaction.

With the two of them safely ensconced behind the locked door, he made quick work of removing her bra and boy shorts, taking in her whole body with his eyes. He stopped at her mouth and pulled her in for a long and luxurious kiss.

When he finally bent Sienna over the back of her chaise, there was nothing quick as he dipped his hand between her legs, making certain she was ready. She heard the telltale opening of the condom package, and at once he entered her.

Nowhere near the sharp entrance she remembered from her marriage, when Carson seated himself inside her in one fell swoop it felt magnificent, decadent, and her soul was complete.

His hands smoothed down her back, taking his time, treasuring, mapping, and learning her body all over again. He kissed a path down and back up her spine, finally coming to a halt behind her ear where he nipped, licked, and whispered how gorgeous she was, while sliding all the way in and out of her tightness. Sienna felt every nerve ending come alive as Carson's length went deep and then torturously pulled out before doing it again.

Sienna's back arched and her body shifted, lifting her butt, begging Carson to be one with her, to make her feel whole.

Fool, falling for him. Completely, totally, irrevocably.

There was nothing she could do to stop herself from grinding back on him, and when he finally pushed inside her, staying there as he pumped in and out at an urgent pace, blanketing her back with his body, bringing his arm around her middle, lifting her higher so he could go deeper, Sienna was certain there was nothing she could do to stop from falling into the abyss known as Carson.

Right before her orgasm exploded through her, he turned her head to the side so he could quiet her screams with his mouth. Together, the two of them came, and then he bundled her in his arms and sat her down on his lap on the couch, holding her tight, not allowing anything to spoil the moment.

He was still touching her, rubbing softly down her back, kissing her lips tenderly while looking right through her with a look that said he felt as overwhelmed as she did. That was how the two of them stayed until she had to get ready to dance again.

The second time onstage for the evening, bubbling over with sex and the peace from her own orgasm, Sienna did fully strip out of her nightie all the way down to her bra and thong, taking the crowd to unparalleled heights with her moves. She taunted the audience with slow gyrations of her hips as she worked the pole, but kept her eyes glued on Carson in anticipation of what they might do later.

As the fast-paced pop song blared through the club, she lost track of her fears and shook her shoulders with reckless abandon as the pressures of the last seven years slipped away. For a few minutes, she was only Sienna Flower, exactly as she had created her to be, but without a dark and hidden past.

She was a carefree stripper who was having fun tormenting all the men with hard-ons, watching with their tongues hanging out. She was a girl who liked a boy. She was a woman who was free to explore what the possibilities might be with a man. She was a lust-filled, hot-blooded, independent woman who couldn't wait to get her man home. And that was what she did as soon as she finished on the stage.

Carson didn't disappoint. When he brought her home, he relaxed her with a bath and coffee like the night before, growing the expectation for what was to come while he lathered each inch of her body with soap, and then he proceeded to keep her up all night, giving her pleasure she'd never even dreamed of. After what seemed like hours of positions she didn't even know existed, Sienna relished in the way he made gentle love to her before they both drifted off to sleep.

Before sleep took them, Carson snuggled her into him like the night before, their legs entwined, a delicious soreness settling throughout her body as his hand wrapped in her long blonde locks.

He opened his mouth, then took in a breath before he said, "Sienna, honey, I need to go back to the East Coast again for three or four days tomorrow. I wish I could put it off, but I can't." He spoke softly, tenderly, as if the words were painful, even for a grown man.

Unable to open the dam of emotions she was feeling, Sienna only replied, "Shh, let's not ruin this perfect moment."

twenty-one

Sunday

THE NEXT morning, over coffee standing on the edge of Sienna's patio overlooking the garden, Carson brought all her mixed emotions back to the surface when he tried to talk about his trip. It was midmorning, and the sun made his black hair shine. She couldn't help running her hands through it while she said, "It's all right. You've got to do what you've got to do."

As do I.

Standing face-to-face, she focused her thumb on the tiny spot of gray along his temple, thinking it only made him more handsome, rugged, and full of experience in life. All of which she wished he could share with her forever.

"I really wish I could stay and work from here, but I can't. I'm going to try and wrap this up as quickly as I can, and then come back and spend a whole month with you. Wouldn't that be fun?" He slid behind her, placing their mugs down on the ground, forcing them to look out at the rocky terrain, then wound his arms tight around her middle while leaning over her side to plant a kiss on her cheek.

While her heart sank knowing she wouldn't be here for that,

Sienna couldn't let on about her plan. She leaned back into his embrace and lifted her arms behind her, sifting her fingers through his hair. It was a quiet and contemplative moment between a man and woman considering what may or may not lie ahead of them.

After they finished their brief solace, Carson swiftly lifted Sienna and flung her over his shoulders. "Let's go back to bed and stay there until you have to go to the Tunnel. I want to soak up my fill of you."

Me, too. If that's possible.

Unable to speak, Sienna enjoyed the view of Carson's ass from her vantage point and let him carry her caveman style to her bedroom. Once inside, the pair abandoned any serious conversation and allowed passion to take over the hours before she had to go back to work.

It felt like minutes.

Time wasn't on Sienna's side. She felt it slipping away as she started to doze in Carson's arms in the early-afternoon light. She woke to Carson pulling her closer to him, his arms reaching for her as though he hadn't had her twice hours earlier.

She didn't care. When it came to Carson, she was as insatiable as he obviously was.

Suddenly, Sienna was fully awake and sliding one of her legs over Carson's hip, giving his fingers easy access to touch her. She was a little tender, but in a delicious way—a reminder of how intimate they'd been earlier into the wee hours of the morning. Sienna ran her fingers down his muscled abs, dropping lower to wrap around him. She began to stroke him evenly, smoothing her thumb over his tip, wetting the rest of him while they made pillow talk, sharing secrets that would stay inside the four walls of her bedroom.

Never the selfish lover, Carson slid his finger deeper into Sienna while she continued to work his length. He added another finger, taking her right to the crest before gently flipping her on her back and sliding his tongue down the whole length of her body. Then he spent a little time biting her nipples, sucking, nipping, and cooling each one with his breath before dipping down to her belly button, and then lower. He didn't tease her like he did that morning when he ran his tongue along the crease in her thigh, hinting at what might come next. This time, Carson went straight to her heat, a quick learner, picking up on what she liked the most.

Sienna burst into hot chills with only a few licks of Carson's tongue. Tiny waves rippled through her whole body as he continued to lightly massage his tongue over her core. Never had she felt more heated for someone or something in her life. As the orgasm rode through her body and she shuddered with pleasure and passion, she felt him holding on to her hips, steadying her while she fell into the black hole of pleasure known as Carson Graham.

He smoothed his finger over her scar, the one from the candleholder piercing her body. The same one she expertly hid behind lotions when naked onstage. She didn't want his hand there. Not because she didn't want to talk about it; she could easily make up a small fib as to where it came from.

She knew it was unfounded, but she felt like his hand being there brought him together with Elon, and the two of them couldn't be farther apart in looks, hearts, or minds. She wanted him to move. She didn't want him to even breathe the same airspace that Elon once occupied with his iron fist. Sienna grasped at Carson's broad shoulders, pulling him toward her.

"I want you," she whispered.

"You don't even have to ask, love."

With those words, Carson was once again buried deep inside Sienna, and she never wanted him to leave.

The problem was, she had to go.

WHILE SIENNA napped, Carson pondered going back east, which he wanted to do about as much as he wanted to blow his foot off. He had to put this whole thing to rest, and prove he was wrong. Sienna wasn't the woman he'd been looking for over the last few months. He was letting his mind run away with him.

Either way, he had to get himself off this case.

Perhaps he could have Alex refer someone else. There were too many unknowns with the current information he'd been handed, and he knew that the miserable family was full of shit. There was a reason why the parents weren't the slightest bit forthcoming. In fact, he'd bet money they were withholding information. But why?

If they really wanted their daughter back, why were they paying him to go on a wild-goose chase? He didn't need the money, and they clearly did, so why were they wasting the cash?

One thing was clear—they wanted their daughter less than they desperately wanted their in-laws back. Geez, they were so messed up. To love indifferent in-laws more than their own child was a crime. Was it that crucial they be related to these people in their community?

Carson had a number of stones to uncover as soon as he touched down in New York, but first and foremost, he wanted to assure himself he was wrong about everything regarding the case and its potential connection to Sienna. Then he wanted to get the hell back to her on the first plane to Vegas.

He could pick up several lucrative government contracts, spend his free time watching Sienna dance, and end his nights in her bed. Sounded like fucking perfection. He needed to be rid of this awful case, and fast.

Carson couldn't reveal any of this to Sienna, nor could he let on he noticed a strange expression pass over her face in the morning. It was when she told him to do "what he needed to do" in discussing him going back east. What was it about? Did she not believe him that he had to leave? Was she making her own secret plans?

He pretended to not see her indecision, but planned to ask her about it and look fully into it later.

No way I'm losing her.

At the moment, he was rubbing Sienna's back and wanted to let her continue to doze. Her sleeping in his arms had suddenly become his favorite way to pass idle time. However, suddenly he was in no mood to be idle.

He nuzzled Sienna's neck, breathing in her scent, allowing her hair to tickle his nose while his hands traveled around front, making their way south.

"Mmm, Carson," she said as she scooted back even closer, her tight ass grazing his dick as she turned and threw her leg over his hip.

"Nothing better than hearing you say my name, baby."

"Carson."

He smiled. He knew she couldn't see it because his face was buried in her mass of blonde hair, inhaling her scent, but still he smiled to himself.

"I like hearing you say mine, too," Sienna admitted to him.

Sometimes she was so open with her thoughts, and he liked that. Were there no games because she had never learned to play them in the first place? He found it hard to believe, but it seemed as though she was the real deal, telling the truth when she claimed to be inexperienced with dating.

"Good, baby. I like saying it, especially when I'm deep inside you."

Something else altogether took over Carson in that moment, and he spoke without thinking. "I never asked, is Sienna your real name or a stage name? Your secret is safe with me, if you care to share," he said with a wink.

Carson realized he was only half-joking.

Shit, I just put my foot in my mouth.

He expected Sienna to stiffen and pull away. What happened next stunned him.

Sienna continued to touch him, stroking his abs while obviously reveling in his touching of her when she said, "Lila. Sienna's been my name for so long, and everyone calls me that. I barely remember my birth name, but Lila, that's what it was."

As soon as the words came out of her mouth, Carson knew with certainty that the woman he was falling in love with was the missing woman from Brooklyn he'd been chasing. Not wanting to spark fear in Sienna, or Lila, Carson didn't give up what he figured out. Struggling to keep his breathing steady, he continued to kiss Sienna's neck and played the whole thing off like the pillow talk it appeared to be.

He reminded himself of his first priority: To keep her safe. He would figure out the ghastly reason why she ran, and then decide how to deceive his client. For the first time ever.

"Lila, it's a beautiful name," he said. "Suits you, but so does Sienna. Your beauty runs so deep, I don't think it matters what your name is or what anyone calls you. Everything anyone needs to know is in your smile, your eyes, the way you listen intently."

He pulled her up so they were eye to eye. Keeping her close, kissing the top of her head, he vowed to himself to protect her, even if it went against his work ethics.

Carson made love to Sienna one more time, memorizing her body and how it felt when joined with his as one, before driving her to the Electric Tunnel. Since it was Sunday, she only danced once, so Carson stayed and watched.

He couldn't help but get the feeling that this was his last time watching her for a while, and he hated it. He didn't know why he felt that way, other than he had a crazy work situation staring him in the face.

Oh, and I'm in love with the very missing person I'm supposed to be handing over to whom I now consider the enemy.

When Sienna was done for the night, Carson drove her back to her place, tucked her in, and waited until she fell asleep to leave. He went back to his hotel in order to pack and prepare for something he never had to do in his career so far. Lie to a client, break a contract, and admit to himself he got emotionally involved in a case.

Carson denied himself staying at Sienna's because he knew if he spent one more night, he would never leave. Then he'd never get closure on this fucking hell of a situation, and he just wanted it to be resolved, and done for good.

So he could get back to Sienna and never fucking go anywhere else.

twenty-two

Monday

DEEP LONELINESS set in like a dark cloud when Sienna woke up in her bed without Carson. She knew he wasn't going to be there, but still caught herself reaching for him.

Reaching for and missing a man who as of a few weeks ago wasn't even part of my life or plan?

This wasn't what she bargained for when she decided to let herself have a little fun. Funny that now thoughts and visions of love were consuming her, debilitating her thought process when it came to trying to simply survive.

Shoving all thoughts of happily-ever-after to the back of her mind in favor of dirtier ideas, Sienna dragged herself from bed, made coffee, and was deep in thought when her doorbell rang. Immediately, the back of her neck tingled with nerves. She didn't know if they were good or bad ones; no one ever rang her doorbell. Asher typically just walked in after keying in the code on the security keypad, and Petal and Sydney texted first.

Could it be Carson? He usually knocks, but who knows?

Despite knowing somewhere deep inside it wasn't Carson, Sienna couldn't help the little jolt of excitement flowing through her, so she cracked the door open without asking who was there.

An arm reached out and pushed the door open the rest of the way, slamming Sienna into the entryway table. Her hip dug sharply into the corner of the table and she winced in pain. The unwelcome intruder kicked the door shut with his foot and started walking toward her.

Stunned, it took her a moment to stand back up and take stock of what was happening. When Sienna finally righted herself and looked up, Sam Charles, minus his cowboy hat, was standing over her, holding a gun pointed at her forehead.

How did he get back here to my carriage house without being spotted? This is why love is bad. I've been in love for all of forty-eight hours, and now I open the door without checking to a complete crazy person with a gun.

"Come on, missy," he said roughly. "I've wasted enough time chasing your ass around this town for my insane employers. I'm ready to get the hell out of here and you're coming with me."

"W-what do you want with me?" she stammered. "Who are you?"

"Sam Charles, adult movie producer extraordinaire in the flesh, and *you* are my very next star," he said in the cockiest tone Sienna had ever heard.

Anger slammed through her entire body, giving her courage. "No. Asher won't let you leave this property with me. He's probably calling the authorities and the bouncers as we speak." She stood up and braced herself on the same side table she'd slammed into as the man moved with her, keeping the gun trained on her face.

Sienna did her best to remain calm and appear as though she held on to some type of control. Although calm was absolutely the last emotion she felt as she was being held hostage by a fucking nut job who wanted to take her back to wherever he was from…to make porn.

He shook his head. "Nope, sorry, honey. Been watching Asher, he got called away late last night to deal with a problem with that whore, Natalie. He's busy with her and couldn't care less about you right now. Not a soul knows I'm here, not even your detective boyfriend. What a dumb shit he was. Dropped you off all alone last night and jumped on an early flight back home, leaving you here totally alone." He flashed her a shit-eating grin.

Sienna couldn't believe what she was hearing. Who the hell did this guy think he was? She wasn't going to star in his movies. How did he know so much about her life and everyone around her? Why did he even care?

"Get out!" she yelled. "I'm going to start screaming louder. The neighbors behind me will hear and call the cops." She inched backward.

"Out of luck again. They're out for the morning. It's Monday. They work nice white-collar jobs unlike you, you little cunt bitch. Not everyone can sell their soul and pussy like you do."

Sienna's mind raced as she desperately tried to come up with a plan. She didn't run away from Elon just to let this jerk have his way with her.

Where was her phone? Damn, it was still back in her bedroom. If she could just get to her phone, she could dial 911.

With Sam still looming over her with the gun, Sienna couldn't make a run for it, but he wasn't going to shoot. He wanted her to come with him, so she had to pretend to do so.

"Okay, I guess I have no choice. You win." She stood up with her hands in the air. "I need a few tampons, though, it's that time of the month. And pants, seeing as how I'm half-naked," she said, trying to buy herself time. She waved her hand down toward the lower half of her very naked body. She was still wearing just a long T-shirt and underwear. He certainly couldn't take her anywhere like that.

Sam nudged her with the gun toward her room, and said, "Get pants. Make it quick and hurry the hell up with your woman stuff."

Sienna breathed a sigh of relief, stupidly thinking he wasn't going to accompany her. No such luck. The asshole followed her back to her bedroom and stood in the doorway with the gun still trained on her head. Sienna took a pair of leggings out of the closet and slowly slipped them on, trying to distract him with her body. It wasn't working.

Finally, her eye caught her stainless sculpture for Vegas Adult Entertainer of the Year sitting on the shelf. She reached for it, intending to grab it and throw it at Sam's head, but he grabbed her and stuck her with a syringe.

Instantly, a burning numbness spread through Sienna's body. As her legs gave out beneath her, she felt Sam grasp her underneath her arms and hold up her weight, grumbling, "I told that fucker, Elon, you weren't worth it, but his family is so damn money hungry, they only wanted you in their movies. I hope they don't get outed to their damn friends how they actually make their money, because they owe me a shit load of cash."

The last thing Sienna remembered hearing before passing out cold was, "They just *had* to have you. They couldn't leave it alone, thought they already owned you. Dumb, if you ask me."

CARSON THOUGHT about having a drink to settle his nerves when he nabbed a seat on an earlier flight out of Vegas. Since he made it a habit not to drink on early-morning flights, he abstained, especially with what he would have to deal with upon his arrival. He dreaded the upcoming meeting with his clients, who also happened to be the parents of the woman he had fallen in love with. It was time to confront them about their true intentions in looking for Lila. With absolute certainty, she was Lila to him now. He'd meant it when he said he didn't care what she called herself and that she was beautiful inside and out. But the moment he was certain she *was* Lila, that was the name he heard in his mind when he thought of her. She should be free to be whoever she wants to be. Lila. Sienna. Mrs. Graham.

The plane was mostly empty, since who wanted to leave Vegas first thing in the morning when they could have the whole day? Him, for one. Carson wanted to make this trip as short and sweet as possible, and get back to whatever was happening with Lila and him.

He needed to figure out what exactly Lila had run away from, so he could devise the best strategy possible. One thing was certain, he couldn't leave any loose ends where she was concerned. He wanted her to live free. With him.

As the plane began its descent outside New York, he knew one thing for certain. All roads would lead back to that crazy husband, Elon, who'd basically appeared out of nowhere. Why didn't her family tell him about the guy originally? His best guess was that either they were estranged from him, or he didn't want the investigation.

Something was very wrong, and it was time for Carson to use his brain and not his dick. He had to think, plan, and implement. Period.

Elon. Even the asshole's name made him shudder. The bastard seemed to have slid out of the picture after Lila ran away. Was it because he didn't want them to know the hand he'd played in her leaving? What hand was that, exactly?

No matter how he dissected the situation, Carson knew it wasn't a good one. Lila's parents obviously didn't know why she ran from her life, namely Elon, or they wouldn't need him.

He knew whatever it was, it was bad, and Lila wanted to save her family from that, or did they not listen to her? How could a mom and dad do that to their own daughter? It had to be Lila protecting them. She was that type of person, always protecting those around her. He'd seen her do it enough with Asher and Petal in the short time he'd known her.

It was still so strange how her parents were always talking about making things right with their in-laws, not concentrating on reuniting with their warm and sensitive daughter. Shouldn't Lila being gone for close to seven years be their focus?

His mind flicked to Lila's scar, the long and skinny abrasion along her hip bone. It melted into her skin and was often disguised under her glittery lotion. They never talked about it. In fact, when he touched it, Lila often moved him, changed the course of their action, deflecting him away from it. He shouldn't have been so consumed with his feelings for her not to take notice and inquire about it. Damn him.

Switching his thoughts back to Elon, who he had started to think of as *the bastard*, Carson figured the ass had probably been playing the role of bereft husband or a lover scorned for the last seven years. No doubt, he was anything but that. Fuck, Carson needed to get himself in check or he was going to rip the guy to shreds. He couldn't afford to let on he knew where Lila was when he got in front of Elon, or namely, that he had caught on to who the jerk actually was.

Carson needed to remain even-keeled, pragmatic, and capable, but let Lila's parents know he was unable to finish the case. Not enough information? Not the right match? He was going to learn what he needed, get the family and the husband off the hunt for Lila, wipe his hands of them all, and then save the woman he wanted for himself.

Unethical, maybe? He didn't care.

Returning a woman to a violent husband was even more unethical, so his current plan trumped that idea.

Carson had a feeling that Elon, the religious freak, was the worst kind of violent husband, one who hid behind the cloth. Damn it, his blood pumped just thinking about it.

The second the plane touched down, Carson was out of his first-class seat, rushing the door to get out while turning on his phone. As soon as the thing powered up, it started to vibrate with messages. What the fuck?

Asher? *Strange…why would he call me now?*

Carson pressed the Listen To Message button immediately as the plane's door finally opened and he made his way up the Jetway. When he heard the agony in Asher's roar, his stomach dropped out from under him.

> *Carson, dude. I'm sick to leave a message about this but I don't know what else to do. I don't even know if I should trust you to tell you this, but fuck, if you're at all involved, know this. We're on to you, and if not, you got to know. Sienna is missing. MISSING! I spent the night at Natalie's after you and I talked at the bar. I thought you were at Sienna's so it would be okay, but this morning when I got back home, Sienna's door was ajar and a few things were broken in her place. Doesn't feel right to me. Jesus, my Sienna is GONE!*

Staring at this phone, trying to collect his thoughts and contain his emotions, Carson saw a number of texts from Asher and Mike, basically relaying the same information as the voice message from Asher.

Once inside the concourse, the big, bad PI stood back and pressed his weight into a wall, attempting to cage and contain himself from throwing a full-on rage in the middle of a very public place.

Carson ran his hand through his short hair, the same hair Lila had run her fingers through the day before. He tried to make sense of the whole fucking mess while trying not to be consumed by waves of loss. His entire being felt empty and cold.

Sam Charles. It had to be him. Carson had misread who he actually was, and the serious ramifications of his underestimating him was hitting home like a ton of bricks. Carson just knew that fuckface had his gorgeous and innocent Lila, and was doing God only knew what with her.

Needing to vent, he turned and slammed the toe of his boot against the wall, which earned him a few concerned glances from passersby, but he ignored them. He was going to murder the asshole with his own two hands.

Carson needed to regroup. He no longer needed to rush back to Lila and make her safe. Because Lila wasn't safe, and she wasn't there.

Now more than ever, he needed to rid himself of the case and fast, so he could find Lila before the worst happened. He stalked toward to the rental car desk like a madman with zero regard for anyone who dared cross his path.

Little did he know that while he was flying in first class, the woman he never thought he wanted or deserved was probably being kidnapped by someone he had dismissed as being irrelevant.

And it was all his fault.

twenty-three

CARSON'S NEED to find Lila was as basic as taking his next breath. Obviously, he had to call in more favors from Ray in order to get his hands on some quick information. Time was of the essence, and he had to operate on all cylinders.

With a few keystrokes on his phone, he had his old FBI buddy pulling flight records, pictures from toll booth cameras, and everything there was to know about Sam Charles, right down to his tax forms and birthmarks on his body.

Jumping into a rental car he had waiting for him, Carson drove straight to Brooklyn to have a come-to-Jesus meeting with Lila's family, and then he was going to hunt down Elon while he waited for the information on Charles.

As for his mood, he was trying to steel himself against reality. Gripping the steering wheel as if it were the bastard's neck, he imagined choking the life out of Elon.

Was there the possibility Lila had left of her own volition? The damage in her house certainly didn't suggest her leaving on her own. Which meant she could be hurt, dead, or being tortured at that very moment. Carson's mind was running wild with horrible thoughts, and he knew if he was to be effective in finding her, he had to stop those thoughts and make better use of his energy.

He pulled himself together, using focusing techniques he'd learned in the academy and during training. If he allowed himself to get overly emotional, he would make things worse, possibly screwing up the entire situation. He took long, overly deep breaths, dragging the oxygen in, then forcing the carbon dioxide out, eventually controlling his ability to take air in and out of his lungs.

Christ, where was Lila? Now it was even more imperative to question the family for more information, and get a read on the asshole husband who'd showed up out of the blue.

As he sped toward Brooklyn, cursing as he had to fight rush-hour traffic, his mind was running through every possible scenario. Maybe Sam Charles actually was a PI who was also looking for Lila, but sent by whom? Was Sam Charles wanting to cast who he knew as Sienna in his porn films just a coincidence to the abduction? Perhaps Carson was being played, and the family hired an investigator to keep an eye on him, that investigator being Sam Charles, leading them and Elon right to Lila.

Whatever the case, he was certain it wasn't some strange cosmic coincidence, and Sam Fucking Charles definitely had a role in Lila's disappearance. Just how and why, he didn't know.

Carson was playing out in his mind how he was going to torture the information out of Sam Charles when he pulled up to his first destination. The small Brooklyn brownstone where Lila, his Lila, had grown up sat directly in front of him. Although he'd been there before, it now held a brand new significance.

Taking a deep breath, Carson got out of the car and walked confidently to the front door, then rang the bell. It was past dinnertime, so he assumed they would be home. He needed the family now more than ever to give him potential clues as to where Lila might be, and he wasn't sure whether he could expect them to cooperate. There was no fucking way he was going to allow them to railroad him as they, or Elon, had been doing thus far. Whoever was pulling the puppet strings was finished. He was going to make sure of that.

He also didn't expect Elon, the bastard, the goddamn husband, to answer the door, but it was a welcome surprise. Carson had a feeling this would make his fact-finding mission that much easier. He also was pretty certain he had just discovered the puppeteer.

Unfortunately, he wasn't such a welcome surprise to the man

standing opposite him, judging by the quick flash of anxiety that crossed the jerk's face. And the way he greeted him while growling, "Hello, Mr. Graham. What brings you here today?"

Bringing up his acting skills, Carson pretended not to notice his animosity. "Hey, glad you're here, man. I was just coming to check in with your in-laws and get some more information to help my ongoing search for your wife," he said, cool as a cucumber.

Just using the word *wife* with regard to Lila and this asshole made him cringe inside.

"This works out well," he went on. "I can kill two birds with one stone now that you're here. I'm really looking forward to getting to the end of this case for you and your in-laws. You must be so anxious to find your wife." Carson continued to play it cool. He even stuck out his hand to shake the fucker's hand.

"I was here checking on my in-laws," Elon said carefully. "I actually think this whole crazy chase hasn't been good for their health. I told them long ago, Lilach decided she didn't want this life, and they should just let her go." He crowded the doorway, obviously trying to keep the conversation at the front stoop.

Carson gave Elon his best shark smile, then stepped into the hallway, shouldering his way past the bastard. He did his best to ignore the fury that passed briefly on Elon's face as he pulled the large door partially closed behind him.

The detective in him noted the extra emphasis on the "ch" in the old-fashioned pronunciation of Lila's name that Elon had used. What was that about? Claiming his stake?

He pushed it to the back of his mind and put himself on high alert, searching for any clues, desperate to be sure nothing slipped by him. The stakes were too high. He walked farther into the entryway and faced his newfound enemy head-on, then asked, "Weren't you worried about your wife, though, despite her not wanting this life?"

Elon stood stiffly in the hallway, his face impassive before he slid a sad but resigned look on his face. "At first, yes, but then I reflected back on the few years we were together, and she always mentioned wanting something more out of life. Not this life here, apparently. I guess she's happy somewhere now." The bastard stepped forward, using his personal space to attempt to push Carson back toward the door.

Yeah, right, motherfucker. More like she ran as fast as she could away from you, but why?

222

electrified

Carson continued with their dance and prowled right on ahead, heading toward the sitting room where he'd met with the family before, pushing himself further into a space where he clearly wasn't welcome.

"Did she ever file divorce papers," he asked, "or did you think about it? Did you want to move on, make a life with someone else, presuming she was happier now that she was gone?" Carson couldn't help but goad the asshole a little bit, standing in the narrow hallway. It was the only way he could avoid physically attacking him.

Elon pressed his lips together. "She didn't, but that's all right. Lilach is my one true love, and I will stay married to her for as long as I live. I only wanted to know if she's happy, which is why I allowed my in-laws some leeway with this little investigation. But we will never know, I fear." He shook his head in mock concern.

Unreal. Carson couldn't believe the lies that were coming out of Elon's mouth, but worse, he couldn't stomach him saying the name, Lilach. Carson had just learned Lila's real name the night before, and he was still enjoying it coming off his own lips. He didn't want it tarnished by this motherfucker.

"Hmm, so you're not in favor of your in-laws following through with their search? Because I may have a lead," he said, deciding to give Elon exactly what he *didn't* want. He would make them think the case was close to being solved, forcing Elon to put an end to it all. And more than likely he could follow Elon to exactly who he wanted...Lila.

Elon frowned. "I think their health is more important, don't you?"

He shook his head. "I don't know, Elon. Your wife, their daughter, is out there somewhere. She didn't just disappear into thin air. I'd think you would want them to find her, see that she's happy for themselves."

Carson continued to prod and provoke, toying with the jerk's mind. If Elon had the slightest inkling that Carson might have a lead on his wife, Carson knew he would fire him.

Bingo! That was exactly what happened.

Elon's face tightened and he crossed his arms over his chest. "Yes, while I agree we should find her, I'm taking over. I'm hiring my own investigator. My in-laws have run out of funds, and I'm choosing to work with someone less judgmental. I'm taking control of the situation. I will decide what information my in-laws receive," Elon threw back at him.

Even better than a confession of guilt. It was done. Carson found himself off the case without having to do it on his own, and there was no better proof of Elon misleading Lila's parents than Elon dismissing him from the case.

He knew Elon didn't have any real plans of doing a search for Lila's parents' benefit. It would be for himself, and Lord only knew what he would do to Lila.

Carson needed to find Lila, and Elon was his first clue, now that he was free to watch the fucker.

He needed to continue to play poker, though, so Carson simply said, "That's your choice, but I do need to hear it from the people who hired me."

Elon pointed toward the sitting room just off the hallway, where Lila's father sat in an armchair. He'd obviously overheard the entire conversation.

Mr. Dasher nodded his head, but wouldn't meet his eyes. "Yes, I'm sorry. We're out of funds, and have handed the reins of the search over to Elon." Lila's father's gaze flicked to Elon, as if looking resigned to Elon being in charge.

Thank God. Now he needed to get the hell out of there and find Lila, rescuing her from this crazy-ass situation for once and for all.

But where the hell was she?

Unfortunately, he knew Elon would end up being the biggest clue in finding Lila, so he couldn't free himself of the ass-wipe. He needed to stay close to the bastard in order to learn what he intended to do now that he'd taken Carson off the investigation.

After saying his good-byes, Carson walked down the steps of the house back toward his car, dialing Ray along the way. He knew deep in his gut that none of what Ray had to say would be good.

"Talk to me," was all Ray said upon answering the phone. He knew it was Carson from the Caller ID.

"You talk to me, buddy. I'm trying to find my girl, who coincidentally turns out to be the person of interest in my recently fired-from-as-of-a-minute-ago case."

Ray exploded. "Shut the fuck up, man. How did you fall for the person of interest? Christ, I thought you were asking me for favors only for your case, I didn't know you were emotionally involved. Could this be any more unlike you?"

He let out a long sigh which Ray heard, but thankfully he didn't see the way his body shook. "Not the time for this, Ray. I didn't know she was the same girl I was hired to find because I'm a dumb fuck." Carson moved the phone to his other ear as he got into his car and started it.

"I was working a case out west, looking for a religious nut, a young woman gone missing in the middle of the night seven years ago. The family who hired me sent me on a snipe hunt, and didn't bother to tell me about the estranged husband, Elon, until last week. Probably because he wanted me out of the way, the bastard."

Ray snorted and said, "You gotta be kidding me."

Carson switched his cell phone to speaker, then tossed it into the center console as he looked over his shoulder before pulling out into the street. He raised his voice as he continued his story. "So I started spending some time in Vegas on the weekends and got involved with a woman who worked in a club there. Turns out she's the missing woman reincarnated as a stripper. The rest you know. Now she's gone, more than likely at the hands of this Sam Charles I have you chasing down, and I don't have time for any more chitchat. I need to find her before the lunatic husband does."

Eyes on the traffic ahead, he tapped his fingers on the wheel and wished he could push his speed, allow it to take him away from the stress building inside his head.

Ray let out a sympathetic grunt, then said, "Okay, tough guy. I found out that this Sam Charles isn't exactly a nobody in the porn industry. He did start out making small potatoes for films, but about a year ago he was brought in by a big-time production company. The company does it all—movies, live webcams, print. They run a private LLC called Mystique with all these entities, but I was able to connect the dots with Mystique and Religion Plus Press. It took some technical digging, so the average Joe wouldn't be able to put it together. Do you know who owns Religion Plus Press?"

Carson was just pulling onto the interstate as he said, "Uh, no. If I did, I wouldn't need you. Hurry the hell up and tell me."

"Well, I'm not sure if it's the same person, but one of the major shareholders of Religion Plus is Elon Finder."

The car swerved, and he narrowly missed being the cause of a multi-car pileup. "Fuck! You have to be shitting me! Elon Finder? He's the husband, which means he's running Religion Plus as a front for Mystique, acting all high and mighty when he's nothing but a perv. This also means Sam Charles works for Elon, which makes me think Elon has Lila as we speak. Sam fucking kidnapped her from her place for Elon." He slammed the steering wheel with the palm of his hand as he ground out, "Fuck me."

"Yeah, dude, I think you're right."

"Did you find out where this Mystique houses their production facilities? My guess is they keep it away from the religious shit."

"Exactly," Ray said. "The religious stuff is done in two locations. One located in Jersey, which is probably how they originally connected with Sam Charles. The other in Brooklyn at a small printing press and warehouse, but get this. Around the corner from that warehouse is a large unfinished building leased to S. Charles, LLC by none other than Mystique, LLC. These people are really robbing Peter to pay Paul. My best guess is they pay Charles to run the webcams and he sublets the space from them, while they make print and movies there. No matter what, none of it appears to be on the up-and-up."

"Fucking hell," was all Carson could say.

Ray went on. "As an added bonus, my man, I'm now interested in the whole shebang because it looks like Mystique is not crossing all their t's and dotting all their i's. Which opens them up to violating a number of federal offenses and who knows what else. I'm gonna keep digging and find more shit on these assholes."

Carson fought the anger rising within him and asked, "What's the fucking address, Ray?"

Those were the last words Carson spoke before disconnecting the call and plugging the address into his phone's GPS. As he followed the directions, he called Asher and brought him up to speed. It wasn't a conversation either of them wanted to have, but Carson was determined to make it all right. Or die trying.

The address took him to a dilapidated warehouse building. The area was run-down; most of the streetlights had been broken by vandals, which left the area extremely dark. On the outside it was decrepit, but a stealthy walk around the perimeter and quick peek inside a window or two showed him the inside was a different story. Someone had invested a ton of money in expensive film equipment and a pornography scene setup.

For the most part, the inside of the building was quiet except for some live webcam action he caught in the corner. Thanks to the infrared goggles he'd invested in a while back, which he fortunately was carrying in his travel bag, Carson learned there were only a few video and sound people in the building, in addition to the actors on the live sets. Although Carson watched the warehouse for several hours, it continued to be quiet. Dawn would arrive soon, which would make his stakeout more difficult.

No one else came or went.

Where the hell is Lila?

Carson was losing patience, which was bad on a stakeout. Especially an unauthorized one for his own personal cause; one where he had no jurisdiction or warrants. He started to think either Elon or Sam didn't have Lila, or if they did, they took her somewhere else. His phone rang just as he decided to get a hotel room and do some Internet research.

Ray didn't bother to identify himself, and got right down to business. "Got a turnpike pic of Charles. He's with an unidentified big black dude and a smaller woman lying in the backseat, driving across the country. Appears they're heading toward New York, buddy. Last time they were captured on camera was on I-70 in western Kansas."

"Of course, they couldn't fly with Lila. She doesn't have any real identification to get on a commercial flight, plus they have to know Asher is looking for her, not to mention me. A private plane would be a bad idea, even if they wanted to cough up the cash for it. Wait, what do you mean she's lying in the backseat, like drugged?"

"Probably how they took her. Shot her up with a sedative. They had to know a few tough guys would be looking for her. Needed her quiet," Ray said, musing out loud.

"Fuck! I'm going to go apeshit when I find those assholes." Carson went to punch a nearby brick wall, stopping centimeters from shattering his hand. His entire body vibrated with rage. The slew of curse words coming from his mouth didn't even take the edge off.

Ray's low voice came over the line. "You gotta stay calm, Carson."

He took a deep breath and tried to corral his emotions. "Well, I checked the building out. There's a good bit of equipment and the means to make a shitload of pornographic content, but pretty quiet at the moment other than the webcams running. Jesus, fuck, they better get here soon. I want Lila back safe and sound."

Ray paused, then said, "Listen, I was thinking, Carson, what if we went after this even harder than just rescuing Lila. I've been digging deep, and these jerks don't have all their paperwork, permits, and clearances lined up. The Bureau can bust them up on some charges of child pornography and/or trafficking of a minor, and get their shit all tied up, in addition to freeing Lila while hitting them with abduction, too."

"I'm listening," Carson said as he paced the alleyway, needing to burn off nervous energy.

"I'm betting this would put Lila in the clear of running anymore, leaving her free to live her life if we bring this Elon down for who he truly is—a scumbag, pedophile, borderline pimp."

Carson nodded, even though his friend couldn't see him. "I like where your head is at. Let's collect all the shit we need and do it fast. This will be a good bust for the Bureau. The only thing is I don't want to hold on too long. We have to estimate how long it'll take them to get Lila here, because once they have her in that building, Christ, there's no telling what they will do. I don't want anything to go wrong on that end, Ray."

"I hear you."

"Do you?" Carson said tersely. "Because if something looks fucked up when it comes to Lila, I *will* abandon ship when it comes to anything official for the FBI. You got me?"

"Loud and clear," Ray said with a sigh. "I'm hanging up to go to work on the information. In the meantime, I'm getting a ground team down with you to keep watch on the building and give you guys some cover. I'll have them call your cellular when they arrive."

Carson hung up without even a good-bye. He did some quick calculations in his head and determined that the soonest Sam Charles could arrive in Brooklyn, driving cross country with another guy to spell him at the wheel, would be sometime Wednesday.

He hoped to God whatever they gave Lila was almost out of her system. Fucking whackos better have not given her too much; so much could have gone wrong between Vegas and Kansas. He couldn't even think of the worst.

What if they defiled her while she was out? If they even laid a hand on her...

CAUGHT UP in a horrific line of thinking as he watched the warehouse through Monday night and into Tuesday, Carson didn't realize how much time had passed until the ground team arrived. Too worried to think about food or other needs, he hadn't moved from his spot except to take a piss in the alley, and there hadn't been any more movement going on in the building. He desperately wanted to get into the bakery truck doubling as a surveillance van to see if there were any more traffic photos of Sam Charles and Lila.

There was no need for anything more than quick introductions with the FBI guys. Even though he was no longer with the agency, Ray pulled some strings and made sure he was allowed to tag along for the bust. Carson brought them this fucking case, and that was his woman, doped and being driven across state lines. He knew that they wouldn't want to apprehend Lila outside the building. She needed to be inside so the Bureau could also take command of everything else illegal happening inside the four walls.

Carson knew Ray was doing what he needed to do. This case would be a big win for him, and would push him up the ranks a bit. The public loved when the FBI busted anything perverse and nailed the sucker responsible. Elon Finder was going to go down like the flaming bag of shit he was, freeing Lila from a life of hiding.

He had to admit, it was a stroke of brilliance on Ray's part to hand the case to the Bureau, therefore opening up the impending bust to the media. The public eye would eat this shit up, and Lila would get redemption for why she left. Her family and friends would know who she really was married to, and why she left quietly without a trace. Her husband was a monster.

Carson was thrilled when the van arrived so he could do some research of his own. He had everything he needed at his disposal inside the van, and the ground guys would take turns keeping their eyes on the warehouse. They'd also have supplies, food and drinks, so they could stay on-site with no need to leave.

More excruciating hours passed before Carson saw what he was desperately waiting for…another picture of Lila. This time, Charles and the black guy were both up front as they drove through Ohio. He could see Lila propped up against the window in the back.

Is this Charles fucker so dense and stupid, he didn't think I would pull in favors? Check traffic cameras?

Lucky for him, Charles underestimated him.

AFTER A long night of sitting in a cramped van, taking turns dozing off, Carson and the ground team finally saw some activity Wednesday morning as what looked to be production crew and "actors" showed up and entered the back of the building. Hours went by, then they caught a glimpse of Elon entering the warehouse on Wednesday afternoon.

That was their cue; the action was about to go down. Carson

checked in with Ray, who was five minutes out with reams of paperwork and bullshit he'd pulled on Charles and Finder. Lack of permits was going to be the least of their problems, because the two young women Carson saw working in front of the webcams were definitely not a day over sixteen years old.

The whole scene made Carson sick to his stomach, and that was before he watched the dark SUV pull up, and saw Charles get out and proceed to start pulling Lila out of the backseat. Carson had to convince himself to remain in the van and stay on task. He wasn't sure he could make it when Elon Finder replaced Sam Charles, dragging Lila into the warehouse by her hair without any regard for her safety.

Carson was ready to pounce even though he knew it wasn't prudent. Lesson number one was always let the enemy get comfortable and drop their guard when doing a stakeout.

It was sheer bad luck that Lila's husband, Elon, only hid behind a religious career, but in reality was in the middle of the underbelly of the porn industry, enabling him to find her even though she was aligned with others who were decent and good. The smug bastard actually thought he was going to get away with this.

Carson flexed his muscles, eyed his weapon, and blew out a long breath. Well, Finder fucking met his match in him, and he was in no mood to be decent or good.

twenty-four

Wednesday

S IENNA FELT someone pulling on her arm, jostling her awake.
Where am I? What happened?

She had to clear her head. It felt so heavy, and her whole body was limp and weak. She tried to remember why as she slowly opened her eyes.

Sam Charles took her. He injected her with something and kidnapped her from her home to make porn movies. She vaguely remembered being woken somewhere near a rest stop, allowed to use the bathroom with the door open, and then being injected again before being pushed back into the vehicle. In fact, she vaguely remembered more than one rest stop, and wondered how long she'd been held.

Her head was so foggy, and she couldn't understand why Sam Charles only wanted her with all the money-hungry strippers in Vegas willing to do anything to be a star.

Then it hit her, sending the air right from her lungs. Somehow Elon was involved. His family wanted her for their movies.

His family thought they owned me.

They made movies? Porno flicks was what they wanted her for?

Charles had said something like that right before he stuck her with the needle the first time. Now his grubby hand was trying to awaken her. For what? To make porn for her in-laws?

That couldn't be true. They were religious, faithful people with a deep belief in God. They owned a publishing house specializing in religious educational materials. They didn't make porno movies. Their son had a screw loose, but not them.

Could this all be true?

Not knowing what to make of anything, and barely able to open her eyes to the light, Sienna took in her surroundings. She was in the back of an SUV, winding through the streets of Brooklyn. How did she get here? Had she been asleep all this time? It would have taken days to drive cross country. Her hand immediately went to pat her body, checking for her clothes being in the right place and making sure she wasn't injured. Her mouth felt like something had died in it, and she would kill for a cup of hot tea.

Sam Charles was riding in the passenger seat while an enormous black guy she'd never seen before drove the SUV. Sam was trying to rouse her again as they pulled up in front of an abandoned warehouse. She shook her head, not wanting to get up and meet the fate in front of her.

Sienna's mind might be cloudy, but she knew this wasn't good. Not good at all. As the black guy parked the car, Sienna tried to come up with a quick plan, but her head was fuzzy and it was difficult to concentrate.

If nothing else, when Sam opened the door to get her out, she could kick and hit him in the family jewels. And if the black guy took his time walking around the car, she could do the same to him. But when the door opened, Sam wasn't there for long. He was quickly replaced by someone else.

Sienna lifted her head and locked eyes with Elon. Standing tall in a black suit, his hair and beard trimmed short, the very image of a religious man, he said, "Hello, Lilach."

She didn't answer. Words screamed in her head, her body twitched with wanting to take action, but Sienna remained stock-still and silent. She couldn't respond or make her way out as her worst nightmare came to life before her eyes.

When Elon grabbed her hair and pulled her toward the building, all the fight left Sienna. Instantly, she was a scared and timid Lila. She knew Elon was going to destroy her. She felt it deep in every bone in her body; she wasn't making it out of this alive, and if she did, she would be a hollow shell of a person.

Either he was going to beat the living hell out of her, or this movie thing was for real and he would make her do whatever he wanted for the camera. The latter scenario was almost worse. Lurid visions ran through Lila's mind.

Then, all of a sudden, Lila remembered Carson and how beautiful it had been when they finally came together as one and were intimate together. Fear like none other swept over her. Carson's safety was the first thought that crossed her mind, but then something much more dark and sinister took over her thoughts.

Was he part of this? Working with Sam Charles? Did he lure her in with his charms and leave her vulnerable to Sam coming to steal her?

Did their lovemaking mean nothing? Was it all an act?

It all made sense in her muddled mind. Carson didn't stay over on their last evening together, leaving Sam Charles to know where to find her and that she'd be alone, ripe for the taking.

They weren't making love, as she'd fooled herself into believing, or anything remotely close to it. It was a play on Carson's part, even though it had felt so real. She'd never know real love.

This was her destiny.

Elon no longer needed to pull her inside the deserted warehouse. She had nowhere to escape to, nothing to believe in, no hope left. This was her destiny, and she went willingly with Elon.

Lila dragged her feet as she was led into the deserted, remote building in the center of the city she had run from seven long years ago, leading her to the only life she would know from now forward. A life in which she'd be humiliated, shamed, and shunned.

Inside what appeared to be a run-down warehouse from the outside, was anything but that. It was a completely renovated modern studio filled with expensive cameras and sound equipment that was in complete contradiction to the facade.

As Lila made her way slowly and painfully through the building, she saw many active scenes set up with live cams recording whatever raunchy sexual act the actors were performing. Lila lowered her gaze to the ground, unable to take in all the body parts and lewd acts on display. Ironic that she'd be embarrassed by them, since she was a stripper.

The warehouse was an epicenter of female debasement, broadcasting all that was happening to anyone with an Internet connection who would pay to watch.

As Elon continued to draw her deeper into the building, they walked through a darkened movie set, complete with a bed and a shower. A shudder ran through Lila as she became certain her future involved that bed of filth.

At the opposite side of where they entered was a door to an office, which Elon opened and shoved Lila inside, trapping her inside the room alone with him. In her mind, this was a worse fate than the looming scene she just witnessed.

Elon started right in, not allowing her a minute to breathe or take in her surroundings. "Well, well. Thought you'd get away from me, Lila? Or do you prefer Sienna now?"

He didn't give her time to answer, not that she would have. He just clenched his fists and spat out, "It would have been a perfect cover, I'll give you that. Except for the fact that I work in the industry. I know it's a bit of a shock, but we couldn't turn down this type of money." Now pumping his fists open and closed, he rocked back and forth as rage, sheer excitement, or both propelled him.

Lila could tell he was holding back. Even so, she was silent with fear. No telling when his control would break.

Elon laughed, an evil sound that sent a chill running through her. "It's made me laugh every day for the last seven years you were gone. Your parents were so upset you ran away from a nice, good family with money. Little did they know what we really do for all that 'hard-earned cash.' Of course, it started out legitimate with printing books and magazines, educational shit, but then the offers came for the nudie mags. Damn, those people who print that shit have deep pockets, and soon they were paying us an arm and a leg to shoot the scenes here."

Lila, still stunned silent, braced herself against the wall she was leaning against. The thought crossed her mind to pray for someone to rescue her, but she pushed it away.

First of all, there was no way they would even know where she was. This whole scenario was so absurd, how would anyone even dream it up, let alone figure it out? Especially when no one really knew all the facts of her past. Sure, Asher knew some, but not enough to connect these crazy dots.

Furthermore, she'd do anything to keep Asher and Mike out of harm's way. A few hours ago, she considered Carson to be part of that group. There was no way Lila even wanted her friends to find her and risk them getting in trouble with the law, or hurt. This was her fate, whether she fell for Carson or not. She always knew her past would come knocking on her door. She just never imagined she would fall for the guy who might have brought them right up the walkway.

Elon's voice came booming through the office, pulling her from her line of thought.

"After my pretty little seemingly religious wife left me, I had time on my hands to work on bigger and better deals like film and webcams. Everyone thought I was occupied looking for you. Who knew my little cash cow would lead me right to you, Sienna?"

He leered at her, obviously enjoying rubbing it in how stupid and unaware she'd been. "About two years ago, we started looking for a few big headliners for our movies. Where better to look than Vegas? Right there before my fucking eyes was my wife. My fucking wife, Vegas adult entertainer of the year. Of course, you don't look anything like the frumpy piece of shit I married. No, you dolled yourself up for all those men to whack off to—nose job, curves, hair like a seductress, sticking your tits in anyone's face who will look. My fucking wife!"

As Elon trembled with emotion, she realized that he was losing what little control he had. He slammed his hand against a file cabinet, putting a dent in the steel, and she was certain her face was next.

"Good thing my partner, Sam, found you and was able to act so damn stupid in that cowboy hat, all your little protectors discredited him. Who's the idiot now? I got you back lock, stock, and barrel. You're fucking mine, and I plan for you to make good on that starting right now. I own Sienna Fucking Flower, and she's going to do a private show for me. Come on, take your clothes off, babe, and show me what you got. Then we'll put those luscious titties and ass on film and make millions."

Lila finally found her voice. "You're not going to get away with this, Elon. I ran from you, and you know exactly why I did. Quite frankly, I did you a favor by not revealing the true reason. I never told anyone, I just wanted my peace. People are going to be looking for me." She wished she could fade into the wall, close her eyes tight and disappear forever.

She really didn't know who would be looking for her, but she had to try to scare Elon somehow. She hadn't spent all these years trying to stay alive just to end up in a warehouse doing porn.

"No one is going to find you," he spat out. "Your parents had some dumb shit rescue mission going that I just put an end to. They'd never dream you take your clothes off for money, have sex with men who pay you. It's fucking ironic that the good little religious girl is nothing but a whore. One who is about to make me even richer. Now, strip!"

Lila trembled all over, from fear as well as fury. *I'm not a whore.*

She needed to accept this as her punishment for running away that dark night so many years ago. Elon was right—her parents would never imagine something like this. Her few friends in Vegas knew so little about her past, they'd never dream to look for her wherever she was at the moment. As for Carson, she had no clue whether he was good, bad, or where he fit into this nightmare. It didn't matter anymore.

Even if he was one of the good ones, like she was fooled to believe, he wasn't going to want her after he learned about her past. Nor would he want her after she was defiled, as she was about to be in any number of ways.

There was no paper trail of Lila or Sienna, zero clues, and it was pretty likely Carson was involved, no matter what she tried to tell herself.

Lila kept her face down but started to take her clothes off, accepting whatever was about to happen.

She had no other choice.

twenty-five

THE LAST thirty-six hours had been hell, and Carson felt the weight of the world on his shoulders while he waited. He needed to make sure Lila was safe, and then figure out how to tell her who he was and why he was really out west. And he hoped to do all this without severing his chances with the beautiful woman.

Did she feel the same about him? Or was he just a badly needed fling?

He didn't have to time to question himself or Lila's feelings. He knew how he felt and what he had to do. Unfortunately, time was standing still outside the warehouse. Inside it was a much different story, but he continued to wait outside with the rest of the ground team after Elon dragged Lila inside.

He could tell the asshole was manhandling her, and that severely strained the little patience he had left. Come on already, he thought. Clear the way for them to enter the building. Carson continued to pace the small interior of the van, desperate for some clue as to what was going on inside. This was the problem with getting emotionally involved in a case; you became a liability, and that was what he was. A big fucking liability who needed his woman back safe and sound.

Lila was in that building, and what the fuck were they doing with her?

The ground team, now multiplied by ten, was hidden and scattered all around the warehouse with a slight sight line into what was happening inside. Carson and Ray were running command from the van. Over the secure line, the team kept the two of them apprised of what was happening.

"Leading subject through building."

"Webcam scenes still running. Confirmed, both women actors definitely appear to be minors."

"Main subject looks to be fine. Walking on her own. Clearly absorbing all around her, confused but alert."

"Finder and Charles now guiding subject beyond quiet movie sets to an office."

"In office, door closed, sight line dark."

Lᴵᴸᴬ ᴛᴏᴏᴋ her clothes off as slowly as possible while silently counting backward from a hundred in an effort to remain calm. Despite already resolving herself to a very bad ending, a small part of Lila hoped someone would find her. For some reason, she couldn't extinguish the little spark of hope.

Mike, Asher, Carson. Any one of them would be fine.

"Good girl. Now get down on your knees," Elon commanded as she finished removing her clothes.

It was ironic to think that only a few days before, she had found some sort of strength in stripping, taking her clothes off and dancing for a crowd. Now all Lila felt was naked, alone, and scared.

She had no other choice but to do as Elon said, so she lowered herself to a submissive position on her knees, surrendering any control she had left. She didn't move fast enough, and Elon shoved her down the final few inches. The cold, hard floor sent a chill through her spine and her knees ached, but not nearly as much as her heart.

Elon tied her hands behind her and then blindfolded her, making the room go black for Lila. Perhaps this was for the best; she wanted to witness as little as possible. Lila tried to listen to what was happening, but only the worst, most evil and sordid thoughts ran through her mind, distracting her from the sounds in the room.

She took in a deep breath, but all she smelled was stale cologne and dirty, raunchy sweat. Then the door opened and she prayed Elon was leaving her alone, but that was only a pipe dream.

Lila heard what sounded like the footsteps of two more men enter the room. One smelled like he was greased up in coconut oil, and she couldn't even allow herself to think why.

"Stan, take your camera to the far corner. Peter, position yourself in front of the whore," Elon instructed.

Lila's blood coursed through her veins at rapid speed. What was he going to make her do? On camera? With oil-slicked "Peter?" She shivered from the top of her head all the way down to her toes, an ice-cold sensation running through her spine, coating her insides and seeping out to her extremities, overwhelming her with dread.

Bile started to rise up her throat. Tears filled her eyes, and she pinched her eyelids tighter even though she was wearing a blindfold. She wanted, needed to close out whatever was happening, even more than the blindfold already did. The darkness of the blindfold wasn't enough.

She started thinking about holding her breath in hopes of passing out, when she felt something making a path along her neck, stroking as it trailed down to her cleavage and back.

That isn't a hand.

There was no longer any need to force holding her breath, Lila was on the verge of passing out all on her own when she realized it was a penis making its way around her neck and face. She felt the tip of Peter's penis dripping with fluid, rubbing all over her.

Pinching her mouth shut as tightly as her eyes, she tried to hold both her tears and screams at bay.

She had never given oral sex. Just a few days ago, she thought she might give it a whirl sometime soon, but with Carson, not Peter or anyone else. This wasn't how she expected to do it. Blindfolded on her knees with a dirty porn star slathered with oil, while being filmed, and her deceitful husband directing the scene.

Elon had approached and tried to pry her mouth open, insisting that she cooperate and "make nice," when she heard the outer door of the building slam open and the sound of shouting fill the building. She had no idea what any of it meant, but somehow Lila discovered a newfound resolve to hold her mouth closed.

Are those the good guys outside? Did Asher send someone?

CARSON HAD waited long enough. Since hearing Lila was currently locked in a back office with no clear sight line from the ground team, his body shook with rational and irrational thoughts.

"I'm going in, Ray," he insisted tersely. "NOW!"

"Carson, let them just get settled for three minutes, then we go. Three minutes, that's it. You know it works better when we have the element of surprise," Ray countered.

He clenched his teeth so tightly he thought his jaw might snap. "I'm getting ready to go. You count or do whatever you need, but at the strike of three minutes, I'm heading in, so your team better be ready."

As Ray gave the instructions to the ground team, Carson checked that he was armed, then tossed his jacket on to conceal his weapons. He waited at the back door to the van, tapping off the seconds with his foot, carefully counting each tap so he wouldn't think about what could be happening inside the building.

When the count reached 179, Carson leaped away from the van and sprinted toward the building. The ground team met him at the door, and quickly and efficiently busted it down.

Shouts from the team rang out. "FBI, stay where you are, you are under a siege and search! Cooperate and this won't be difficult!"

"Where is Elon Finder? You! Behind the camera, step forward to answer my questions!"

The cameraman slowly edged toward the team, but one of the actresses tried to make a run for it. Commands were shouted louder and with more urgency as the team dispersed to lock down everyone in the building.

With all the chaos, Carson found it easy to sneak back toward the closed office where they knew Elon was holding Lila. He grabbed the doorknob and yanked the door open with such force, one of the hinges came loose, and the door hung, swinging at an angle.

Even with all the crazy irrational thoughts he had earlier, there was no way Carson could be prepared for what he saw before him. There was Lila, blindfolded and naked, on her knees on a dirty, cracked floor with a greased-up scumbag trying to stick his dick in her mouth, and Elon attempting to pry her jaw open.

Tears had seeped under Lila's blindfold, staining her cheeks while she used every bit of her strength to keep her mouth locked tight. With her arms tied behind her, Lila struggled, jerking her whole body forward as she tried to knock the men away from her.

Elon looked to be on the verge of losing his patience. He was cajoling Lila to "open up" with clenched teeth, sweat running down his brow and pools of wetness staining his shirt.

Sam Charles stood next to a cameraman recording the disgusting scene, huge bulges evident in both their pants.

Sick fucks.

Carson took in the entire scene in less than a second. He felt vomit racing up his throat but tamped it down, knowing he needed to be there for Lila. He yelled for Elon to stop, but the man was so enraged and determined, he didn't even notice.

Sam Charles looked up, and noting Carson standing in the doorway, shouted, "Oh, shit! Stop, Elon, stop. We're fucked!" He then tried to slip around Carson and get out of the office.

Carson's attention was diverted when Elon grabbed Lila by her hair and dragged her up to her feet, pulling her in tight against his body, squeezing the life out of her, claiming her when he had no right to claim.

Thank God Ray was right behind Carson. He grabbed Charles and handcuffed him, then began reading him his rights. He'd be charged with kidnapping, taking a victim across too many state lines to count, and God only knew what else they could pin on that sucker.

The stupid-as-nails actor and the even dumber cameraman were no problem; they quickly submitted to the ground team. They were ready to roll on anyone to save their own asses, not fighting at all, walking easily out of the office and already spilling what they knew.

With the others under control and in custody, Carson was left to deal with Elon. He couldn't take his eyes off Lila, fearing the worst.

Carson squeezed his fists open and closed, felt his biceps straining against his vest, wanted to pummel the bastard into the cold, dank floor, couldn't stop imagining his skull fractured in a million pieces. He'd never experienced so many violent thoughts as he was when it came to his woman's safety. He needed to reel himself way back in.

He inhaled deeply, deciding how to handle Elon, who currently had a death grip on Lila. He knew there would be dark bruises where Elon was tightening his filthy hands on her slim body, and that was enough to make him implode, but he had to remain calm, in control, and on task.

He noticed the veins that expanded and throbbed in Elon's neck, making physical the rage running through the man's body. He could practically see the gross thoughts the man was having, and when the asshole started to talk, Carson saw red.

Fuck staying on task.

L ILA'S EYES burned as more tears formed. She was sure they were leaking out of the blindfold when the yelling outside the office grew louder, closer. Elon was in such a state, he didn't even seem to hear the commotion, and continued his efforts to pry her mouth open.

Elon was going to shove some random guy's dirty, more than likely diseased penis in her mouth. She could feel it.

Why? She was still his wife, after all. Did he not value her? But he never did, so why would he start now?

With her face growing wet with salty tears, her jaw aching from trying to keep her mouth sealed, sick to her stomach from smelling the nasty man's arousal, and her arms straining against the zip tie holding them behind her back, Lila felt Elon's slap rip across her face at the same moment she heard the door slam open.

Elon yelled, "Open up, you slutty bitch. You're gonna suck this guy off and he's going to come all over your moneymaker face. I'll make fucking millions."

His tone and words were so much a direct opposite from the man she married, she wasn't even sure who he was or used to be. The only certainty Lila knew was Elon was an animal, no matter what he said or did.

With a huge cracking noise, the door slammed open, the sound of many heavy footsteps in the building drifting through the doorway.

Lila knew Carson was near even with the blindfold on. She could smell his aftershave and feel the familiar electric current that passed between the two of them whenever they were in proximity. The sad thing was, she didn't yet know if he was there as friend or foe.

Then he spoke. "You better back the fuck up and keep your hands to yourself. You're done, Finder. Now, shove that nasty fucker with his even nastier cock hanging out away from Lila."

At those words, one of the men—Sam Charles?—tried to leave the office, but she heard a different guy grab him, slap handcuffs on him, and read him his rights. Who was that? A partner of Carson's?

Lila didn't have time to ponder it because Elon suddenly lifted her by her hair, so quickly she didn't have time to register the pain. He hoisted her tight against him, his nasty grip squeezing her so tightly she couldn't breathe, much less speak.

"Did you hear me?" Carson said firmly. "You're done, Finder. The FBI has enough evidence on you to put you away for a long time, not to mention the huge scandal that's about to go public in your community. Instead of being revered as a religious and successful man, you'll be known as the perverted fuck you really are. Now, get your scummy hands off of Lila."

He was speaking calmly, but there was an authority to Carson's voice. He wasn't to be messed with, but Elon didn't release her, so Lila began to shake. It was obvious Elon was throwing caution to the wind. Either he had no idea who Carson was, or he didn't care because he was about to lose everything.

"She's my fucking wife to do what I want with, till death do us part, you asshole," Elon roared.

"Keep telling yourself that, Finder. She ran as far away from you as she could, and my guess is she'd rather die than be in your arms right now. Lucky for me, she's not going to die now that I'm here, but *you* will if you don't let go right the fuck now!"

A tiny piece of Lila surrendered to the idea of Carson being there to save her. She breathed a silent sigh of relief.

Elon snorted, then yelled, "Fine, no need to point that gun at me. I really couldn't care less about Lila. She's nothing, not worth the effort. The bitch couldn't even have babies for me. I was just going to give her one last chance to make me some money now that she's a whore." But he didn't loosen his grip on her.

Lila shuddered at the thought of a weapon. She didn't even want to know what kind or what was happening on the other side of the blindfold.

"You deserve to die for saying that alone, calling Lila a whore, but I'm going to have mercy on you and let you rot in prison." Carson's voice sounded smug as he said, "There it'll be your turn to feel what it's like to have a dude shove his dick in your mouth, as well as other places."

"Look, take her if you want, but I need a deal," Elon said as he shoved Lila toward Carson.

Stunned at the sudden movement, Lila stumbled since she was still blindfolded and couldn't see what was going on. Thank God, she didn't think she could watch what just happened. It was bad enough hearing it, but seeing Carson face off with Elon would be too much for her to handle.

Carson caught her as she went flying forward and tucked her behind his back, keeping one arm behind him, holding her close to him. She buried her head into his back, breathing him in.

Carson isn't part of this. He's who he said he is, ex-FBI.

He's actually rescuing me!

"Good thing you're a dumb fuck, Elon," Carson said. "See, if you want a deal, you need to hang on to the bargaining chip. Now I have Lila, and Ray's coming to get you. No deals, my man."

Lila heard the other man grab Elon and restrain him in handcuffs, like he did to Sam Charles.

The room was silent other than the man called Ray reading Elon his rights as Elon cursed and spit at him, and the noise drifting in from outside the office. Lila felt her arms being released from the ties behind her back. Carson took a moment to massage her sore muscles, then she felt herself being slipped into her yoga pants and tank top, the same clothes she had been wearing when she was taken from her house. They smelled awful, but she didn't care.

Warmth flooded her when she was wrapped in a soft blanket and lifted into Carson's arms. She didn't even realize she was shivering until then. Cradled like a baby, her face snuggled into Carson's neck, Lila let out a long sigh as he started walking.

She was so relieved to be covered up physically from whatever waited for her outside this room. Still without her sight, her eyes covered tightly in the blindfold, she wasn't in a hurry to take in any more of the awful warehouse and its activities.

"Lila, leave the blindfold on until we get out of the building. I don't want you to have any more memories of this place than you already do," Carson whispered in her ear, verbalizing her exact thoughts, emphasizing their connection, and making her feel even more secure.

It also occurred to her that he was only referring to her as Lila, not Sienna. She wondered how much he knew about her past and what had brought her to this terrible place, but she stayed silent, still processing everything that had happened.

Carson dipped his chin and pressed his cheek against hers. "I got you now, and I'm not letting go. I'm going to take you someplace safe, and make it all better."

Lila felt him smooth her hair down her back, brushing it behind her ear when he said softly, just loud enough for her to hear, "Lila.

electrified

You're safe, honey. You can stop running. You can be whoever you want to be. With me, I hope. But first I'm going to get you the hell out of here."

twenty-six

CARSON COULDN'T shake the bad feeling that nagged him, despite the fact that he finally had Lila in his arms. As soon as he could, he settled her into the back of a town car he'd called when it looked like the takedown was actually going to happen, not wanting to let Lila out of his sight long enough to drive. Someone from the Bureau could return his car. Adrenaline still coursed through his body as he slid in next to her, then pulled her onto his lap. He had saved his girl, busted the bad guys, and made the FBI look damn good in the process.

Technically, he was a "hero," but he felt like anything but that. The truth had to finally come out about who he really was, what he was doing out west, and why he found and rescued her so quickly. And he dreaded Lila's reaction.

Once settled into the backseat with Lila in his lap and the privacy screen up, Carson ran his hand down the side of her face, grazing his thumb along her temple, and gently removed the blindfold. She looked spent, emotionally and physically. Leftover eye makeup was smeared across her lids, both eyes were bloodshot, her soft, natural green eye color dulled from exhaustion, and her cheeks pale from stress. But the tiny fleck of spirit behind her eyes was still alive.

She was stunning.

electrified

He finally understood what the mysterious draw, the gaze that captivated him from the beginning, had been in her eyes. It was life, love, and unbridled passion waiting to be unleashed. It was only a little speck, but so vibrant it stood out from behind colored contacts and a well-constructed persona.

Carson expected the tiny flecks of life to grow bigger in time. He was trying to be hopeful that they would expand with him, and not after Lila ditched him. Would she dump him after learning the truth?

He nuzzled Lila closer to his body, careful to be extra gentle. He didn't want to hurt her any more than she already had been by Elon. They settled into an embrace, faces buried in each other's necks, while he silently convinced himself they were both okay. He breathed in and she breathed out as the car took them away from the warehouse.

There were still a lot of blanks to fill in with Lila's story, but Carson had a pretty good idea of what had happened years ago. She probably always wanted to love, be loved, and grasp life in every way possible. Her awful, violent, and painful marriage didn't break that desire. Lila had to tamp it down in order to survive.

She kept her desires hidden down deep, but it left a little twinkle, even behind contacts and spotlights. With the floodgates open to a new release on life about to be opened, Lila would be able to allow her eyes to shine all she wanted. Whether that was with him was to be determined, and that scared the shit out of him.

Carson didn't care what all this emotion said about him. He never thought he'd have anything like this in his lifetime. He wasn't even sure he deserved it, but he had something so precious in his arms, he wasn't giving it up.

Not only had he convinced himself he didn't deserve it, for years he told himself he didn't want or need it. He never thought this would be the path his life took, but at the moment, he was damn happy. He needed Lila; he hoped she needed him, too.

She stirred in his arms, and he looked up to find her completely focused on him.

Lila just stared at Carson for the longest time, and he gave her that. He didn't want to force her to talk, so he bit his tongue and gave her time to adjust at her own pace.

When she finally spoke, she said, "I'm sorry."

You're sorry?

"No, baby, don't say that," Carson started to say, but Lila interrupted

247

him, shaking her head from side to side.

Running her finger mindlessly along his tattoo on his forearm, leaning into him, Lila said, "I don't mean about today, but lying to you about my past. I had to protect myself. Oh God, I can't believe you're here and had to witness all that and him, Elon. I don't know how much you know now. I assume you know that he was my husband, and he clearly still is a violent and mean man. I didn't know he was in the porn business. Guess that's how he found me, because people in my culture really don't embrace public sensuality, or anything sexual, for that matter." She hid in his chest, wiped her tears on his shirt, and continued to quietly cry and shake in his tight hold.

Carson listened without interrupting, merely stroked her arm gently and nodded, encouraging her to continue.

"He beat me when we were married. My parents were so enamored with him, I knew they wouldn't believe it. They never wanted to hear about his controlling side, so I ran away. I ran to Vegas and started dancing because I thought I was safe in a world so far removed from the one I came from. I never meant to get involved, to fall for someone and get them stuck in this whole mess, like I did with you."

"Shh," Carson said as he traced a path with his hand along her face, stopping at the nape of her neck. He pulled her close to drop a kiss on her forehead, then placed tiny ones along her brow, and finally a small one on her lips. "I know, I was able to piece most of this together in the last couple of days." He continued to run his hands all over Lila, now rubbing up and down her sore legs, massaging her muscles.

"But, baby," he went on, "I'm the one who should be sorry. You see, the missing person I was looking for out west was you. I didn't know it until the last night we were together, and I was heading back east to drop the case. I was putting together a game plan for making you safe when you were taken from your place. It's me who should be apologizing, not you." He dropped his head and hoped for forgiveness.

Lila gasped. "What?"

"Yeah, this is so hard. Your parents hired me to find you, Lilach," he said, deliberately using her full name, loving how it sounded rolling off his lips. "At first, I only met your mom and dad, not Elon. I didn't even know you were married. Your parents just told me they wanted their daughter back, and their friends and community were paying my bill."

Her eyes widened as he said, "I caught on pretty quickly that they were less than honest, and then I met Elon. The way they talked, it became obvious they wanted you back only so they could be back in their in-laws' good graces. It killed me when I realized the search had very little to do with you. Honey, I'm sorry."

When she shuddered but didn't say anything, Carson continued talking, filling in the holes, how he came to put it all together, and when and why he finally brought the Bureau in to help.

Lila looked up at him, her expression so filled with so much pain it broke his heart. "I can't believe this. My own family…and you…you must think I come from terrible people."

He entwined his hand with hers and squeezed it gently. "No, baby. Your parents are misguided, but that has nothing to do with you. They told me the girl I was looking for was confused and wanted a new life, probably out west. They crafted this whole story about you wanting a new culture, but it was based on what Elon told them."

He went on to explain how he wasn't sure when Elon caught on to him, but he definitely was the source of evil playing on her parents' emotions and purse strings. He didn't go into how frightened he had been when she was taken, or how panicked Asher was when he discovered she was gone. She was so fragile at the moment and had enough to digest with the situation with her parents.

Lila continued to look at Carson with a blank face. Not wanting to push her for a reaction, he was only happy she hadn't moved out of his arms. He hoped she was just processing everything, and not planning on letting him go.

Drawing his one and only love closer, he said, "I had my hunches, but I wasn't a hundred percent certain until you told me your real name was Lila. Then I knew I had to come to Brooklyn and drop the case, because one thing I knew for certain—you wouldn't have run away if there wasn't a valid reason. I was heading east to dump your parents as clients and hurrying back to make a plan to keep you safe when you were taken. That changed everything."

Lila held his face in her hands, ran her fingers along his two-day stubble, and stared deep into his eyes. "Carson, thank you. You saved me."

He shook his head. "All that matters is I got you back, and now you don't have to hide, especially from Asher and the girls back home. They're on their way here right now to see you with their own eyes. I've been keeping a very antsy Asher up-to-date for the last forty-eight hours. You have a lot of people who love you, Lila, including me." Carson tucked her head under his and placed another kiss on the top of her head. He couldn't see her eyes, so he wasn't sure if she heard his admission.

Then Lila looked up with her head cocked to the side, some of the light coming back into her eyes, her expression questioning.

"Yes, you heard me right. I fell in love with you, Sienna, Lila, or whatever you want to call yourself. I don't care. Inside, you're the most beautiful woman with a huge heart and I love you. You're a flower who hasn't even fully bloomed, and I want to watch you come into your own."

Carson saw tears welling up in Lila's eyes once again, yet this time, he believed they were happy tears and not ones of fear.

"What do you mean, a flower?" she asked. "Because of my tattoo?" With a shaky finger, she traced along her own collarbone.

Yeah, he was right; those were happy tears. Carson knew exactly what she was fishing for in asking that question.

"No, nothing at all to do with your tattoo, love. I know what Lilach means in your religion. It means flower, and you're a bud getting ready to bloom. I knew it way before I knew who you were in relation to my case and what that meant, but I understood it much better when you were taken and I put it all together."

He shook his head and said, "What must have happened for you to run and hide in Vegas, I can't even think about it. You hid pretty damn well, I have to admit. You had no clue that asshole ex-husband of yours would be involved in illegal pornography. So, no, I mean you're a gorgeous bloom in waiting, and I know exactly what that means, Li."

Lila gasped and covered her mouth with her hand to conceal her intake of breath. "I'm pretty sure I feel the same, but I have too many mixed-up thoughts at the moment to say it back." She raised her gaze to meet his and blushed, guilt written all over her face. "And there's a little problem…I'm still married. How can I love you and still be married to that awful man? What am I going to do about that? I have to make sense of all this, and I can't even take it all in."

Carson pulled her tight against him. "Of course. I wouldn't want you to say anything now. Just feel. I want you to know that this is real for me, and I'm all the way in it with you. For you. Whatever you need or want, go ahead and take it from me."

Lila leaned in and kissed Carson softly on the cheek, letting her lips linger and graze along his stubble. He heard her inhale and breathe in his scent. He liked that a lot, and wanted her to keep doing it for however long she damn well wanted.

"Thank you," she said softly. "I don't even know what to say. I feel bad you had to use up so many favors. I want to be able to tell you how I feel about you, but it feels wrong to do that while I'm still married to Elon. I need a divorce, and he's not one to grant something like that, so I have no idea how that's all going to work out."

"Baby, you got to know this. The FBI just cracked an enormous case in that warehouse. Elon, Sam Charles…they're going away for a long time. The FBI owes both you and me. Either way, I would have used up all my favors and called in a million markers if needed. Don't worry about all that. Right now, you have to think about what you want, and if you want a divorce, you'll get one."

"How?"

"Elon is screwed, baby. He's going to do a lot of time, and his crimes will be smeared all through the news. I'm pretty sure his family, the government, his legal counsel will all put pressure on him to at least do one right thing and grant you a divorce."

She just nodded, but didn't say anything.

Carson sighed, not wanting to overwhelm her any more than she already was. "Right now you only have to decide this. Do you want to go see your parents, or do you want to go to a hotel and eat, shower, and rest? I'm pretty certain your parents have heard the news of what went down by now, but it's up to you to tell them what you want, when you want."

"I need a shower and clean clothes," she said while staring down at her disheveled clothing, then corrected herself. "Come to think of it, I don't have any, but I think I should stop by my parents' house. Let them know I'm in one piece, and then go take a bath and maybe get some clothes at the hotel?"

He had a feeling that stopping to see her parents wouldn't bring the reaction Lila was expecting, but there was nothing he could do. He had to let Lila see for herself where her parents' true allegiance lay.

"That'll work. It will also give you a little time for a nap before Asher and the Vegas gang arrive. The Tunnel is running on a bare-bones crew at the moment, I'd guess. Asher, Mike, Petal, Sydney, and Penelope are all on their way here as we speak. I doubt they're going to let you rest or let me have you all to myself." He growled, lightening the moment, but made his point. He was looking forward to being with her, and only her.

"Two things, though," Lila said firmly. "I'm thirsty and I have to use a bathroom. Do you think the driver can make a pit stop at a corner store?"

Carson shook his head, annoyed at himself. "I'm so stupid, I should've thought of that, but I was so nervous about getting you back and telling you the truth. Of course, bathroom and water it is, and maybe a coffee?" He gave her a wink and smiled at her.

Lila kissed him fervently, letting all the emotion run out of her system straight into him. It might have only lasted a few seconds, but he felt her completely relax in his arms while her lips moved with his. Her kiss didn't feel lust-filled. Instead it felt tender. More like love.

Carson took down the security window and alerted the driver to the stop, and went right back to kissing Lila after putting it back up. As they held each other, he hoped their passion wasn't only a promise of what they already knew worked between the sheets, but of togetherness. Something lasting that would bond the two of them forever.

He didn't want to push the boundaries too far with all Lila had just been through. Realizing she was in an overly emotional state, he pulled back and settled her head back against his chest, while he gently rubbed his hands up and down her back to soothe her, stopping to massage her neck.

After a moment, Lila sat up and said, "Carson. I don't know what to say. I've never had this kind of caring in my life, no one ever took care of me and I was always the caretaker. Back in Vegas, I wanted more than anything to have something like this with you, but I was sure I had to leave and let you go, because I was putting every one at risk. Then when I was taken, I worried that you were maybe behind it all. I'm so ashamed that I doubted you."

Carson shook his head and said, "Don't think about that, Li. It's over. You don't have to leave, you can have someone take care of you, and love you."

"I know it's over, I just don't believe it," was all Lila would say before they made a quick bathroom break.

S OON AFTER that, they pulled up in front of her parents' house. Both her parents and another couple—the in-laws, he'd guess, based on Lila's gasp—came rushing out the front door.

The in-laws?

Lila took a deep breath and seemed to steady herself before getting out of the car. Her parents looked overjoyed to see her, but what followed shocked Carson.

"Oh, Lila, we're so glad we found you," Lila's mother said. "And don't worry about Elon…it's all a big mistake." She glanced at the other couple, then told Lila, "Mr. and Mrs. Finder are so happy to have you home, they're willing to overlook where you went and what you did. They don't even want to know."

She patted Lila's arm reassuringly. "They're going to get Elon the best legal team, and before you know it, you can go back to life as it was before, as our daughter and their daughter-in-law. You'll be a Finder again."

Carson wasn't surprised, but the look on Lila's face told him that she was. There was no hug, kiss, or long embrace for the daughter she hadn't seen in seven years.

Then the woman had the nerve to smile condescendingly at her daughter, as if everything had been Lila's fault. As if the seven years since they'd seen each other didn't matter, and the fact that Elon had just been busted for abuse of minors, conspiracy to kidnap, and running an illegal pornography ring had never happened.

"What?" Lila asked. It came out as a whisper, but Carson heard it, and the pain in that one syllable had him seeing red. Before he could say or do anything to put an end to this charade, she said, "Mom, Dad…I don't want to be a Finder. That's why I ran away. Elon is a mean and cruel person who's going to be dragged through the mud, and rightfully so, for the terrible things he's done. Both to me and to other people. And the Finders are all going to go down with him, don't you see? They should, they knew exactly what he was up to. Maybe not how he was beating me up all the time, but definitely about all the porn. Don't you get that?"

Her father frowned and shook his head. "None of that is going to happen, Lila. The Finders are good people, and Elon went off track when you left. We're going to make it all right." Then in a commanding and authoritative tone, he said, "You and Elon will both forgive each other. He'll let it go that you ran away and left him desperate, Lila, and in a few months, it will be like this never happened. Don't let your overactive imagination take over."

Carson didn't quite understand. Did these assholes really just try to blame Lila for what Elon did? He was about to step in and intervene when Lila found her voice.

"No! I'm never going to apologize to Elon. He beat me black and blue daily when we were married. He just had me abducted from my home, drugged and tortured, and only an hour ago, he was taken away by the FBI for filming pornographic movies starring minors."

Tears began to stream down her face, but she pressed her lips together and straightened her shoulders before saying, "You're obviously more concerned with the Finders, so you're welcome to them, but you can't have me, too. If you choose to believe the lies they tell you about what Elon was really doing, so be it. But the truth is that he's nothing more than a violent, sick, twisted man. He's a criminal." Her voice hitched as she said, "And this is good-bye from me to you. Officially, this time."

Lila was steady on her feet as she made this declaration, but Carson couldn't help but wrap his arm around her, wanting to be sure she knew he supported her.

Mrs. Dasher's eyebrows drew together as she looked on Lila with pity in her eyes. "Lila, maybe you need to talk to someone. Perhaps you're creating something in your head like your father said, making this all bigger than it really is." Her expression grew disgusted as she added, "*This* can't be what you want," and her husband nodded in agreement.

Both of Lila's parents turned to glare at Carson, apparently understanding for the first time that the PI they'd hired meant something to Lila.

His arms wrapped tightly around their daughter was probably a pretty good clue, he mused. Let them try to say something to him; they would be sorry real quick.

Lila didn't give them a chance to speak with Carson, nor did she even respond to them. She turned and began to climb back in the car when her brothers ran out of the house. It was clear they had been watching the reunion from inside the house, and no doubt knew what their parents' message was.

"Lila!" they all shouted. The three men circled Lila and pulled in her for a tight hug. None of them had a dry eye and they kept repeating, "Lila, we were so worried. Love you, Lila."

Carson knew that this type of touching, even between siblings, was unusual in their religion, but so were the circumstances. He stepped back to let Lila have her moment, and could see how torn she was. She obviously wanted to stay and revel in her brothers' warm kindness, but she needed to get away from her parents, and fast.

With quick promises to spend some time with her brothers over the next few days, Lila excused herself to go back to the hotel. He knew she needed to clean up and rest, but she probably also needed some time to herself to figure out what she was going to do now that her true identity was revealed. And he hoped she'd decide to make a go of it with him.

There was nothing left for her at that brownstone. He wanted to make the whole memory disappear for her. Carson would be Lila's home now, if she would have him.

As they settled into the town car and prepared to pull away, a police cruiser pulled up. Carson watched the officers load Elon's parents into the backseat, then drive off with blue and red lights flashing.

Lila turned her head into his shoulder, blocking her own view.

twenty-seven

LILA DESPERATELY needed some time to herself when she finally made it to the hotel, time to digest all that had occurred in the last two days. Her entire life—past, present, and future—had collided in a way she never would have believed. Like a multiple-car pileup, all the facets of her life were crashing into one another, shattering into tiny bits and shards, leaving everything she ever knew in a state of disarray.

Anything she had ever subscribed to, believed in, or told herself had been crushed in three short days, and there was no simple way to reconcile that, let alone push on without misgivings. Lila needed to put the pieces of her short life back together, and figure out what she wanted moving forward. Neither would happen overnight, so she decided to give herself a break and mourn for the irrefutable loss of her parents, and the Sienna persona she had carefully constructed to be her suit of armor.

No matter what happened, she wasn't going to be the same Sienna she'd been for the last several years, nor would she be the Lila of her past. Neither identity existed anymore, now that all she was and had ever been was laid out on the table for everyone to see.

Carson had said he wanted her. Wanted what from her? She wasn't even sure who or what she was anymore.

Was she a good girl? A dirty stripper? Or just a nonbeliever?

As they approached their hotel, Carson instructed their driver to use a back entrance in order to avoid the media camped out in the lobby. For this alone, Lila would be eternally grateful. Forget how she looked, she wasn't in the mood to reveal to the press how devastated she was as Lila, Sienna, or whomever they believed her to be.

She wasn't even sure at the moment, so how could they know who she was?

Lila never wanted any kind of press coverage or notoriety, which was why she ran in the dark hours of the night. Sienna wouldn't have wanted this type of information leaked to the press. Sienna heavily guarded anything other than the glitzy side of stripping, the perfectionism she brought to the industry, and her image at the Tunnel.

Lila and Sienna were two totally different women, one crafted to secure the safety of the other. They were light years apart when it came to their life experiences and expectations. Except when it came to Carson. He claimed to be able to see through Sienna, catching quick glimpses of the girl underneath.

It was true, at the core of each persona was Lila, the real Lila. Who that was at the moment, was anyone's best guess.

With Lila being safe and all of her secrets exposed to those who mattered, where did Sienna fit? Could she go back to her life as Sienna Flower with the people who loved her more than the family she had been born into?

And if she went back to Vegas as Sienna, what would happen to Lila, the woman deep inside her soul?

Lila clung to Carson as the car came to a stop, afraid of the decisions she would need to make soon after she left the vehicle. She needed to understand who she was now that her past was behind her; frankly, something she never considered to be a possibility. Was she Sienna or Lila? Sienna had built a good life for herself over the last few years with decent people in it, and now she had Carson, so he said.

Carson. He fell for Sienna. He said he loved her whether her name was Lila or Sienna, but how could he know that? He had only just learned who she really was, where she came from, and why she ran away from it all. Escaped to a life she once would have called morally degrading.

Would Carson still love her now that her true colors were revealed?

Could she be Lila in real life with Carson and Sienna onstage to her fans? Would he accept that?

The woman winding through the hotel hallway, walking to her room at the moment would never say stripping or working in a place like the Tunnel was degrading. No, the Tunnel and the people that came with the club took care of and protected her when they didn't even know what they were guarding her against. Those same individuals were on their way to see her at this very moment, to simply be with her, love her, and make it all better.

She could never give up Sienna totally. Sienna had given her what she was about to receive. A new family.

Her Las Vegas family thought she was beautiful inside and out, thought she was sweet and funny. They loved spending time with her. They didn't yell or hit, only supported her unconditionally.

She would never desert them or what they grew together. Carson would have to understand. She needed these people to survive.

Her parents obviously didn't get the ugliness she ran from and wanted to tear her away from the beauty she made instead. Lila knew she'd never reunite with them as long as she lived. It used to hurt when she thought about them over the years, but now she realized she'd believed what she wanted to about them. They weren't the caring individuals Lila thought them to be from when she was a young girl. Her parents had an agenda to move up in their narrow world, and Lila was a pawn in their plan.

Lila had too much making up for lost time to do to burden herself with trying to figure it all out.

Her new family—Asher, Mike, Penelope, Petal, and Sydney—were on a private plane to New York to be with her, whether she was Lila or Sienna. Even Petey, who she heard stayed behind to watch the club, was closer to her than her mom and dad. She knew her new family loved her, and wanted to do whatever necessary while she healed from the kidnapping and attack. She didn't need Carson to tell her that, but he did.

Their affection and Carson's reassurance was more than her own parents offered her. Ever.

Carson hadn't left her side. She wanted to let herself believe what he said in the car. He loved her. It wasn't a fairy tale, but it was more than she ever expected.

Was it true? Could she allow herself to have it? To take the sweetness in front of her?

electrified

AFTER SHOWERING and resting for a couple of hours, Lila woke to find her friends waiting in the hotel suite. They ordered a late dinner to be delivered up to the suite, and while they ate, she told them the entire story about what happened to her before coming to Vegas, revealing details she'd never told anyone. They cried right alongside Lila over how she was battered and bruised, yet brave enough to climb through that window, get on a bus, and find them.

It was because of this family that Lila began the healing process she never quite started years before.

She needed to stop thinking about the what-ifs and should'ves, and start believing in a good life, Asher told her over and over again while tucking her into his side on the couch, stealing her away from Carson.

They were a motley group, all with their own skeletons in the closet, but together they were surviving, and that was what Lila needed. As a whole, the group decided to call her Lila in private. It was such a pretty name, a survivor's name. But when she finally made it back to Vegas—and she was going to get back there, they weren't taking no for an answer—she'd always be Sienna at the Tunnel.

She could be Lila with those who really knew her, and Sienna for her fans. Carson, despite being her biggest fan, was also the one who knew her best. To him, she became "Li" all the time.

During those first days in New York after her rescue, Carson held her, promised her everything would work out, and waited patiently for her to make sense of her future and what felt right. He didn't push for her to say she loved him, but he made sure she knew he loved her without any reservation.

She went to sleep each night wrapped in Carson's warmth. They didn't make love. She wasn't ready after what she'd been subjected to in the warehouse, and she wanted to get her mind in the right place so she could be completely attentive to Carson. He told her he understood and allowed her to keep control, but she relished in holding and kissing him without any secrets between them.

Lila made peace with her brothers. All three of them came to see her at the hotel and visited. Carson remained in the background, just in case Lila changed her mind or became uncomfortable. They all blamed themselves for not seeing any warning signs or stepping in when Lila needed them most, or when her parents chose the Finders over her. Her oldest brother, Daniel, seemed especially burdened by guilt over their part.

But Lila wouldn't allow them to take on any of the burden. They were good men, and never doubted her parents would want anything but the best for Lila. Unfortunately, they had been wrong.

After all the emotions and reunions had run their course, Lila had to help the Bureau tie up loose ends surrounding the case.

Carson sat by her side the whole time she was debriefed by the FBI. He didn't patronize or coddle her, but let her reveal the nasty truth about her life seven years ago, the details of her escape back then, and everything else all the way up to her abduction. She knew none of it was easy for Carson to hear, but she needed to control the information and make sure this time everyone knew the truth.

Carson had been right; Elon faced serious charges and lengthy prison time. It wasn't hard to press him to divorce her. Filing the paperwork to dissolve her miserable marriage was the last thing Lila did before leaving New York.

twenty-eight

WITH HER real identification in hand, thanks to the Bureau, Lila left for Philadelphia to see where Carson lived. It was the first trip she had taken as Lila.

Carson had made plans for her to go back to Philadelphia with him while she spent time with her thoughts in the suite in New York City. He wanted to show her his condo before taking her on vacation, to the Bahamas.

Lila was apprehensive. She felt obligated to get back to the club and dance, to help ensure her friends were successful, and she'd never taken a vacation other than an overnight here and there in Red Rock with Asher. Not once had she gone a multicity adventure, let alone out of the country.

One call from Asher, and she was left with no more fears or excuses. He insisted she go, promised he'd take a long trip when she returned, and made her believe she deserved it. It amused her to think how he and Carson had obviously become fast friends.

Carson rented a car, a fast one, to drive them back to Philadelphia. Lila enjoyed the drive, taking in the passing scenery. She'd never been outside New York before she ran away, and when she did leave last time, it was on a bus and dark outside. Her most recent car trip back east was also less than pleasant, plus she'd been heavily drugged during the entire journey.

Once she and Carson left the big city and were on the large expanse of freeway, they sped by farms, green pastures, and gorgeous mountains. Lila took it all in like a little girl. She caught Carson smiling at her many times during the ride, and reveled in it for a second before begging him to put his eyes back on the road.

After shifting into high gear, Carson held Lila's hand, rubbing his thumb back and forth over hers, lending her his strength and confidence without ever uttering a word. It was such a simple indulgence, holding hands while driving free, but it held such intense significance for Lila. She was free to be Lila and live, love, and move on.

Parking in Carson's garage brought on a whole new set of jitters for Lila. She was there, at Carson's place. Walking in from the garage, she caught a glimpse of his motorcycle parked next to the wall. She looked at the bike, then at him, and his brown eyes twinkled. "You want to go for a ride?" he asked, his dimples in full bloom.

She grinned and pretended to shoot her head. "No way. I was thinking with how fast you drive a car, I can't imagine what you do on that thing. It's probably scary."

"Definitely scary. Scary fun. I missed my bike when I was out west, but not nearly as much as I missed being inside you the last few days. Come on." He lifted her up, threw her over his shoulder like it was nothing, playfully smacked her butt, and carried her to the elevator. She laughed to herself as she remembered the last time he went caveman on her.

Carson lived in a posh, huge condo in the center of Philadelphia. There was nothing compact about it, as she recalled him telling her he had a "small place" when they first had coffee.

The space wasn't homey like hers, though. She was saddened to see Carson had very little on the walls, nothing but beer in the built-in stainless fridge, and little more furniture than a sectional sofa and a huge entertainment center complete with the largest TV Lila had ever seen. The minimalist decor and feeling screamed *lonely* to Lila, but she would deal with that later because before she could take in any more, Carson scooped her up for the second time and showed her his bedroom, which held only a king-sized bed.

He gently placed her down on the bed and rested beside her, propped up on one elbow. They just lay there staring into each other's

lectrified

yes, Lila's green and Carson's brown, and let their gazes do the talking. Their eyes were both filled with equal parts love, lust, need, and want.

Both of them were two lonely, hopeless souls before they met. Neither believed they deserved something to last, a little touch of sweetness, and now that they had more good than they knew what to do with, there were no words to express it. Only actions.

Carson smoothed her long hair behind her back and pressed his mouth to hers. What started out as a soft kiss quickly grew to a delicious blend of lips, tongues, and teeth. They fed off each other's heat, racing toward more tasting, touching, and melding their bodies together in the most magnificent of ways.

Lila knew he wanted to put his mouth elsewhere, kiss her where he hadn't been in a while, and make her scream his name. Which she most definitely wanted, but she wanted to be the first to incite the passion. Forcing herself to pull away from his mouth, she kissed along his neck, lapped around his nipples with her hands slowly roaming south, then began inching down his body.

Her fingers found his button fly and opened his jeans, pushing them down and finally off with her foot. She grasped him, all of him, running her hand up and down his smooth shaft, caressing the silky tip with her thumb. Carson let out a deep moan right before she lowered her head and took him completely in her mouth.

She really didn't know what to do, but took cues from his moans as she sank deeper on him with her lips. She slid back up and down again at a slow rhythm, moistening all of him, savoring his salty taste, loving her first experience with this.

This being her first blow job.

Carson lifted his hips so he could slide a bit deeper in her mouth, and she started to move a little faster. He wound his hands in her hair, keeping her at the current pace, obviously liking the faster way she was skimming up and down him.

She moved one of her hands up his abs and chest to slowly graze his nipples while she continued to suck him below with her mouth.

Now she understood how it turned him on so much to pleasure her with his mouth. The sounds he was making, the way he kept pressing into her, the sight of his head falling back on the pillow in ecstasy had her so turned on, she was ready for anything.

Carson broke the moment. "Lila, oh God, you feel incredible, but I'm not going to last and I want you."

He stilled her and pulled her back up his body, then met her mouth with his and kissed her passionately. He stroked his tongue against hers before flipping on top of her and pushing her thighs apart with his legs. She could feel how hard he was against her core.

Her body had a mind of its own and was straining toward him, begging him to dive inside. She was wet and more than ready. She felt his hand brush over her dripping core, and without pause, he entered her, filling and consuming her at once.

For the first time since they met, they were Lila and Carson with no secrets or barriers between them. She was certain this made it even better. They were suspended in time as one; her body ached for more every time he slid in and out of her.

He held her hip tightly, rubbing his thumb along her scar as though he was scrubbing the memory from her mind and replacing it with a happier one, as he went deeper and deeper. She didn't have to tell him what the scar was; she knew he knew. He was making it all go away with each time he drove inside her.

Lila squeezed his ass every time he landed in her depths, silently asking for him to not stop what he was doing. It was carnal, passionate, and beautiful all at the same time.

They devoured each other, and Lila felt her orgasm tunneling through her veins, seeping out from her bones, and igniting her soul. She couldn't hold the force of it back, and when he gave her a long, soulful thrust, she came with Carson's name on her tongue.

He shuddered inside her as she rode out the last waves of her climax, shivering all around him, reveling in hearing her name from his mouth. Her real name, all hoarse and gravelly, deep from his throat while he was planted inside her, surrounded by infinite pleasure and a feeling she'd never felt before.

"I love you, Carson."

The words slipped out all on their own, and Lila realized that was the feeling she was experiencing so deliciously. Love. Love without strings or demands. Unadulterated love. She said and meant it, and had to believe Carson wasn't lying when he told her earlier.

He whispered sweet words of love to her, and then proceeded to spend the next few hours showing her how he felt.

electrified

SPENDING THE entire day and night in bed, only getting up to answer the door for takeout, Lila didn't see any of Philadelphia until twenty-four hours after arriving. She didn't care. She was seeing all she wanted to see in Carson's eyes.

Eventually, he did take a little time to show her around the city. She took in the architecture and history, met his friend Alex, who was somewhat like a brother and clearly important, but mostly enjoyed being alone with Carson at home with no pretense, making love, and exploring each other.

They even took a short ride on his bike. A short, painfully fast excursion where Lila lost herself in leaning into his muscular back, reveled in having her arms folded tightly around his waist, and thought if it weren't so dangerous, motorcycle riding behind him wasn't half bad.

After a few days, Carson made true on his promise to go to the Bahamas. Something he told Lila he planned to do without her when he finished the case that brought them together, but was going to be much better with her.

And it was so fabulous together. Just the two of them. After a week of indulging in each other on their veranda, in the sand with the ocean waves rolling in the background, and on the enormous bed in their cabana at an exclusive resort, Lila finally had to face going back to life and what that meant. She couldn't stay in paradise forever.

It was easy to lose herself in the tranquility and easiness of being Carson and Lila in the most stunning place ever, forgetting where they came from, and what was waiting for her at home. She had a life to get back to, even though her identity had been destroyed. There were people she cared about waiting for her, depending on her for help and success.

She owed those people, and she had to get back to them. But she also owed Carson and wanted to stay with him. Did he want to stay with her? How would that work?

Their last evening in the Bahamas, while dining under the stars at a private table set for two outside their little bungalow, she asked Carson, "So, will we visit each other, see each other. How will this work?"

He set his fork down, sat up straight, and smoothed his hand across his face. "Li, baby, there will be no visiting."

Lila couldn't stop herself from frowning, her eyes immediately welling up with tears. She couldn't control her face and emotions betraying her, showing every bit of her sadness and remorse.

"Lila, I'm kidding. Kidding. There will be no visiting because I'm moving to Vegas with you. That is, if you'll have me." He laughed loudly, bared his big beautiful smile, leaned over and planted a big kiss on her lips.

She brought her fingers up to her mouth, tracing where he just left, and tilted her head to the side. "What? How? You have a life, a job, a condo."

"Is that an excuse? Are you looking for a way out? We never discussed your religion, is that it? The one you were raised in, it's obviously not the same as mine, which is nonexistent. Is that a problem? I don't know what to suggest. I only want to be with you, for always."

She shifted in her seat. "It's not an excuse! I don't care what religion you are. I'm not the same person I was back in Brooklyn. I don't believe in many of the old customs anymore. They didn't help me when I needed them the most. I do believe someone was looking out for me, though, because I met you. And now you want to be with me? It's just, I can't believe this is happening. All my dreams are coming true. That's not supposed to happen."

Carson nodded and snared her gaze with his. "It's true and should be for you of all people, you deserve it and more. Listen, I work for myself, and I want to be with you. Period. I can live anywhere, but I want to be with you. Does that work for you?" He got out of his chair, picked her up by her hips, and lifted her so they were eye to eye.

With her legs now wrapped around his waist and the biggest smile ever, Lila only said, "Absolutely!"

Sporting a tiny glint in his eyes and his dimple peeking out, Carson ended the conversation with, "I'm bringing my bike. No doubt about that."

He kissed her before she could reply.

epilogue

Two years later

CARSON LANDED at the private airstrip, practically *jumped out of the plane*, hopped on his bike, and headed toward home. Screw debriefing his client. He solved the case, found the person of interest, delivered them, and wanted to get the fuck home. As soon as he had deposited the individual in question with the authorities, he'd demanded the plane get right back up in the air. He mostly flew private these days.

The flying, an added perk to his elevated career status, was only superseded by being able to charge exorbitant rates after he had handed the FBI such a big tip-off and case with Elon Finder and Mystique. He would have done it no matter what for Lila.

His private work was steady as usual, but now he could be even more particular in choosing jobs, since the FBI now called him to consult on certain cases they couldn't get a solid lead on, or to pass along cases the government didn't want to be involved with. He was in high demand, and he liked it that way.

Hence, his current client could wait. Their software programming was safe now. Carson found and apprehended the idiot who had tried to run away with the code for himself. Some people got so greedy, thinking they could have it all.

Like him. He did. He had it all. Yeah, he was a smug shit, but considering he came from not much, Carson was proud of where life had landed him.

Lila wouldn't be happy he was on his bike. He hoped the fact he was home a day early would make up for it. She hated his fast driving, whether it was his sports car or his treasured bike.

It was who he was. He drove fast when they met. What did she expect?

With the wind buffeting his back as Carson pushed his speed a little faster, his thoughts drifted back to when he first picked Lila up in the rental car in Vegas. She'd gripped the side bar back then as though her life depended on it. To think of it, she still did as he continued to speed around town whenever they were out.

He could see her point. Sort of. What did she want him to get? A minivan?

No fucking way.

He ran through all of his options on his ride home. He had to settle on some type of compromise, because it wasn't going to be just the two of them for much longer.

After he parked his beloved bike in the garage and slipped into the house quietly, he caught a glance of his wife sitting on the back porch, hands on her round stomach, shadows from the palm trees moving over her, their fronds gently waving in the ocean air.

They had moved to Santa Monica permanently a year ago. Their Spanish-style ranch house with huge windows and big wide-open spaces was the exact opposite of Lila's life growing up. In New York, she was shut inside, forced to hide her bruises in the darkness, and expected to remain separate from the outside world.

He didn't want that for her ever again.

Carson was pretty sure Lila missed Vegas from time to time, but she never admitted it. The glitz, action, and dancing were all she knew for most of her young adult life. For many years, all that was her safety net and her only family. It was ironic that the crazy, on-the-edge adult entertainment industry had protected her when she was hiding from a painful and secluded past.

He took care of her now. At least, that was what he told himself, but he knew she could take care of herself. Lila was strong and capable. She was a survivor; he'd never believed anything different. It was her resilience that allowed her to build a life in Vegas instead of wallowing in self-pity when she escaped New York.

That was why he didn't say a word when Lila continued to dance as Sienna Flower for the first six months they were officially together. He had to put his feelings aside and let her do what she wanted.

She needed to make her own decision to quit when it felt right.

Which finally happened when Asher's personal life quieted down after a painful few months, a time during which the two men became extremely close, thanks to their shitty but similar pasts. Lila started working toward her business degree; she knew it was the right move. She was almost thirty years old at that point. It was time to do something else other than dance, but she couldn't turn her back on her adopted family.

Lila never mentioned Carson being a part of her decision to retire from dancing. He let her have that. She knew what he wanted, but after spending the early years of her life with every decision made for her, he knew she needed to make her own choices. With Asher making a life of his own, both he and Lila decided to expand the club. He wanted to make sure they both could reap enough from the business. Carson owed the man everything, and now that Asher had settled down, the pair was almost even.

Between Lila's recent experience in business school and her years of being the top adult dancer in Vegas, she was more than ready to build and run more clubs. Their first expansion was in Los Angeles, which was what brought Lila and Carson to Santa Monica. Thank God he could work anywhere, because he was going to follow her wherever she went.

Lila now oversaw the entire operation in California. She took each dancer under her wing as only Sienna Flower could—giving them confidence, pride, and survival tips. She made sure each one saved money, took good care of herself, and never let any one of them get down on themselves. On any given day, Carson would come home to a house full of gorgeous women, lounging around with coffee or wine, laughing, relaxing, unwinding, and sharing the stress of the week.

He was the envy of all his buddies.

Carson gave Lila many of the same things she gave the girls—peace, strength, pride, and love—and he loved doing it. He liked nothing better than to relax on the patio with his wife, beer in his hand and a hot cup of coffee in hers, while she snuggled up to him. There was something special about kicking back as waves crashed nearby, the ocean air whipping around, wrapping them up in its salty essence, and helping take away all the strain of life.

Which was what he wanted to do right now, once he could stop staring at the beauty in front of him.

The LA club, the Electric Cove, was way in the black after just one year. Lila did that, too. She worked tirelessly, a perfectionist at heart. Carson didn't ever mention her upcoming maternity leave and what would happen afterward. Another little way he let Lila be her own woman. He knew she was handling it.

Petey had traveled to LA with Lila to set up and run the security at the club, and she had recently moved him into the role of club manager. Petey was happy as fuck with his new title and his twenty-five percent stake in the joint. Whatever plans Lila and Petey made once she had the baby, he knew they'd be solid.

Lila's oldest brother, Daniel, who had been most affected by the discovery of her and the circumstances around why she ran, couldn't make peace with their family or religion afterward. He and his wife separated. Since they didn't have kids, he made a clean break and moved to LA to reacquaint himself with Lila. He visited the club from time to time during nonbusiness hours, and now did the accounting for them. Carson knew he had tremendous guilt, and this was his way of atoning for it.

Lila was still getting used to having one family member back in her life, but he could tell she liked it. Her parents kept their distance, just as Lila asked. Unfortunately, making it right with their daughter was less important than being excommunicated from their community.

Although Lila was an innocent victim in all of Elon's actions, her parents associated her with him and refused to absolve her, which trickled out to the rest of the neighborhood. Their motives in hiring Carson and finding her were never sincere. They just wanted to be related to the Finder family.

Then when everything went south, they changed their tune and didn't want anything to do with the Finders. Ironically, that included their own daughter, who had been a Finder in name.

Lila never talked about her ex-husband. Never, and Carson was fine with that. It was over for Lila and Elon before it really started. Lila went to therapy for the first year after the kidnapping, and made peace with the idea that none of it was her fault.

She also resolved and strengthened her belief her work as a stripper was decent. It kept her safe for many years, and now she used the knowledge she gained from that experience to help other women make money in an industry that often stripped them of their pride. She showed them how to avoid that at all costs.

Personally, for Carson, all he cared about was keeping Lila safe.

electrified

After Elon gave her the civil divorce from prison, she was granted a religious divorce. Elon was tied up for a very long time in the system. He wasn't coming back, but just in case, Carson had someone keep a constant eye on him.

He and Lila went back to the Bahamas a year after their first trip there and were married in a small ceremony on the beach. It was an anniversary and a birth all in one—the one-year mark of when Lila had stopped living in fear, and the beginning of a new life with a husband who adored her. Since her entire Tunnel family was in attendance, it was also a going-away party for Lila and Carson right before they moved to California.

They all would be back together soon with a number of upcoming arrivals, his and Lila's baby being only one of them.

He knew Lila was making the most of every second until their baby arrived. Last week, she and Asher broke ground on the birth of their next club, the Electric Wave in Miami. Lila had gone to scout locations, but now that she wasn't traveling, Asher took over for the time being.

Big Mike and Lila talked on the phone daily, and Carson was pretty sure he was the one she missed the most. He wasn't the least bit surprised when Lila told him she was sending Big Mike to Florida to take over the club. Giving back to the people who had helped her was important to her, and she wanted to do everything she could to be sure they all succeeded.

As much as she was making the most of every last minute before becoming a mom, Lila was also determined to deliver on her due date, so she'd make the club opening set for two months after the day their baby was due to arrive.

There was nothing Carson could do to stop her from going. The Tunnel franchise was her first baby.

Carson went in and out of LA almost weekly on cases, always rushing back to Lila. He loved the weeks where he had nothing but preliminary research and he could spend the whole week at home. Recently, he was back to a lot of cross-country travel, which would come to an end for a while after the baby came. Although he knew Lila wouldn't let him keep that up for long.

Lila...she wanted the best for everyone. Wanted each and every person in her life to have success. She loved so big after allowing her walls to come down completely. He tried not to think about rescuing her anymore or how they began. He was proud of her, though.

Christ, she was amazing, and he knew it would only get better with the birth of their baby.

He didn't know what kind of dad he would be. He hoped he'd be pretty decent with Lila's help. He did know for certain she was the kind of mom he never had but always wished for, and was thrilled that his son would have that.

Looking out the window, Carson took note of Lila talking, no doubt sharing all her love with their soon-to-be-born son. His heart swelling with love, he made a decision.

I'm getting a fucking tank, one of those big SUVs with enough steel to protect my family.

Sliding the glass door open, he peeked out, trying to hear what Lila was saying to their son.

"You're going to grow up to be big and strong like your daddy, but you're going to use all that strength for good just like him. I know you'll really be gentle and kind and never mean."

Lila turned her gaze up, her glowing green eyes meeting Carson's as a huge smile played on her face. From the pleased look on her face, he knew his dimple must be showing again. He was constantly electrified with life by his wife.

"Welcome home," she said as she moved her hands up and down her stomach.

He glanced at what she was wearing, and they both burst out laughing at her Superwoman T-shirt stretched out across her huge pregnant belly. Carson smiled on the inside now, remembering Sienna on the pole wearing nothing but hot pants and the Superwoman T-shirt tied in a knot, and what they did afterward. She was a Superwoman, and he wanted her all to himself, whether she was a dancer or not.

He wanted it all, and he got it.

Read on for a Sneak Peek of Asher's story in *Smoldered*

sneak peek
smoldered

Five years ago, Sunday

BREATHED A sigh of relief. This was exactly what I needed tonight. All it took was one lap through the Pink Leop—or the Leop, as it was known—and I felt like I was transported to some of my dirtier fantasies. By dirty, I meant the gritty, baser shit I tended to think about, but didn't act on—too frequently, anyway. I was no angel, and never claimed to be one. I'd had a lot of women, and tonight, I really needed to get off hard.

I didn't do drugs. I did sex, and the not the missionary-style, lovey-dovey stuff.

Snaking my way around the main bar and heading toward a side stage in the back of the club, I set my eyes on where I wanted to land.

The Leop was set up differently from my club. Instead of a main stage there were four small stages, one per corner, each platform featuring a different tantalizing vignette. I couldn't walk fast enough to the back right. I licked my lips as my feet ate up the floor, my heart pounding as I neared the tiny platform.

At my club, the Electric Tunnel, we had a single main stage looping around the front of the club where we featured either one main act, like my Sienna Flower, or two or three scenes simultaneously at different ends or corners. Our lap dance business was most likely quadruple what the Leop did, by the looks of it. Here the customers—mostly men, but a few women, too— worked their way around the room as they checked out the different stages, which was wasted time, in my opinion.

Not wasting mine right now. That fucking scene playing out is hot, and my dick and I have to get closer.

My club had one main focal point, but not everyone could get close enough, so we brought the act right to their seats with a private lap dance. It was a win/win for everyone. More money for the dancers and me, and a much better view for the customer.

As I neared the end of the bar, the regular head bartender, Ryan, reached over and grabbed my shoulder. "Look what the cat dragged in! None other than Asher Peterson, the guy remaking the stripper biz on the other side of town."

I laughed, stretched my hand over to shake his, and answered, "You got that right, but no harm in swinging by and checking out the competition. That way I get to catch up with assholes like you."

Ryan chuckled. "I'm kidding, dude. We all know you got your sights set on something bigger and better over at the Electric Tunnel. Just happy to see you can still slum it over at our fine establishment. We know our market, and you're it." He slapped my back in jest and asked what I wanted to drink.

I ordered a shot. I figured it would be quick, and I was practically hopping back and forth on my feet, fighting my desire to get to the action.

Finally, he poured, I lifted the little glass, tossed the burning liquid down my throat, and gave the dude a small chin lift in thanks. "Catch you later, Ryan," I said and moved like a leopard on the prowl.

Earlier, I told myself I wanted to check out the competition, so I could convince myself I was doing better than them. But it was really something more. I had my limits, and I was nearing them. I needed to get off. Period.

The Pink Leop had been around for a while, and had a reputation for allowing quite a bit of crazy shit to go down. Word on the street was you could get just about anything you wanted done to you, or for you, in the private rooms. And for the right price, you could take a girl back to your place with you for the night. It was exactly what I didn't want for the Tunnel, but it didn't mean I was immune to the stench of sex when I walked through its doors, or that I didn't want to partake a little bit. I did. It was exactly why I was here, pushing a few gross fat and sweaty men out of my way so I could get closer to the action.

So what if the owners lost money in lap dances? They obviously made up for it in their private rooms. Yeah, some of the shit they allowed wasn't exactly on the up-and-up. "Heavy touching" was probably putting it nicely, but hey, what the hell did I care? I didn't own the place. I was here for a good time like the next guy. If they got into trouble with the law, it wasn't my problem.

Finally, I sank down into a worn-out red suede chair to the side of the scene that caught my eye. I couldn't be bothered with how grubby the shitty chair was, pushing out all thoughts of what may have touched its gross fabric over the years. *Thank fuck, mine are leather at the Tunnel.*

I was fully laid out in the piece of crap, sticky as all get-out, and I couldn't be bothered because the two women directly in front of me were *hot.* Smoking hot, and it had absolutely nothing to do with the fake haze whirling all around them from the smoke machine.

I wanted to take both of them home and test out what they were doing onstage with me in the middle, preferably without any clothes in the way. The girls were both completely naked other than the thongs they wore, one red and the other gold. They stood on either side of a chair set in the middle of the stage, long messy hair falling all around soft and demure shoulders and touching the tips of their nipples, grinding on either end of the piece of furniture while leaning over and groping each other's tits.

I was rigid everywhere as I watched in anticipation of what the two would do next. Christ, the way they twisted each other's nipples, moaning and groaning like it felt better than anything they ever had before, appeared to be incredibly hot. The two luscious babes stared deep into each other's eyes as if they were soul mates, doing exactly what they would be doing at home, but I knew the truth. They'd much rather be at home on their couch, drinking wine and watching a chick flick.

My line of work let me see behind the curtain, so I knew it was a ruse, a charade, nothing but pretend, but I couldn't bring myself to care. They were doing what they were paid to do, which was to titillate the audience, and they were doing a mighty fine job of it from where I was sitting. My eyes focused on the women, even though I could only see their hazy profiles. My dick twitched, anxious to be released from my pants, screaming, "Let me out to play," and my mind was running through an endless stream of scenes involving the two women and me.

I motioned to one of the Leop's managers on the floor. When he appeared by my side, I asked him how much it would cost to take the pair back to a private room. I made a mental note to feel them out and see if one or both of them would accompany me back to my house. Of course, I was hoping for both, but I'd settle for one. I needed some action. Badly.

The manager set out the deal and I agreed to the terms. I had cash to burn, with a growing business and no real responsibilities at home. After paying for the first hour in advance, I headed to the back to wait for the women in my private booth. Yeah, I stroked myself over my pants a little while waiting for them. So, sue me.

When the song changed out in the main club, I heard two pairs of heels clicking down the hallway toward the room where I waited. My breathing sped up in time with my heartbeat, and I sat up and waited for the delicious duo to open the door.

Here they come.

The outer door opened and closed, then two curvy silhouettes entered my little corner and turned around. I blinked. Then blinked again, hard. I tried to clear my eyes, to get them to focus in the dim, red-hued light.

Why the hell was everything in this ugly fucking club red?

I didn't have time to ponder that right now. Instead I stood up and crossed the space in between the couch where I was sitting and the door in two steps and said, "Holy shit! Natalie, what the fuck are you doing here?"

Not stopping to wait for an answer, I opened the door and pushed the other girl outside the room toward the nearest bouncer. "Never mind," I told him. "I changed my mind. I only want one girl. This girl." I gestured behind me to Natalie. "Keep the extra money." The girl glanced back at me, a confused look on her face as she tottered toward the bouncer, then I slammed the door shut.

I stared at the door for an extra moment, trying to contain myself. Thank God there was no one else in the high-backed booth on either side of me because I feared I was about to lose my shit.

Turning back around slowly, I said, "Natalie...Jesus Christ, it's been years. I can't even think about how long it's been, but what the hell are you doing in a raunchy place like this? You were taking classes, making a life for yourself the last we talked." When she didn't respond, I said, "I've got to get you the hell out of here."

Natalie shrank away from me, backing up until her shapely calves hit the sofa. She stared in horror at my eyes boring down on her.

I shoved a hand through my hair and paced back and forth like a madman. I had no idea whether I was whispering or yelling, I was so furious.

With her gaze lowered, her long lashes covering her big, beautiful eyes, she walked toward me and pleaded, "Shh. They know me as Natasha here, and I need this gig, Asher. Stop making a scene…please."

I could still see the younger Natalie somewhere inside the hard woman talking to me. Her long brown hair hung way down her shoulders, heavy bangs sweeping over her eyes, which were decorated with glitter and dark black eyeliner. Underneath all that caked-on shit, my "little doll," the girl who used play kickball out in the alley and chase after the neighborhood boys, was there.

I threw my hands up in the air. "Nat, I don't want to hear that you need this job. This isn't the fucking place for you, babe. You want to strip, come work for me. My girls are respected. You want to do something else, go do it. What you aren't going to do is work in this shithole, one step away from being a prostitute."

She shuddered. I felt Natalie's whole body shiver under my hand, which had found its way to rest on her hip as she faced off with me. It made me want to wrap her up in my arms and carry her out of the mess she was currently wrapped up in.

I completely forgot that I was at the Leop to get a little action. Instead, it looked like I was going to have to rescue the girl like a fucking superhero.

Shit.

Coming Fall 2014

Domestic violence is a serious situation and one that should never be ignored. If you or someone you love is in a violent or hostile situation, you can find anonymous help here:
National Domestic Violence Hotline
http://www.thehotline.org
1-800-799-7233

acknowledgments

So, I get these wild ideas every now and again, like inventing products and changing careers. This time around I wanted to write a fiction book. Actually, I've wanted to write one ever since I received a D+ on a paper in AP English. It only took me twenty-four years to do it.

Thanks to my husband and kids, who support all my adventures in writing, running, inventing, donut eating, and cleaning. I love you all. *Please don't forget to make your beds.*

I could *not* have written this book without the writing mentorship and editing capabilities of Pam Berehulke at Bulletproof Editing. I may not be able to pronounce your last name without instructions, but I can't write without you. Your endless patience, gentle pushing for me to do better, introduction to words like *ham hocks*, and ability to get rid of my ellipsis addiction have all been crucial to my process. I thank you from the bottom of my heart.

There are a few authors who took time to encourage me to reach for my dream, or perhaps just fly my romance-author freak flag. Thank you, Madeline Sheehan. Notice, I don't beg you for your next installment anymore? Well, not entirely now that I know how hard this thing we call writing really is, but I still want it.

Thank you, Heidi McLaughlin, for smiling at me at a book signing and opening up your virtual arms when I needed them.

Tara Sivec, something about you made me not scared to use my own voice, find my own cadence, and put it out there. Thanks.

And the bloggers. Being one myself, I could never forget you. Sarah at *Smart Bitches/Trashy Books*, we went to high school together, reconnected on the World Wide Web, and now I can't take a vacation without your recs. Thanks for the never-ending advice to make sure my ass was seated in my desk chair. To Virginia at *Love N. Books*. You cheered for me when my book was only a speck of an idea, and encouraged me to move forward. Although I don't typically jump up and down, I may for you.

Special thanks to my friends. I know I tend to hole up with my creative projects and disappear. I appreciate your patience when I don't come out to play. *Who wants to have a cocktail?*

SJP (the other one), please make sure I continue to get out to drink wine, eat fried tofu, and learn how to cook a turkey. Thanks for reading this book in its most primitive form.

To my betas—Tiffany, Gretchen, Jill, and Lori—thank you, ladies. You loved my characters from the beginning, some more than others, and begged for me to keep writing when I would leave you hanging. I couldn't have done this without you. And Tiffany, I still am going to visit you and see your floor coated in recycled book pages.

I would be remiss if I didn't mention my cousin Ed, who made sure I knew a guy with feelings wasn't a wuss and helped me find my inner-male voice.

Most of all, thanks to you for reading and recommending this book. This would be a great big nothing without YOU!

about the author

Rachel Blaufeld is a social worker/entrepreneur/blogger turned
author. Fearless about sharing her opinion, Rachel captured the ear
of stay-at-home and working moms on her blog, *BacknGrooveMom*,
chronicling her adventures in parenting tweens and inventing
a product, often at the same time. She has also blogged for *The
Huffington Post*, *Modern Mom*, and *StartupNation*.
Turning her focus on her sometimes wild-and-crazy creative side, it
only took Rachel two decades to do exactly what she wanted to do—
write a fiction novel. Now she spends way too many hours in local
coffee shops plotting her ideas. Her tales may all come with a side of
angst and naughtiness, but end lusciously.
Rachel lives around the corner from her childhood home in
Pennsylvania with her family and two dogs. Her obsessions include
running, coffee, icing-filled doughnuts, antiheroes, and mighty fine
epilogues.

Please connect with me on:
www.rachelblaufeld.com
Facebook: www.facebook.com/rachelblaufeldtheauthor
Twitter: twitter.com/rachelblaufeld

about the book

Everyone knows her as Sienna Flower.

Her curves and long lashes tease and taunt from her very own billboard where the desert meets the Las Vegas Strip. She's the hottest stripper in town, known for her sultry and indecent moves coupled with her virginal eyes.

She's a heady and unique combination, and a mystery to all who come to see her.

Sienna captivates crowds nightly at the Electric Tunnel, leaving them wanting to know more about the sensual enigma. But no one ever sees beyond the heavily guarded stripper onstage. She is Sienna Flower 24/7.

No one other than her closest friend and boss, Asher Peterson, who helped turn a young and frightened girl into who Sienna is today. Together they created the sexual illusion known as Sienna Flower. They will go to any lengths to protect her image, which is why Sienna is convinced she must remain unattached and alone.

Like everyone else in Vegas, Sienna is hiding something and playing a role. A good girl in her former life, she was raised to be obedient and accepting of her fate, but there are some circumstances no one should be expected to accept. She escaped to a world light years away from the one she was subjected to…the Electric Tunnel.

Now she can never be anything other than Sienna Flower. Not only would she be hurt, but everyone around her would suffer the consequences.

That is, until she meets private detective Carson Graham, the dark and mysterious ex-FBI agent who watches her dance every weekend. With his dark hair and chocolate-brown eyes, Carson begins to heat Sienna's heart and body, melting away the layers and secrets. Sienna doesn't want to get attached to Carson, but when another man surfaces and starts hunting her down, bringing out the scars of her old life, she can't help but seek comfort in Carson's protection.

With everyone trading on the secrets of her past, Sienna finds herself caught in an awful web of lies. Her ultimate fear is hurting her friends at the Tunnel, but she doesn't know who to trust. Namely, Carson. Is he good? Or bad? Does she have the luxury of finding out?

www.ingramcontent.com/pod-product-compliance
Lightning Source LLC
Chambersburg PA
CBHW021508240626
47154CB00002B/547